THE MIND OF JOHN MEREDITH

An ancient curse echoes down the centuries and lays its shadow across the household at High Perwyl, the Welsh Border Castle where John Meredith is trying to regain both physical and spiritual health after long and terrible war service coupled with cruel personal loss.

Why does young Sir Martin Lauder-Treaves fly into a rage merely because his charming American wife, Finella-Lou, drinks accidentally from his glass? What is the origin of the great marauding dog—if dog it is—that roams the countryside about High Perwyl at night?

As these and other sinister questions become increasingly urgent, the old spirit comes to life again in Sir John and he rouses himself to track down and destroy the evil thing that is poisoning the lives of his friends and hosts.

THE MIND OF JOHN MEREDITH

Francis Gérard

MYSTERY

First published 1952
by
MacDonald & Co (Publishers) Ltd
This edition 1990 by Chivers Press
published by arrangement with
the author's estate

ISBN 0 86220 794 0

Foreword copyright © John Kennedy Melling, 1990

British Library Cataloguing in Publication Data

Gerard, Francis
　The mind of John Meredith.
　I. Title
　823.912 [F]

ISBN 0-86220-794-0

Printed and bound in Great Britain by
Redwood Press Limited, Melksham, Wiltshire

FOREWORD

DURING THE YEARS of the Second World War and immediately afterwards, there was a surprising number of paperback imprints and publishers—perhaps a score or more. My father, a voracious reader, particularly of crime stories, was always handing me a positive galaxy of titles by many authors, some of whom, like Francis Gérard, are in my opinion well overdue for reissue and revival.

The first thing I noticed about Gérard's books was their alliterative and euphonious titles—*Concrete Castle, Dictatorship of the Dove, Emerald Embassy, Fatal Friday,* and *Golden Guilt* on to *Prince of Paradise, Red Rope, Secret Sceptre* and *Transparent Traitor.* I have since found out that there were many more titles written between 1936 and 1952. Little seemed to be known of this author; in fact, in his monumental survey of crime fiction, *Murder for Pleasure* (1942), Howard Haycraft asked if Francis Gérard and Gerald Fairley (note the initials) were the same man. When Fairley (who continued the 'Bulldog Drummond' series) died, I was, through the courtesy of criminology experts J. H. H. Gaute and Robin Odell, able to ask this question of Mrs Fairley, who categorically stated that her late husband never wrote other than in his own name.

Remembering Gérard had also written three 'Sanders of the River' novels by permission of the Edgar Wallace Estate, I asked Wallace's daughter, Penelope, a former CWA Chairman, and she put me in touch with the present Organiser of the Edgar Wallace Society, Colonel John A. Hogan, who gave me some facts.

Born in 1906, the son of French-born Maurice Gérard, and with his boyhood spent in France, this lover of Edgar Wallace books became a Major in the Essex Regiment during the War, serving in Malta. He married Anne Valerie—to whom this book is dedicated—and they lived at 22 Caroline Terrace, near Hyde Park Corner, but he was so frustrated at the problems of getting some wood for shelves in his library that he emigrated to Natal on 22nd December, 1946. He became a South African citizen and died there in the early 1960s.

Gérard had written for Edgar Wallace's magazine *The Thriller*, and published his first book featuring his detective John Meredith in 1934, thus slightly preceding Michael Innes, both of whom gradually promoted their sleuths from Inspector to Commissioner, with a knighthood *en route. The Mind of John Meredith* appeared in 1952, and Francis Gérard features in it himself as a serving army officer meeting Brigadier Meredith, who has just received his knighthood. Meredith is suffering both from his War service in Intelligence and from the loss from a V1 bomb of his beautiful wife, his son and his elegant house. Sent to a stately home to recuperate, he finds himself in the middle of a family mystery involving murder and lycanthropy. This brings me to the third notable factor which impressed me so much as a schoolboy reader, for Gérard frequently starts his books with a Prologue, set in the past or in a far or primitive country but which seems to govern the lives and minds of the characters today.

The Welsh Border Castle of High Perwyl is the hereditary home of Sir Martin Lauder-Treaves, whose ancestor was cursed by a Welsh chieftain he was torturing—and now the baronet finds every indication that he is turning into a wolf! Anyone who saw Lon Chaney Junior in one of the many 'Werewolf' films will recognise the signs—a large dog roams the estate by night, he finds the scent of animals on his body—so he lashes himself to a chair at night for protection. Is lycanthropy possible, as some writers like Baring-Gould tell us? Are the family records foretelling a terrible future for Martin and his American wife? Can his cousin Yves help him escape? The pressure increases, as does the terror, but as in all Gérard's books, there is, in spite of the authentic gothic atmosphere, a down-to-earth explanation.

Gérard has a felicitous turn of phrase, and I am delighted and proud to be able to bring a book by this first-rate author into the Black Dagger series and to contribute this Foreword to mark his re-emergence.

JOHN KENNEDY MELLING

John Kennedy Melling, the Editor of the Black Dagger series, has been a crime book reviewer for BBC Radio both in London and Essex. As a crime and fiction historian he has specialised in parody and pastiche in the genre.

THE BLACK DAGGER CRIME SERIES

The Black Dagger Crime series is a result of a joint effort between Chivers Press and a sub-committee of the Crime Writers' Association, consisting of Marian Babson, Peter Chambers and chaired by John Kennedy Melling. It is designed to select outstanding examples of every type of detective story, so that enthusiasts will have the opportunity to read once more classics that have been scarce for years, while at the same time introducing them to a new generation who have not previously had the chance to enjoy them.

MY DEAR,

Were I to follow my instinct this dedication would be couched in somewhat fulsome, not to say flamboyant, phrases. But such usage is quite foreign to your nature. I will content myself, therefore, with something more direct and say simply: "This is for Anne, with my love."

FRANCIS.

CONTENTS

		PAGE
	Prologue: THE WELSH MARCHES, A.D. 1164	7
CHAPTER		
I.	EMPTY WELCOME	15
II.	MEREDITH ON THE THRESHOLD	29
III.	FINELLA-LOU	40
IV.	THE FAMILY AT HIGH PERWYL	48
V.	MIKE	58
VI.	"AS THROUGH A GLASS DARKLY"	70
VII.	THE DAM BREAKS	77
VIII.	THE DISCIPLINE OF THE DOGS	83
IX.	DEATH OF AN INNOCENT	89
X.	TOOTH AND CLAW	97
XI.	DEUS EX MACHINA	106
XII.	BROWN BRUMMY	114
XIII.	HISTORY	119
XIV.	THE STAYLEY DOCUMENT	126
XV.	PERWYL'S BANE	136
XVI.	PSYCHIATRIST'S OPINION	142
XVII.	VIRGINIA'S BIRTHDAY	152
XVIII.	THE MARK OF THE BEAST	158
XIX.	"FROM THE POWER . . . O LORD DELIVER US."	173
XX.	LULL BEFORE THE STORM	180

CONTENTS

CHAPTER		PAGE
XXI.	ROSE WITHOUT A THORN	192
XXII.	UNHAPPY BIRTHDAY	199
XXIII.	THE ACCUSATION OF THE DOGS	205
XXIV.	DARK EXIT	226
XXV.	THE KILL	229
XXVI.	MEREDITH EXPLAINS	242
XXVII.	COMING EVENTS	252

THE MIND OF JOHN MEREDITH

PROLOGUE

THE WELSH MARCHES, A.D. 1164

THE man was dying—slowly and excruciatingly—but it would be long before that giant frame and those enormous thews granted him the release for which his spirit would not permit him to cry aloud to his enemy. Slowly, very slowly, the spit on which he was impaled revolved. The archer at the windlass was sweating freely, more so than the man who, beneath his ministrations, was dying. There was an explanation for this, for the sweat upon Rhodri Mawr's face and naked body evaporated swiftly in the heat rising from the fire below him.

The garrison watched him, fascinated and rather fearfully, bearing in mind his reputation as a warlock. True, fire had ever been Mother Church's cure for such disease, but a humble archer or man-at-arms could not be sure. The folk from the small but ever-growing burgh at the foot of the hill watched him with all the sympathy prompted by the admixture of blood which was the heritage of such people on the Welsh Marches, who counted their breeding within a century of raid and counter-raid, foray and reprisal, and all that it left behind it in savage sireing of progeny. This man who was dying before their eyes was a prince among his own kind and of a kindred stock to theirs.

A sound, part-prayer, part-curse, part-moan issued from the tortured man's lips. Yves de Tréves pricked his ears and nodded to the big man-at-arms who stood, stripped of his jerkin, at the opposite end of the spit to the archer who exerted his own giant strength to turning the weight which was his labour. At once the fellow raised a great pitcher to cast water upon the flames rising from the faggot fire. Again Sir Yves nodded and a second vessel of water emptied its contents over the naked body of the Welsh prince. Steam and smoke rose, enveloping the dying man, and the hiss which came to the ears of those within hearing was not only from the fire, but from Rhodri Mawr's body which turned the drops of water to steam in its heat.

The pain of this rude bathing was so great that, despite the rigid iron driven through his thighs and forearms, the man straightened convulsively and emitted a shuddering groan, instantly caught back between the bars of his lips, almost as rigid as the brutal metal upon which he was suspended. "The dog dies hard," commented Yves de Tréves, "more faggots to the fire! Let it not be said that we did not grant warm welcome in King Henry's name."

. . . . . .

It was Evan ap Price who brought the news. He arrived at dusk on a sweating hill pony which he had ridden into a white lather. The thunder of their arrival alone was sufficient to warn the tribesmen of the tref that something was amiss for, in those days of raid and counter-raid, no man but approached his own holding in silence and the wariness of suspicion. In war between Norman and Celt, treachery was but another name for ruse. The tref folk heard his stuttered message with dismay. This was, indeed, the blackest tidings. From tref to cantref the news travelled by rider and runner, until there was not a tribesman in all the wild hills of Gwynedd, or even in the sister-land of Powys, who had not learned the dread tidings.

Rhodri, the hope of Gwynedd, was taken at last.

Worse, of all those bloody men who held the Marches from Montgomery in the north to Pembroke in the south for the Angevin Henry of England, it had to be into the ruthless hands of Yves de Tréves that he had fallen. All Wales, even as far south as the half-hearted Deheubarth, knew what the Wolf had sworn to do to Rhodri Mawr should he take him.

. . . . .

THE WELSH MARCHES, A.D. 1164

It had been with the dawn of the new year that the Celtic chiefs had risen against their titular overlord, Henry II. The King had been in Aquitaine at the time, engaged upon his eternal quarrel with his cousin of France, and it had been in no kindly mood that he had been obliged to return to his unruly kingdom across the Channel to teach his Welsh subjects something of the weight of his hand. His mood had not been softened when, after storming north at the head of a confident army of Normans and bastard-Saxons, he had been decisively worsted in the field by the rebels. The heavily armed Norman troops were no match for the tribesmen fighting on their own ground, nor did they understand war as waged by these hillmen who struck and vanished into the screen of their damned eternal mists before the mailed men could recover from the initial shock. Smarting under this defeat, which was an affront to his high majesty, Henry cast about for some object upon which to vent his royal spleen. With those protruding eyes of his gorged with blood and squinting slightly with the weight of the uncontrollable rage which one day would occasion the murder of an Archbishop of Canterbury, Henry recalled the hostages. These, the sons and daughters of Celtic chiefs, he had held for some three years and had, to do him justice, lodged them fairly and according to their station. Now they were become less and more than the heirs and daughters of princely enemies. They were small children, the means by which to inflict upon the rebel dogs a hurt as great as that which he himself had suffered. For the boys, the heated iron and the empty and withered eye-socket. For the girls, the sudden sharp pain which deprived them of their childish beauty and left them to face life noseless and without ears.

With the callous brutality of the age Henry sent the children home that the Welshmen might learn that it was not with impunity they could affront the king's high majesty. It was a mistaken gesture, for the hot-blooded Celts swore upon the heads of their horribly mutilated children that they would not rest until they had avenged the outrage.

Among these pathetic hostages had been Rhodri Mawr's three children: Howel and Mervyn, the boys; and Aila, the girl. It had been Owen, the brother of Evan ap Price, who had brought them back riding upon sturdy little Welsh cobs. Owen, himself, had been set free by the Keepers of the Marches, for in place of his hands there were left to him naught but shapeless stumps, roughly encrusted with dried tar. Rhodri had gathered his children in his arms, kissed them and, handing them over to the care of the wise-woman who had been their nurse since their mother's death, went out from his holding with his face to the east. At his back rode fifty dalesman who had fled the Marches when the Normans came and who had old scores to pay off against the hated foreigner.

Not yet thirty, Rhodri, himself descended from that Rhodri Mawr who had been king of all the land of the Cymry nigh on three hundred years before, was one of whom the stuff of legend is made. His mother, Aila of the Long Hand, was of the fey people of Anglesey, a strange woman of strange powers in whose presence many of the rude hillmen made the horns— for safety's sake. She knew the power of healing and, some said, its opposite. It is undoubted that she had the Sight and foretold the day, the hour and the place of her husband's death, though in the manner of his passing she had been at fault, for it had been a spear and not a sword which had pierced his side. Her son, Rhodri, was liker his dam than his sire, though he inherited from the latter his enormous stature and phenomenal strength. Men said of Rhodri Mawr that he had scant need of his weapons and it is true that once, at least, he struck down his enemy merely by holding him with his eyes. Rhodri had been unarmed at the time of the encounter and his adversary, a maurading, thieving Breton of the following of Yves de Tréves, had swung up a battle-axe and then, with the Welshman's eyes upon his face, had stood unmoving until the axe fell from his hand and he turned and shambled away, staggering and lurching in his gait as one in wine. The Norman garrisons upon the border said uneasily that the man was a warlock and swore that the big grey cob he rode was in truth a kelpie. Certes, in all the forays in which he had carried his master the pale cob had taken never a scratch, though he came out of the fight almost piebald with blood—from others.

It was three days after the return of Howel, Mervyn and Aila to their father's cantref that a strange little procession was seen approaching the dour fortalice which housed the Wolf of Tréves and his garrison. When Sir Yves learned the manner and condition of the newcomers, his rage knew no bounds. They were thirty men-at-arms, long overdue replacements for his depleted muster. Eagerly awaited, they came now in parlous state. Rhodri Mawr and his dalesmen had ambushed them and sent them on their way to their master without their eyes, their ears, their noses or their hands.

Yves le Loup de Tréves sat that night over his stock-fish, the victuals in the fortress were getting low, and thought as to how he could best acquaint Henry with the story and a request for fresh reinforcements. The devil was in that gross-bellied king in Westminster, and one scarce knew whether the great stomach would shake and shudder with laughter at the tidings or whether the bulging eyes would glare in lunatic anger. The news would go up and down the Marches and he, himself, would become the butt of his fellows' wit. It was not to be borne. These damned Norman earls—Yves, as a Breton, despised them—who held the other great keeps along the border must not be allowed with impunity to scoff at the wolf-banner. He had the name for being the most ruthless of all the king's wardens and he would keep it.

When the courier came at last to Westminster, the tale he bore occasioned his royal hearer considerable satisfaction for of all the Celtic chieftains of the Cymry, Henry judged Rhodri Mawr the most dangerous.

"A gift for Sir Yves," said Henry in high good humour and throwing the courier his purse. "Bear this to your master with my love and pleasure, an you will, bidding him hold the rascal fast."

"Hélas, my fair and sovereign lord," sighed the courier, "it were no longer possible, even for the Wolf of Tréves."

The king's protruding eyes began to darken. "How now, sirrah, are the Wolf's fangs falling with age that they have lost their grip?"

"Even the arm of your dread majesty, my sweet liege, could

no longer hold Rhodri Mawr for, it is to be hoped, the devil himself will be holding him now."

The royal belly began to heave and shake. "Dead?" he asked in high delight.

"As yester-night's flagon, an it please, your grace."

"And the manner of his passing?"

The courier told him.

. . . . .

It was the late afternoon some three days before the courier came to Westminster that Rhodri Mawr was led out to die.

The infamous manner in which de Tréves had secured the person of the Welsh chieftain was one which pleased his cunning spirit mightily. Following the arrival of those maimed and useless men-at-arms at his fortress, which the tribesmen had come to name High Peril, the Wolf, curbing his instinct to ride out openly against his enemy, kept strict watch from the battlements of his frowning keep. During the days that followed, the occasional unwary flash of a weapon in the woods across the river spoke eloquently of the continued presence of the Welshmen. After the lapse of a week there came a great blowing of trumpets, stamping of horses, shouting of orders, ring of hammers and all the attendant bustle and turmoil of an armed force setting out on the march. All this was duly reported to Rhodri Mawr, who lay a few miles back at the tref belonging to a kinsman. He rode forward to where he had left his fringe of scouts in time to witness the departure of the Seneschal and what appeared to be almost his entire garrison, riding under the blue wolf-banner, that banner which had become the terror and the bane of the greater part of Gwynedd. The column moved westward, maintaining an orderly march discipline and quietly shepherded on the flanks by the unseen Celtic tribesmen. It appeared that the objective of the expedition lay north towards Anglesey. For five days or so the wolf-banner moved resolutely on and Rhodri Mawr gathered the hillmen from far and wide to make an end of the Warden and his company.

It was almost a week after the expedition had set out from High Peril that Rhodri Mawr's scouts made capture of young Bertrand de Tréves, who was squire and own nephew to Sir Yves. He was brought into the presence of Rhodri Mawr, a pretty fellow and unarmed save for the straight sword which hung at his hip. He seemed no wit abashed by the peril of his condition.

"It seems," said Rhodri, "that in stooping at the wolf I have first fleshed the cub."

"Nenni, Sir Rhodri," smiled young Bertrand easily, "bethink you with what ease your men took me. Will you not wonder an it were not by my uncle's design?"

"I have yet to learn that Sir Yves would willingly make me such a gift," replied Rhodri Mawr, frowning, "and, by my hilt, *timeo danaos et dona ferentes*."

"What, learning from a barbarian?" queried Bertrand in supercilious surprise. "But a truce to such quips. I am come at my uncle's desire to acquaint you with his terms."

"Terms, an it please you?" observed his captor. "An it come to terms, certes, it is for me to speak, for I hold Sir Yves and all his following in the hollow of my hand."

The Breton laughed. "Get you home, my master," he advised, his ringed fingers playing with his little beard. "Get you home, you and," he looked disdainfully around him at the ragged circle of his enemies, "and these unwashed dogs. Go visit your cantref, your holdings, your villages. Why, by the bowels of God, you shall find much to warm you. That I may promise you."

"Speak fast, Sir Bertrand," snarled Rhodri Mawr, "and make your meaning plain, or else you will not speak again this side of the sod."

There was little to tell. With ever-growing fury and dismay the Welshmen learned how they had been duped by the cunning of the Wolf. He, himself, had never ridden with the main body of his forces. The great figure whom they had seen ride out was but a man-at-arms bedight in Yves' own ponderous armour. While Rhodri Mawr and all the tribesmen of North Gwynedd had been shepherding the Norman column over the hills and through the valleys, Sir Yves, with a second force lightly armed, had swept through the trefs, burning and pillaging as he went and was even now safe back within his fortalice together with the women and children of the principal tribesmen whom he had taken in his withdrawal.

"Thus, then, speaks the Seneschal, my uncle," nodded Bertrand de Tréves. "Withdraw your men and yield safe passage to the company under my banner. No blow shall be struck. Nor injury offered. I will stay my hand for the space of one sennight until the feast of the Blessed St. Barnabas. Upon that day all those of my company will be returned unscathed together with the person of Sir Rhodri Mawr, whose life is forfeit to me by reason of his dastardly attack upon my garrison. Fail to comply with these my commands and from the day of the feast of St. Barnabas I will each morning, from my battlements, hang six women and six children and so I will do each dawning until my terms are fulfilled. This I have sworn to do upon my head and upon my soul and by the honour of the Wolf."

When Bertrand ceased speaking, there was a moment's stupefied silence and then he stood very still, for the Welshmen bayed him like dogs and only Rhodri Mawr's giant arm saved him from being torn to pieces by the pack.

Thus it was that Yves de Tréves took the most dangerous man in all Gwynedd in his own hills without a fight, for Rhodri Mawr went down into England and to death upon the feast day of St. Barnabas.

. . . . .

The man was dying—slowly and excruciatingly. The great head was hanging back now, the cords in the throat standing out under the strain. His huge physique and enormous vitality were not the only reasons why he took so wondrous a time a-dying, for his tormentors, under the skilled instructions of the Wolf of Tréves, never allowed the fire to blaze up under the impaled body to the point of consuming it. This was torture at its most refined, as well as execution. Yet even the brutal Seneschal could not altogether prevent the smoke from entering the air passages and Rhodri Mawr was nearing the time when, if life continued, pain would be no more. Just before he finally lost consciousness, Sir Yves came striding towards the spit and stood, arms akimbo and laughed his great belly-laugh at what he saw. The Welshman's eyelids flickered and the eyes, drunken and glazed with agony, fixed themselves upon the huge figure of his enemy.

"Wine," he gasped. "Wine. I would speak."

"And wine you shall have, Welsh cur, for you have provided merrier sport than I have known in others in your case. And I have known many."

An archer brought a small skin of wine and poured it clumsily into the dying man's mouth. Much of it ran down his face and hissed into the fire. After that reviving draught the tired eyes closed momentarily and then they opened again and in them was so fell a light, that the archer who had brought the wine involuntarily stepped back a pace as though that poor trussed thing could harm him.

"Hearken, then, Yves, whom men rightly call the Wolf," came the hoarse words from those cracked lips. "Men in after time shall have yet greater cause so to name you and those who spring from your loins."

Only Sir Yves, the archer at the windlass, his fellow with the wineskin and the man-at-arms holding a fresh pitcher of water, heard what the dying Welshman said. Afterwards not one of Sir Yves' three companions would speak of it. They shook their heads when questioned by their fellows and hastily crossed themselves at any mention of it. It is a fact that all three died within the year, but the Wolf lived on and begat himself sons and a daughter and from that night on knew a great and fearful rue.

CHAPTER I

EMPTY WELCOME

THERE were only the three of us in the car, for Geoffrey had dispensed with his ATS driver and was driving himself and, at the last moment, McAllister had been unable to get away owing to Monty putting in one of his sudden appearances in London. Stella and I sat in the back and, though we had not seen each other for some months, found little to say. Geoffrey Tracy, very magnificent with his red tabs and hat-band, was also far from the ebullience he usually displayed. In any case, these last few years at the War Office had taken much of the leaven out of him and he was growing as grey as a badger. Though the act of welcoming home an old friend is one usually attended by a spirit of gaiety, and though that was the mission upon which we were bound, our mood was melancholy.

The weather didn't help. It rarely did in this infernal country. It was early June 1945 and, as usual, it was a filthy day, raining cats and dogs. The flat East Anglian countryside looked dismal, damp and damned under a low mantle of swift-scudding clouds driven on by the whiplash of frequent squalls which flung the rain horizontally against the windscreen.

For some while, when we struck the Chelmsford by-pass, we were completely silent, only the harsh spatter of the rain, the hiss of the tyres, over the wet macadam and the tock-tock-tock of the windscreen-wiper provided a dreary accompaniment to our thoughts.

We were going to meet John Meredith, to welcome him home, and we were sad at the prospect.

My mind wandered back to the man as I had known him before the war. Physically a magnificent specimen, with those rather hard-bitten good looks which you find only in a certain type of Englishman, he was a singularly attractive fellow. He exuded an atmosphere of quiet confidence. One felt that here was a man who would have to think twice as to how to spell the word panic. All his history, indeed, bore this out. His unusual upbringing in India, largely influenced by his father's Pathan bearer, had provided him with an approach to things generally rare among his own kind. He had been schooled in self-sufficiency and his resource was infinite. I suppose he was an egoist, though he rarely spoke about himself, and such data as had been necessary to me in recording his more successful cases for the benefit of the police archives had had to be dragged out of him piecemeal. To only one person had Meredith really made surrender of himself. That was to his wife, Juanita. I shied away from my thoughts at this point, wondering miserably how the thing would have affected him.

My mind wandered once again and I recalled the last occasion upon which I had seen Meredith before he disappeared on the mission from which he was now returning, that mission upon which the Prime Minister, himself, had commented as being "in my opinion an example of personal fortitude, individual resource and consistent ingenuity unsurpassed by any one man in all the gallant catalogue of the last six years." Those words had been repeated in the *Gazette* announcing the award of the K.C.M.G. to Brigadier Sir John Meredith for "outstanding services to the Allied cause". The story of what Meredith had done to earn this signal award was still under a security ban and might so be for many years to come if, indeed, it were ever made public. I was privy to much of it, for my brigadier had warned me that Meredith had already expressed a wish through his chief, Sir Hector McAllister, for my assistance in writing his secret report.

I had seen John Meredith last in Malta. I was I.O. there at the time. It was July 1941. I had been coming up those innumerable stone steps from War Headquarters to my own office, overlooking Grand Harbour, when I had heard my name called and, turning, beheld a very tall figure clad in the service dress of a brigadier. Automatically I straightened and saluted and instead of acknowledging my gesture the other grinned. "You did that quite nicely," he said. " You don't look as funny as a soldier as I thought you would."

I stared. "Well, blow me bloody well sideways!" I exclaimed, "Meredith!"

He grinned, nodded and held out his hand. "Not so loud, Gérard," he said, "I'm a hell of a swell now, and am travelling under an alias."

"Gosh," said I, very impressed. "What's your official monicker?"

The blue eyes in the lean face twinkled and his mouth went up at the side in that charming, crooked little smile of his. "Tracy," he said, and we both burst out laughing.

I took him along to the Union Club and went into the Hall Bar. We sat down alone at the far end and, over a pink gin, I asked him what he was up to.

"I suppose you're with Sir Hector and the Regent's Park boys?" I suggested and he nodded. "Going on to Mid-East?"

"That's the next stop," said Meredith.

"And then?" I queried.

"And then," he replied, "into the blue." He paused, took a drag at his cigarette, exhaled a cloud of blue smoke from his lungs and added: "It's big game this time, Gérard. I'm going on *shikar* for the biggest game of all. And even *that* you're to keep under your hat."

At that moment the Defence Security Officer came into the bar and joined us and I was very annoyed to discover that he had been privy to Meredith's arrival while I had been told nothing in advance. The Luftwaffe arrived just about then and kicked tin cans about the roof while the Bofors and the heavies all round Grand Harbour and Sliema banged away with the usual Malta welcome.

Meredith was not going on until next day, as the Sunderland in which he had arrived had had engine trouble on the lap from Gib. and was now in the hands of its physician. So he came back to my little house at St. Julian's for the night. After dinner there was the usual start to the night's activities and we sat smoking on my little terrace so that he could see for himself what the Malta show was really like. His comment after the third raid was quite unaffected and absolutely in keeping with the man. He said: "You know, Gérard, it's much more fun out here. You've got a ringside seat and can really watch the fun. In London you see damn-all."

Well, that was one point of view. He left just before sundown the following evening from Kalafrana.

My mood of reminiscence was interrupted by Stella Tracy saying at my elbow: "Francis, how much does John know about Juanita and the boy?"

I shook my head. "I'm not sure," I replied. "He knows about it, of course, but in what circumstances he was told and by whom I haven't the least idea."

"It's bloody," said Geoffrey, from behind the driving-wheel. "Just unutterably, damnably bloody. Poor old John."

"Sir Hector," said Stella, "tells me that he's in pretty bad shape, too."

I nodded. "Yes," I said, "he's taken a pretty savage beating, in more ways than one."

"I hope they looked after him properly at that place in Sweden," went on Stella.

"Oh, I should think so," I assured her. "The Swedes were pretty decent and, of course, our own people at the Embassy were there to see that he got proper treatment."

"Poor old John," sighed Geoffrey again.

"Oh, Geoffrey," snapped his wife irritably, "for God's sake don't keep on moaning about poor old John."

"Well, what the hell do you want me to say?" he growled.

"For Pete's sake, shut up, you two," I admonished them savagely.

We were all of us very much on edge and Geoffrey, never able to leave well alone, continued to worry away like a man with an aching tooth.

"Anyway, Francis," he said, disagreeably, "you haven't had to listen to a lecture as I have ever since we left Queen's Elm this morning. 'Now mind you don't say this' or 'be sure not to mention that' or 'for heaven's sake be careful and don't put your foot in it'. Anyone would think I was a half-wit."

"Not anyone, my darling," said Stella, sweetly, "just me."

"Pipe down, you harpy," suggested her husband, "and make yourself useful for once, instead of merely decorative, and light me a cigarette."

Stella complied with his wish and leaning forward inadvertently thanks to the motion of the car, touched the lobe of his ear with the lighted end. At any other time this would have been the signal for a display on Geoffrey's part which would have made Berry look like the merest beginner, but it was typical of our common mood that he merely swore under his breath and took the cigarette between his fingers.

"Sorry, darling," said Stella, absent-mindedly.

We drove on again in silence, and after another twenty minutes or so I leaned forward and peered ahead.

"We should be nearly there," I said and Geoffrey nodded and pointed with one hand.

"There's a stocking or sock or whatever the RAF call their jolly little windbags which tell them which way to go."

We drew up before a big gate, bristling with barbed wire, and the blue-clad RAF policeman came forward to examine our passes. He peered into the car. "Colonel Tracy?"

"That's me," said Geoffrey.

"Major Gérard?"

"Here," I said.

"I'm not so sure, sir," he said, addressing Geoffrey, "about this lady's pass."

"It's all right, corporal, she's my wife."

"Well, would you be good enough, sir, to drive up to the C.O.'s office there and report?"

"Certainly," said Geoffrey and let in the clutch as the big gate was drawn aside.

In the office of the Wing-Commander of the Transport Command airfield we learned that a w/t message from the aircraft, a Skymaster, had stated that they were meeting unexpected headwinds and would be some thirty minutes late on schedule. That meant that we should have at least an hour to wait, for we had allowed ourselves a spare thirty minutes in case the formalities were stricter than, in fact, they had proved.

"I expect," said the Wing-Commander, "you'd like to go into the waiting-room. It's more comfortable there."

He escorted us across to a long, low building set at right-angles to his own office and explained to us, as we went, that it had been the mess ante-room of a bomber squadron, now on its way to the Far East.

The room, when we entered it, looked almost as though its previous young occupants might return at any moment from a raid over Germany. There were wicker tables and arm-chairs scattered about, the former still littered untidily with copies of illustrated magazines. The walls were unashamedly adorned with a picture gallery, largely supported by tin-tacks or pieces of sticky paper, devoted exclusively to the female form divine.

"By Jove!" said Geoffrey, screwing in his monocle. "What ho, what ho!"

"Oh come and sit down, Geoff, and don't be revolting," said Stella and Colonel Tracy, M.C., M.B.E., of the War Office, meekly sat down and picked up a four-month-old copy of *Esquire* from which all the jolly bits had been cut out.

I wandered round the long room and noted the scrawled signatures on the walls, the charcoal outlines of fantastic Gremlins and, over in one corner, where a telephone had been removed from the wall, a list of women's names and phone numbers which would have kept Casanova busy for several generations. I wondered idly where the scribblers were now and how many of them were still able to note a telephone number on a wall. It was sad to think that the brave, noisy fellowship which this room had known was now reduced to the gloomy companionship of three middle-aged people waiting cheerlessly in dreary silence.

It was at this point in my sombre reflections that the door opened and a blue-clad orderly appeared who saluted and said: "Major Gérard, sir?" I nodded. "The C.O.'s compliments and would you mind stepping down to the orderly room for a moment? London's on the blower for you." He corrected himself hastily, adding: "I mean phone, sir."

Both Stella and Geoffrey glanced up at the information and, muttering something about not being long, I followed the orderly back to the office where we had been received by the Wing-Commander. It was the latter who indicated the telephone as I came in, saying: "There's a General McAllister on the line for you, Gérard. Seemed to think it was bloody urgent."

"Hello," I said, into the phone, "Gérard here, Sir Hector."

"Thank goodness I've got you," came the voice of the big Scotsman, who was chief of the only Intelligence Department which really mattered. "Has that plane come in yet?"

"No, sir," said I, "they made a signal a little while ago saying they'd be late."

"Thank God," breathed the telephone.

"I gather something's wrong," I suggested.

"Like hell it is," said Sir Hector. "Listen, Gérard, between the Swedish specialist who was looking after Meredith and our own people at the Embassy, they've balled the whole thing up. I mean about Juanita and the boy," he added, as though in explanation.

I frowned down at the phone, slow in the uptake. "What *about* his wife and son?" And then it dawned on me. "D'you mean . . ."

"Yes, I do," came McAllister's voice, "the bloody fools have let him leave Sweden in ignorance of what's happened."

I nearly dropped the telephone. "Oh, Christ!" I exclaimed helplessly.

"I don't know what you're going to do about it, but you and the Tracys will have to think pretty fast. I'm awfully sorry about this, Gérard, but now, I'm afraid, it's up to you."

"Okay, Sir Hector," I said hopelessly, "we'll cope, somehow. G'bye."

"'Hang on a second. Tell the Tracys that unless they hear to the contrary I'll get down to Queen's Elm some time this evening, if only for a few minutes."

"Right-ho, sir."

I made two boss shots at replacing the phone in its cradle before I hit it off. The Wing-Commander stared at me curiously. "Something gone wrong?" he asked.

I looked at him for a moment or two without replying. Though I had heard what he said it hadn't immediately registered. I nodded.

"Do you know who's coming in on this plane?" I asked him.

"Yes, I've got a list here," he replied. "Chap who's our Press Attaché in Stockholm, a couple of N.O.'s who've been playing games with the Swedes and one V.I.P."

"Very Important Person," I echoed. "Know who he is?" The other shook his head. "In that case I suppose I'm not at liberty to tell you, but I can tell you what's gone wrong. He's a chap who's done a hell of a job of work. Been . . . overseas for some years. He's been knocked about and pretty well played out. He's coming home now and he hasn't got a home and he hasn't got a wife and he hasn't got a son. The whole lot written off by a bloody V1."

"And he doesn't know? Phew! You've got a jolly job, haven't you?"

"You can call it that," I said, and went out of the office.

I walked back to the ante-room-cum-waiting-room and, without wasting words, told the Tracys what Sir Hector had said. Neither of them uttered a sound. Stella looked white and ill and poor old Geoff seemed to shrivel up. It was he who, at last, broke the long, pregnant silence. "Who tells him?" His voice was a harsh croak.

As though they were controlled by a single string both Geoffrey's and my head turned slowly towards his wife. Stella looked horribly distressed.

"Recommend me," she sighed, "to a couple of soldiers for moral courage."

"Honestly, old girl," Geoffrey was beginning, when she cut him short.

"I didn't mean it," she said, "only it does seem so grossly unfair this sort of thing always has to be done by a woman. Of course I'll do it. Poor darling," she ended.

"But what does the poor old chap *think*?" exclaimed Geoffrey, lighting a cigarette with an unsteady hand.

"God knows," said I. I stared around me vaguely. "I wonder if that Wingco could rustle up a couple of drinks?"

"Oh, heavens," said Stella.

"It does help, you know," nodded her husband.

However, there wasn't time for, at that moment, we became conscious of the sound of an approaching aircraft and a moment or so later the same orderly appeared at the door to inform us that this was the plane we were expecting.

"Circling the airfield, now, sir. C.O.'s compliments, and, if you care to, you can come out onto the runway with him."

The ground was still pretty wet but, thank God, it had stopped raining. As we stood aside for Stella to go through the door I heard her gasp as though she were suddenly being plunged into ice-cold water. Instinctively, I did one of those things which, in a man, is so well-meaning and so often misfires. I slipped an arm round her shoulders and kissed her cheek. She was deathly cold and trembling like a frightened filly. She pushed me away almost roughly. "Oh, don't, Francis," she said, "or I shall howl."

Geoffrey moved up on the other side of her and took her hand. She seemed grateful for it. With sick apprehension the three of us, who were to welcome poor old Meredith home, walked out onto the runway.

The huge aircraft, its powerful engines roaring thunderously, swept overhead only a few hundred feet up and I stared at its great hull, striving to catch a first glimpse of Meredith. I wondered, suddenly, whether, perhaps, he might not be expecting Juanita and young Rupert to be. . . . My stomach turned over and I thought for one frightful moment that I was actually going to vomit. I felt like hell and, glancing at my companions' faces, saw that they looked like death warmed up.

The Skymaster made a lovely three-point landing some hundred yards to the north of where we were standing and then swung majestically round and ambled in an astonishingly amiable manner towards us. It came slowly to rest and we moved forward into the shadow of the giant wing. A couple of Erks trundled forward the stepped gangway to the side of the hull and the smoothly fitting door swung open.

One of the crew emerged carrying a small case and then there seemed to be some sort of a mix-up. Eventually I saw that there was some chap being assisted out by two other men. I wondered impatiently whether he were the Press

Attaché, but he didn't look sufficiently alert for that sort of a job. White-headed old chap, using a couple of arm-crutches. Thin, to the point of emaciation, too, but still rather a distinguished-looking old boy. I looked eagerly past him for some sign of Meredith and it was Stella's whispered: "Oh, my God!" at my elbow which prompted the truth. That withered, helpless old cripple, whose clothes hung on him like sacks, was Meredith.

One of the things that I have discovered during the course of this war is that men cry more easily than is generally supposed or admitted. I've seen a number of them cry for a variety of reasons and can recall a naval doctor in a destroyer actually weeping over the appalling wound in an Italian submariner's back. I thought, just after realising that I was looking at Meredith, that I was crying. I wasn't, but I almost suffocated. I found myself literally breathless. K.C.M.G., I thought! Not even a bloody dukedom would compensate for this.

With the first whimper which broke from Stella's lips, Geoffrey turned on her savagely.

"Shut up!" he snarled. "If you go to pieces I'll . . . so help me, Stella, I'll. . . ." He gripped her arm above the elbow and urged her forward. I went with them, my feet moving reluctantly.

Meredith and his two helpers had reached the ground and, though his voice was weak as he turned to thank them, it hadn't changed, thank heaven. And then I saw the ghost of the old crooked little smile as he looked up and saw us standing there. Impulsively, Stella ran forward and flung her arms round him. There was no question of not crying now. She howled all over him, sobbing convulsively and Meredith, dropping one of his short crutches, patted her helplessly on the back. Geoffrey and I couldn't find a hand to shake, so we stood and patted Meredith. It sounds ridiculous but it was too deeply affecting adequately to be described in words.

And then, then I saw that the really ghastly moment had arrived. Those washed-out blue eyes, once so brilliant and now pale and muddy, were searching beyond us. And then it came. "I suppose," asked the husky voice, "I suppose Juanita is still not well enough to come?"

I saw Stella's face crumple up like a baby's and then set rigidly.

"No," she said, gently. "Look, John dear," she went on, "let's get off this beastly damp stuff, there's a comfortable room just across there. Can you make it, old boy?"

"Oh, yes, rather," Meredith nodded. "I'm getting quite good with these things now."

I'd had a word with the C.O. while we were standing waiting for the plane to land and, like the good fellow he was, he had arranged for us to have the exclusive use of the waiting-room. As we went slowly towards it he came up and caught my elbow.

"I say, Gérard," he said, *sotto voce*, "I've had a bottle of brandy, a siphon and some glasses shoved in there for you."

"Brandy?" I said, stupidly.

"*Bisquit du Bouché*," he winked.

"My dear fellow," I said, "that's extraordinarily handsome of you and devilishly thoughtful, but are you sure that you can . . . ?"

"That's all right," he said, rather shyly, "we get . . . well, we get a few bits and pieces coming in from the other side, you know."

We settled Meredith in one of the wicker arm-chairs and he said yes to being asked if he were allowed a spot of brandy. It was as Stella placed the glass in his hand that she looked at her husband and me and gave the faintest jerk of her head towards the door.

"Oh—er—yes," said Geoffrey, inanely, while I hastily murmured something about having to clear our permits before leaving the airfield. We went out and I think we shared a mood of both thankfulness and reluctance.

I never learned just what took place at that dreadful little interview, but it was not until some three-quarters of an hour later that Stella came out and joined us in the C.O.'s office, leaving Meredith alone. Her expression was strangely peaceful. We asked her if he were all right and she nodded. "It was almost," she said, "as though he were prescient, and, in any case, I think he has suffered so much in whatever he's been doing that he is, somehow, beyond further suffering, even such as this. John is . . . changed isn't the word. He's . . . he's somehow not quite in this world."

"D'you mean," I asked bluntly, "he's not quite in his right mind?"

She hesitated. "N-no, I don't, I mean. . . ." She looked up suddenly, her lips parted. "D'you know, I've just realised I can tell you exactly what I mean. John has today that kind of suggestion of being . . . of being disembodied which, you know, you find in a genuine mystic. That queer lack of animation which seems to spring from a real carelessness as to the things which *we* think matter. I know that sounds awfully involved and rather high-falutin', but that *is* what I mean. You'll see it for yourselves. The old John, the John we knew before the war has . . . well, he just isn't there."

Geoffrey shook his honest head. This was all much too esoteric for him. "Oh, I expect old John'll perk up when he's had some decent grub and a good lie-around in the country. A few weeks down at Queen's Elm and you won't know him. Or rather, going by what Stella says, you probably will."

As I was to learn subsequently, Stella's womanly intuition had been singularly and irritatingly right. Anyway, Meredith didn't look very different when we went to collect him in the car to drive him off to the Tracys' place in Hampshire. It was as we were waiting for the gate onto the main road to be opened that a big staff car drew up outside so abruptly that the tyres screamed on the macadam, while the brakes ground horribly. A very immaculate young Guardsman with three pips on his shoulder leaped out, flourished a pass at the gate policeman who was even then making a road for us. He started at a run towards the administrative buildings and then hesitated as he saw our car. He came across, caught sight of Geoffrey's red tabs and saluted smartly.

"Forgive me, sir," he said, "but I'm from War Cabinet offices, may I ask if one of you gentlemen is Sir John Meredith?"

Geoffrey nodded and jerked his thumb over his shoulder to the back of the car. I turned to where Meredith sat at Stella's side, his gloved hands tucked under a heavy rug.

"My name's Hawtrey, Sir John," the young Coldstreamer explained. "I must apologise for not being down here to meet you. The P.M. particularly requested that I should be, but we were given to understand that your plane was not getting in until this afternoon. It was quite by chance that General McAllister put us right. I do apologise, sir. I have been commanded by the P.M. to give you this."

Meredith took the thick blue envelope and opened it. The letter inside was written in ink and ran to two pages of the none-too-familiar script. Meredith read it through without a word, then, handing the letter to Stella, he turned to the boy standing beside the car and said quietly: "Would you thank the Prime Minister very much from me? I will, of course, reply myself, but please be good enough to thank him. Thank you also for bringing it."

"Certainly, sir, I'll give your message and . . ." He looked suddenly shy. "I . . . I would have liked," he stammered, "I mean, I would have liked to have been here to have shaken hands with you, sir. I . . . you see, Sir John, I know what you've done."

Without the flicker of a smile Meredith extended a thin hand through the lowered window of the car. The boy took it and then drew himself up to attention and his hand went up in the salute which you only learn at Wellington Barracks.

As Geoffrey let in the clutch, I took the letter which Stella was holding out to me. It was an extraordinary letter, written by an extraordinary man. It was the sort of document which a man is apt to treasure and to show his children when they are able to understand it. It was signed: "Winston Churchill."

Meredith received it in silence, folded it and placed it in his wallet. The gate swung open, the car rolled forward and turned south towards Hampshire.

CHAPTER II

MEREDITH ON THE THRESHOLD

To Meredith, Queen's Elm, the Tracys' lovely Queen Anne house on the sweeping Hampshire hillside, was familiar of old. He knew and loved the warm, rose brick and gracious rooms almost as much as that other house of the same period which, before the explosion of that fateful V1, had been his home. With anxious tact Lady Mary had put him in the opposite wing to that which had housed him in the past, when he had been there with Juanita, and the windows of his rooms gave him a view of the Dutch water-garden which stretched as far as the great semi-circular hedge which told of the yew maze beyond. It had been impressed upon him by his hostess that he was to please himself and do exactly as he wanted. In consequence, apart from an occasional halting stroll with his crutches over the wide lawns beneath the spreading cedars, Meredith spent most of his time during those first few days seated in a deep, chintz-covered armchair at his bedroom window.

He was completely docile, eating what he was told to eat and drinking his half-bottle of claret each evening with his dinner, a gift, did he but realise it, of very real affection in these days of sadly depleted cellars.

Geoffrey had gone back to the War Office after driving him down to Hampshire and, apart from the family and the servants, Meredith had seen nobody except McAllister, who had driven down and spent an hour with him on the night of his arrival. In consequence, the telephone message that morning sent Lady Mary Tracy in hurried search of her daughter-in-law. She found Stella helping the ancient housemaid who, apart from the cook, was now the only indoor servant, to make the beds.

"We have a problem, Stella," she announced, pushing back a wisp of hair from her forehead with that characteristic gesture of hers. "Sergeant Beef's rung up and wants to come down and see John."

"Well, it's very natural," replied her daughter-in-law.

"Yes, but he sounded frightfully excited," said Lady Mary, "and you know what the old boy's like. Hardly the soul of tact. He's sure to put his foot in it."

Stella straightened herself from arranging the counterpane on the bed and regarded her mother-in-law with a little frown.

"I'm just wondering, you know, whether we're right in cosseting John like this. I feel he might be more likely to snap out of it if we were to study him less."

"I think, darling, we'd better wait to hear what Sir Hector's man has to say about that. John's body will mend now of its own accord. The psychological side of it is too tricky for us to play about with."

"Still, I shouldn't worry too much if I were you, mother, we can have a word with old Beef beforehand and warn him."

Ex-Detective Sergeant Matthew Beef, who had been Meredith's assistant at Scotland Yard for many years, who had retired with him and who had helped him on many of the queer cases entrusted to him by Sir Hector McAllister's department, was a very literal-minded person. In her telephone conversation with him, Lady Mary had suggested that he should "come to lunch and come early so that you can have plenty of time with Sir John." Beef, who had to travel into southern Hampshire from north of Colchester, arrived the following morning just after Stella and her mother-in-law had finished their breakfast.

"Good heavens!" exclaimed Lady Mary, as Beef was shown into the morning-room where they were sitting. "How d'you do, Sergeant? *Whatever* time did you start?"

"Mornin', Lady Mary. Mornin', Mrs. Geoffrey," said Beef. "Yes, thank you, I could do with a nice cuppa. It seems a long time since I 'ad my little bit o' spam and pickles as Mrs. Beef got me for my brekker."

Lady Mary concealed a shudder as she handed her stout, red-faced guest tea in one of her best Crown Derby cups.

"Nice to see these coloured pieces again," nodded Beef appreciatively, "I gets heartily sick of this white utility muck."

Beef had brought his bowler hat into the morning-room with him and it now reposed on his knee. As he raised his cup to a widely-opened mouth he inadvertently caught his sleeve against the hat, after which he put in an astonishing display of juggling before he replaced the empty cup and its saucer on the table, while Lady Mary's heart returned to its normal position.

"Arh!" breathed Beef happily, wiping his large moustache with a downward circular motion of one finger. "And 'ow might you be keeping, m'lady?"

"Very well, thank you, Sergeant Beef, and you?"

"Mustn't grumble." He turned to Stella. "You look just your usual bloomin' self, Mrs. Geoffrey, if I may be permitted."

"You may be permitted a great deal," said Stella, "if you say nice things like that."

"It's just a way I 'ave, Ma'am," nodded Beef complacently, "and now, ladies, 'ow about Sir John?"

He stood up as though to proceed to the interview. Lady Mary smiled. "Not so fast," she said gently. Beef sat down again. "Before you see him, Sergeant," she went on, "of course I know that you'll be the soul of tact. . . ."

"That's right," said Beef.

". . . But I feel I ought to warn you that you will find a great change in Sir John."

"Arh," agreed the old C.I.D. man, "bound to be. A-course I don't know *exactly* what Sir John's been up to, seeing as 'ow I am relegated to unemployment, so to speak, but knowing 'im I'll bet it was where it really mattered and where it 'urt most. Larkin' about with them ruddy Nazis, like as not."

"I don't know, either, what he's been doing," said Lady Mary, "but whatever it is, it has taken it out of him mentally as well as physically."

Beef's big mouth opened and his jaw hung. "You don't mean . . . you don't mean as . . . as he's gone *nuts* ?"

"Good heavens, no! Nothing like that, but . . . well, it's very difficult to explain, you'll see for yourself that he seems sort of disinterested."

Beef nodded. "You leave it to me, m'lady," he reassured her. "Why, bless you, I know Sir John's moods and tenses, as you might say, like the back of my 'and. I'll just treat 'im the same as I always did. I shan't say nothin' to upset 'im."

In point of fact Beef was entirely right in his boast, though you mightn't have guessed it had you stood at Lady Mary's side as she opened the door into John's room and said: "Here's a visitor for you."

Meredith's head turned slowly. From his arm-chair by the window he regarded the newcomer quizzically and then, for a moment, just as though one magic-lantern slide had replaced its fellow and then been withdrawn again, the old Meredith appeared briefly in the characteristic little smile which twisted up one corner of his mouth.

"Good lord," he said, in that far-away voice. "Beef!"

Beef, for his part, stared incredulously, his eyes goggling. Then, crashing in where even an archangel would have tiptoed, he treated Lady Mary to a display of tact which almost made her faint.

"'Oly Moses!" he gasped. "Gawd rot me rops! What've they *done* to you, Sir John? You look *aw-ful*!"

Lady Mary put out a hand to the post of the door, while the other went to her heart. She inhaled deeply and then stood without breathing. Then, why then, something totally unexpected happened. Meredith's eyes crinkled up at the corners and he laughed, the first laugh he had known for many, many weary months.

Lady Mary found herself, willy-nilly, joining in and then she couldn't stop. Beef, feeling instinctively that he'd done something clever, opened his big mouth and bellowed.

"Why, that's the ticket, Sir John," he spluttered. "Just for a moment I reely thought you looked as if they'd unscrewed your mainspring. Lumme, give me quite a turn, you did, seeing you sitting there. Well, 'ow *are* you, sir?"

"Very much all the better for seeing you," replied Meredith, and wincing slightly at the bear-like grip and pumping which was Beef's handshake.

"Well, well," went on Beef, unexpected tears in his foolish, honest eyes. "Well, well, 'ere we are again."

Seeing that the situation was now, comparatively, in hand, Lady Mary left them together and went downstairs to babble to Stella about the fact that John had actually laughed.

"Kill-or-cure Beef from Harley Street—or thereabouts," said Stella, stupefied.

Meanwhile the two old friends were sitting facing each other, Beef's eyes hungrily examining the wasted lines of his old chief's face.

"Can't say you look in the pink, Sir John," he said at last, shaking his head. "Pretty bloody awful time you've 'ad, I gather. I 'ope you've done them Jerries a bit of no good."

"Yes," said Meredith quietly, just that and no more.

Beef waited, but nothing further was forthcoming. "Secret, I suppose," he suggested. "Very 'ush-'ush, eh, Sir John?"

"Yes, Beef," said Meredith. "I'm . . . not permitted to say anything about it."

"That's all right, Sir John, I never was one to pry, except in me job, o' course. Never stick your nose into what don't concern you and then you'll keep it clean, that's me motter. Nothin' very 'ush-'ush about my job, now."

"What *have* you been doing?"

"To start with just a bit o' this and a bit o' that," said Beef. "At the very beginnin' I did a lot o' this evacuation stuff, mostly mothers as was expectin'. Lumme, some of them was expectin' all right, *and* they wasn't disappointed, neether. I tell you, Sir John, I learned a thing or three on that job. Why, these East End London nippers was getting themselves born all over Essex, in Greenline Coaches, in the back o' me car. Somethin' chronic, it was. But that didn't last long, and then I did a bit of ARPin', sort o' all round stuff, and then I specialise, as it were. I blossomed out." He slapped his knee a resounding whack. "You're lookin',

Sir John, at Beef the fire-fighter, and no mistake. Blimey, when I joined the NFS I really got a move on. All over the place. Colchester, London and even once as far as Sout'ampton. All through the blitz there was old Beef and 'is 'ose, pumpin' in the stuff for dear life. Cor, it was a proper do! I can't say I didn't enjoy it. Seemed to take years off me to find meself really useful again, and they was a fine bunch of chaps to work with." Beef glanced hastily at the door and then hitched his chair closer. "Tell you, though, Sir John, I made a bloody awful bloomer one night and got a rep for it from the big white chief, though 'ow the 'ell we were to know what was doin', I don't know. It was one night when Jerry was plasterin' incendaries all over a big aircraft plant at . . ." He broke off, pulled at his ear and said, hesitatingly: "Maybe I'd better not say where, we got our security in the NFS same as you 'ave in your job. Anyway, Jerry, was givin' this place a proper doin' over. It was in an area as we didn't know. We'd been brought in from outside a long way and as we neared what I took to be our destination, we come across a lot of buildings blazin' their 'eads off. It was a *lovely* fire. Before you could say knife, Sir John, I 'ad me chaps stuck into it good and proper. We done that fire a bit of no good and just as we got the 'ole thing out, up comes one of them army staff cars and a flock o' brass 'ats tumbled out, one of them yelling: 'Oo's the bloody fool in charge of this goddam outfit?' 'Me,' says I. 'Well, what's your name?' says 'e. 'Beef,' says I. 'Why?' 'Because I'm reportin' you for inefficiency,' says 'e. 'Inefficiency?' I says. 'We got this ruddy fire out quicker nor any o' your lousy outfits round 'ere could 'ave done.' 'Why, you blitherin' idiot,' says 'e, very 'ot, 'you've extinguished the biggest decoy-fire we'd established in the area!'"

Meredith kept Beef reminiscing until it was time for lunch, and soon after the meal Beef took his leave of his hostess and Stella dropped him off at the station in the dog-cart on her way to the Royal Air Force convalescent home, where she was a voluntary worker.

. . . . .

It was the following morning that General McAllister looked up in surprise from the file he had been studying as his secretary came into the office and said: "Brigadier Meredith's here to see you, Sir Hector."

"What, *here*?"

"He's waiting in my office." She glanced at the little watch on her neat wrist and added: "You can give him half-an-hour before you're due for your appointment with the Minister."

"At a pinch, my dear," said Sir Hector, "the Minister *could* wait, but Sir John can't. Bring him in at once."

He was waiting at the door of his office when Meredith came slowly into the room. "My dear fellow, I'm delighted to see you," said his chief, "but you shouldn't have come up from Hampshire."

John Meredith sank gratefully into the deep, leather armchair set across from the other's big desk and glanced round him with a little frown.

"A lot's happened since I sat here last," he observed. "Yes, a hell of a lot," he nodded drearily. He appeared to make an effort and went on: "I had to come up and see you as I couldn't very well say what I wanted over the phone without a scrambler, and I felt it might be unwise to commit it to paper."

The big Highlander waited patiently, his shrewd, kindly eyes observant of all the detail betraying the shocking change in his *vis-à-vis*. He pushed a box of cigarettes across his table towards the other and then, realising that Meredith would still not be able to reach it without rising, picked it up and walked quickly round the end of his desk to hold it out for the other man.

"Thanks," said Meredith, accepting a light from the other. "I'm afraid I'm smoking too many of these things. I came up this morning, incidentally I almost had to fight my way out of Queen's Elm, I came up to talk to you about this infernal report of mine."

"My dear fellow," said Sir Hector quickly, "it can wait. I thought I'd impressed that on you the other day. The P.M.

has, at my request, sent a personal letter to the President and our Ambassador in Moscow has had a word with Molotov. I heard, only this morning, that the White House is prepared to wait almost indefinitely and Uncle Joe, ever the realist, replied that the fact was what he was interested in, its record was largely of academic interest." Sir Hector broke off for a moment and shot a keen glance at Meredith before continuing. "Incidentally, John, I'm afraid you'll have to make up your mind to accepting a few more things to hang about you."

Meredith's eyes queried these last words and McAllister went on: "I know that these things don't really mean very much to you . . . now," he said awkwardly, "but I'm afraid you'll have to accept them, otherwise not only you but we will be giving offences to our Allies. The Russians are giving you the Order of Suvarov and the Yanks haven't said yet what they're turning in for you, but I gather it's something pretty high-powered."

John Meredith nodded with complete indifference and went on as though Sir Hector had not spoken at all. "I came to talk to you about this report of mine," he said. "I'm not interested in whether the powers-that-be want my report in or not. *I* want to get it off my mind. You were good enough to agree for me with Gérard's department that he should write it and I'd like to get on with it. I've made a few notes on a bit of paper and I can give Gérard a pretty good outline of the thing in an hour or so's conversation. So I was wondering. . . ."

"Look, John," said the big man, leaning forward and interrupting, "I know that you want to be shot of this thing as soon as possible, and I quite understand and am in complete sympathy, but you can't rush this, my dear fellow. I realise you're worn out and sick to death of the whole thing, but this report, together with the three copies of that sworn document which are held in London, Washington and Moscow, may well prove the most important documents in the political history of modern times. I know that sounds very pompous, but just think, John. If Germany ever attempts to resuscitate this particular thing, we've got her cold with those documents in our possession. Not six propaganda ministries, entirely staffed by men of the calibre of Goebbels, could break down that acid proof which we could flourish before the world." He shook his head and looked very straightly at Meredith. " No, no, John, I'm talking to you now, not as a friend, but as your superior officer. This report which you and Gérard will write between you must be completely detailed and documented. It must start at A and work through without any omission to Z. *I* know the kind of report I want from you and I realised that it was not a task upon which you were, at the moment, physically capable of embarking, and that's why I got the P.M. to explain any delay that our friends might have kicked at. As I see it, this is a job which may well take you months and, quite frankly, I think it would be useless as well as unfair to Gérard to bring him in at all at this stage. I know that he will write the finished draft, but it will be *your* draft and before he can begin to attempt it, he must have down on paper a hell of a lot of facts. Gérard's own department has sent me a whole lot of documents, which they have prepared in the course of their routine duties, which you will be able to use and I think you will find that a great deal of what they have recorded about facts and personalities in Germany will help to refresh your memory as you get your notes down."

McAllister finished speaking and regarded the other with an expression of bland assurance which veiled a keen anxiety, for Meredith had leaned back in his chair and closed his eyes as though the prospect before him were one of deathly weariness. The eyes in the wasted face did not open even when he, in turn, began to speak.

"I've lived with this thing now, Sir Hector," he said, "for almost seven years. You remember that, after that business with von Wallenfels before the war, I told you that I thought that that was only a beginning.[1] You remember that I went into *purdah* for nearly a year and then came to you and told you that I could speak perfect German? I knew in my bones that I'd have to use it and I was right. Well, that was one

[1] See the author's *Wotan's Wedge*.

year. Then came that time of intensive study until July '41, when I went in."

The weary voice broke off and McAllister sat very still and silent, watching the twitching mouth of the man in the deep chair opposite. The silence continued and the big Highlander, noting that nervous twitch and all the other signs which, in another man than Meredith, might well have been beyond the border of complete physical and mental collapse, recalled, with horrified pity, the man as he had known him before he went upon his dreadful mission. When Meredith again began speaking he seemed, at first, to have gone off at a tangent.

"You remember my father's bearer, Yussuf Khan?"

"Am I likely to forget him?" asked Sir Hector. "He died in the service of my department."

"Yes," nodded Meredith, "I sometimes think he was lucky. In India, when I was a child, Yussuf Khan taught me the elementary principles of *yoga*. One of the exercises was to empty the mind and then to induce reception of ideas and principles totally foreign to one's own personality. I made good use of his tuition while I was in Germany. *You* know the job I was on and you know too, that it *had* to succeed. For the first time in my life I allowed nothing, you understand, Sir Hector, *nothing* to stand in my way or to cause me to deviate one iota from my purpose. It involved . . . considerable sacrifice."

The last two words were barely audible to McAllister and in the silence which followed them he saw the other's face creased, as though in sudden pain and heard the long shuddering sigh which accompanied the grimace.

"You can be perfect in the language, you can carry yourself with the same loathsome assurance as those bastards, but unless your mind is receptively tuned-in to theirs, no agent could ever hope to get away with it—particularly a foreigner, as I was. When I was alone at night I used to get out the training manuals of instruction issued to the higher ranks of the Gestapo and the Waffen-SS. I used to spend about an hour doing the exercises which Yussef Khan had taught me so long ago and then I would spend half the night reading those damned publications until my mind had soaked it all up, absorbed it and, believe it or not, relished it. But for that nightly outrage upon my mind I could never have gone through with the things I was called upon both to witness and to do myself. For three solid years I've lived with the Nazi filth in my mouth and I tell you, Sir Hector, I can't go on with it. I feel my mind needs a complete purge—and quickly." Meredith's eyes opened and for a moment Sir Hector saw the old familiar blaze. And then it was gone and Meredith was just a broken man asking to be let off.

The big Scotsman rose to his feet and, hands in pockets, walked slowly up and down the room. The inter-office communication on the desk buzzed and McAllister, irritably, turned up the switch.

"You're due for your appointment with the Minister," came his secretary's voice.

"God bless the man," said Sir Hector, "I'd forgotten all about him. Ring through and tell him I'll get in touch with him this afternoon. Tell him . . . tell him I've had to go down to Downing Street. *He's* not likely to be there."

He pressed down the switch again, cutting off the sound of his secretary's delighted chuckle, and seated himself across the corner of his desk.

"Look, John," he said, "I think the thing for you to do is to forget all about this blasted report for the time being. Go away and do nothing. Concentrate on getting yourself physically fit and let the thing go hang. When you, yourself, feel that you can bear to turn in a proper job of work, come and tell me. Nobody knows better than I do what you've been through, and I also know that even I can't appreciate the half."

"Where can I go?" asked Meredith helplessly.

"You don't feel like staying on with the Tracys?"

John Meredith shook his head. "No," he said slowly. "They're sweet and kind, but I feel as though I'd rather be with people who didn't know me. I thought I'd get away, if possible, to some farm somewhere or other out in the wilds where, as my legs got better, I'd walk a bit. I . . . I asked old Beef, who came to see me yesterday, if Mike was still alive."

"Mike?" queried McAllister.

"That Sealyham of mine," explained John. "I thought I'd like to have him with me."

"Good idea," agreed the other. "He's probably the best company you could possibly have."

"It seems damn' silly," said Meredith, "but he's actually the only company I want."

"Still, you'll have to be somewhere where you can have your massage and all the rest of it."

"Yes, that's true, blast it, I'd forgotten that."

"Well, you get along back to Hampshire. I believe I've got an idea."

CHAPTER III

FINELLA-LOU

FOR some time after Meredith left, General McAllister sat in silence, his eyes staring blankly and unseeing through the window. At last he roused himself, glanced at his wrist and rose to his feet. He pressed the buzzer on his desk and was putting on his Sam Browne when his secretary came into the room.

"Just ring down for my car, will you? I shall be lunching at the club if I'm wanted."

The ATS lance-corporal saluted smartly as she held the door of the car for the man to whom, in her off-moments, she referred as "my old duck".

"Thank you, m'dear," said Sir Hector, who, after more than five years, could still never regard women as just "other ranks". "Take me to White's."

During the drive down through Baker Street and across Mayfair, Sir Hector's mind was still busy with the man who had so recently left his office. It was as he got out of his car in St. James's Street outside his club, that he heard a voice, with that lovely soft drawl which comes from only one part of the world, say: "Hector, darling! What luck! You can take me to lunch."

McAllister stared, as well he might, for he found himself looking at the girl with whom his thoughts had been tied up.

"Finella-Lou!" he exclaimed, "this is *kismet*!"

Finella-Lou was obliged to stand on tip-toe as, with complete naturalness, she put her face up to be kissed. Sir Hector hesitated, for a moment, as he caught the wooden expression on the face of his ATS driver and then stooped from his great height and saluted the girl on her cheek. He was obliged to straighten himself very hurriedly to return the salutes of two red-caps of the C.M.P., one of whom, without moving his lips, like a ventriloquist, observed to his companion: "What price the General and 'is bit?" To which his side-kick replied, apparently through his ear: "Nice piece of 'omework, too."

"Where shall we go?" asked Finella-Lou. "We can't go in there because White's despises women."

McAllister pointed with his stick down the street.

"Prunier's," he said, "and just hope for a table." He turned to his driver. "Let my secretary know where I am, will you?"

"Very good, sir."

They were fortunate and a few minutes later were seated across a table surveying each other with unmixed pleasure. McAllister, ever appreciative of a pretty woman, awarded this niece of his sister's full marks for looks. That was largely due to her personality, for Finella-Lou was by no means a beauty, according to the usually accepted standards. Her mouth was too wide, her nose too tip-tilted, her eyes too widely set apart in the neat head to measure up to classical acceptances, but she was a piquant little person with the charm of mischief in her face and she used her really lovely hands with all the infectious gaiety and vivacity of a French woman. Finella-Lou was from the South, the Deep South, and the Louisiana family from which she came was, in fact, sprung from old French stock. Her life, prior to her marrying an Englishman, had been divided between the lovely old *manoir*, Belle Allée just outside New Orleans, and her aunt's (Sir Hector's sister's) Colonial house in Kentucky. Between the two she had grown up in the atmosphere of two traditions, the one exquisitely formal and with the grace which once obtained in France, the other redolent of the old English squirearchy, where horses mattered more than men. She had been raised with all the heady perfume of magnolias and the clean vigour of Blue Grass. The result was Finella-Lou, a very exceptional little person, for she combined all the vigour and staying-power of the modern young woman with the disarming charm of those manners which are fragrant of the eighteenth century.

Over their *bisque homard* which, thanks to war-time difficulties, was more *bisque* than *homard*, Sir Hector asked: "And how's Martin?"

At once the little face which, a moment before, had been full of life and gaiety, lost all its fun and the twinkle dying out of the big grey eyes left them clouded and faintly puzzled.

She didn't answer at once. She put up her hands and removed the tenderly idiotic little hat from her smooth black hair, which she wore parted simply in the middle and drawn back into a loose knot upon her neck. Slowly she shook her head, as though the removal of that minute piece of tulle and feather from above one eyebrow had relieved her of a crushing burden. Her companion eyed her shrewdly and wondered what precisely was going wrong in the Lauder-Treaves family. He was too wise, however, to repeat his question and continued to eat his soup as though he had observed no hesitation in her reply. Presently the girl leaned forward and he could tell the gravity of her mood by the manner in which she addressed him, for he was not, in fact, her uncle. "Uncle Hector," she said, frowning down at her plate and fiddling with her roll. "I'm worried, quite desperately worried."

"Is it his wound troubling him again?"

Gently she shook her sleek head. "No. It's nothing to do with that. I don't know what it is." She hesitated a moment and then said, her voice very low, "He's shut himself out of my bedroom."

She glanced up and McAllister saw that her eyes were

swimming with unshed tears. He smiled very kindly and reached across and patted her hand. "Come on, dear, tell your old Hector all about it."

Finella-Lou blew her nose with commendable vigour and said: "Sorry to go all maudlin on you. I don't know what you must think of me bawling in public like this."

"A friend of mine," said Sir Hector, "once told a woman, in what I should imagine to have been very similar circumstances, that she looked like a little, drowned fairy."

"He sounds delightful," said Finella-Lou miserably. "Maybe I ought to meet him."

"Maybe you will," agreed McAllister. "But, seriously, Finella-Lou, what's Martin up to? Is it . . . it isn't . . ."

"Another woman?" finished the girl for him. She gave a twisted little smile. "No, it's nothing like that. I wish it were. I could deal with any other filly ever foaled."

"I should think you could," agreed her companion, allowing an honest admiration to appear in his face.

She twinkled faintly in instinctive response. Then her face sobered and she went on: "No, Uncle Hector, it's . . . it's something queer."

"Good heavens!" exclaimed Sir Hector, "not *another* borderline case of the mind?"

Finella-Lou looked up quickly and said: "Why do you say that?"

"Nothing really. Go on, my dear."

"Well," said Lady Lauder-Treaves, "it sounds absurd, but the thing seemed to start . . . you won't laugh, will you, dear? . . . With a toothbrush."

"A *toothbrush!*" echoed the man incredulously.

"Fact. That's where it seemed to start, as far as I can remember." She shrugged helplessly. "It all sounds so *silly*, but it isn't silly any longer. It's . . . pretty horrible, really. I mean, Martin and I were so awfully happy. Of course there's this damn business of my still not having a baby, though we've tried and tried. However, old Doctor Blackie says there's nothing really to worry about and it's true Mummy didn't have her first until she'd been married eight years."

"Has that any bearing on the present trouble, do you think?" asked Sir Hector diffidently.

"I'm sure it hasn't. No, Martin's gone all funny on me."

"Tell me about the toothbrush."

"You know the arrangement of our rooms at High Perwyl, don't you?"

"Not all the bedrooms," replied McAllister.

"Well, Martin and I have our room—that is until this recent business—at the head of Great Stairs. To the right is Martin's dressing-room, where he's now sleeping, and between is our bathroom. During the war, that is, since he came back, with the difficulty of getting fuel for the central heating, Martin hasn't used his dressing-room much where, ordinarily, he used to shave, do his teeth and so on. We've both been using the basin in the bathroom."

She glanced anxiously at her companion and said miserably, "I know this sounds awfully petty and stupid, but you've *got* to understand these absurd details before you can appreciate the rest. On either side of the shelf above the basin is a bracket to hold our tooth-glasses. In those glasses our toothbrushes live, Martin's on the left, a blue one and mine, which is pink, on the right."

She broke off in her queer little domestic narrative to seek reassurance that she was not being foolish, but the man's eyes were quiet and steady and very interested.

She gave a tremulous little smile and continued: "Not the stuff of which tragedy is made, is it? Well, anyway, it was about a fortnight ago that I got up first one morning and went into the bathroom and cleaned my teeth. Then I came back into the bedroom and drank my early morning tea while Martin went into the bathroom. He left the door between the rooms open and I heard the taps turned on. Then there was silence. Of course, at the time, these things didn't record themselves as anything in particular. It was only in thinking back afterwards, in cudgeling my brain for an explanation, that I worked out these very mundane details. I know, at least, that the taps couldn't have been running at the time, because I so distinctly heard his exclamation. I heard him say, and his voice held a kind of horrified incredulity, I heard him say: 'Oh, dear God! Not that!' I called out to him to know what was wrong and was half-way out of bed to go to him, so great had been the frightful urgency of his tone. Then he appeared in the bedroom door. In his hand he held my pink toothbrush. His face was as white as a sheet, he was trembling violently and his eyes regarded me with an expression which seemed like horror. 'Which toothbrush did you use?' he shouted. I was bewildered and said: 'Mine, of course.' 'Damn it, don't be a fool,' he went on, still shouting, 'look at *this*,' and he thrust my toothbrush almost under my nose. 'For the love of God, Finella-Lou, *think*. Did you or didn't you use this brush?' 'Darling,' I said, 'what *is* all this? I *suppose* I used my own toothbrush. I always do. What are you fussing about?' He came up to me and caught me by the wrist and I cried out that he was hurting me. He took no notice, but looked at me like a lunatic. I could see that his face was clammy with sweat. Oh, it was horrible! I've never seen him like that before. I thought he'd gone mad, or something. He certainly *looked* like it. He made an obvious effort to control himself, but he was still shaking like a leaf when he said, more quietly: 'Listen, Finella-Lou, *your* toothbrush, this one, was in my glass on the left. It's dry. Feel it. Mine, the blue one, was in your glass on the right. Now think, I *beg* of you, which brush did you, in fact, use?' 'Martin, darling, I don't *know*. I went in there, half-asleep, and reached up automatically to the right and took down the glass and brush that was there.' 'But did you *use* it?' he screamed at me. By this time, Uncle Hector, I was crying foolishly. The whole thing was so . . . so idiotic. I said: 'I don't know. If I've used your toothbrush, Martin, I'm awfully sorry but . . . !' Martin shut his eyes tight as though he couldn't bear to look at me and then he caught me to him convulsively and kissed my forehead and my hair and I felt something wet. I think he was crying. Without another word he flung out of the room, through the bathroom and into his dressing-room. I heard the door slam and the key turned in the lock. By this time I was really *frightened* and I ran after him and knocked on the door. 'Martin!' I called, 'Martin! Answer me! What are you doing in there? Darling, for God's *sake* come out. You'll catch your death of cold in that icy room in your pyjamas.' But he wouldn't answer, nor would he let me in and I stood there, feeling the cold draught on my bare feet from under his door and then I heard . . . I heard him crying."

She broke off. Sir Hector watched the little white face with its clear mat skin and read tragedy, complete and absolute, in its expression.

"That was almost a fortnight ago," she went on. "Since then he's not referred to the incident and has taken to sleeping in his dressing-room. He's removed his toothbrush from the bathroom and never enters the room except to take his bath. He locks his door at night. I wait to hear him do it. He's miserably unhappy and . . . so am I," she ended in a whisper.

They had reached the coffee stage in their lunch and Sir Hector stirred his cup for some moments, in silence, after the girl had finished speaking. He knew Martin Lauder-Treaves well, had known him most of his life and, while it is true the boy had been very nervy after being knocked about so badly in that Commando raid, his behaviour over this ridiculous affair of the toothbrush was entirely out of character. Mc-Allister realised that this was no "shaggy dog" story and that something very serious underlay and explained Martin Lauder-Treaves' behaviour.

Still in silence he held out his cigarette case to the girl and then snapped on his lighter. He inhaled deeply and blew a cloud of smoke from his lungs.

"Have you talked to Martin's cousin about this?" he asked quietly.

"Yves? Oh, no." She hesitated. "The whole thing is so peculiar and . . . so intimate that, though I treat Yves like a brother, I can't quite bring myself to discuss it with him. Mind you, he's far too sensitive not to know something's wrong. I'm sure he guesses and he's been very sweet with me. I've caught him watching Martin surreptitiously and I've seen how worried and anxious he is—for both of us. He's a very sweet person, Yves."

"He's a very shrewd person," commented Sir Hector.

She shook her head again. "Somehow I wouldn't have thought of Yves as shrewd, he's always dreaming in some other world. Not at all a practical person."

"That's as may be," said Sir Hector, dismissing the subject. "The question is, what's to be done about that husband of yours. What about that psychiatrist fellow who looked after him during his long convalescence?"

"Miles Langtrey? I had thought of talking to him, but this seems totally different from the quite natural nightmarish reaction he had after that show near Calais. *This* is something to do with me. Besides, I can't have Langtrey up to High Perwyl casually, just like that. Martin would know at once that I had sent for him and would resent it. I mean, the last time he was under his care he was in a physician's hands at the same time and realised that he was ill and not normal. He quite voluntarily accepted Miles Langtrey and his hocus-pocus, then. No, I don't think, somehow, that this is Langtrey's pidgin. I just don't know what it is and frankly, Hector dear, I'm terrified."

"But what possible basis could there be for this haroosh about the toothbrush? It sounds crazy."

"Yes," said Finella-Lou, her voice rather breathless, and they stared at each other in silence.

"Tell me," he said slowly, "are you still running that convalescent home at High Perwyl?"

"Not really," said Finella-Lou, "it's more or less petered out as we haven't been getting any more cases. Of course, Sergeant-Major Briars is still with us, but he's hardly a case any longer and anyway he's been living down at the Truelove's for some months."

"Pity," said Sir Hector, "I've got a case for you, or, at least, I've been thinking about it."

"There's no reason why he shouldn't come," the girl assured him. "There's plenty of room and if he just wants quiet and fresh air, heaven knows we can supply that. He's a Commando, of course?"

McAllister looked astonished. "Do you only take Commandos?"

Lady Lauder-Treaves nodded and said: "Yes, Martin made that a condition when he threw open the house for this purpose. He . . . liked having his own fellows around and I must say they were delightfully docile and well-behaved."

"No. The chap I had in mind isn't exactly a Commando, though I expect that in his day he could have given points to most of them. He's a very close friend of mine in my own department and he's had just about as bad a time as a man can have and get away with it. Would it be possible to make an exception?"

"Oh, I should think so."

"One other small thing. Could he bring his dog with him? It's a Sealyham."

Finella-Lou smiled. "He might get a sticky welcome from the Big Three." Sir Hector raised his eyebrows and she added: "Our own Sealyhams—Franklin, Joe and Winnie. When would he be coming? I mean, both of them."

"I don't know yet," said McAllister. He summoned a waiter and settled his bill. "Look, my dear, with regard to this business we've been talking about, don't worry too much and just leave it to your Uncle Hector."

Outside the restaurant Sir Hector's car was waiting for him and they parted, he bound for his office, she in search of a taxi which should bear her on the first stage of her journey back to that centuries-old building, half manor-house, half castle, on the Welsh border of Shropshire, which had sheltered her husband's family for close on nine hundred years.

CHAPTER IV

THE FAMILY AT HIGH PERWYL

IT was just after six o'clock. The evening was fine and clear and as Yves Lauder-Treaves stepped out of the trees crowning the long slope of Hollow Hill with the three dogs at his heels, the sun, then at his back, was casting long horizontal shadows and painting the gracious landscape with bars of alternate gold and indigo. From where he stood the prospect before him was rich indeed. The long, smiling valley stretched across his view north and south, its lush water-meadows following the course of the swift-flowing Perwyl, now dancing and sparkling in the light of the westering sun. Behind him the woods, through which he had been walking, loomed darkly, their thick foliage impenetrable to the sun's rays, while beyond them rose the sudden, dramatic, little Welsh hills which for countless generations had marked the refuge of the Celt. Across the valley rose the last big hill of any consequence before the long sweep down to the rolling country of Shropshire and on this hill stood the weather-worn stone and brick and timber of High Perwyl, which was his home.

Yves sat down for a moment on the carpet of pine needles at the wood's edge to feast his eyes upon this small corner of England which he loved so well. His keen eye marked the swirl in the water above the little stone bridge which spoke of scum and driftwood again collecting. He would have to speak to Truelove and get it cleared, otherwise the Duchy Meadows would be swamped again this year. He noted the tone in the lowing of the small cattle, all now assembled at the top end of Great Yield and glanced at his watch. The man was more than half-an-hour late again. Truelove would have to be told, though, heaven knew, it was difficult enough without experienced labour now-a-days. Still, those land-girls they'd got ought to be able to do it by now. His ear detected the creak and grind in the belt and bucket chain which was only a modernised version of the same method of feeding the big stone sluices which in turn shot the water into the moat which had been used eight centuries ago. Wanted greasing. Yves made a mental note. Every field and covert, spinney and pool, every stick and stone, tree and ditch, Yves knew and loved with a passion which he had known for nothing else. High Perwyl, its farms and holdings, was in the heritage of his blood. He could conceive of no other place to live. Transplant Yves Lauder-Treaves and he would wither.

Winnie, the Sealyham bitch, came snuffling up to him, wrinkling up her nose and showing her front teeth in a wide grin. Yves, in his turn, crinkled up his nose at her and she panted delightedly and hung out her tongue. Joe and Franklin immediately materialised from behind a bush, unchivalrously shouldered her out of the way and jumped at his face. Joe put a paw in his eye, Franklin bumped his chin, while Winnie ki-yied in the background and nipped them both in the behind to demonstrate her displeasure.

At such a moment Yves was at his best. He had a huge attraction for all animals and was always attending to the hurt or the sick, provided his patients bore fur, hide or feather. Finella-Lou used to call it doing his St. Francis-stuff. He was, in fact, a singularly attractive fellow. Martin, his cousin, was one of the "black Treaves", but Yves was ash-fair and Saxon-eyed. His naturally curly hair was usually all over the place and the casual manner of his dress, though fastidious as to linen and shoes, might well have lent him a somewhat effeminate appearance had it not been for the good sweep of jaw below the well-shaped mouth. He was extraordinarily fascinating to women, but seemed unaware, or completely careless, of his affect and was inclined, by nature, to be something of a solitary. Though his colouring was very English he had, oddly enough, his Spanish mother to thank for it, for she had been one of those rare blue-eyed blonde women from just south of the Pyrennes. She had been rare in other ways as well, though not exactly exclusive.

His father and Martin's father had been twin brothers, only some twenty minutes separating the two boys, though they were totally dissimilar in both looks and character. Yves' father, Gervase, had appeared to take after "mad, bad Treaves", who had been an intimate of the infamous Duke of Wharton and whose conduct had been so abominable that even Prinny withdrew the light of his countenance and, with the withdrawal of the Prince Regent's favour, "mad, bad Treaves" had been run out of the country. Gervase had resembled his notorious forebear to such an extent that old Sir Yves had kicked him out and told him to go to the devil "in your own time, but not on my ground". He had gone to the devil most successfully with the able assistance of his incredibly beautiful wife, Conchita, who was not only entirely delicious, but equally vicious. Together they traipsed about Europe, successfully raising the devil wherever they went, until Gervase died in raving delirium tremens in a more than doubtful hotel in Budapest, while Conchita had the final grace to succumb to double-pneumonia in Istanbul some four months later. Their one and only child, Yves, was born in the station waiting-room at Milano. At three years old, on the death of his mother, he had been rescued by a distant relative, who dumped him down at High Perwyl and said: "He's a Lauder-Treaves, and this is his home." And so it was.

Yves followed the footpath down Hollow Hill to the bridge, the three Sealyhams rocketing ahead of him and barking in noisy chorus. He followed them across the bridge and up the steep footpath the other side, which came at last to the wrought-iron gate which led into the terraced gardens, now, alas, no longer so trim as before the war, which had been cut out of the solid hillside below the sweep of road which led up to the moat. He crossed the stone causeway to the great door and swung it open, the Big Three wrangling amiably for precedence.

Here he found himself in the lovely Jacobean hall which represented the most modern part of High Perwyl. The enormous house had been fashioned over a period of centuries and now was shaped in the form of a left-handed L with its base to the north and the long column pointing due south. The surrounding moat, the water of which was visible only in patches, thanks to the profusion of great water-lily pads, formed an accurate rectangle about the building. Only the great keep, situated at the north-east corner, now remained of the original Norman castle which had been built by the descendant of that Breton adventurer who had stormed into England at the heels of hook-nosed William of Normandy. The remainder of the house was late Elizabethan with the exception of the big hall which, being almost gutted by fire, had been rebuilt in the time of James II. Despite its architectural anomaly, High Perwyl was a proudly gracious house and, in the lambent light of the sinking sun, it possessed the beauty which comes of age and serenity alone.

He had hardly swung the door to again when he heard the sound of a car arriving outside. He looked out of one of the windows and saw Lady Lauder-Treaves getting out of the station taxi. He opened the door for her as she crossed the causeway.

"Hello, 'Lou," he smiled. "Enjoy your jaunt to London?"

"So-so," said the girl after they had kissed each other in greeting. "Where's Martin?"

Yves shrugged and gave her his attractive grin as he looked down at her and said: "My sweet and lovely cousin, judging by his behaviour during the last two days, Sir Martin glowers in gloomy solitude—er—by himself, somewhere or other."

"Oh, dear," sighed Finella-Lou wearily and pulling off her hat any-old-how.

She riffled through the letters which awaited her on the Georgian salver on the hall-table while Yves watched her, slowly filling his pipe.

"Look," he said, blowing smoke and shaking out the match, "what's wrong, 'Lou? I mean, between you and Martin. No, don't shake your head at me. I know you both far too well. The old boy's working himself up into a shocking lather about something. It happened about two weeks ago, didn't it?" he asked shrewdly. He took the pipe from his mouth and pursed his lips to blow smoke over her head. Finella-Lou saw the quizzical little smile in the blue eyes which regarded her so kindly and amiably.

"Well, then," said Yves, when the girl made no reply. "I'll tell *you* something. Martin has been working up for this for weeks."

Finella-Lou looked startled. "Do you mean before . . . more than a fortnight?"

The man nodded, his expression sympathetic. "'Fraid so, my sweet. I've been watching him and I'm damned if I know what's the matter with him. I know him so well, you see, and, I was going to add, better than you," he said gently.

"I think that's true," returned the girl, frowning slightly. "You see, Yves, you *know* him, but I . . . I just love him."

"Well, so do I, I suppose. Never stopped to think about it. We're more like brothers than cousins. But something's biting old Martin pretty damn badly and I'm going to get to the bottom of it."

"Oh, no, don't do anything just yet, Yves," said Finella-Lou quickly and laying a hand on his arm.

"Why so vehement?" Yves queried, cocking one eyebrow at her. "Well . . ." She was evasive. "Well . . . not just yet. I want to give the poor darling a chance to sort things out for himself," she concluded lamely.

He carried her suitcase and dressing-case up Great Stairs to her room for her and was just leaving when he was swept aside by a huge presence which materialised suddenly and came bustling into the room in a swirl of vast petticoats and black, gesticulating hands.

"Nobody done told me you was back, honey-chile. My, my, but you is lookin' mighty tired, Miss Finella-Lou."

The big negress turned to Yves, who stood watching her amusedly. "Now, you-all, Master Wives, you be off. Shoo!"

Yves accepted his *congé* and Magnolia Lincoln was left with the girl for whom she had cared since her mother weaned her.

Magnolia was an institution. When young Sir Martin Lauder-Treaves had gone a-courting at Belle Allée shortly before the war, it was Finella-Lou's big "Mammy" who had confronted him with a demand as to his intentions long before any member of the girl's family would have dreamed of broaching the subject. Upon being assured that his intentions were strictly honourable, she had observed that that was all right, but that he must realise that "you-all, Master Sir Martin, has gotta marry me too. Where Miss 'Lou goes, I goes too." Laughing, Martin had encircled her enormous waist with his arm and planted a resounding kiss on her shining black cheek. He had vowed that nothing would give him greater pleasure than to marry her as well. To this Magnolia, looking at him somewhat askance, had observed that she didn't mean man-and-woman marrying and Martin, with perfect gravity, had told her that he fully understood. So Magnolia crossed the Atlantic and, on being shown her new home, had observed that it was jus'-like them movies and complained at the absence of melons.

. . . . .

In the deep embrasure of the tall, mullioned windows which overlooked the moat at the south end of the lofty library, Martin Lauder-Treaves stood and stared unseeing at the old, disused quarry which scarred the hillside towards which his face was turned. Major Sir Martin Lauder-Treaves, D.S.O., was, at this time, some two months past his thirtieth birthday. He was a tall fellow, standing almost two inches above his cousin, Yves, who was an easy six foot. He had the powerful shoulders and small flanks of a first-class fighting-man, though the former now drooped dejectedly with no indication of their ever having known a soldierly bearing. He stood, one hand thrust deep into a pocket of his jodhpurs, the other plucking nervously at the collar of his high-necked sweater. His left hip was pressed against a heavy oak settle so that he could rest his wounded leg upon the toe of his shoe, as it was hurting like the devil.

The face, with its big cleft chin, its deep-set, grey eyes which were placed just a fraction too closely together, the long, somewhat pointed nose and high cheek bones, bore an expression over-saturnine for one of his years. Ordinarily, the inherent gaiety which had ever been his, up to so short a time ago, had relieved the naturally taciturn appearance of his face which it assumed in repose. His mouth was his real redeeming feature, for there was a gentleness about his lips denied by the rest of his features. Like all the other "black Treaves" his hair was almost as dark as his wife's and Finella-Lou's hair followed the fashion of the raven's wing. He wore his hair somewhat longer at the sides than was necessary, as he was conscious of his puck-like ears with their marked points.

From where he stood at the open window Martin had heard his wife's taxi grinding up the long hill from Stayley station. He had walked to the north windows of the library to satisfy himself that it was Finella-Lou's taxi, and had seen it swing round the corner and disappear to the front of the house. He made no effort to leave the library, to greet her, but turned away from the window and limped irresolutely about the big room. His course appeared quite aimless, picking up an ornament here or a book there and looking at them without, in the least, realising what it was he had in his hand. His eye lingered on the big, gilt French clock on the wall above the open stone fireplace and he found himself counting the rays of the sunburst superimposed one upon the other. Suddenly conscious of what he was doing, he noted the time. He hesitated a moment and then crossed to one of the three enormous tables which graced the long room and picked up the house-telephone. He pressed down the button of his wife's bedroom, and then, in sudden panic, replaced the telephone in its cradle. He stood with his hands still upon it, trembling violently. He passed a hand over his upper lip to wipe away the sudden sweat which had resulted from his impetuous action. He stood breathing deeply like a man who has just sprinted the hundred yards. He turned away from the telephone, turned back again and then, automatically making an effort to straighten his drooping shoulders, swallowed hard and picked up the telephone. His hand was shaking abominably when Finella-Lou's voice answered and he put up the other to steady the mouth-piece near to his chin.

"Hello," he said, speaking very quickly. "Look, I'm in a sweater and tweed coat. I don't want to change into anything else for dinner. Is that all right for you?"

"Yes, of course, darling," came the girl's voice. "Where are you?"

"In the library. See you at dinner."

He hung up and stood by the big table and buried his face in his hands. Oh God, he'd not even given her *one* word of welcome. Why hadn't he thought before using that blasted phone? He ought to have thought it out beforehand. No occasion to penalise her like this.

He began again limping aimlessly round and round the library, his eyes upon the floor, his mind turning and twisting and ever returning to its starting point. It couldn't go on. He'd have to do something about it. He'd been telling himself this for weeks, now, and ever at this point he's shied away from what would have to be done. He thought again, for the thousandth time, that, perhaps, he would talk to Yves about it. After all, Yves knew as much as he did, but how different were their positions. By a freak of birth it was he and not Yves who must bear it. Often he had brought himself to the resolve to take Yves into his confidence but, somehow, at the last moment, close as his cousin was to him, he had held back, bound by the shackles of his pride. All through their childhood, and when at Eton together, it had always been Yves who had come to him for help, advice, consolation and protection. Yves had ever been of more delicate substance than he, more easily hurt, less able to look after himself. The habits of a life-time die hard and Martin found it almost impossible to envisage himself going to Yves in a reversal of their instinctive rôles. Yet if not Yves, who? Who was there that he could go to? Who could *possibly* help him? Finella-Lou was out of the question, simply because she was Finella-Lou and because he loved her too much to take the risk.

He went across to one of the gilt-wired bookshelves which entirely lined the walls of the lofty room. He pulled the keychain from his pocket and unlocked the door and swung it back. On the shelf facing him reposed the tooled edition of *Brantôme* which had been his father's particular joy. Four of the big books were thrust further forward than their fellows on the shelf. He put in a hand and lifted out two of the great volumes and took out, also, the bottle of whisky and glass which they had concealed. He filled the small tumbler and once more concealed the bottle in its hiding place. He glanced at the clock and nodded, as though assured that he would have plenty of time in which to induce a mood that would pass muster at the dinner-table. He sat down in an embroidered winged-chair close to *Brantôme* and drank steadily. Presently the whisky began to induce that heaven-sent sense of carelessness and irresponsibility in which, alone, he knew an escape from what he feared. It was pretty damn silly, really, when you came to think of it. This was the twentieth century, and it just *didn't* happen. Hell! What he was worrying about he really didn't know. Damn lot of tripe. How old Yves would despise him if he knew that he had been allowing this sort of poppy-cock to get him down. No, not despise him but . . . well, anyway, what did it matter. He was Major Lauder-Treaves, D.S.O., of No. 17 Commando. There hadn't been much of the willies about him that night on the coast near Calais when he'd gone in with his sergeant-major, old "Basher" Briars. He laughed in sudden savage reminiscence as he recalled the German officer's expression of stupefied astonishment as Briars had kicked the door in and said: "Here, chum, catch!" and had then put a short burst from his tommy-gun through the other's mid-section. God, it *had* been a night! He knew a glow which pervaded every little part of him and which was by no means entirely whisky-induced as he thought of how, wounded though they both were, they had tumbled back to the beach laughing like a couple of boys who'd successfully robbed the apple orchard. His mind jerked back to the present. He'd walk down and see Briars tomorrow. That ex-sergeant-major of his made him feel all right, as though this other thing didn't exist at all. As for Finella-Lou, well, she'd have to take her chance. What was he thinking about? Finella-Lou? He shook his head stupidly. No, no hanky-panky with Finella-Lou. Of course, it was all nonsense, but . . . still, better be on the safe side. Couldn't take any risk with 'Lou. I mean, damn it, well, you just didn't take those sort of risks with your wife, not when you'd got one like . . .

The thing was back again, worse than before. For the first time the whisky had failed him. He stared about him, his mouth half-open, as though to cry out aloud. His eyes were panic-stricken. It was at this moment that the library door opened and his butler appeared.

"'Dinner is . . .'" began the old man, when he caught

sight of his young master's expression. "In the name of God, Sir Martin, what's the matter?"

The young baronet's head turned slowly towards Plum, who had advanced into the room. "What did you say?" he asked dazedly.

"Are you all right, lad?" asked Plum, who had served the boy's father and forgot himself in his anxiety.

"Yes, of course," replied Lauder-Treaves irritably. "What the devil's the matter with you?"

The butler shook his head. "There's nothing the matter with *me*, Sir Martin," he said drily.

"Then what are you havering about?"

"I came to tell you that dinner is served," replied old Plum quietly.

CHAPTER V

MIKE

IT was at Hayley that Meredith made his mistake. In view of the fact that he had been travelling for almost seven hours and was pretty well played out, he may be excused, for Stayley, which was his actual destination, is very similar in name to the place where, in fact, he descended from the train.

It was nearly three weeks after Finella-Lou had lunched with McAllister that John Meredith found himself standing on the platform at Hayley Junction, and the arrangements and negotiations which had brought him there had been of Hector McAllister's organising. It is true that Meredith, himself, had known little of what was going on and the big Scotsman had displayed a bland cunning in getting Meredith from A to B which would not have disgraced Machiavelli.

"But I can't just go and dump myself on people I don't know," Meredith had protested, when it had been suggested that he should go and vegetate at some place oddly named High Peril (for so it was still pronounced).

"Nonsense," McAllister had returned. "You're not being dumped at all. These people turned over a large part of their house for convalescents during the war and they're only too delighted to have you. I know them well and I wouldn't suggest your going there if I wasn't quite sure that it would be the sort of place which would just suit you down to the ground."

"Will I be able to take Mike with me?" Meredith had asked.

"Yes, I've fixed that for you and you can leave all the arrangements to my secretary. I'll produce a railway-warrant for you. After all, you're on leave and you won't have to think of a thing except just going there."

Meredith, still in that distressingly docile mood, had accepted the arrangement and, after a fortnight during which he progressed under the masseur's attentions from crutches to sticks, he started, in company with Mike, for High Perwyl.

His reunion with the little dog had been oddly affecting and, at the Sealyham's frenzied display of pleasure, amounting to ecstasy, had shown the first signs of emotion since his return to this country. Mike had constituted himself Meredith's inseparable companion and refused, unless dragged out by the collar when he swore abominably, to leave his master's side. The two of them spent their afternoons at Queen's Elm in the lovely old gardens, now so neglected, Meredith moving haltingly on his sticks, Mike running and shouting before his lord. The dog had been with Juanita and young Rupert upon that dreadful day when all three of them had been buried by the flying bomb. The Sealyham, alone, had emerged alive and had vented his displeasure at the occasion by biting the heavy-rescue worker smartly through the wrist.

On the journey up from London to Shrewsbury, Mike had been obliged for a time to travel in the guard's-van, but from Shrewsbury on they shared a compartment of the branch-line train, the Sealyham cocking a wary eye every time the man moved lest they again be separated. Meredith was in a doze when the train ran into Hayley Junction and he opened his eyes in time to see a part of the name-board of the station which spelt "ayley". Without more ado Meredith clambered to his feet and got down onto the platform. He started towards the rear of the train where, presumably, his luggage would be decanted, while Mike paid some urgent, if indelicate, attentions to an empty chocolate machine. To his surprise, no luggage was forthcoming and he was nearing the luggage-van when the train pulled out of the station and went winding upon its way into the hills.

"Damn and blast," said Meredith mildly.

Turning, he saw the name-board to his left and again swore. He went up the platform towards the booking-office where a seedy individual, who proved to be porter-cum-ticket-collector-cum-station-master, was in conversation with a short, stocky fellow who was attired in breeches, leggings and a much-worn leather jerkin.

"T'ain't my fault, Missur Briars," the representative of the railway company was protesting as Meredith came up. "All goods assigned to 'ayley Junction comes to 'ayley, so they do an' all."

"Like hell, they do," commented the other in a voice that Meredith recognised as that of a Londoner. "This bloody thing hasn't come, has it? I've drove over all the way from Stayley to pick it up."

"Did you say Stayley?" asked Meredith.

"That's what I said," nodded the little man whom Meredith now noted as looking remarkably tough, with the battered face of some old-time pug.

"I seem to have made a mistake," said Meredith. "I was supposed to get out there."

"So you 'ave an' all," nodded the railwayman complacently. "Stayley's not 'ayley, nor 'ayley Stayley. Neether one being t'other. You done a proper muck-up, missur, so you 'ave an' all." He shook his head gloomily. "Arh, a *proper* muck-up," he repeated with relish. "There ain't no other trains from 'ayley to Stayley, not now, not until six o'clock tomorrer mornin'. Ay, a proper muck-up, a wonerful proper muck-up."

He broke off and nodded happily to himself and then

straightened suddenly to roar: "Oi! Look at that liddle dawg o' yours, missur. 'E be a-piddlin' on them ducks an' they don' loike it. No more do I."

Meredith called the Sealyham to heel from the slatted crate which had been the object of Mike's attentions and asked if there were a car he could hire to get him to Stayley.

"Car, sez 'e!" echoed the porter, turning to his other companion and jerking his head sideways at Meredith.

"Well, I've got a car, haven't I?" asked the other.

Meredith perked up and smiled. "You appear to be a bit more helpful than this representative of a company which is supposed to treat its passengers with care and consideration, to say nothing of courtesy."

The stocky little man nodded and regarded the railwayman unfavourably. "Him and his mucks-up," he said. "Him and his ruddy company have mucked-up delivery of the gasket for my tractor. Jacks-in-office, that's what they are. Too many of 'em in this country now, a ruddy good dose of the army's what they want. I'll give you a lift to Stayley, sir."

"That's uncommon good of you," said Meredith.

He followed the other out of the station to where a much-battered Austin stood waiting. They got in, the other politely holding the door for Meredith the more easily to manipulate his sticks. Mike was put in the back where he stood on the seat with his fore-paws on the front seat and breathed gently in their ears.

"What about your luggage, sir?" asked his companion.

"I expect they'll kick it out at Stayley," returned Meredith, "and I can pick it up later. What was *your* regiment?"

"Commandos."

"I wonder if you know the chap where I'm going?" asked Meredith. "Fellow called Lauder-Treaves?"

"Are you going to High Perwyl? Lumme, you must be the brigadier! Merridew, is it, sir?"

"Meredith."

The other shot a glance out of the corner of his eye at John and then said, shyly: "Name of Briars, sir. Albert Briars. I was Major Lauder-Treaves' C.S.M."

Meredith stuck out his right hand. "How do you do, Sergeant-Major."

"How d'you do, sir." He grinned. "It's the first brigadier I ever shook hands with, though I 'ave shook hands with the King."

"Decoration?"

"D.C.M., sir." He hesitated a moment. "You copped it pretty badly, sir?"

"Oh, I'm on the mend now."

"Would you mind, sir, if we drove round by Home Farm? Of course, I'll drive you up to the house and run down and get your luggage for you after. Only I want to let 'em know at the farm about that ruddy gasket. We'll have to use the old tractor now and she'll want to be oiled up. Pity. She's a fair bitch."

"I wouldn't *dream* of your fetching my luggage, I'll make some other arrangement," said Meredith.

"That's all right, sir," returned Briars. "Only too glad to do anything for a friend of the Major's." He shook his head. "He's a one, he is. You know, sir, you bein' a brigadier, I hardly like to say what I was going to say."

"Spit it out, man."

"Well," went on the other, slowly, "you know, sir, from the point of view of us chaps, I mean other ranks, officers is all sorts and conditions, so to speak. Pretty good on the whole, I suppose, but sometimes you find one that's a real treat. That's what the Major was. Mind you, you mustn't think he was a cissy with us chaps. Tough! Cor blimey, he was tough all right, but fair, you see. I seen some pretty good officers in the old Commandos, but they didn't come better than him. He was . . . super, as you might say. Why, if it hadn't been for him I'd never have got my bit of ribbon. All I did was just follow him. D.S.O., they give him," he added disgustedly. "D.S.O.! It ought to've been a V.C. He was a one, and no mistake, sir. Between you and me and that there dog of yours, sir, I haven't been easy in my mind about him recent. Not himself and it isn't his wound neether. Seems like he was sickening for somethin' or somethin' and that there Doctor Blackie, well, he's all right if you got a belly-ache or somethin' simple like that, but with the Major it's different. He's a highly complicated bit of mechanism, as it were, delicate in parts. Not physical, mark you, but nervous, like a good horse. Ah, well, I expect it will all come out in the wash, but I'm glad you're going up to the castle. Be a bit of company for him, like. And you'll have a bit of company, too, won't you, boy?" He added, turning his face to the Sealyham who was leaning over his shoulder. "What's his name, sir?"

"Mike," said Meredith.

"Mike?" echoed Briars. "Hello, Mike, boy." The dog, somewhat overcome by this sudden publicity, barked violently between their heads, whacked Meredith on one ear with his chops and did his best to lick Briars' left eye out.

"Blimey," said the latter, rubbing his eye. "Proper chummy, isn't he, sir? Here we are at Home Farm."

Briars descended from the car and walked across the spotless courtyard which was enclosed on three sides by the farm buildings. He disappeared into the nearest of these, a solid, stone-built house whose steel-frame lattice windows were at variance with the age-old walls, but bespoke the good and careful landlord. Meredith turned to look out of the other window of the car and found himself almost nose to nose with a little, round-eyed face which was regarding him solemnly. He lowered the window between them and the little girl crammed her flaxen head with its two neat plaits through the aperture and regarded him quizzically.

"Hello," said John Meredith. "Who are you?"

"I'm Ginnie," replied the child. "I live here with my Mummy and her Mummy and Daddy. They're my grandparents, you see," she explained. "Albert says he's got a brig-dear in the car. Are you a brig-dear?" Meredith nodded solemnly. "What's that?" asked the small Virginia.

"It's a kind of soldier," said Meredith.

"Are you a big one, I mean, a nimportant one? My Daddy was a nimportant sailor."

"Isn't he any longer?" asked Meredith smiling.

The child shook her head and the small brow furrowed slightly, the gentian-blue eyes looking faintly puzzled. "No," she said slowly, "he was a Chee-Petty-Off'cer, but he got lost at sea. Is it very easy to lose your way at sea?"

"Sometimes it's all *too* easy," Meredith answered gently.

"It's funny, that," went on Ginnie in a speculative tone of voice. "'Cos I never knew Daddy to loose his way . . . at land. Is a Chee-Petty-Off'cer a more nimportant man than a brig-dear?"

"Much more important," Meredith assured her, and Ginnie gave him so lovely a smile that the man, despite his present aloofness from the human scene, felt his heart respond.

At that moment Mike, who had been thinking deep thoughts on the floor of the car, suddenly reared himself up at the window. The black truffle on the end of his nose wiggled within an inch of the child's chin.

"Oo!" she exclaimed. "Isn't he a *pet!* May I get in with him . . . with him and you?"

When Briars returned to the car he found the three of them sitting in amiable converse on the back seat of the car.

"I hope she's not bothering you, sir," he said.

"Not a bit, I've loved it," said Meredith truthfully.

"Susan!" roared Briars over his shoulder and a very pretty fair-haired girl came running out of the house at his call.

She looked absurdly young to be the mother of a six-year-old and possessed a colt-like grace more usually associated with one's teens.

"I hope she hasn't been a nuisance, sir," she said, lifting the child out of the car.

"A-course I haven't," protested Ginnie. "This is my Mummy," she went on, turning back to Meredith, "and her name is Mrs. Mills. My Daddy was called Chee-Petty-Off'cer Mills, R.N., that's why she isn't Miss Truelove any more. That's what Grandpa says."

Susan Mills looked apologetically at Meredith. "She will run on, sir."

John smiled and the irrepressible Ginnie chipped in excitedly. "Do *you* know 'tinker, tailor, soldier, sailor'?"

"'Rich man, poor man, beggar man, thief!'" ended Meredith.

Ginnie clapped her hands together delightedly. "You see, *he* knows," she nodded to her mother.

"Go along with you, you little devil," said Briars, in dulcet tones. "That's enough now."

"'Tisn't!" protested Ginnie. "He's a nice man and a brig-dear and I like him." She turned her little face once more to Meredith and said: "Grandpa says that Mummy's going to change it."

"Change it?" asked Meredith, his head on one side.

"That's enough now, Virginia," said her mother, blushing furiously. "It's a *secret*."

"Is it?" asked Ginnie, round-eyed. "Grandpa knows and Granny knows and you know and even Albert knows." The little face began to crumple dangerously, the tender lips trembling warningly. "I did *so* want to tell my brig-dear. He's nice and he let me play with Mike who's *awful* nice and all I wanted to tell him was that Grandpa said it would soon be 'tinker, tailor, sailor, soldier'."

"Oh, you little horror!" gasped Susan Mills, red as a peony and, sweeping the child up into her arms, she ran back to the house with her.

The two men caught each other's eye. Quite deliberately, and as though at the word of command, brigadier and sergeant-major winked at one another.

The seven-hour journey must have tired Meredith far more than he had realised, for, as Briars assisted him to get out of the car on the causeway at High Perwyl, his head swam suddenly and he almost fainted.

"Here, catch 'old, sir," said Briars, slipping an arm round him and thumping on the great door with the toe of his boot. "Hang on a jiffy, sir, and we'll get you nice and comfortable."

Meredith had a confused memory of being helped up enormous and, seemingly, never-ending stairs by the ex-

Commando and a tall, fair fellow who panted under the strain almost as much as the man he was assisting. He was vaguely conscious of being helped to undress by this latter individual and became convinced of a semi-delirium by the apparent presence of a colossal black woman. Then he was in bed and he slipped away into a dreamless sleep of sheer exhaustion.

It was about nine-thirty that night that he opened his eyes to find himself lying in a wonderfully comfortable canopied four-poster in a room which would have made a Hollywood producer sick with envy, for this was the real thing. The panelling was linen-fold, the furniture was Jacobean and the big fire-dogs he later discovered to be of beaten, time-worn silver. The heavy brocade curtains were drawn against the dying light and the standard lamp upon the bedside table scarcely competed with the cheerful glow of the dancing fire in the big open grate, which cast a warm, flickering light over picture and ornament and a great Chinese bowl of tea-roses on a polished mahogany table between the windows.

Meredith raised himself upon one elbow, the better to survey this princely room and Mike, who had been curled up on the bed at his master's side, thrust a wet nose into his neck.

"I don't think you ought to be on *this* bed," said Meredith doubtfully and the Sealyham wagged his tail as though agreeing, but made no effort to move.

The door opened and Magnolia Lincoln came into the room. "Hello," said Meredith. "You *are* real."

Magnolia dazzled him with a flash of her splendid teeth. "Sho I'se real," she nodded, "and mighty glad to see you-all a-settin' up and takin' notice."

Meredith smiled and then frowned. "I'm afraid I was a bit of a nuisance when I arrived. I can't think what made me behave like that."

"Lawdy-lawdy, never plague yo'self. You'se been a mighty sick man so Miss Finella-Lou says, but you sho have come to the right place for getting a well man. Yes, sir! We done had a lot o' poor gentlemen in the castle and they gone away again feelin' fine. I come to see if you was aimin' to eat a little somethin'. You done had no dinner along of you-all sleepin' like a piccaninny. I was reckonin' to fix you some *bouillon*. How'se about it, honey?"

Meredith smiled at this vast, benignant creature who seemed to exude the very spirit of kindliness. "I think I'd like that very much," he said, "if it wouldn't be too much trouble."

"Why, the good Lawd bless you! I'se here for that. When they was a-bringin' you up them stairs I said to Miss Finella-Lou, I said: 'That man needs Magnolia.' And I'se Magnolia," she added in explanation.

She fussed over him while he had a light meal of a most appetising clear soup, a comforting dry sherry, toast Melba and a big, fat peach which Magnolia explained was grown in the small hothouse which was all they could now maintain. "When we got more coal," Magnolia told him, "Master Sir Martin has promised me he'll done try to grow old Magnolia a melon."

Sergeant-Major Briars had been as good as his word and had fetched Meredith's luggage, together with Mike's basket, from Stayley station. And, after the Sealyham had been taken downstairs by Magnolia to "look at a tree", the two of them settled down for the night. That short sleep of his seemed, unfortunately, to have restored Meredith to the point of wakefulness. He switched his light on and off and then on again and again off, but his efforts to induce sleep were not helped by Mike, who displayed a restlessness which may have sprung from finding himself in unfamiliar surroundings. Finally, Meredith gave up the struggle, and, wrapping himself in his dressing-gown, he went across to a well-filled bookcase which stood between the two doors to his room. He took out the first volume of Winston Churchill's *Marlborough* and settled down in a deep winged-chair before the fire. Mike promptly got out of his basket and came across and slumped down with a deep sigh at his feet. Meredith read steadily until long after twelve. It was somewhere about the half-hour when he became aware that the Sealyham, who was stretched upon his side on the deep rug, had jerked his head up into an attitude of attention. Meredith marked his place with his forefinger and lowered his book.

"What is it, old man?" he asked.

The dog took no notice, but came to a sitting position, his ears pricked.

"What is it, Mike? Is it a mouse?"

The dog turned his head and gave his master a quick glance and wagged his tail slightly and then immediately resumed his attitude of alertness. Meredith stared idly about the room and stood up, puzzled by the dog's behaviour. At once Mike ran to the door and stood there listening. Meredith followed him and put his hand out to the handle.

"Now you're not to bark, Mike."

The Sealyham shot him a glance of obvious impatience and Meredith opened the door into the corridor. Without haste Mike walked out of the room and once again stood listening. Now Meredith could hear what he thought was troubling the dog. Far away, somewhere across the intervening space of many rooms, somewhere from downstairs, came a confused yapping chorus of small dogs. Meredith was about to grab Mike by the scruff in case he should go charging off in quest of the barkers but, to his astonishment, the dog grumbled to himself and trotted back into the bedroom. In the middle of the carpet the Sealyham paused and raised one fore-paw as though he were about to point. Then he lowered his paw to the ground and stood, his small head on one side, slowly turning as though he would twist it off.

"What the *devil's* the matter with you, Mike?" grumbled Meredith. "Come and lie down."

Mike stood irresolute and then whined. He trotted across to one of the big windows and stuck his head between the curtains which reached down to the floor. Then he disappeared behind the curtains, and, from the way in which they then billowed about, Meredith realised that the dog was standing on his hind-legs.

Meredith frowned and pulled the curtain slightly to one

side and picked the dog up. He could feel the small body trembling with excitement.

"What is it, old man?"

His query earned him a swift lick and then the dog's muzzle pointed once more towards the window.

"Something outside?" he asked, stretching out his hand to open the window.

His action produced a violent struggling in the Sealyham, who was quite definitely interested in "something outside".

Meredith took a firmer grip of the dog, opened the window and peered out. Below him the moat glimmered faintly under a fitful moon. He was conscious that the dog had become very still and then, his eyes becoming more accustomed to the half light outside, he saw a dim shape move along the far side of the moat. It was impossible to see what it was, but Meredith gathered an impression of movement instinct with stealth. Any speculation as to its nature was swiftly terminated in no uncertain manner by Mike who, beginning somewhere deep down inside his small person, produced a throaty, malignant growl which would have done justice to a Great Dane. Instantly, Meredith caught him by the muzzle and the Sealyham muttered unprintable expressions of disapproval at his action.

"Shut up!" hissed Meredith. "If you bark I'll wring your damned neck!"

Meredith closed the window and drew the curtains again. The Sealyham was standing just behind him, his tough little body set squarely on his short legs, the expressive ears flattened to his head, his lip curled up as though about to bite. Meredith regarded him in astonishment.

"Don't be such a chump, Mike," he admonished the small dog. "There's nothing to worry about."

But there John Meredith was wrong. Did he but realise it the Sealyham had been nearer, in those moments, to the thing that hung like a deathly pall over High Perwyl, the evil thing which had known blood and terror almost indescribable in the past and which was to know them yet again.

CHAPTER VI

"AS THROUGH A GLASS DARKLY"

A WEEK passed, during which Meredith did little but eat and rest. His dull routine was broken when he was driven into Shrewsbury for massage and ultra-violet ray treatment. He made the acquaintance of his hosts and Mike of his, though the manner of *their* introduction was not precisely similar, for the four dogs, upon meeting, dissolved immediately into an apparently fluid mass of Sealyham which rolled rapidly across the causeway to break up into its component parts the other side. Having established themselves as proper dogs, the Big Three quite happily accepted the newcomer so long as he did not approach the bitch too closely.

John Meredith was walking a great deal better now and, by the end of the first seven days, was able to venture beyond the terraced gardens and seek the solitude of the woods. During his small wanderings he several times encountered the ex-sergeant-major with whom Meredith felt immediately at home. From him he learned a bit more about the family at High Perwyl and something of the Home Farm household. Briars, himself, had been invalided out of the army and had decided to cast in his lot with his former company-commander. Briars was a Cockney, a sturdy, reliable and quietly cheerful sort of chap. His father kept a fish-and-chip shop in the Lambeth Road and the small Albert had been reared with a view to taking over the business later.

"It's a rum thing, you know, sir," he explained to Meredith, "that though I was born in The Smoke, I've got much more of a feelin' for . . . well, for this," and he waved his hand vaguely and inarticulately at the pleasant countryside stretching from Great Yield down the valley to Duchy Meadows. "Of course, I like to get up to little old London now and then for a jag, as you might say, but to *live* in," he shook his head, "give me a nice little bit o' green."

"So you're going to be a farmer," suggested Meredith.

The other nodded. "Sort of," he agreed. "You see, sir, Mr. Truelove, he's the Major's bailiff, never had no kids other than Susan. They wanted a boy real bad on account of there havin' been a Truelove at the Home Farm well, almost as long as the family up at the castle. Then Susan went and married Harry Mills." He broke off and sucked at his pipe. "I reckon, you know, sir, that Mills must have been a bit of all right, goin' by the way Susan speaks of him. He was a local man and when the war was over he was comin' out of the Navy to help Mr. Truelove and, eventual-like, take over from him. *That's* what Sir Martin's training me for now. He's been ruddy good to me, he has."

"Seems a bit nervy, doesn't he?" asked Meredith.

Briars nodded. His rather battered face looked puzzled. "Yes," he said slowly, "and it's only come on recent, too. Mind you, he was always 'ighly strung. I can remember him when we was goin' in to have a bash at Jerry. Nervous as a kitten he was and anyone who didn't know him would think, my Gawd, this chap won't be much good. But they'd have been wrong. Once started he was a holy terror. But there, I mustn't wander on like this. I got work to do. Good arternoon to you, sir."

Yves Lauder-Treaves was another whom Meredith encountered about the place. He found him a singularly pleasant companion and the man's knowledge of, and obvious love for, the estate was refreshing.

Meredith was sitting on the little stone bridge over the Perwyl late one afternoon with Mike, when Yves swung into view coming down the footpath from Hollow Hill.

"Hello, Sir John," he said as he came up, "are you gracing the drinking-match this evening?"

"Drinking-match?" queried Meredith.

"Yes, every Thursday at six. Finella-Lou is a big noise in the local WVS, but there is an even bigger noise, as you will discover if you come up for drinks, in the person of Mrs. Mawdley-Hay-Mawdley—believe it or not. Old Mother M.H.M. is a very wonderful person. Martin and I have known her all our lives and we are, occasionally, privileged to address her as Hey-Hey Maud. Thursday is her day for conferring, as she calls it, with my little cousin. Though in point of fact all she does is to relate all the latest dirt she's collected during the week. She comes for a good gossip and a mild blind saying, quite frankly, that High Perwyl's the only place where she gets her whack these days. I strongly advise you to come. It's worth it. We do it in style for the old girl's sake and use the Lacquer Room for some esoteric reason known only to Finella-Lou. By the way, I ought to warn you she's a bit deaf."

The two men walked slowly up the hill to the castle and on the way encountered Doctor Blackie, the family's physician, toiling in the same general direction. Blackie was definitely "past it". He had retired some years before the war, but had come out of his kennel at the clarion call of Mr. Churchill in 1940.

"You're walking better," he wheezed at Meredith, "than when you first came down here."

"I'm walking towards a drink," smiled John.

"A drink?" queried the other with heavy puzzlement.

"It's Thursday," said Yves drily.

"Thursday?" echoed the old man, stopping in exaggerated astonishment. "God bless my soul! It had entirely slipped my memory."

Yves smiled disarmingly and took the old doctor's arm. "You lying old blackguard," he said affectionately. "You know damn well you turn up every Thursday at this time."

Doctor Blackie drew himself up and said with dignity: "When you reach my age, Master Yves, you will long ago have realised the truth of the saying that 'a little of what you fancy does you good'."

In the Lacquer Room the three men found Finella-Lou and Mrs. Mawdley-Hay-Mawdley deep in converse, while Martin Lauder-Treaves shook drinks in the background. He was frowning heavily, as though he found it difficult to concentrate on what he was doing and looked white and drawn. To Meredith, his appearance was no particular shock since he had never seen him look any other way, but Doctor Blackie paused at the sight of him, violently adjusted a pair of horn-rimmed spectacles and emitted a noise like an elephant trumpeting.

"You're looking damn rotten, Martin," he said frankly, employing his customary hell-and-brimstone bedside-manner. "Are you takin' that stuff I gave you?"

"Yes," said the young baronet wearily.

"What's that?" yelled Mrs. Mawdley-Hay-Mawdley. "What stuff? All a lot of fiddle-faddle, I'll bet. What you want to do, Martin," she roared, "is to take some new salts I've discovered, Monty something-or-other, you only want a pinch, only a pinch, mind you, and you never have any trouble at all. Look at me, fit as a flea at seventy and as regular as clockwork."

Meredith regarded this formidable lady with genuine interest. Her customary conversational tone was a sustained bellow. She was built on the heroic side with plenty of this and a bit more of that, she wore tweeds as hairy as a bearskin and high fawn-coloured spats over beautiful crocodile shoes. On the top of her untidy white hair was perched what looked like a man's brown Homburg hat, with a feather which, judging by its proportions, must have been plucked from the Great Auk itself, sticking straight up in front. Cameo brooches, rings, chains, fob-watches, and similar doo-dabs cluttered up all available space. She used a lorgnette.

"Amy, dear, may I introduce Sir John Meredith? . . . Mrs. Mawdley-Hay-Mawdley," said Finella-Lou.

"How-de-do," shouted the old lady. "Where's my whisky?"

"Here, Hey-Hey," said Yves, grabbing a *very* tall tumbler filled with an amber-coloured fluid from Martin's table and thrusting it into her hand. "Choke yourself on this."

"Dear boy," cooed the old lady in the tones of a drill-sergeant and, to Meredith's complete fascination, up-ended the huge glass and drank it down with the same proficiency as a Heidelberg student dealing with a small *stein* of light beer. Mrs. Mawdley-Hay-Mawdley sat very still, as though that overwhelming draught had turned her to solid concrete. Meredith thought the woman was ill, but then her lips opened to emit a sudden blast which was, for her, a deep sigh of satisfaction. "My father," she explained to Meredith and favouring him with a display of enormous false teeth, "my father always used to say when I was a gal that whisky should be drunk quickly. As in most other things I have ever found him to be singularly right."

Conversation then became general with Martin, however, taking little part in it. Every now and then Finella-Lou or Yves would attempt to draw him into the circle, but his replies to such attempts were invariably monosyllabic. Meredith moved over to where the young man was standing and said: "Now that I can get about a bit more I'm able to appreciate what a very lovely place you have here. You must be very proud of it."

Lauder-Treaves looked at him in astonishment. "Proud?" he echoed, as though bewildered by the suggestion. His face showed a sudden infinite distress and though he was staring at Meredith, the latter realised that he didn't see him. "Proud," he said again, his voice lower, his tone speculative. "Yes," he went on slowly, as though speaking to himself. "Yes," he said, "I was."

He turned away to concern himself once more with the bottles and decanters, but Meredith noted the tense he had employed. It was at this moment that Finella-Lou made the remark which was the prelude to the extraordinary behaviour of her husband. Meredith was to remember later the exact positions of everybody in that lovely room, that room with its glowing lacquer and flamboyant masses of colour. Yves Lauder-Treaves had his back to the fireplace and was talking animatedly to the old lady, who was roaring with laughter and in imminent danger of slopping over yet another of those monumental whiskies of hers. Doctor Blackie had lumbered across to Meredith and was holding forth in a voice of complete authority and with a profound ignorance on the subject of penicillin. Finella-Lou rose suddenly from where she had been sitting at Mrs. Mawdley-Hay-Mawdley's side and looked round her.

"Where's my glass?" she said. "Ah, there it is." She walked across to a small table on which stood a half-empty glass containing some of the cocktail which Martin had been shaking. She picked the glass up and was about to drink when there came a sudden strangled sound from her husband and everyone looked up at him.

The man was shaking like a leaf. His face was so colourless as almost to resemble the underside of a dead fish. His trembling mouth was open and his whole aspect suggested so great a terror, that complete and utter silence descended on the room.

"Finella-Lou," whispered Martin, making an obvious effort to speak normally, "are you *sure* that's your glass?"

The girl's brow wrinkled and she looked down at it and then up again at her husband with wonder. She shook her head.

"I . . . I *think* so," she said, "but if it isn't, it's yours."

"Don't touch it," came that strangled whisper again from her husband.

Meredith stared, his eyes slightly narrowed, at the distraught face which his host exhibited. There could be no doubt of the seriousness of the matter in the fellow's mind. What, in the name of God, was it all about?

Said Yves, speaking from where he stood before the fire-place: "What's the matter, Martin? Swopped glasses, or something? For that matter," he glanced at the glass in his own hand, "for that matter I'm not sure *I* didn't pick up a glass at random from that table. Would *you* know your particular brand of lipstick, Martin?" he ended, attempting to infuse a lighter note into the uncomfortable tension in which the room was held.

"Fiddle-faddle!" roared Mrs. Mawdley-Hay-Mawdley suddenly. "Behave yourself, Martin. You're frightening the poor girl to death. Such a to-do about a glass."

Martin Lauder-Treaves never so much as turned his head, his eyes remained fixed on that glass in his wife's hand, yet no one in the room but knew to whom his remark was made when he spoke. "Please be good enough not to interfere," he said acidly.

"*Darling!*" exclaimed Finella-Lou.

"Put that glass down!" said Martin harshly. "Damn it!" he shrieked suddenly. "Do as I *tell* you!"

"Martin!" breathed Finella-Lou faintly. "Darling, this . . . this is outrageous."

Doctor Blackie took a step forward as though to go to his young host. It seemed he felt that a doctor's attentions would not be inappropriate. Meredith shared these views and was annoyed to realise that his heart was beating violently. He felt his flesh crawl suddenly as though there was something evil in the room—as indeed there was.

Before the old doctor had made more than one step forward Martin had flung himself across the intervening space between himself and his wife and, to everyone's unutterable astonishment, had dashed the glass from her hand. It shattered into a thousand pieces on the table above which she had been holding it, its contents rushing in a small cascade onto the carpet.

Before anyone could make so much as an exclamation at this conduct, young Lauder-Treaves swung round to where his cousin was standing.

"It doesn't matter about the others," he said thickly, "they're drinking whisky, and I couldn't be mistaken. Now yours too, please, Yves."

For a long moment the two young men stood facing each other without moving. From where he stood Meredith could see Yves' face. Slowly, as though at something which he read in his cousin's expression, some frightful knowledge which was written there, his face drained of colour and Meredith saw the dawn of a reflected fear come slowly into the wide blue eyes.

"No, Martin. No," he said urgently.

"Yes," insisted his cousin. "Don't be a fool, Yves."

Yves' glance fell to the glass in his hand. He stared at it as though suddenly it had grown monstrous. With a quick little shiver, as though of distaste, he handed it to his cousin.

"Thank you," said the latter huskily and tossed the glass into the fireplace, where it shivered to pieces as had its fellow.

CHAPTER VII

THE DAM BREAKS

When Meredith went up to his room that night, he knew the thing was coming on. He'd had one go while in hospital in Sweden and the thought of another quite frankly terrified him. On that last occasion the big Swedish doctor had used a needle on him, but he had told him afterwards that such treatment could not be continued. It wasn't so much that he was tired, as one normally understands it, though the very bones of his body ached with fatigue, it was a terrible lassitude of his own fundamental essence, an infinite weariness and inertia of spirit. It was as though he were being subjected to some colossal and psychological atmospheric pressure, as if the core of him, his soul, if you will, were being crushed by some appalling yet intangible weight.

In his room he sank bonelessly into a chair, feeling as though a dockside crane would not be capable of lifting him out of it again. This frightful inertia brought no relaxation with it. The thing could only be described in contradictory terms. It was a ghastly lassitude at high tension. Inside this mind-suffocating envelope of collapse there was a mad nucleus of frenzied turmoil. It was as though the thing which was essentially himself was turning and twisting in crazy and useless revolt against some overpowering constriction, a constriction which was more in the nature of an abnegation.

Meredith lay back in his chair supine and listless, immovable save for the sudden occasional twitch of hand or mouth.

Downstairs, Finella-Lou took the supper-tray which Plum had prepared and, emerging into the Inner Hall, commenced to climb Second Stairs. Meredith had been advised by his physician to rest as much as possible, and it was at his hosts' insistence that he had his evening meal served in his room, to have in bed or not as he pleased. Tonight, Magnolia, who commonly waited on him, had taken, if not her harp to a party, her banjo to a village concert in Stayley. Miss Lincoln's deep, mellifluous voice and her rendering of plantation songs were something of a star-turn upon such occasions. Coming to Meredith's door, Finella-Lou knocked and, receiving no reply, went into the room. Her own spirit in travail at the evening's fresh instance of her young husband's abnormality, she took one look at Meredith and stood still with sudden shock. She put down the tray and hurried across to him, feeling singularly helpless and with her mind running on fits as she watched that white and twitching face.

"Sir John," she cried, with soft urgency, "what's the matter? Sir John, are you feeling ill?"

The closed eyelids fluttered and opened slightly. She saw that the eyes were looking at her, but that their owner was oblivious of her presence. She put a slim hand onto his forehead and found that he was in a cold sweat. She regarded him in increased dismay and made helpless, fluttering little gestures with her hands. She turned resolutely away towards the door, but before she could reach it Meredith spoke to her. She didn't catch what he said and she turned back to him in anxious enquiry. It was evident that the man was having great difficulty in speaking at all and she came back to him and took his limp hand and fluttered over him and made funny little crooning sounds for his benefit.

"What is it, my dear?" she said clearly and distinctly.

"No doctor," came the whispered request. He paused and closed his eyes momentarily, as though the effort of bringing out those two words had exhausted him. Then he opened his eyes once more and said more distinctly: "No good, I know. Please. No doctor. On the bed," he ended indistinctly.

When she attempted to help him out of the chair, it rapidly became borne in upon Finella-Lou that she would not be able to manage him without assistance. She said: "I'll just go and get Plum to give me a hand," and at Meredith's almost imperceptible nod fled out of the room on winged feet. She had forgotten the bell.

Between them, she and her butler got John Meredith onto the bed and, since he was still a big man despite his wasted condition, were both panting heavily before it was achieved.

"Might I suggest a little brandy, my lady?" said old Plum.

"I don't know if it's a good thing or not," returned the girl helplessly.

"No. No brandy," said Meredith with difficulty.

Plum went downstairs, leaving his mistress with her patient and about five minutes later Meredith was sitting up in bed and, if somewhat white about the gills, was talking quite rationally and behaving in a comparatively normal manner. Finella-Lou was sitting on the side of his bed and they regarded one another ruefully.

"My dear Sir John, you gave me an awful fright," said the girl gently and still watching his face with obvious anxiety.

"I'm so sorry you should have had to have witnessed it. Another few minutes and you wouldn't have been bothered."

Impulsively she leant forward and laid a small hand on his. The big grey eyes were very gentle and kind. "I'm not," she said softly. "I'm only too glad you had someone with you. It helps, doesn't it?"

The tired face among the pillows smiled wanly. "It helps a lot."

Meredith ate his meal with an appetite which surprised the girl. It seemed as if nature was insisting on his restoring lost energy.

"Now, are you sure you have everything you want for the night?" asked Finella-Lou solicitously.

"Everything, thank you very much," nodded Meredith, "except, I wonder if it would be too much trouble to get someone to give Mike an airing."

"Of course not. I will myself. I was just going to walk round the moat anyway with the Big Three."

Meredith had not eaten his dinner in bed, but on a table before the fire and afterwards had sat in his chair and continued resolutely with Churchill's *Marlborough*. However, despite the interest of his subject and the extraordinary ability of the author, Meredith, in his condition, could not bring his mind to bear. He put the book down and rose suddenly and walked across to the bookcase. On the bottom shelf were a number of novels and he was amused to see one of my books among them. He took it out and idly flicked over the pages. It was the usual Gérard, a fictionised rehash of one of Meredith's own cases. He carried the book back to his chair and sat down, changed his mind and undressed. When he emerged from the bathroom which adjoined his room, he found that Mike had been returned in his absence and had put himself to bed in his basket. Meredith got into bed and picking up my book opened it at random. That did it.

You must remember that for the last three years Meredith had been figuratively, literally and actually *not himself*. He had, in his own peculiar and inimitable way, sunk his own identity, almost to the point of destruction, into the individuality of one Gerhardt Trantz; that he had first removed this man and then stepped into his skin; that he had, quite deliberately, assimilated the doctrine, beliefs, loyalties and, indeed, the hopes of a member of the Nazi Party. You must recall that Meredith had a theory about these things which had been proved in practice, that if you want to be *thought* an individual other than yourself you must use all your powers to *be* that individual. The process *can* be accomplished, but only at great danger to your own mental balance and Meredith had subjected himself, voluntarily and successfully, to the frightful experiment of assuming a personality which was alien in every sense of the word. During this period he had submitted his mind to outrage and had assisted open-eyed at the rape of his own ego *while still maintaining an inner core of purpose which, in its turn, was completely hostile to the individuality into which he had sunk himself*. The effort and strain which had been necessary to this successful achievement had told and was now telling on him with the removal of the necessity for maintaining the odious existence of the thing to which he had, for so long, played Frankenstein.

The long and dreadful schooling to which he had been obliged to submit himself, the incredible harsh self-discipline he had applied, had blunted his sensibilities and had made his finer feelings into a gross caricature of what he had known before his long ordeal. He had practised his self-imposed exercise so fully and for so long a time that he had actually become incapable of ordinary humane instincts and the gentler dispositions. Thus, when he returned to this country to learn that, in addition to his father's death early in 1940, he had also to face the normally overwhelming loss of his wife and little son, his long self-imposed habit had asserted itself and his deliberately brutalised sensibilities had not reacted immediately even to so frightful a shock. No man, however, may hope to side-step sorrow which he is capable of feeling, and the thing merely burrowed into his sub-conscious, a delayed-action threat biding its time.

That evening at High Perwyl Meredith was *loosened up* by his recent nervous attack and when the shock came, it found him receptive to its impact and it knocked him for six.

He found himself reading a page of my book. It was, as I have said, a fictionised account of a kidnapping case which Meredith had handled in association with Scotland Yard after his retirement from the Metropolitan Police. The page at which Meredith found himself looking described, with an unfortunate vividness, a scene which took place at his own home, Radfield Place. As his eyes took in the words he found himself once more living through that scene which had taken place with Juanita and the boy. Juanita and Rupert. That's when the thing hit him.

It must have been about an hour or so later that a small figure appeared in the doorway of his room. It was Finella-Lou, looking very small and fragile in an oyster-coloured quilted dressing-gown, her dark hair about her shoulders. Mike raised his head from his basket and the slight thwack-thwack-thwack against its side signalled his greeting to her. She paused just inside the room looking towards the shadows of the great bed, the man in which was barely illuminated by the bedside lamp.

"Are you awake?" she asked softly. "I just thought I'd come to see if you were all right."

The head on the pillow turned slightly in her direction and she went quietly across to him. She stood looking down at him and her hand went to her cheek as she saw that Meredith's face was again wet, but this time it was not with perspiration. Slow, painful tears rolled down his cheeks and fell unheeded to the pillow.

A little cry of genuine distress was wrung from her. "Oh, you *poor* dear," she crooned and sat down on the bed and made as though to take him in her arms.

Meredith turned his head away and muttered and made as though to thrust her from the bed, but in that moment she was the eternal feminine and the comfort of her shoulder was very sweet and very near. With an inarticulate sound Meredith dropped his head to her embrace and, for the first time for many years, knew the utter relief of unchecked tears.

An hour later he was sleeping like a child and Finella-Lou gently disengaged herself from the frenzied clutch which had actually bruised her. She bent down and smoothed the hair from his forehead. She hesitated a moment and then stooped and laid her soft cheek against his.

"Poor, *poor* John," she breathed and, almost as though he had heard her, the man gave a little smile in his sleep.

Back in her own room she lay long awake, pondering the things she had learned or guessed at during that terrible hour of Meredith's emotional collapse. Over and over again she thanked Providence that she had been there to help him, for the man had suffered almost beyond the bounds of bearing and his loss had been complete and absolute. Much of his raving she had not understood, for he had spoken as much in German as in English and she had no knowledge of the language. There had been constant repetition of a woman's name other than Juanita whom she realised was Meredith's dead wife. This other woman, too, was dead, though in what circumstances she had died she had not gathered. Some of the things to which Meredith had given utterance had made her flesh crawl with horror and disgust and she had been given a glimpse of a positive hell of obscenity as made in Germany. Yes, she thought, the man had been through the mill and it had ground exceeding small.

CHAPTER VIII

THE DISCIPLINE OF THE DOGS

It is a singular fact that, until Meredith woke the following morning, only one person on the estate at High Perwyl walked in danger, but with the opening of Meredith's eyes a second individual went beneath a threat. Of this the person concerned was quite unaware as, indeed, was Meredith himself. For in waking up that morning Meredith opened his eyes in more ways than one.

He was, at first, quite unaware of any great change in himself. Yet, as he sipped his early morning tea, he became slowly more and more conscious of a return of something which long had been absent in himself. He remembered the events of the night without dismay. Oddly, he felt no shame at the recollection, but a kind of melancholy relief which was coupled with a very warm feeling for the girl who had been his witness and his comforter. He wondered suddenly whether he were not just a fraction in love with his charming little hostess. The momentary flash of introspection, ordinarily so foreign to his nature, brought a smile to his lips which went up at one corner in the manner of his old self. The thought of Juanita and the boy was no longer a cold thing at the back of his skull, but an honest, human sorrow, the edge of which he realised quite well would be blunted with time. In fact, Meredith, for the first time, realised that life still stretched before him to be used as capably as possible.

Whoever had brought in his tea had taken Mike down with them for, at that moment, the door was opened slightly and the little dog erupted into the room, catapulted onto one chair, ricochetted off another and finally launched himself, apparently by jet-propulsion, from the floor smack into the middle of Meredith's stomach. He then walked slowly up his master's chest, licked him firmly in one eye and, still on Meredith's supine body, turned right round and surveyed the room in a satisfied manner with his small behind right in his master's face. John Meredith inhaled and blew hard. The small erect tail was clapped down promptly into place and Mike sat down on the bed and surveyed his owner with a good-humoured brown eye.

"Allow me to point out," said Meredith pompously, "that your manner of entering my bedroom just now was positively scandalous."

Mike swung round and bit himself violently in the small of the back where matters of some urgency required immediate attention.

Finella-Lou was writing letters at her desk in the Lacquer Room when Meredith found her. He came in, walking steadily, if slowly, his hands in his pockets. The sleek, dark head was tilted and the wide, grey eyes regarded him quietly. Then the pencilled brows were raised and she said, shaking her head slightly: "No sticks?"

Meredith shook his head in his turn. "No sticks," he said gently.

Despite the peculiar intimacy of what had taken place between them the previous night, neither of them felt the slightest embarrassment.

"I don't suppose," said Meredith, walking over to where she sat, "that this is at all the thing to do, but none the less I'm going to do it." And he stooped and kissed her lightly on the cheek.

"La, Sir John!" she twinkled at him, fluttering her lashes rapidly. "An you please, it were delightful, I vow."

"Dear my lady," sighed John and they smiled with one another, thoroughly pleased with themselves, with each other and, momentarily, with the world in general.

"Seriously, my dear," said Finella-Lou, regarding him, her head cocked attractively to one side, "I'd hardly have known you. You look . . ." She shrugged. "You look *quite* different."

Meredith took her hand and firmly kissed the slim wrist. "I *mean* that," he said seriously. "You've done more for me than all the doctors and masseurs put together."

"I don't think that's really true," she replied slowly, "but it's sweet of you to say it. I think it was a combination of circumstances rather than anything I did. All I did was to provide a shoulder," she smiled wistfully. "I only wish . . . I only wish I were always as . . . successful," she ended in a whisper.

"You mean?"

She looked miserably at him and said: "I mean Martin."

Meredith nodded. "I . . . I was rather hoping you might feel you could talk to me about him, Finella-Lou . . . May I call you that?"

"Please," she said, laying a hand on his, "John. I'd like to awfully. . . . Only we must get away out of this house to talk." She shivered suddenly. "Somehow I can't talk to you here about it. Look," she went on, "you'll be driving into Shrewsbury this afternoon for your massage. I can easily make an excuse to come with you and we'll talk then."

"It's a date," said Meredith.

In the hall, as he was going out, he encountered Yves Lauder-Treaves who was explaining to the three Sealyhams, who sat regarding him expectantly, that he would not be able to take them.

"They can come with me," said Meredith, "if they will. Mike and I were just going for a stroll anyway."

"That's very good of you, sir," said Yves and added suddenly: "What, no sticks? This is an occasion."

"No sticks," agreed Meredith, looking rather smug and nodding complacently.

"Now listen, you three, you go with the brigadier and do as he tells you."

The three Sealyhams regarded Meredith with an expression plainly indicative of their opinion of the arrangement. However, on the opening of the door they tumbled through it shouting, in company with Mike, who got nipped for crowding Winnie at the gate.

Across the causeway Meredith turned left and made his way down the hill towards the old disused quarry which scarred the hillside above Great Yield, intending to skirt it and make his way round it to Home Farm. He followed the course of the little river until he was parallel with the quarry and then struck down half-right across Great Yield. The enormous field, almost a small down, was under grass and the four Sealyhams ran ahead, occasionally bouncing like rubber balls into the air to obtain a better view of their own small prospect. It was when Meredith had reached a point due west of the quarry that a very extraordinary thing happened. One of the dogs, it was Joe as far as he could tell, suddenly put up a hare. Meredith discovered afterwards that the dog had actually blundered onto the seat where the little beast was cowering. Away went the hare, head up, ears back, moving with that display of superlative speed which is its one defence against its enemies. Mike, suddenly conscious of game afoot, bounced nearly three feet into the air, sighted the streaking quarry, fell back to earth, emitted a sound which was half-bellow, half-squeak and flashed away in bounding pursuit. Poor Mike never stood even the proverbial dog's chance, but he disappeared rapidly into the distance roaring, squealing and yapping in the frenzy of excitement of a proper Sealyham about his lawful occasions.

So interested was Meredith in the chase which was heading for the bend of the river to the south of Hollow Hill, that he had not immediately become conscious of the totally unexpected behaviour of the other three dogs. By rights, in any normally constituted doggy confraternity, there should have been a cascade of Sealyhams after that hare, but only Mike had entered upon the sport so unexpectedly provided. The other three dogs, including Joe, who had himself put up the hare, were standing rigid. Their small bodies were shivering with tense excitement. All three had their ears pricked and their muzzles turned towards where Mike and his quarry had disappeared. The bitch was even whining with eagerness and she glanced uncertainly once or twice at Meredith. There could be no doubt in the beholder's mind of their desire to join

Mike in the pursuit, yet they stood like soldiers, unmoving, rooted to the spot.

"Go on!" urged Meredith. "Go on, go get him!"

They came running to him, barking and jumping up at him and waltzing round and round in excited circles, but though Meredith again urged them on not one of the three Sealyhams belonging to High Perwyl made a movement in the direction which the hare had taken. It was one of the most astounding exhibitions Meredith had ever seen and contrary to all instinct and nature.

"What's the matter with you three?" he asked, looking down at the little dogs who now sat down round him panting and occasionally casting obviously wistful glances towards Hollow Hill. "Well," commented Meredith, "you're the rummiest little beggars I've ever encountered."

At that moment a small white figure appeared at the far end of Great Yield toiling towards them. He'd got burrs all over him and he'd evidently been through brambles, for a small thorny branch still clung to his under-carriage, making him hop every so often with discomfort. He was very hot and his tongue was hanging out as he panted up to them, but he had the pleased expression of one who'd had a jolly good run for his money and now awaits the next treat.

As Meredith stooped to remove the bramble from Mike's tummy the bitch flew at the newcomer and immediately Meredith was in the middle of a pile of dogs biting and snapping and yelling their heads off. He cuffed them all indiscriminately and swung one out into the air by his tail before order was restored, but there could be no doubt of the home-team resenting Mike's performance.

It was as Meredith reached Home Farm that a car came along the Shrewsbury road and pulled up in the yard. Yves got out and was greeted rapturously by the Big Three.

"I'll take them over now if you like, Sir John," he offered.

"If it isn't too much," agreed Meredith. "They've just had a scrap with my tyke."

"Oh, I'm sorry," said Yves penitently. "No damage done, I hope?"

John shook his head. "Nothing to speak of," he said, "more bad language than bite. But something damn funny happened. We were over in Great Yield and one of your dogs put up a hare and . . ."

Yves looked suddenly startled and Meredith broke off as he caught his expression. "What's the matter?" he asked.

"Nothing. Go on."

"Well," went on Meredith slowly, "off went the hare with my chap in full-cry on his scut. The extraordinary thing was that your three dogs just stood and looked on. Made no effort to go after the beast. It was the rummiest thing I've ever seen."

Yves frowned and looked away, avoiding Meredith's eye. He looked like a small boy caught in the jam cupboard. He opened his mouth to say something and then closed it again. "Well, you see," he said hesitantly at last. "You see, no High Perwyl dog ever . . . ever touches a wild animal."

"*What!*" said Meredith incredulously.

Yves nodded, a lock of fair hair tumbling forward over his forehead. He caught his lower lip between his teeth. He looked horribly embarrassed.

"It's a fact," he said. "It's . . . it's damn silly, really, I suppose, but, well, it's something to do with . . . with the family," he ended shyly.

The infection of awkwardness spread to Meredith and he said in a small voice: "I haven't the least wish to stick my nose into things that don't concern me."

Yves suddenly favoured him with a dazzling smile. "My dear chap," he said, "there's nothing for *you* to feel embarrassed about. It's just that . . . do you know anything about my family?" he ended on a query.

"Well, no."

"Well, we're a devilish queer lot," said Yves, shooting a glance at him from under his lashes. "We're a very old family, of course, and . . . and I sometimes think we're a bit nuts."

John Meredith's eyes narrowed. "Mad?" he half echoed softly. "Your cousin?" he asked directly.

Yves shot another of those sidelong glances at him and then smiled. "Old Martin?" he shook his head. "No, there's nothing *really* wrong with Martin. He's a bit moody at times, but nothing more. You ought to read up the family history sometime," Yves suggested. "That isn't just snobbery. It really *is* better than a thriller, especially when you get 'mad, bad Treaves' disgracing the story. He was one of the Hellfire boys of Wharton's. And the hare business comes into it. Silly, isn't it?" he grinned suddenly. "Read on, gentle reader. To be continued in our next. See the next smashing instalment. Look," he ended, "I really must get on if you'll excuse me."

He got back into the car, evidently having changed his mind about what had brought him to Home Farm and he drove off with Franklin, Joe and Winnie bickering for the place next to him on the driving-seat.

When he had gone, Meredith stood for a long time staring after the car. Smashed cocktail glasses . . . Yves Lauder-Treaves' embarrassment at his discovery of the strange idiosyncrasy of the three Sealyhams. . . . Finella-Lou's unhappiness . . . family history . . . yes, and damn it, what about Mike's behaviour the other night? . . . Meredith stared after the car. He looked puzzled, worried, but not for himself. John Meredith was beginning, once more, to think objectively—and in that fact was born both threat and rescue.

CHAPTER IX

DEATH OF AN INNOCENT

MEREDITH's reflections were terminated by a small voice at his side which said: "Good morning, brig-dear."

He looked down to encounter the wide gaze of Mistress Virginia. The child laid a hand on his arm, stood on tip-toe and tilted up her face.

"Good morning, Ginnie," said Meredith with a smile and he bent and kissed the small cheek. It occurred to him, with some surprise, that he was doing more kissing today than he had done for many, many a weary month.

"You smell quite different to Albert," said the child decidedly. "But I think I like you equal as much. Would you like to see the sheep?"

Meredith said he'd love to see the sheep and the two of them set off hand in hand from the court-yard, Ginnie suiting her eager pace to the man's less certain gait.

"I hope it won't be too far for you," said the little girl solicitously, "but we can go by the short way. It's over at Trennion Deep. That's one of the farms. There are five farms on the 'state; Home Farm, where I live, Trennion Deep, where we're going, Hordle Hold, the Gawpe and Nocking Thicket. We're going over to Trennions'. Now you know," she ended solemnly.

Meredith took a cigarette from his case and produced a box of matches.

"Please may I blow it out?" asked Ginnie, and the small ritual was duly carried out, the child carefully wiping Meredith's sleeve where she had spat a little in her excitement.

They went in amiable converse by way of a long, grassy ride through age-old woods, Virginia occasionally leaving him to flash ahead on twinkling legs while Mike barked joyfully at her side.

"'Fraid you're getting tired, brig-dear," suggested Virginia after they had come some way and Meredith agreed that it would be pleasant to sit down.

They seated themselves side by side on the bole of a big fallen beech and Virginia entertained him artlessly with a description of life at Home Farm.

"Do you wear long woolly drawers, brig-dear?" asked Meredith's small companion, out of the blue.

"Good heavens, no!" he laughed.

"What kind do you wear?"

"Well, if you must know, you very forward young woman, I wear short linen ones. But why on earth do you want to know?

"Well, Albert suffers from rude-matics because of his wound, you see, and Mummy wants him to be sensible and wear long, woolly drawers like Grandpa. Mummy says he wouldn't have rude-matics any more. Mummy said that Albert forgot himself when he said no, that he wouldn't. He was afraid of something, I think, 'cos he said he'd be," and here she used a word which made Meredith gape at her, "if he did."

Meredith shouted with laughter at this ingenuous disclosure of the intimacies of the household at Home Farm and he had the greatest difficulty in providing Ginnie with an explanation of the word which she had used and which evidently intrigued her greatly. To take her mind off this fascinating problem, Meredith made magic for his small companion and obligingly produced smoke from his ears. This proved even more absorbing than the minor etymological mystery.

"Oh, how *lovely*!" sighed Ginnie ecstatically, shaking her head from side to side so that the small plaits with their blue bows swung gaily. "Could Albert do that, do you think?"

"I don't know," replied Meredith. "He might choke himself."

"What, choke himself dead?" The child pondered the possibility of this tragedy and then said regretfully: "I suppose he'd better not, otherwise I wouldn't have a new Daddy an' Albert's awful nice."

"I think so, too," agreed Meredith, "and I'm sure he'll be a very nice Daddy to have."

"I've practically got him now," said the small realist. The light of sudden mischief came into her eyes and she added, instinctively lowering her voice to impart the information: "D'you know, brig-dear, Albert and me have secrets which we don't even tell Mummy. Isn't that *fun*?" and she regarded Meredith, her eyes alight with pleasure.

"I think it's simply enormous fun," agreed the man and they went on again, hand in hand, and presently emerged from the grassy ride through the trees onto the slope of a long open field in which sheep were grazing.

Over to the left was a picturesque huddle of farm buildings, presumably Trennion Deep. Meredith noted with appreciation that the hedges of the fair prospect before him were all trimmed, the fences kept in perfect repair and each field which was not under grass spruce and clean as though those who farmed the land loved what they worked. Over in a corner of the big field, which stretched away from where he stood with Virginia, a small part had been penned off with hurdles. Within this reserve were four creatures, one of them dead.

"There it is!" cried Virginia, pointing towards the little group. "Granny said I shouldn't see it, but Grandpa said it couldn't do me any harm. That's Grandpa down there with the grey cob and *his* name's Day's Delight. You can see him talking to Mr. Yves."

"What's the other thing with them?" asked Meredith, shading his eyes with his hand.

"That's the sheep," said Ginnie, regarding the scene somewhat solemnly. "Dead as mutton, poor thing. She's one of our late February ewes."

"But you don't kill out in the fields here, do you?" asked Meredith, puzzled.

"Oh, no!" replied the child, shaking her head violently. "We didn't do it. There's a sheep-killer," she explained.

The two of them walked down the slope until they came to the sheep-hurdles beyond which Yves was talking to Benjamin Truelove, who stood, hand in pocket, the reins of the stout grey cob looped over his arm. At their feet lay a part-grown sheep, stiff and cold in death, its head back rigid in the last attitude of its dying agony. There were wounds in the throat from which much blood had run and other dragging incisions in the haunch.

"Grandpa, this is my brig-dear," said Virginia.

Old Truelove raised his hat courteously and held out one hand across the sheep-hurdles.

"You'll be Sir John Meredith, I take it?" he said smiling. "I'm glad to know you, sir."

"How d'you do," said Meredith, shaking the old man's thin hand.

"I hope this young terror hasn't been plaguing you, sir."

John shook his head. "Not at all," he assured the other.

"She's brought me a very charming walk, though the end of it's a bit messy," he added, jerking his chin towards the dead ewe. "Dog?" he queried.

"Aye," agreed Truelove, "it's a dog all right, but that's the puzzle. Must have come from miles off."

Meredith turned to Yves Lauder-Treaves, who stood frowning down at the corpse of the innocent victim. "Doesn't the rule apply to *domestic* animals?" he asked quizzically.

Yves looked somewhat taken aback. "It wouldn't be one of the estate dogs," he replied shortly.

. . . . .

It was after lunch that John Meredith and Finella-Lou got into the latter's little Hillman to drive into Shrewsbury as they had agreed. Lady Lauder-Treaves had an additional quota of petrol for her W.V.S. and Red Cross work and the local Petroleum Officer had kicked in with extra coupons to enable Meredith to go in three times a week for his treatment. Finella-Lou drove with Meredith sitting at her side, Mike on his knee. She glanced at her watch suddenly and said: "We're in lots of time and I want to be able to think while I'm talking to you, so we'll pull in at a spot I know and smoke a cigarette."

On a small hog's-back, which gave a lovely view to both the north and south, the girl brought the car to a halt. She accepted a cigarette from her companion.

"Now," said John, exhaling a deep cloud of smoke and throwing the match out of the car window.

The girl knit her charming brows before replying and then said: "I'm going to begin with a question."

Meredith was watching her and he could see the effort she made in putting her question.

"Do you think," she asked slowly and rather breathlessly, "that Martin is mad?"

John hesitated. "My dear, that's a question which could only be put with any hope of an accurate answer to a psychoanalyst. After all, we're going in nowadays for such a welter of psychiatry that I should think more or less *anyone*, if they were analysed, would trot out all sorts of jolly little hugaboos. But you've asked me a direct question and," he smiled, "like Hyman Kaplan you want 'a strong, plain enswer'. No, I do *not* think your husband is mad, but I would say that he was at an almost unbearable tension and that there was a danger of a snap. You know him better than I do but, from what little I've seen of him, that is my considered opinion."

Finella-Lou nodded her sleek head. "It's really rather what I feel," she agreed. "But what to do? Hector made me promise to do nothing, which was odd. I couldn't understand that."

"Hector?" Meredith queried.

"Hector McAllister," she explained. "I went up and wept on his shoulder."

Meredith looked bewildered. "But where on earth does McAllister fit into this? What does he know about it?"

"Nothing beyond what I told him," she replied.

"And what *did* you tell him?"

"I told him about the toothbrush and how it had seemed *that* which had started the whole miserable business. Oh, of course, you don't know about that."

Meredith learned for the first time of the apparently inexplicable behaviour of the baronet on that morning when he had behaved like a lunatic in the Great Toothbrush Mystery. He listened in silence until Finella-Lou finished speaking, then he said slowly: "It does tie up, doesn't it, with his glass-smashing display of the other night?"

"Does it?" she asked wide-eyed, her expression avid with sudden hope as though Meredith might pull the answer straight out of the hat.

Meredith laid a gentle hand on hers. "My dear Finella-Lou," he said, "don't look at me like that. I'm no witch-doctor, but I *can* see a possible explanation to link the two events. He evidently doesn't want you using things which he has touched with his mouth."

Meredith saw the little white face turned to his fall. The droop of the tender lips was pathetic. She shook her head very sadly. "No, it's not that," she said. "I thought the same thing. I've thought round and round in circles and it occurred to me that my poor sweet might think he was suffering from some frightful disease or other and didn't want to give it to me. I actually tackled him with that and begged him to go up to Harley Street and have a thorough check-up. I'm quite convinced from his reaction to my suggestion that it isn't that. He was so absolutely adamant that there was nothing a doctor could do for him."

For a moment or so there was silence in the car and then Meredith said, speaking very carefully: "Has it occurred to you that my explanation might work both ways? That Martin might think . . ."

"Oh, *no*," breathed Finella-Lou. "He couldn't. There's nothing the matter with me. Besides, I know Martin and . . . and I'm sure that, in spite of everything, he loves me very much, still loves me. You don't know Martin, he wouldn't . . . shy away from me if I *had* anything. No, it's something quite different, something. . . . It seems silly to say, sitting here in broad daylight, but I really do mean that it's something evil."

"Well, I can't help still thinking that it's a job for a psychiatrist. What I don't get is Hector McAllister's advice to you."

"To do nothing?"

"To do nothing," nodded John. "He can't possibly know any more than you do, can he?"

"No, I don't think that would be possible."

"I wish I knew what the old devil was up to," grumbled Meredith. "Is there anyone who sort of takes your husband a bit out of himself?" he added.

"Yes," said Finella-Lou promptly and rather bitterly. "His old sergeant-major, Briars. Somehow, it's as though he were the only person with whom Martin can feel really at home and normal, though I know that Briars has noticed Martin's condition. He said so to me only the other day. Said he was worried about the Major."

"They're very fond of one another, aren't they?"

"Very," nodded the girl, "and I must say I think Albert Briars is an awfully nice man."

"So do I," agreed Meredith. "He's a tough 'un all right, but sound as a bell and steady as a rock."

"It's rather sweet, really," said Finella-Lou smiling wanly, "to hear them talk about each other. Their mutual admiration and devotion is touching. From Martin's account you would think that Briars won his D.S.O. for him, and to hear Briars, you'd think Martin had done the whole thing single-handed."

"I should encourage Martin to be with the chap as much as possible. I should think Sergeant-Major Briars is probably about the best medicine he could have. Have you talked to your husband's cousin about all this?"

The girl hesitated. "Well, yes, I have, in a way, but I have to be a bit careful because their relationship, while very close, is also just a little bit peculiar. Martin's approach is always to 'young Yves' if you see what I mean."

"You mean he's always looked after the younger boy?"

Finella-Lou nodded again. "Yes," she said, "Martin is . . . touchy, you know. Very much lord-of-the-manor. He doesn't obtrude that side of him, but if there is a discussion affecting the estate, his word is absolute law. For instance, a little while ago, before all this horrible business started, there was almost a scene one night with Yves. Yves knows the estate just as well as Martin and I sometimes think even better. He certainly loves it and during the war has practically run it with old Benjy Truelove. I suppose he'd grown used to having his way and one evening when I was there he said to Truelove: 'We'll put Great Yield under the plough this year.' Martin, who had only recently come back from the hospital, looked up and said: 'I don't wish Great Yield touched this season.' 'But that's nonsense,' said Yves. 'Of course we must plough it up.' Martin didn't even answer him, but turned to Truelove and said: 'My orders are that Great Yield is to stay under grass.' So you see," she ended, "I don't want to do anything that might make for additional irritation and, while he is very, very fond of Yves, he might regard anything on his part as interference."

"I see," said Meredith doubtfully. "Mind if I talk to Yves about it? I think he's genuinely concerned about your husband's state of mind."

"Oh, I'm sure of that."

"What's *almost* the most puzzling thing in the whole issue," said Meredith speculatively, "is old Hector McAllister's telling you not to do anything. He's a pretty *wise* old bird."

CHAPTER X

TOOTH AND CLAW

NIGHT must fall. The phrase came unbidden to his mind and he shivered suddenly, though the air which came through the open window at which he stood, high above the moat, was warm and balmy. He stood and watched the dying day, his spirit clinging, like a mariner lost at sea clings to a spa, to the last pale glimmers of the fading light on the hills beyond the river. The eyes in the haggard young face were frightened, apprehensive with that dreadful apprehension and sick fear which he, himself, had once seen in the eyes of a man before he shot him. Downstairs, from the open windows of the south drawing-room, he could hear the sound of voices which told of warmth and light and companionship, all things from which he knew himself to be exiled.

He turned suddenly from the window and went heavily across to an Empire *escritoire* which stood against the wall at the far end of the room. From his pocket he pulled a keychain and unlocked one of the drawers. He stood staring down at his old Service revolver, that revolver which he had no business to have and which he should have handed in to company-stores when he was invalided out. He picked up the gun, broke it and satisfied himself that it was loaded. Here, in his hand, lay release. Was it the coward's way? He found himself thinking quite objectively about the point. One day, one day soon, perhaps, he would make up his mind or, maybe, his subconscious would take charge. It wouldn't be very difficult to do, if only . . . if only he could be sure that it *would* be release, escape. He sighed deeply and put the gun back in the drawer.

From the same drawer he took something else which clinked and jangled and then a small key. He walked across to his bed and put the pair of handcuffs down on the eiderdown. Then he undressed and got into his pyjamas, dressing-gown and slippers. He felt very, very tired, so tired that he knew that if he lay down upon the bed he would probably sleep and he didn't want to sleep. He was afraid of sleep, of sleep and that . . . that other thing which might, or might not be sleep. Wearily he seated himself in a massive, high-backed Elizabethan armchair of black oak. As a piece of furniture it was very beautiful, with its lovely carving and statuesque proportions, but, as a place in which to sit, it could, in no way, be described as comfortable. He did not wish it other than what it was. Quite deliberately he put his right wrist into one circle of the manacles and snapped it shut. The other he fastened about the arm of his chair. The key remained in the open drawer of the writing-desk. Major Sir Martin Lauder-Treaves, D.S.O., was ready for the night. . . .

. . . . .

Meredith and Finella-Lou had the drawing-room to themselves after dinner that night, for the baronet had taken himself off to his room immediately after swallowing his medicine and Yves had retired to his office-study in the old keep to work on his own version of the family history which he was re-writing and bringing up to date.

The girl put down her coffee-cup and, breaking a long silence, said: "I can't go on like this, you know, John."

Meredith's eyes sought permission and he struck a match and lit his pipe before replying. He seemed to have gone off at a tangent when he spoke, for he said: "I had thought of running up to town tomorrow. There's something I want to ask a man."

"Still worrying away at Hector McAllister's advice?" she suggested shrewdly.

"Yes, it seems so damned odd in the circumstances and if it had come from anybody but McAllister I might have dismissed it, but he knows how many beans make five. I've got to know what he has in his mind."

"Won't it be too much of a strain for you? Your journey up knocked you up quite a bit."

Meredith shook his head. "But I'm far better than I was. I ran a few yards today," he ended with naïve pride.

Finella-Lou cocked her head at him and noted that the man's face seemed less wasted than when she had first seen him, that some of the lines etched in appeared to have been smoothed out. "You're looking younger," she pronounced at last.

"Largely your doing," he replied smiling. "By the way," he went on, "what was it that especially upset your husband at dinner tonight?" She hesitated and he continued without waiting for her answer. "It seemed to me that it was this business of the sheep-killing. Did you notice that he shied away from the subject when his cousin brought it up?"

"It's funny, that," agreed the girl, "because Martin's particularly good when it's a question of any action to be taken. He's essentially a man of action, but he seemed to haver around the thing almost . . . almost as if he didn't want anything done, which is absurd."

"Anyway," said Meredith, "I think I'll go up to London. I could, of course, telephone but, somehow, I feel that McAllister will need a bit of prising open."

It was shortly after that that the girl announced her intention of going up to bed. She was looking very tired and anxious and Meredith put his arm about her shoulders momentarily as he bade her goodnight. They smiled at one another and she went along the gallery towards the Great Hall while Meredith opened the long windows of the drawing-room and stepped out to give Mike his last airing.

The walls of the house did not drop sheer to the foundations set in the moat. Around the house there ran a strip of lawn about half-a-dozen yards in width. He walked slowly along this, his eyes on the still surface of the water below him, while Mike went about his business, performing balancing feats which would not have shamed a *première danseuse*, kicking energetically backwards with his hind-legs, grunting, coughing and blowing and generally settling his small interior-economy for the next few hours.

When Meredith reached the north-east corner of the building he could go no further, for here the lawn terminated suddenly in the sheer wall of the old Norman keep which still maintained a resolute air of impregnability and reached down sheer into the protecting water. Above his head lights shone from an open window in the massive wall and told of Yves, presumably, engaged upon his family history. John Meredith turned to a small door at his left and went into the house. The man and dog found themselves in a wide corridor which was half-museum, half-picture gallery. To their right, shallow stone stairs led up into the thickness of the keep. At the opposite end of the gallery a door led into the library which had to be crossed to a further door in order to reach the Inner Hall. Meredith and Mike went up Second Stairs to the first floor and so to their bedroom

Meredith was nobody's fool and he had worked with Sir Hector McAllister in various Intelligence jobs now over a number of years. He knew the workings of the big man's mind almost as well as he knew his own and he had a pretty shrewd suspicion as to the reason for the Scotsman's advice to Finella-Lou. He undressed and got into bed and lay relaxed, his mind still playing with his little problem until he had thought himself into complete wakefulness. He reached for a cigarette from the box beside his bed and in so doing noticed that Mike was standing up in his basket, his small head cocked on one side.

"Oh, for heaven's sake," grumbled Meredith, "we're not going to play those games again, are we?"

The dog wagged his tail slightly, but did not turn his head to his master. Slowly and in silence the Sealyham stepped out of his basket and advanced to the middle of the room.

"Go back to bed, Mike! And don't be a chump. Go on!"

And then Meredith himself was out of bed as he remembered that there *had* been reason for the dog's uneasiness on the former occasion. Swiftly he pulled on a pair of grey flannel trousers and a polo-sweater over his pyjamas, thrust his bare feet into a pair of soft, desert-boots with crêpe soles and, seizing a stick, moved towards the door. Mike's reaction to these signs of evident preparation was a wild excitement, in which he ran round the room whining and was waiting tremblingly by the door when Meredith approached it.

In the corridor outside, Meredith once more heard that doggy chorus from somewhere downstairs, so it was evidently not only Mike who was disturbed. In company they descended Great Stairs and turned right at the bottom to the door which led to the Inner Hall. From beyond this they could hear Franklin, Joe and Winnie lifting up their voices in no uncertain manner.

. . . . .

In the room almost immediately above their heads the big standard-lamp beside the fire-place was still alight. Near to it stood the massive Elizabethan oak chair. Upon the floor to one side of it lay a tumbled heap of shoes and clothing. It consisted of a dressing-gown, a pair of pyjamas and a pair of bedroom slippers. The right sleeve of both the dressing-gown and the pyjamas had been ripped to ribbons to get them off. Upon the rug in front of the heavy oaken chair and still shackled to its arm lay Martin Lauder-Treaves. He was quite naked.

He was sprawled face down upon the rug and lay very still. At rare intervals he twitched suddenly and violently as a dog does when it's dreaming and at such times a small whimper broke from him. The eyes in the white face were not quite shut.

. . . . .

Meredith opened the door to the Inner Hall and a cascade of small dogs rocketed over his instep and raced clamouring to the front door. He followed them and had some difficulty with the huge and massive bolts which held the ponderous timber against the night. He got it open at last and swung it wide, all four dogs rushing out across the causeway to the drive beyond the moat. As Meredith was about to follow them, his eye fell on a big electric-torch lying on one of the hall tables and he snatched it up.

At the end of the causeway the dogs seemed to be at fault, at least the High Perwyl dogs stood hesitating. Mike continued in a bow-legged run some yards further and then checked, his ears pricked, the black truffle on the end of his nose wiggling to beat the band. Then he raised one forepaw and pointed. Meredith, who by this time had reached his four small companions, noticed that they all had their hackles up, the tall ridges along their shoulders and back standing out quite distinctly. Whatever it was that was agitating them they both feared and hated it.

This momentary hesitation, on the part of one of the dogs, was suddenly terminated by Mike producing a deep, savage growl and then he was off. He went like an arrow from the bow straight, straight out into the darkness and was lost to view.

"Hey, Mike!" shouted Meredith. "Come here, you little devil! Heel! Heel, I say! Mike!"

But Mike never heeded. He was a Sealyham and knew his job. The other three dogs whined and shivered, but they made no effort to join their fellow who had disappeared into the night.

"Blast it!" swore Meredith and ran unsteadily along the narrow lane of light cast by his torch.

He fetched up short after about thirty yards, his heart pounding in his side as though he'd run a couple of miles. He laboured in his breathing and cursed weakly at his own humiliating condition. He was obliged to pause to regain his breath and then he called again: "Mike! Mike! Where are you?"

A light was flashed on, on the first floor and a window opened.

"What is it?" cried Finella-Lou's voice.

"It's me," Meredith called back. "It's all right, only the dogs agitated about something." And he went plunging down the hill in the general direction his dog had taken.

After that one deep growl to announce his coming, Mike ran mute. The tough little body above the stocky legs went bounding down the hillside towards the thing which he knew to be his enemy. He knew, instinctively, that this thing towards which he was racing, with every intention of giving battle, was much bigger than he was, but Mike had his own methods with dogs bigger than himself—dogs or other things—— He had developed his own technique of fighting and with an adversary to whom he was giving away considerable weight, it was his practice to run in low, deliver one savage bite in a vital spot (which was not one permitted by Queensberry rules) and then to throw himself on his back and allow the heavy-weight to attack him. This meant that the enormously powerful jaws of a Sealyham could be aided by the tough little hind-legs scrabbling frantically bicycle-fashion so that their claws could lacerate the soft underside of his big adversary. It was a method which had enabled him, in the past, to defeat dogs three and four times his own size. But tonight the little dog was giving away too much weight. The scales were weighted against him and he shot down the hill to meet an enemy which was dangerous in itself, but now doubly dangerous in that it was frantic with fear.

Far behind the little dog could hear Meredith's voice calling him, but he went on and there beside the Perwyl he came face to face with the thing which he had come to fight.

. . . . . .

The twitching of the prostrate body was almost constant now. Hands and feet moved continually in little abrupt gestures, backwards and forwards, backwards and forwards again. He seemed to be straining at that right arm held by the handcuffs and the solid weight of the Elizabethan chair. And then, why then something rather horrible took place.

Laboriously dragging the great chair behind him, Martin Lauder-Treaves began to crawl along the floor.

. . . . .

Meredith never saw what it was that he fell over, but he tripped suddenly and fell flying on the down slope to the right of the terraced gardens. The torch flew out of his hand. Came a sudden crash of broken glass and the light went out. Though the breath was driven from his body the man scrambled to his feet for, by this time, he could hear the fight going on down in the valley. He lurched drunkenly down the remainder of the hill and fetched up in the grass meadow at its foot. The snarling and the other sounds of conflict had ceased now and Meredith went on with a great anxiety in his heart. He kept calling: "Mike! Mike! Where are you, old boy? Here, Mike!"

It wasn't until the old butler Plum had joined him with a second torch that they found the little dog down by the river bank. Meredith took one look at him in the rays of the torch and then went down on one knee at his side.

The Sealyham was terribly mauled. It was impossible there to make a proper examination. Meredith gently laid his hand on the dog's heaving side and one brown eye opened slightly and there came just a ghost of a movement from the short tail. Meredith pulled off his sweater and, with the old man's help, gently eased it under the little dog and then they took two corners apiece and lifted him gingerly. They carried him up the hill and across the causeway into the hall. Here they found Finella-Lou with Magnolia in attendance and the women cried out at the sight of the small hairy thing, so covered was he in blood.

"Can you get a vet?" asked Meredith, his voice not quite steady.

Finella-Lou shook her head. "No, no," she said, "we must find Yves. He's better than any vet."

Meredith and Plum carried Mike into the kitchen quarters where he was laid down on some newspapers in Plum's own chair which he had offered for the purpose. Yves materialised from somewhere and said quietly: "Just leave him to me."

"Are you quite sure?" asked Meredith doubtfully. "The little chap's very uncertain when he's hurt."

Yves smiled. "It's all right, Sir John," he said. "No dog's ever offered to bite me."

"It's quite true, John," Finella-Lou assured him, laying a hand on his arm. "We call this Yves doing his St. Francis stuff. Animals just don't attempt to bite or scratch him."

It is ever the exception which proves the rule for, as Yves stooped down and put out a hand to the little dog, Mike opened his eye again and promptly raised one lip warningly. There was no doubt of the malice of his intent and, as though to clinch the matter, a sort of whispered growl came from deep down inside him. Yves sat back on his haunches. Meredith was to remember afterwards that the young man looked astounded and then, suddenly, frightened.

"I told you he wasn't safe," said Meredith.

"But . . . but it's . . . it's *astounding*," cried Finella-Lou. "I've never known such a thing to happen before with Yves."

Meredith was about to take Yves' place when, with a murmured apology, old Plum bent down and, without any sign of objection from Mike, gently felt about the little dog's body with careful, tender fingers. He looked up at last and said: "Nothing broken as far as I can make out, sir," just as though he had not performed a minor miracle. "If you'll just give me that bowl from the sink, sir, in my pantry, I'll get the little chap washed. Exhaustion as much as anything, I think, sir."

They made the Sealyham as comfortable as they could and Finella-Lou insisted on his having a teaspoonful and a half of the sort of brandy which would have cost twelve-and-six for that amount nowadays. The dog's basket was brought down from upstairs and a towel spread in it. Into this he was gently lifted and the old butler insisted on carrying dog, basket and all, upstairs.

"I think the little chap will be fairly comfortable now, sir," said the old man as he was leaving the bedroom. "It must have been that wretched sheep-killer he came upon."

"Yes, I expect you're right," said Meredith, stooping over the basket and gently rubbing behind one velvety ear with his finger-tips.

. . . . .

It was an hour or so later that, naked and shivering and exhausted, Martin Lauder-Treaves opened his eyes. He discovered that he must have dragged the big chair across the room and was puzzled to find that it stood now before the Empire bureau while he, himself, free of the handcuffs, lay just inside his bedroom door. He stood up and put one hand against the wall. He felt sick and faint and dizzy. He took his hand from the wall and then stood swaying, looking at where it had rested. The wall-surface was smeared with something dark. He lurched away from that accusing imprint and found himself face to face with the long cheval mirror which stood between the windows. Fascinated he moved a drunken step nearer and peered into it. There was something dark at the corner of his mouth, something which had run down his chin, something which was of the same colour as . . . he held up his hands and looked at them. There was blood on them. With an effort as great as though he were lifting some tremendous weight, he raised his head again and looked into the mirror. There was blood upon his mouth and upon his chin.

CHAPTER XI

DEUS EX MACHINA

MEREDITH was at first reluctant, in view of Mike's condition, to fulfil his purpose of going up to town to see McAllister. The vet, however, summoned first thing by telephone, assured him that the little dog was in no danger, despite the number of his wounds. He had lost a fair quantity of blood and was, of course, much weakened, but none of the bites was in a vital part and, thanks to Plum's thorough washing, were quite clean. It would just be a question of careful feeding and nursing. During the vet's visit Mike showed himself to be a contrary little cuss, for Yves put in an appearance and was greeted with every show of approval on the part of the patient. Finella-Lou, Magnolia and Plum all promised Meredith that the dog would be watched constantly and that he could go to London with an easy mind.

John Meredith had telephoned through to General McAllister's secretary to make an appointment for the late afternoon and Sir Hector, on receiving the news from her, rubbed his chin and said: "This is one of two things. Ring up Major Gérard and get him down here too."

Thus I was sitting in McAllister's office when Meredith was shown in. He paused for a moment in the doorway and stood regarding us both, hands in pockets. At the sight of me his mouth went up at one corner in the old Meredith smile. The eyes were laughing too. Here stood Meredith, still far from a fit man and as yet underweight for his build, but the change in him was remarkable.

"Cor, stone the crows!" said I softly.

Meredith's grin widened and he held out both hands and showed us first the backs and then the palms in the manner of a conjuror about to perform a trick. "No sticks," he said, "I thought I'd better get it in first."

I glanced at McAllister, who was looking devilish pleased with himself and frightfully complacent. He looked like the cat that had had the canary.

Meredith shook his head as he closed the door behind him. "I've not come," he said, addressing himself to the Intelligence chief, "to talk to you about *that*," and he pointed directly at me.

"Meaning," I suggested, "no report?"

"No report," he nodded. "I've got something else on for the moment, but I'll be ready to get down to it with you next month, if that's all right with you, Gérard."

"Suits me," I said. "Well, if I don't fit into this picture I'd better go."

"No, you needn't move," replied Meredith. "Stick around

and learn something about the way you're treated as a pawn by the god in the chair, there."

"So it worked," said McAllister quietly. "It wasn't entirely my idea."

Meredith looked surprised. "Not?" he echoed.

"If I'm to stay," I put in, "would somebody please tell me what this is all about?"

"You tell him," suggested Meredith lazily and sinking down into a deep leather arm-chair facing me. "You started it."

The general cocked one grey eyebrow at him and regarded him questioningly. "No hard feelings?" he said.

Meredith laughed. It was good to hear that laugh again. "Why should there be?"

"Well," said Sir Hector, tugging at his neat white moustache, "you remember when I came down and saw you the second time at the Tracys'?" Meredith nodded. "You remember I had a chap with me whom I told you was from the Foreign Office? Well, he wasn't."

"Nut-doctor?" suggested Meredith, looking at Sir Hector through narrowed eyes.

"A vulgarism," said McAllister, "but it's near enough. He was Hartley Frome who, together with Miles Langtry, is at the top of the tree. I just wanted him to have a look at you and talk to you. There was no question, of course, of his being able to make any analysis but . . ." He hesitated a moment. "Well, I just wanted my own opinion confirmed as far as possible."

"Opinion?" queried John.

The big Highlander looked embarrassed and Meredith's eyes crinkled up at the corners again as he smiled, but he made no effort to help the other.

"Well, I felt that you . . ."

"What you're trying to say and spare my feelings at the same time," said Meredith bluntly, "is that I was as near as dammit to sliding over the edge. Isn't that it?"

"Yes," replied the big man quietly, "that was it. But I thought a good deal more than that. I thought that if you could be brought up against someone else who was blundering about in an unhappy fog that your innate sense of fellow-feeling would be aroused. I thought also that if you could be brought close to some little problem your deductive instincts would respond and that you might well start ticking over *as yourself.*"

"And this bughouse wallah confirmed your opinion?"

"Yes," said McAllister.

There was a short silence during which Meredith contemplated the other, his face inscrutable. Presently he shook his head. "One of the last things I remarked to Finella-Lou before leaving High Perwyl this morning was that you were a pretty wise old bird," he said, his voice not quite steady.

McAllister coughed, blew, trumpeted and generally made a lot of blimp noises. "Yes, well, if you haven't come down to talk about your report, what are you doing here?"

"Just to hear what you've already told me," replied Meredith, "but as I'm here I'd like to know if you have any information about young Lauder-Treaves to which I am not privy."

"Well, I've known the boy all his life, but beyond that I can't tell you anything as to the reason for his present *malaise*. In fact, I expect you could tell me a bit. I suppose Finella-Lou's confided in you?"

Meredith didn't reply. He sat and stared at Sir Hector and then said: "Look, I'm staying at my club for the night. What are you doing for dinner?"

"I'm dining with you," said McAllister.

"That's what I thought," nodded Meredith, and after a short exchange with me about later arrangements for getting down to his report, he took his leave.

It was after dinner that night that they settled down in a secluded corner of the smoking-room overlooking St. James's Street. Said Meredith, regarding his companion shrewdly: "I've more than a suspicion that you've got an idea at the back of your mind about this business up at High Perwyl. You have, haven't you?"

The big man rolled his cigar gently between his lips, exhaled an aromatic cloud of blue smoke and nodded: "Yes," he said, "I have a very definite idea, but I don't propose to tell you what it is."

Meredith smiled. "Not going to do my homework for me?"

"Not exactly," replied his companion. "But I don't want to foist any preconceived theories on you. I'd sooner you arrived at your own conclusion which might, after all, be totally different from mine. I'll tell you one thing I think you should do. It would pay you to read up the family history. At least, I think it would."

"That's the second time I've had that piece of advice. Yves told me to do so."

"Did he?" queried McAllister eagerly.

"That fellow knows something, but he's not coming unstuck. He's worried about his cousin, too. I can tell that."

"If I'm right in what I think," Sir Hector said slowly, "Yves will know all right, but you won't get it out of him. They're a jealously loyal, clannish lot, the Lauder-Treaves. A devilish queer family. Yes," he repeated, "a *devilish* queer family."

"Something rattling in the Lauder-Treaves' cupboard?" suggested John Meredith.

"Legend has it that they've not always been able to confine it to the cupboard."

Meredith smiled broadly. "Good heavens," he said, "don't tell me I'm hunting a family ghost or something. I'd find it difficult to track down something I didn't believe in."

"Well, it's *your* problem."

"You *are* making me do my exercises! Tell me though, you say you've known the boy all his life? His service record wouldn't point to his being neurotic, but he strikes me, at the present moment, as suffering from some extreme form of neurosis. What sort of chap is he really?"

"What you're asking, I suppose," suggested McAllister, "is—what is he like today? I can't really answer that, because I've seen practically nothing of him since the beginning of the war. You know his war record. That was a bloody good D.S.O. he got and he had a couple of mentions before that. What I *can* tell you is a little bit about his childhood and adolescence. Nobody was more pleased than I was when I heard that young Martin had bobbed up as a Commando. I remembered him as a small boy as something of a shrinking violet. He was a hyper-sensitive. Took after his mother, who was a Fothergill and a complete fool. Very pretty and with great charm—if you like them that way—but nervy and vapourish. She tried to pamper the boy and that made his father incline towards brutality with him. She died when Martin was just nine, by which time he and his father actively disliked each other. I think he must have been pretty lonely as a boy and would have been lonelier still but for that cousin of his. Yves was Gervase's boy. I knew Gervase quite well and he was a wrong 'un—all the charm in the world covering up something pretty stinking underneath. He had *all* the Lauder-Treaves' family qualities."

"What qualities?" asked Meredith.

"You really *must* read the history of that family," replied his companion. "It's fascinating. They're the real McCoy. In their family record they've managed to cram more disgraceful stories than Hollywood ever thought of about the wicked British aristocracy. I think I'm right in saying that there are now not more than six families who can trace their ancestry back to the Conquest. I forgot who they are, the de Traffords are certainly one and the Lauder-Treaves another. They've got everything in their story. Madness, murder, incest, treason, patricide and even one who was numbered among the English martyrs and died at the stake for his faith. Within that same generation one of the Lauder-Treaves' women was burned as a witch. They've always been a violent, turbulent lot with a definitely bad streak. Twice their tenants have risen against them. The first time was a little after the Black Death, when the countryside rose and sacked the castle and butchered its master in his own hall. They had put up with their younger women being hoicked off to lighten the leisure hours of their lord, but they took a poor view of the girls being expeditiously throttled afterwards. The second time was when the mob went in after Sir Maurice Lauder-Treaves, who was known as 'mad, bad Treaves', at the time of the Prince Regent. They didn't get him. He got away and died obscurely in Virginia."

"Madness, murder, incest, treason and patricide," echoed Meredith. "They seem to have got the lot."

McAllister nodded. "That's not all," he said quietly.

Meredith regarded him amusedly. "Not all?" he repeated. "I don't know where we go beyond that. Into the realms of metaphysics, I should imagine."

"I want you to make up your own mind."

John Meredith frowned. "Are you serious about this?"

"Yes."

Meredith regarded the other in silence. If he was surprised, he didn't show it and he was surprised. General Sir Hector McAllister was a man who dealt in facts. He had no time for things as he would have liked them to have been, but only as they were. No successful Intelligence chief can afford to be lacking in imagination, but it is a quality which he must ride on the curb and with a strong hand. He must, further, be prepared never to give utterance to a lightly considered opinion when dealing with serious matters and, from the gravity of that last yes, Meredith knew that the big man was, in fact, very serious.

"Where was he at school?" asked Meredith.

"He went to Eton," replied Sir Hector, "as did the younger boy, Yves. He improved enormously at school. Blossomed out at games and collected caps and colours. His cousin, always far more delicate, distinguished himself at nothing except tennis. It was in the finals of the Public School doubles that it was first realised that he had a heart. Young Yves and his partner were playing the Beaumont pair and it was a very tight game. Towards the end the Lauder-Treaves boy went to pieces and collapsed and that lost the match for Eton. He was found to have strained his heart and it's been like that ever since. The two boys went up to Oxford together; Martin to Balliol, Yves to New. Martin stayed at the University for nearly three years and did very well. The other boy threw his hand in after he had been at New College barely a year. He has no persistence, that one. Undoubted flashes of brilliance, but gets sick of things very rapidly. Martin then took himself off on a sort of Grand Tour, winding up at my sister's place in Kentucky where he met that delightful child, Finella-Lou. They were married a year later and came back to High Perwyl. In the five years between leaving Oxford and the outbreak of war, Yves proceeded to pull a number of dazzling rabbits out of a polyglot collection of hats."

McAllister leaned forward and gently eased the ash from his cigar with his little finger. "I'm telling you all this about Yves as well," he explained, "because Martin's life is so bound up with his. They're really more like brothers than cousins. The boy, Yves, never could settle to any one thing for long and he left Oxford and popped up a few months later on the stage. In the West End, too, mark you. He was in a bad play, but got awfully good notices himself. Then he appeared in a good play and was either ignored by the critics or received an avuncular pat on the head in the press. Without more ado he turned his back on the theatre and went into *purdah*. Everyone thought he was sulking, but he wasn't. He came out of his retirement with a satirical novel which had our foreign policy, or lack of it, as its main butt. He called it *Raw Lion*. I must say it was astonishingly good and showed signs of great promise. It was *jejune* in parts, but that was no sin in so young a man. Everyone waited for his second novel, but it never came. He published a volume of bad, and, indeed, rather nasty verse and that seemed to end his literary career."

"What did he live on?" asked Meredith.

"Martin," grinned the other. "The Lauder-Treaves are very well off and Martin was very generous, I believe. And that's really about all I can tell you about them, or at least," he corrected himself, "as much as I will tell you."

"Will you answer one direct question?" asked Meredith.

"It rather depends," said the big Scotsman cautiously.

"In your catalogue of some of the charming virtues of the family," said Meredith, "you mentioned madness. Do you think Martin Lauder-Treaves is mad?"

"No, I don't," said Sir Hector promptly.

"I see," said Meredith, but in fact he didn't see at all.

CHAPTER XII

BROWN BRUMMY

THE following evening, when Meredith reached Stayley station, he was surprised and pleased to see his friend, Sergeant-Major Briars, waiting on the platform.

"As a matter of fact, sir," said the ex-Commando, "I didn't come over special, but as I was in Stayley with the car I thought you'd be glad of a lift." He eyed Meredith frankly. "My word, sir, but there's a hell of a change in you since you first come up to High Perwyl. Why, blimey, you look almost twice the size. I thought you was an old man first time I see you. We got that sheep-killer," he ended.

"*Have* you?" said Meredith, interested.

"Well, per'aps that's a bit pre-mature, as you might say. I believe Brown Brummy's bringing him in now."

"Brown Brummy?"

Briars laughed. "As a matter of fact, sir, I don't really know what his proper name is, though I expect Mr. Truelove does. Brown Brummy is what he calls himself. He's a "— Briars tapped himself significantly on the forehead—"he's a bit funny, you know."

Meredith having expressed a wish to see the captive, they got into the car which Briars headed not for the castle but for Home Farm. On the way he told his passenger what he knew about Brown Brummy who was something of a character on the estate. He lived alone in a tumbledown cottage on the Gawpe and resolutely resisted any attempts on Martin's part to have it put in proper repair. He was what the country-folk call a natural and though the parish records may have shown the date of his birth, few people on the estate knew how old he was. He was, in any case, so full of years that whether he were seventy or eighty or ninety didn't really matter. He earned a livelihood by keeping down the rabbits on the five farms and was regarded as something of a wizard, literally, when it came to dealing with rats. For these pests Brown Brummy used no traps or poison. He would arrive at some rat-infested barn and ask to be shown the main rat runways. He would then proceed partially to undress himself, a lengthy business since he wore the tattered remnants of at least six waistcoats, to say nothing of old cardigans and sweaters, the latter usually tied round his neck. From a dilapidated sack he was wont to produce something which he always concealed from the onlooker. This mysterious thing was known to be some kind of wild herb, for he had been seen to crush it up in the dirty palms of his hands and then to spit in it and work it into a kind of paste. This pungent mixture he then rubbed into his nostrils, after which he dropped on all fours and moved slowly through the barn, sniffing as he went. He was locating the king-rat. Brown Brummy had his own methods and rat-bites seemed to be nothing to him. He was in the habit of catching the king-rat, as he called him, with his hands and taking him away in his sack alive. "Oi kills 'un peculiar," he would say and it is a fact that nobody knew how Brown Brummy disposed of his victims. Nobody bothered to enquire. It was probably messy, anyway. All that mattered was that, believe it or not, with the disappearance of their leader the other rats went away.

Brown Brummy was known to do a fair amount of poaching on the side, but he repaid such depredations by keeping his own preserves to himself and other poachers kept away from Brown Brummy's stamping-grounds. He could set a snare for a man as well as for a rabbit. Brown Brummy was an institution.

When Briars brought the car to a standstill in the courtyard of Home Farm they discovered a group of people standing, staring at the captive. There were the Trueloves, their daughter and grand-daughter and an indescribably dirty, little, old man who seemed, at first sight, to be composed almost entirely of filthy wool and hair. Chained to a ring in the wall was a big nondescript lurcher with a wall-eye. He looked a big, savage brute, obviously dangerous if only because he was frightened.

Meredith and Briars joined the group. At their advent Brown Brummy looked up and pointed a filthy finger at Meredith and croaked shrilly. "Oi seen 'ee afore." Then, to Meredith's astonishment the little man came forward on his bow legs and sprang off the ground and kicked both feet together to the left, landed again and then jumped and kicked them together to the right in the immemorial hops of pleasure of the tumbler or musical-hall artiste. He was amazingly nimble.

"That's Brown Brummy's way of saying how do you do," explained Ginnie from her mother's side.

"Hello," said Meredith and stepped back a pace, involuntarily, for the little man stank like a badger. "Did you take that big brute single-handed?"

Brown Brummy looked at Meredith with unutterable contempt, cleared his throat with a vigour which shook his entire frame and spat accurately between his interlocutor's feet. He then turned his back on him. The small Virginia advanced, frowning, on the little man and gave him a sharp slap across the wrist. "Bad manners, Brummy," she scolded. "Go and say you're sorry."

Old Brummy muttered and looked sulky and promptly got another slap from the child. "Do as you're told," she said severely.

The little man turned, looking very much like a disgruntled badger and came and stood before Meredith and glowered at the ground. He then sketched the merest shadow of his jumps and kicks and then walked away and stood lumpishly by himself. "Are you sure this is the sheep-killer?" Meredith asked Truelove.

The other shook his head. "Not for certain, Sir John. No. The beast's got a collar on him, but we haven't been able to handle him yet. Brummy's only just brought him in and it's a chancy brute."

"I'll have a look for you," said Ginnie suddenly and before anyone could stay her the child had advanced fearlessly towards the big dog which took no notice of her approach, but kept an anxious eye on the group of grown-ups.

Susan Mills gave a little cry of distress and started forward as did Briars, swearing under his breath.

"Don't move, anybody," snapped Meredith.

Ginnie had walked up to the chained dog who was rumbling deeply in his chest and flung an arm about the shaggy neck. "Let's have a look, boy," she piped, quite unconcerned by the fears of her elders.

The dog permitted her to drag the collar round upon its neck and slowly to spell out the name and address on the little brass plate.

It was some moments before Virginia could be induced to leave the dog, who appeared to have no objection to her pulling his ears, though he might well have taken the hand off Briars had he tried it.

" 'Harter, Hawley Farm, Wrayne'," said Briars, repeating the name and address from the dog's collar. "Where's Wrayne?"

"Right over the other side of Shrewsbury," said old Mr. Truelove. "It's a wonderful way for the dog to have come."

"I would suggest, if I may," said Meredith diffidently, "that we find out, if possible without warning Harter, whether the dog was missing from its home the night your sheep was killed. It wouldn't be conclusive evidence, but it would be something to go on."

"I agree," nodded Truelove. "Albert, that's a job for you," he said, turning to Briars. "You can take the 8.10 into Shrewsbury tomorrow morning and you can get a bus on to Wrayne. It's only a mile or so beyond. Can I trust you to make discreet enquiries? I don't want any Commando stuff. No getting hold of this Harter chap and throttling the truth out of him."

"That's all right, Mr. Truelove," Basher Briars assured him, "I'll use tack."

"Well, see you're on the right tack," suggested Truelove with a twinkle in his eye and Sergeant-Major Briars was vaguely puzzled by the general laugh which followed.

Meredith refused an offer of a lift up to the castle, saying that he would like the walk. He started off and was surprised to find that Brown Brummy was trudging sturdily at his side.

"Are you coming with me?" he asked.

"Aye," replied the little man and blew his nose dexterously on his fingers. Meredith looked away and presently Brummy went on. "Oi'm mortal shamed, so Oi am. Oi been rewd."

"That's all right, Brummy," said Meredith kindly.

"'Tain't all right, no'ow. It's all along o' my 'avin' a crorse in me grain, leastways so my ould muther always said." He jerked his hairy head backwards over his dirty woolly shoulder. "'Tweren't that there dawg," he added and chuckled wickedly to himself. "Gert fules they be. Ol' Brummy see the marks o' that sheep-eater and they were bigger nor this dawg's paws. This liddle ould dawg ain't big enough, not no'ow."

"You mean," said Meredith, following all this with some difficulty, "that you don't think that dog is the sheep-killer?"

"No more I du."

"Well, what did you bring him in for?"

The little man raised his matted bush of a face to Meredith and in the faded, bloodshot little eyes the latter read malicious mischief.

"They thinks Oi'm simple, see? But Oi know more nor they du. Gert fules!" he exclaimed bad-temperedly. "Natcheral Oi may be but natcheral things Oi know along of it. 'Twon't du them no 'arm to go pickerin'-and-pokerin' arfter this 'ere dawg. An' Oi don't want 'em a-pickerin'-and-pokerin' round 'ere, no more Oi du." He caught Meredith by the sleeve as they breasted the slope of the hill to the castle. "Oi seen 'un," he said in a conspiratorial whisper.

"You've seen what?" asked Meredith.

Brown Brummy made a gesture of impatience and said: "Whoy, t'other one. An' a gert big booger 'e is. Oi seen 'un but 'e 'aven't seen Brown Brummy, nor loikely to. So big as a cart'orse 'e is, and when the loikes o' 'e is runnin' the loikes o' Oi gets up a tree, see?"

Meredith paused and eyed his small companion with astonishment. "D'you mean," he said, "that you've seen another dog, a dog that's the sheep-killer, and you're keeping quiet about it?"

Brown Brummy looked suddenly frightened and Meredith then saw something which was a very real survival from the Dark Ages. The little man crossed his fingers, not as you or I might do with a laugh and an admonition to keep your fingers crossed, but in the age-old gesture known as "making the horns" which was employed by simple folk to ward off evil. With a few muttered words which Meredith couldn't catch, Brown Brummy suddenly swung round and went off at a bow-legged run and disappeared along the way they had come. Meredith stood staring after him and then shrugged his shoulders and went on up the hill to the castle.

CHAPTER XIII

HISTORY

DESPITE the fact that he was immeasurably better than when he had first come to High Perwyl, John Meredith felt very tired after the journey up from London and was grateful for the whisky and soda which Yves offered him before dinner. As the two men and Finella-Lou were sitting in the south drawing-room before the meal, Plum came in to say that Sir Martin wished to be excused and would have a tray sent up to his room. Sir Martin, however, must have changed his mind because, as the butler was removing the soup-plates during dinner, he came limping into the dining-room and seated himself in his usual place without so much as a muttered apology.

"No. No soup, Plum," he said and sat frowning down at the table.

"Glad you've come down, Martin," said Yves who sat facing John across the table. "I want to return to the charge with regard to Great Yield. Really, old man," he said regarding his cousin with a winning smile, "you'll have to come round to it. Truelove is in complete agreement with me. We don't maintain sufficient stock now to warrant our keeping Great Yield under grass. The Duchy Meadows provide ample pasture for the few Herefords we have left."

"We'll restock as soon as we can," replied Martin shortly.

"But that may not be for some years," Yves pointed out amiably, "and in the meantime there's good stuff going to waste. Have you examined the soil of Great Yield?"

Sir Martin Lauder-Treaves jerked his head up and frowned at his cousin. "What precisely do you mean by that question?" he asked with a distinct edge to his voice.

Yves looked surprised at the tone and said: "Well, nothing in particular, but I thought you might not know that . . ."

So far he got when Martin slammed his closed fist down upon the table's edge so that the glasses jumped and tinkled. His ordinarily pale face was suffused with blood in sudden anger. "Might not know!" he repeated slowly and harshly. "Might not know!" he said again. "Do you think, my dear Yves," he went on, "that there is anything about Perwyl that you know that I don't know? Are you suggesting, by any chance, that I am incapable of directing the working of the place? You forget, I think, that before I joined the army I ran Perwyl without your invaluable assistance, that while you were fiddling around, kicking your legs about on the stage or writing trashy novels I was caring for the estate."

Meredith, maintaining a poker-face as a witness of this unhappy family interlude, watched the two men with interest. He saw that Yves first flushed and then went very white at the grossly insulting language which the other had employed. Then he made an obvious effort to recover himself and succeeded in producing a twisted little smile. He sighed. "Whatever you say, old man," he said placatingly. "We won't discuss it any more."

"Oh, but we will," Martin went on with savage, stubbornness. "We will discuss it," he insisted. "We'll discuss it once and for all. No one's indispensable, you know, Yves," he ended, staring very straightly at his cousin.

Finella-Lou had sat frozen and distressed at these exchanges between the two men, but now she broke in and said gently: "Martin, dear, I really can't see what this is all about. You *must* remember that Yves has carried on here during your absence and has taken a great deal off your shoulders since you returned. In any case, darling, you seem to have forgotten that this must all be very distasteful and embarrassing to John."

The young baronet looked up in genuine surprise. It was quite evident that he had forgotten Meredith's presence. He turned to his guest and murmured an apology and then swung round immediately upon his cousin and said: "Let it be understood once and for all, Yves, that I have expressed my wishes as regards Great Yield and that they are final."

"Right you are," said Yves lightly, as though the matter were one of no account, but Meredith noticed that his mouth tightened suddenly as though with effort.

The rest of the dinner passed off without incident, Martin sitting in morose silence with the three others making rather heavy weather of their conversation.

It was as they were leaving the dining-room after the meal that Meredith found himself momentarily alone with Yves and said to him: "I wonder if you could lend me a copy of the family history you were advising me to read?"

The young man stood suddenly still and eyed Meredith with an expression in which amusement and anxiety were nicely blended. Then he ran his fingers through his fair hair and said directly: "Come to the conclusion that we're a damn queer lot?"

Meredith laughed. "Something of the sort maybe," he admitted.

Yves sighed and smiled rather ruefully. "By all means," he said, "come along to my place and I'll dig it out for you."

They walked together through Inner Hall, crossed the library and turned into the gallery which led to the old keep. As they went Yves explained: "The only history which is at all comprehensive was written by the then rector of Stayley in 1850. It's not very good and the old boy, who must have been a bit of a prig, skated skilfully over the nasty bits in case he got his cleric's skirts dirty. As you know, I'm working on the first really complete history of the family ever to be attempted. If you're still interested after reading old Silas I'll give you some of the real stuff to read. Here we are. This is my place. You haven't been in here before, have you?"

Meredith followed his companion up the worn stone steps of the winding staircase which led into the thickness of the keep and passed through an ancient door beneath whose lintel he was obliged to stoop his head. He found himself in a huge circular chamber into the walls of which modern lattice windows had been introduced to replace the ancient arrow slits. Facing him across the big room was another Gothic doorway, the timber of which was ajar, revealing narrow stone steps leading upwards in the massive thickness of the wall.

"Goes up to my bedroom," explained Yves, intercepting Meredith's glance.

The barrel-vaulted and groined ceiling of this great chamber must have been fully thirty-five feet above their heads and for almost half of that height the ancient stone walls were hidden behind tapestries which, today, one does not ordinarily see outside a museum. Modern electric *flambeaux* had been cunningly affixed here and there about the walls so as to utilise the old existing torch-brackets of heavy wrought iron. There were a number of tall bookcases of black Welsh oak, two narrow refectory tables which in their turn were covered with more books, ancient manuscripts, maps and so on, the raw material from which Yves was fashioning his great work. The floor was of worn, polished oak with a few pleasant rugs scattered about. The fireplace to their left was big enough to have stabled a pair of horses. It was an imposing and a very beautiful room.

"My word," said Meredith appreciatively, "this is magnificent. I suppose it's the oldest part of the house?"

"It's all that is really left of the original castle," Yves told him. "There's my bedroom above, the same size as this and then the stairs go on until you come out onto what's left of the old battlements and where now nothing more vigorous takes place than my sun-bathing."

"It really is *quite* lovely," nodded Meredith. "I envy you your quarters. Anything below?"

The other shook his head. "Nothing much," he said. "There's one small room whose windows are just above the level of the moat which is used mostly as a lumber room now. When Martin and I were kids we used to pretend it was one of the dungeons, but there's no record to prove it. I'll take you down some time, there are one or two bits of old junk there that are quite interesting, notably a huge iron spit which is reputed to have played a somewhat sinister part in the family fortunes. Now then, let's see. Where's old Silas got to?"

He began hunting through the piles of books and papers on one of the big tables and eventually found a somewhat battered volume bound in raw calf.

"Here we are," he said, flipping it open at the title page. "'*The History and Chronical of the Family of Lauder-Treaves, the Same Being Seated at High Perwyl in the County of Shropshire*'," he read aloud. "'By Silas Carraway Whistle, Doctor of Divinity, Master of the Arts, Rector of Stayley in Shropshire and Chaplain to Sir Merrilees Lauder-Treaves, Baronet'. Fulsome old boy, isn't he?" ended Yves, handing the book to Meredith.

Meredith took the volume into his hands and glanced at the frontispiece opposite the title page. This showed engravings of two coats-of-arms surmounted by crests. The one to the left displayed upon its shield a small animal rather like a ferret, while above it the crest was that of a wolf's head encircled by an indented collar. The half-plate to the right showed precisely the same shield with the ferret-like animal on it, but the crest was quite different, being a mailed fist grasping a feather.

"What's the significance of that?" asked Meredith. "The coats-of-arms are exactly the same, but the crests are different."

Yves rubbed his jaw and said slowly: "There is, I suppose, the whole story of the family in that frontispiece. The animal on the coat-of-arms is the ermine of Brittany from which the family originally came. Treaves, or Tréves, is not very far from Rennes and the original man who landed in this country with the Conqueror was known simply as Yves de Tréves. The Lauder part of it is an Anglicised corruption of the old boy's nickname, *loup de*. He was pretty tough, I gather, and certainly merited the cognomen. I think that it was in bravado that he adopted the wolf badge rather than the symbol prompting the use of the nickname, though now nobody can be quite sure. The first member of the family to write himself Lauder-Treaves was the unfortunate fellow who was so ill-advised as to come out in the '45 and was duly hanged for his pains. He dropped the wolf crest and adopted that of his wife's family, a Payton."

"Poor old wolf," said Meredith mildly, "he must have been a bit bored being kicked out after all those centuries."

The other looked at him queerly and then smiled. "Yes," he said. "Perhaps he was."

Meredith then went upstairs to his own room to see how Mike was getting on. The Sealyham was showing the usual toughness of his breed and was making a remarkable recovery. He was still inclined to take things easy, but he got stiffly out of his basket at Meredith's entrance and stood surveying his master with every sign of appreciation, including a slowly wagging tail.

Meredith put the book down on his bed and carefully picked the little dog up.

"Like to see a patch of grass, old boy?" he asked and carried Mike downstairs.

The small dog was rather a pathetic sight, for a good deal of him was still bandaged and the usual freedom of his attitudinal ability was sadly hampered. He was inclined to stagger somewhat at certain moments and grumbled to himself loudly.

Tired after his long day, Meredith said his goodnights early and went up to bed. He picked up the Reverend Mr. Whistle's book and settled down to read. Yves had been right. Doubtless a most worthy divine, the man was an appalling prig and prosy and pompous into the bargain. Despite the archaic dullness of his writing, however, the author could not entirely destroy the fascination of the story he had set himself to write. He was, too, an unconscious humorist and once or twice Meredith laughed aloud. Mr. Whistle had his own method of passing over the unpleasant while being true to his calling of historian in dealing with fair fidelity with the facts. There was, for instance, at one point in his narrative, the account of a Treaves returning from Crusade to discover his wife in adultery. Mr. Whistle stated that he passed his sword-belt three times or more about her neck and then hanged her from a hook to perish slowly and miserably. The author, having done his duty to truth, then proceeded to wash his hands as rapidly as possible of the whole distasteful business when he wrote "this disagreeable incident was followed by a period of comparative calm in the fortunes of the family." Meredith particularly liked the word comparative. Again, later, the conscientious cleric was faced with something even more disagreeable, from his point of view, in recounting the deplorable incest of a degenerate of the cadet branch and wrapped up the whole business in such a cloak of words and allusion, metaphor and hyperbole, as to obscure the issue from anyone with a less intuitive mind than Meredith's. Mr. Whistle chronicled the lingering death in prison of this ineffable young man with a Christian satisfaction redolent of the somewhat stale odour of sanctity. It was with enormous relief that the author was able immediately to turn to the Lauder-Treaves who was grilled like a chop by the Queen of England who, by Mr. Whistle, was invariably referred to as Bloody Mary.

Meredith skimmed through the book which, despite the manner of its writing, was of absorbing interest and then thumbed through it more carefully to discover if its author had anywhere enlarged upon a constantly recurring phrase of his own usage. The phrase in question was "the family misfortune" or occasionally "the hereditary burden". These phrases were so vague that they might have meant anything. At one moment Meredith thought that Mr. Whistle, who was an adept at side-stepping the unpleasant, consistent with accuracy, was referring to insanity in the family, but somehow that didn't quite fit in. Meredith laid the book down some time after midnight with a feeling that he had been presented with a puzzle to which there was no key or, at least, no key of Mr. Whistle's providing, and he resolved to question Yves as to what precisely the sanctimonious historian had meant.

CHAPTER XIV

THE STAYLEY DOCUMENT

As John Meredith walked Mike slowly round the lawns above the moat before breakfast the following morning his mind went back to the book which he had been studying the night before. He recalled that Sir Hector McAllister had advised him to study the history of the family at High Perwyl in connection with the problem of Martin's unaccountable behaviour. True, the record had confirmed the fact of insanity in the family, but of this he already knew and, in any case, McAllister had been quite dogmatic on that score as to his opinion of Martin's mental condition. He had said most emphatically that he did not consider the boy was mad.

As he walked slowly after the dog over the dew-soaked grass Meredith passed in mental review some of the leading

players in the story he had been studying. Before his mind
again floated the savage personality of Sir Mordreth de Tréves
who, on returning from the Crusades, had so brutally mur-
dered his faithless wife. According to his chronicler he was
reputed to have been "a man of great corpulence and girth".
He had died raving, probably of hydrophobia, since, shortly
before his death, he was known to have been bitten by one
of the castle dogs. The figure of the gross-bellied Crusader
was followed cinematograph-fashion, in Meredith's mind,
by that of the Prince Regent's friend and boon-companion,
"mad, bad Treaves". This Regency buck, whose notoriety
exceeded even that of the infamous Duke of Wharton,
appeared, from Silas Whistle's account, to have been a
monumental lecher, duellist and drunkard, but in spite of
his nickname showed no signs of actual madness, save that
all gross excess is abnormal.

Meredith was particularly interested in this specimen of
the tribe for, since his day, the family appeared to have
sobered up into a comparative normality until Gervase,
young Yves' father, once more manifested some of the unpleasant characteristics of his house. There had been, of course,
nothing in Mr. Whistle's book about Gervase Lauder-Treaves,
since the learned divine had been writing in the year 1850
and such knowledge as he possessed of the activities of Yves'
father Meredith had been given by McAllister.

John Meredith paused by Mike's side as the dog was
investigating a tuft of grass below the south windows of the
library and he recalled that it had been in that long and
lofty room that the Regency blackguard had once broken his
stick over the shoulders of young Peregrine Fallow, who, it
seemed, had been tutor to the Lauder-Treaves' children.
There had been no explanation offered in Mr. Whistle's
history for the attack and Meredith had assumed that it
had merely been but another manifestation of "mad, bad
Treaves'" ungovernable rage. On thinking back, however,
he wondered if perhaps there hadn't been something very
definite to occasion the flogging which had put the young
man into the hands of the doctors for some weeks, for it was

a fact that many years after, when "Buck" Treaves had died in America, his widow had married Mr. Fallow.

The archaic and pompous manner of the Reverend Mr. Whistle's writing had embalmed the whole story in a prosy dullness which, taken in conjunction with its context, Meredith had found somewhat amusing. Without the pompous deliberations of the author actually before him, Meredith realised that the long history of the Lauder-Treaves family was, in reality, a gallery of horrors. Between them the descendants of that old Breton swordsman seemed to have committed every crime in the calendar and, at times, to have improved upon the original models, for there were undoubtedly records of unmentionable things and nameless sins the reporting of which might well, in justice to Mr. Whistle, have been confined to a pathological treatise.

It was after breakfast that Meredith encountered Yves in the hall.

"Did you sleep all right?" asked the latter.

"Yes, why?"

"Oh, I only wondered if the family goblins would get you."

Meredith shook his head. "Not at second hand," he said. "I've had actual horrors over the last few years that would leave anything you've kept in your cupboard at the post."

"Yes, I suppose so," replied the other soberly. "I don't know what you've been up to, of course, but Finella-Lou gave me to understand you'd had a bad time." He paused a moment and then went on. "But still, it's an interesting record, isn't it?"

Again John nodded. "Very," he said, "but there's one thing I wanted to ask you; your Mr. Whistle, who, by the way, is an absolute joy, keeps on throughout his book constantly sliding round something. It seems as if he's evading some issue."

Yves smiled one-sidedly and nodded. "So you spotted that," he said. "You mean, I suppose, what old Silas labels 'the family misfortune' and 'the hereditary burden'?"

"Yes," said John.

Yves frowned and rubbed his chin, looking rather rueful. "I suppose," he said slowly, "you'd better see the Stayley document. If you can read it," he added.

"Read it?" echoed John Meredith. "Why, is it indecipherable, or so old? Don't tell me it's in Latin."

Yves shook his head. "No, it's in thirteenth century English and I can give you a typed copy. The original is in a very frail condition and I had the copy made by a friend of mine who is a don at Oxford. It takes a bit of understanding though, if you're not familiar with the language they employed at that time."

"Did old Whistle have access to it when he wrote his history?" asked Meredith.

"Apparently not," replied Yves. "It's an astonishing little chronicle and was not written at the request of the family at all. It came into our hands rather queerly. Old Thomas Lauder-Treaves, who flourished at the time of Henry the Eighth, was an old boy with an eye to the main chance—like most of the family, I'm afraid. Anyway he was well in with the Bullens and was tipped off when Henry decided to clamp down on the monasteries. You couldn't expect a Lauder-Treaves not to be up to the elbows in loot when it was going and Thomas conducted his own private Dissolution by walking down to Stayley with his merry men and sacking the old priory. You can still see some of the looted sacred vessels in the gallery next to the library which leads up to my rooms. But he got more than he bargained for. He got old Ranulf's chronicle which I'll show you if you come along to my place now."

A few minutes later Meredith was bending over a small heap of parchment which Yves had taken from a locked wooden case. It was very worn and old, though the penmanship was fine and graceful and imbued with that spirit which made men spend forty years and more illuminating their own Bibles. The document had been subjected to savage treatment. It was evident that, at one time, it had been torn up, for now it was covered both sides of each sheet by transparent adhesive paper. The pieces had been fitted together with loving care, but the elegant calligraphy had suffered. Each sheet was about twenty-four inches in length by some ten inches across. Meredith stooped and peered at the topmost sheet. He deciphered the simple superscription written in that long-dead hand. It read: "Ranulf hys Cronicel."

"You say you have a typewritten copy?" asked Meredith, turning to Yves.

The other nodded and from the bottom of the box which had contained the Stayley document he took an ordinary office folder and handed it to Meredith.

It was a bright sunny morning and some ten minutes afterwards Meredith, having collected the Sealyham under one arm, was seated in a sheltered spot of the terraced gardens overlooking the river. He began to read and noticed, thankfully, that the fellow at Oxford had modernised the spelling, if he had not changed the actual words and language employed.

RANULF HIS CHRONICAL

This scripture is the chronicle of Ranulf hight[1] the Younger, being clerk and exorcist to the worshipful Prior, Fontenay of Clewes, who holds his priorate at Stayley, the same within the county of Shropshire and within the Rape of Haut Peryl.

I write upon the feast-day of the most Holy Circumcision in the year of Our Most Blesséd Lord Jesu one thousand two hundred and six, John, by the grace of God our dread and sovereign liege, keeping his throne over this land.

I write, whether I wold or nold, in obeissance to and at hete[2] of my Lord-Prior, for to descrive that which I have dured though, y-wis,[3] it were passing strange and grimly. Certes,[3] never sith[4] the miracle of our own lief[5] Saint Hickelmure and the stoat hath the like wonder been in this land and I reneye[6] that there be ought of covin[7] in my accompt and to this do I borrow my soul and avow it

[1] called
[2] command
[3] certainly
[4] since
[5] dear
[6] deny
[7] deceit

upon the Ubblie,[1] *Itself. That which befell came to me by virtue of my office in charge of which I came unto the fortalice of Haut Peryl that was the seige of Sir Mordreth yclept*[2] *also Loup de Tréves as the French tongue has it that, an God so willed, I might make his soul at his passing. Hélas, I holp*[3] *him not and this hauteyn*[4] *knight died unshriven and unhouselled*[5] *in manner that were fearing to witness so that or ever I eft*[6] *reached the priory I was flatling*[7] *with dread and everych*[8] *night sith I have dretched*[9] *in my cell an I had been a little child.*

Yesterweek, it then being the eve of the Fourth Sunday in Advent, it betid that Sir Mordreth was stricken sore of his measle[10] *that was of a gree*[11] *so fell that good Master Umsebras, his leech, might in no wise withsay it for all that he might do. Came unto the priory Master Fulk that was page and bachelor to Sir Mordreth and with him a lewd fellow, hight ap Thomas, that was sewer*[12] *to the knight. Saith Master Fulk, God see you, Sir Priest. Wot you well that my lord is wonderly stricken and you shall come foot-hot*[13] *unto his closet an he be anealed*[14] *this side of his peron.*[15] *Nenny, Sir Page, quoth I, how may I come unto Sir Mordreth with my pyx and orisons? For wot you well good Father Peter is own clerk and chaplain to my lord of Haut Peryl. Then spake Fulk saying, Gramercy for your rede,*[16] *good Ranulf, but you would well to hie you to Peryl whether you wold or nold for Father Peter grovels of a palsied leg and may in no wise discharge his holy comfort. Then, said I unto him, I will come but first must I dress*[17] *against my duties and bring the oil and holy vessels from the chapel. And so I did. Then Master Fulk took me up upon the croup of his haut horse and for a short term we rode a great wallop,*[18] *I ever upon the croup, so that my arse was mischieved and I was fain*[19] *to rest up-so-down for a sennight thereft.*[20]

So we came to the courtelage of the castle and I did off my weeds[21] *and gave them to the keeping of an archer and then there brast*[22] *from my lord's own chamber so grimly a cry that it were more like the*

[1] consecrated Host
[2] called, named
[3] helped
[4] haughty
[5] without Communion
[6] again
[7] prostrate
[8] every
[9] troubled in sleep
[10] disease
[11] degree
[12] taster
[13] at once
[14] anointed
[15] tombstone, grave
[16] advice
[17] make ready
[18] gallop
[19] glad
[20] thereafter
[21] outer garments
[22] burst

questing[1] of a hound than human steven.[2] It were unnethe[3] to be borne and I retrayed[4] from the great stairs and would have piked[5] back to the priory but Master Fulk haled me with his hand and spake many foul words anent a priest's courage. I wold not go but he was wonder wight[6] for a youngling and thrang me up the stairs and so by way of many long eftures[7] unto the threshold of Sir Mordreth's chamber. Wake[8] you here, Sir Priest, spake Fulk the Page. Nor shall you hie you from this place. I spake him no word at his going though I was sore careful and his own lears[9] were blank[10] as he went unto Sir Mordreth's own closet beside which I waked.

Now it came to pass that as I waked in the efture my lady of Peryl that was own wife and spouse to Sir Mordreth came unto me and spake me fair for all that she was well nigh daffish[11] of dolour[12] and she did reverence to That Which I carried. And I cried a benison upon her against her sore disadventure that was of her lord's malfortune. Yet ever I bore my eyes upon my sandals for she was a lady beale[13] and nesh[14] and my Lord-Prior wold well I should in no wise rejoice in her in accompt of Mother Eve and her abominable sorceries.

Then came again the young bachelor Fulk and louted[15] to the dame and bid me come unto his lord and I was sore a-drad[16] of the summons and retrayed from that chamber an it had been a lazar-cot[17] outher[18] the barbican of Hell. But Master Fulk spake me naughtily so that I was fain to usurp[19] Sir Mordreth's closet and so we came to that closet, Master Fulk and the dame and I, everych by other.

Now forwhy[20] of the passing strange tidings I discover in this my scripture, at hete of my Lord-Prior, will I descrive the great chamber wherein Sir Mordreth grovelled of his deadly measle. It was haut and of much nobley[21] being germaine[22] an it were to a kingly hall rather a pallet-chamber for a fortalice. Two great parclos[23] departed[24] the chamber unto three parts, the same of wood wonderly bedecked with paintures of beasts and birds outher paintures

[1] howling, barking
[2] voice
[3] scarcely
[4] withdrew
[5] stolen away
[6] strong
[7] passages
[8] wait, watch
[9] cheeks
[10] white
[11] deranged
[12] grief
[13] beautiful
[14] soft
[15] bowed
[16] afraid
[17] leper-house
[18] or
[19] encroach upon
[20] because
[21] splendour
[22] closely allied to
[23] partitions
[24] divided

of venery¹ that it were wondrous cunning to behold, ne² had other brother of Stayley Priory beheld the like. And I bethought me that mayhap I be impeached³ of bobaunce⁴ at so descriving yet will I borrow my soul an it were not so. So too was the hauteyn pallet⁵ of Sir Mordreth of great noblesse and girt about with samite,⁶ the same which he had fetched out of Outremer⁷ upon Crusade sith he was a man of masteries upon the damnéd heathen Saracen and gained much worship by his glaive.⁸

But the knight that was master of this beale chamber was in great duresse being laced all about and everych way with wight cords that he was liker a trussed fowl or other a man and might in nowise traverse⁹ from his pallet. Not for then he wrothe and so wrought that he weltered with many braids¹⁰ and flang about an he were a fiendly serpent rather a man. And I feared exceeding lest the cords brast to-fore his essaying. And ever he roared like unto a beast at the mort.¹¹ I was much adoubted and had no lust to adventure myself unto that fell¹² pallet for, wot you well, I wagged¹³ to the marrow for I wist not what ailed Sir Mordreth and, certes, it were not seemly measle but a vile enchantment.

Then did I to my marrow-bones and did great praising and loving to God in orison that He allow Sir Mordreth his soul assoilment¹⁴ outher He be greed to grant aligement¹⁵ of the brim¹⁶ dolour of Sir Mordreth his body, and to peace him. But or ever I had made orison enow Sir Mordreth, writhing everych way in brim fury of his duresse by his cords, cried high and dolourous an he had the semblant of a hound. Then wept heavily his dame and stert¹⁷ from out the chamber saying that the woodness¹⁸ had eft come to her lord. And so good Master Fulk bode with me and came endlong¹⁹ to me that we might courage everych other.

Now do I avow by sweet Jesu My Lord and by His Fair Mother Our Most Blesséd Lady that what then befell was as I am making discovery in this my chronicle. And to this also does the young bachelor

¹ hunting
² nor
³ accused
⁴ exaggeration
⁵ bed
⁶ brocade
⁷ Over-Sea (Holy Land)
⁸ sword
⁹ move away
¹⁰ quick movements
¹¹ death
¹² dangerous
¹³ shook
¹⁴ absolution
¹⁵ alleviation
¹⁶ fierce
¹⁷ started up
¹⁸ madness
¹⁹ beside

134   THE MIND OF JOHN MEREDITH

Master Fulk avow, by Saint Hubert that he is nesh[1] *to, and to this is his hand and seal that I discover ought that did not befall.*

Then spake Sir Mordreth, and, perdy,[2] *his steven was unnethe that of a man that it smote upon the ear with mal engine.*[3] *Quoth Sir Mordreth, I am a-cursèd, I and all the heirs gotten of my body. Behold aforetime the grimly thing was done. Wot time Yves the Breton, that was of my fathers, meddled with Rhodri hight also Rhodri Mawr that was a haut prince of the Welsh land. And my fore-sire that was Yves the Breton took this prince that was his enemy by guile and flang him in a bawdy donjon and thereft did him to death in grievous manner so that Sir Rhodri might in no wise escape great dolour. Gramercy, it were a dog's death, for Sir Rhodri was he foined*[4] *through of an iron spit from his arse even unto his shoulder and thereft halsed*[5] *about with fire that he was mischieved unto death. Yet or ever he passed he cursed my fore-sire and spake him foully that it were a marvel. And this man that was a Welsh prince was of perilous stock, certes, he was a clerk of necromancy and had complished divers enchantments, sorceries and the like aforetime and had foiled his enemies that were come against him and him sans*[6] *harness and with naked hands.*

Then did Sir Mordreth learn me and Fulk the bachelor the manner of the Welshman's spell that was wrought upon Sir Yves his forebear and all to follow him of his body. They should go like beasts and pareil[7] *to that beast that was their device, a fiendly wolf, for, wot you well, the lords of Haut Peryl were named in the French manner Wolf of Tréves. A score of years and ten they should go in kindly manner but thereft they would be adoubted for Rhodri's mal*[8] *engine*[8] *would come upon them for all they might do. And then they that were of Yves' blood and bone should go upon their bellies, grovelling after the manner of a wolf and seeking ever to devour even those that were lief unto them. And they would be doted and daffish of their shenship*[9] *and their souls would dwine*[10] *before God that the sins of their fathers might be visited upon them.*

And thus do I avow spake Sir Mordreth unto Fulk that was his

[1] tender
[2] *par Dieu*
[3] force
[4] pierced
[5] encompassed
[6] without (Fr.)
[7] similar
[8] evil intent
[9] disgrace
[10] shrivel

THE STAYLEY DOCUMENT

page and unto me, Ranulf that was a clerk come to housel him. But Fulk learned me then that Sir Mordreth was wood[1] of his measle for that he had grown stricken eft he were bitten of a brachet[2] that was about his lady's bower.

Then came I unto the haut pallet and gat the holy pyx from my weeds and with loving to God did take from it the Ubblie that by Its virtue Sir Mordreth might be sacring[3] his soul but or ever I came nigh unto him he so hurled and flang and weltered in his duresse against the cords that I adoubted sore lest he sacrilege the Ubblie and was fain to put It by. And ever Sir Mordreth roared an he were a hound or, certes, a wolf beneath black Rhodri's spell and so roaring he dwined and was speechless and then he gave up his ghost and was peaced.

And when the knight was dead I came forth and with me ever Fulk the bachelor and we were sore apaired[4] and wagging an we had been children flogged. And the dame caused me to be put up upon a jennet[5] that was of a kind and douce courage and wore an scarlet arson[6] on which I sat. So came I back upon the jennet to the priory and was fain to be so. Then spake I to my Lord-Prior and learned him well what had befallen and of the marvels which betid at Sir Mordreth's passing. Wherefore my Lord-Prior bid me eft descrive the knight's words by which he discovered the peril of his breed and so I did. Then did my father in God give me hete to set down in scripture the marvels I had dured and required good Master Fulk to place his mark upon the same that this my chronicle might in no wise be impeached of covin or un-truth. And so we did. Yet ever I was sore shend[7] as to body forwhy my arse was yet mischieved of that great wallop upon the croup of Fulk's horse, as to spirit forwhy I dretched and adoubted exceeding of nights lest Sir Mordreth might in no wise lie clean[8] beneath his peron. And so ends the chronicle of Ranulf that hight the Younger of the Priory of Stayley. Deo gratias.

[1] mad
[2] small dog
[3] consecrating
[4] weakened
[5] small horse
[6] saddle
[7] harmed
[8] at peace

CHAPTER XV

PERWYL'S BANE

MEREDITH read to the end of this astonishing document and then collected the typewritten pages of the copy and returned them to their folder. He placed this at his side on the wooden bench and reached for his cigarette-case. He inhaled deeply and allowed the smoke to trickle slowly from his nostrils as he stared blankly across the little valley to the wooded slopes of Hollow Hill opposite.

So that was it. He shook his head in wonderment, marvelling at the childishness of human nature. He frowned incredulously as though he found it difficult to credit the fact that a grown man in this age of mechanical materialism should be in the least affected by this medieval nonsense. Lycanthropy, werewolves, hugaboo, hobgoblins and things-that-go-bump-in-the-night. Had I been a Victorian novelist I might aptly have described Meredith's reaction to this balderdash in the word or written sound "Pshaw!" As it is I am obliged to relate that Meredith gave vent to his feelings as an ordinary sort of chap does in *another* word of five letters. He laughed contemptuously, pityingly and felt almost angry. This thing was an outrage on common sense.

Meredith flipped away the butt of his cigarette and rose to his feet. He walked slowly down and out of the gardens towards the bank of the little river. Here, where he had found Mike on the night of his fight, he stood in thought. His first instinct was to go to Martin Lauder-Treaves and tackle him straight away with this idiotic obsession and to tell him to snap out of it. He was prepared to point out to him in no uncertain terms that he'd no business to go worrying his young wife to death like this over a crack-brain superstition which wouldn't frighten a healthy child of ten. Witches, warlocks, wizards, werewolves! Meredith used a string of very naughty words as he thought of it. He started off up the hill at a round pace, intending to seek out the young baronet and charge in right away, but he had not gone sixty yards up the steep hill when he found he was labouring sadly. He was, as yet, he discovered, far from fit and he was obliged to pause to recover his breath. He would, in any case, have had to have waited for Mike who gave vent to a short bark of protest at being expected to go up-hill at such a pace. As Meredith stood on the hillside catching his breath, his mood began to change and he grew reflective. However stupid the thing was, there could be no doubt that young Martin deeply believed it. There must be some reason for this. Everything that he had learned about the youngster showed that up to a short while ago he was perfectly normal or, at least, betrayed no symptoms of obsession of any kind. Finella-Lou wasn't playing the fool about the thing. Her distress was too real and evident not to be believed and she seemed to date the change in her young husband from that morning when he had behaved like a fool over the toothbrush.

Meredith rubbed his chin. Toothbrush? What the devil had that got to do with a belief in lycanthropy? He frowned again. Maybe it might be better to hold his horses until . . . until he knew a bit more about the damn-fool thing. The whole obsession was tripe, of course, *but* it remained an obsession. He recalled that evening before dinner in the Lacquer Room when Martin had broken the cocktail glasses. That white, agonised face swam before his eyes again. H'm, the fellow was scared all right, bloody frightened, in fact. That sick fear had not been a pleasant thing to witness and whatever its cause it had been and, Meredith supposed, remained a real thing, a factor to be taken into account and not dismissed too lightly. Hell, this wasn't a case for a detective. This was a psychiatrist's pidgin. If he went off at half-cock he might frighten the fellow into a fit. Still, anyway, now that they knew what was the cause of the thing it ought to be simple enough to choke it out. Meredith went on slowly up the hill. Rum, he thought, how these old superstitions could still persist. What a hell of a thing to keep in the family cupboard—a werewolf. Bit smelly, unless he were taken out and brushed and combed every day and bathed occasionally. Wonder what you'd feed the brute on? Spratt's Human-Flesh Wolf-Biscuits, probably, and have to give it Bob Martin's Condition Powders to make it a Plus Werewolf. Meredith grinned at his own nonsense and walked across the causeway to the frontdoor.

Indoors he went in search of Yves and made his way through the corridors to the latter's quarters in the old keep. He went into Yves' study, office or whatever he called it, but it was empty. He went to the foot of the winding staircase which opened off the other side of the room and called, but Yves was evidently out about his business on the estate. Meredith put down the folder containing the typewritten transcription of old Ranulf's chronicle on one of the tables and noted as he did so a pile of old documents, letters chiefly, under a paper-weight. Idly he removed this and glanced at the documents from which Yves was drawing so much of the material for his book. The beginning of one of these letters caught his eye. The ink was brown and faded, but the handwriting was large, rounded and eminently legible. It was obviously a woman's writing. It was dated the twentieth of May, 1816, and began "My dear and well-beloved Perry". Still with what was only an idle interest Meredith extracted it from the heap, having marked with his eye the place from which he had taken it. He turned to the signature and read the boldly inscribed "Lucinda". Meredith's interest quickened as he recalled that Lucinda had been the unfortunate wife of the Prince Regent's scoundrelly friend "mad, bad Treaves" and it seemed very probable that her "dear and well-beloved Perry" was the young Mr. Peregrine Fallow who had received such a sound thrashing at the hands of his employer.

Meredith turned the letter over and began to read. *My dear and well-beloved Perry, I am writing to acquaint you with the joyous news that Roderick is now happily recovered from his recent indisposition and bids me send you his love and duty. As for me, you may, my dearest, judge of my content and joy. When the boy was stricken down I felt I might well run mad with fear lest he too should follow in the footsteps of his poor unhappy brothers. Thank God my Roderick is of cleaner stock, for I had thought that when, like Merrilees and Rupert, he sickened that perhaps it was I, their mother, who had bequeathed to them their sickly health. Oh Perry, my dearest, there now remains nothing that can. . . .*

So far Meredith read when the door of the room, which he had not completely closed behind him, swung open and Yves Lauder-Treaves appeared. He stood very still just inside the door, staring at Meredith. His expression was troubled. "Have you read it?" he asked low-voiced.

Meredith smiled and nodded. "Yes," he said, "and I must say that Ranulf is an improvement on Whistle when it comes to style."

"Oh," said Yves blankly.

"I hope you don't mind," went on Meredith, replacing Lucinda's letter where he had found it, "but I was just glancing through some more of your raw material. I haven't misplaced anything."

Yves shot a glance at the other from under his long lashes and asked casually: "Was that one of Lucinda's effusions to her 'dear and well-beloved Perry' that you were reading?"

"Yes," said Meredith, "something about the children's health. In skimming through Whistle I hadn't realised that two of the three boys died."

Yves nodded. "Yes," he said, "the two elder boys kicked off and Roderick succeeded. What did you think of the Stayley document?"

Meredith regarded the other amusedly. "What do *you* think of it?"

Yves hesitated. "Well," he said, reluctantly, "it's . . . it's a remarkable statement."

"It's all that," agreed Meredith, "but the thing's perfectly plain. Old Mordreth was bitten by 'his lady's brachet', contracted hydrophobia and died off his head."

"Oh, I think *that's* true enough," agreed Yves, "but . . . but what about the story which he unwittingly revealed to Ranulf in his ravings?"

"You don't *believe* it, do you?"

"N-no," said Yves slowly and with evident embarrassment. Meredith's eyes narrowed momentarily and then his face became blank of all expression. This was absurd. Here was another member of the family havering about the tribal legend.

Yves reached for a cigarette from a silver box on the table among his papers and lit it absent-mindedly without offering one to his companion. He squared his shoulders and said frankly: "I expect it sounds awful rot to you."

"Frankly," said Meredith, "it does."

Yves grinned. "You're refreshingly matter-of-fact," he admitted.

"But, good God, man," began Meredith, when the other shook his head and interrupted him.

"No," he said, quietly, "it isn't really quite as simple as all that." He began to walk slowly about the big room, puffing frequently at his cigarette. "On the face of it there's no doubt whatsoever that the thing is nonsense, but the family has bred some pretty queer specimens and at times when there was no medical science to pronounce upon their . . . well, shall we be polite and call them ailments? I mean, one or two or more of the family have been as mad as hatters and there is at least evidence that they themselves believed that they were suffering from something for which no certain cure was known. Do you know anything about lycanthropy?" he asked suddenly.

"Practically nothing," said Meredith. "It's true that once, when I was in India as a boy, my father handled a murder case in a village in Rajputana and, until he caught the murderer, the local boys profoundly believed that the murders were committed by a weretiger. Even after the arrest they were still convinced that it had been in the form of a tiger that the chap had committed his abominations. That's the only personal experience I've had of the belief. But, again, you're not going to tell me that *you* believe this lycanthropy business?"

"No," said Yves frowning, "I don't *believe*, but . . . but when you've grown up with the knowledge that the head of your family is fore-doomed to something unpleasant *and* you also know that quite a lot of your ancestors have been pretty bloody queer, it isn't so much that you believe the thing as that . . ."

"You don't disbelieve?" suggested Meredith.

Yves ran his fingers through his untidy curls and scratched the back of his head. "Damned if I know how to put it," he said, "but there *is* a devilish unpleasant sort of feeling that . . . well, that it *might* be so."

"And your cousin?" queried John Meredith. "Does he not disbelieve?"

He was not quite prepared for Yves' reaction to this query. The man looked up, wide-eyed, and stared directly at him. He looked startled and more than startled. "Look, Meredith," he said urgently, "Martin's a rum sort of cove, but the old boy's all right . . . he's all right, I tell you."

"I think he's all wrong," said Meredith bluntly. "I'm afraid I don't agree with you at all. The thing sticks out a mile and what's more, my dear chap, you've known all along."

Yves Lauder-Treaves sank down into a high-backed chair near the fireplace. He passed a hand wearily over his face, sighed deeply and turned to his companion. Meredith could see that the barriers of family loyalty were down.

"Yes," said Yves, almost in a whisper, "you're quite right. Old Martin *is* all wrong."

"But, good grief," said Meredith, "the thing's a lot of clotted nonsense. Surely to God you're not going to sit down, suspecting as you do, that you know what's the matter with him, and do nothing about it?"

Yves shook his head slowly from side to side. "My dear fellow," he said, "I just haven't known *what* to do. I had poor little Finella-Lou to think about. I couldn't very well go to her and tell her . . . that her husband thinks, or at least fears, that he might be a werewolf. I mean, it sounds completely crazy to anyone who is not really of the family. Look at your own reaction. I simply didn't know what to do."

"Well, I don't know *what* I'm going to do, but I'm going to do *something*. To start with, the man's got to be seen by a psychoanalyst."

"He won't see *any* kind of doctor," said Yves sullenly.

"He won't know," Meredith assured him.

"Yes, but for a psychiatrist to be able to help a patient he must have the willing assistance of the individual concerned," Yves pointed out.

"I quite realise that," said Meredith, "but we can at least get a professional opinion as to how best to tackle the thing. You haven't discussed it with Martin at all, have you?"

Yves shook his head. "No," he said, "I haven't."

"Well, don't then," advised Meredith, "and leave it to me. By the way, no mention of anything to Finella-Lou."

Yves nodded and then rose to his feet and stood facing the other. "I say," he began, and hesitated, looking very young and shy. "I say," he said again, "I do think it's awfully decent of you to bother with us. I mean, I'm so bloody glad to have someone else in this with me. It's been frightful watching the poor old boy day by day, scrabbling around on the border-line. I know that a few minutes ago I suggested that there was a nasty feeling in us that there might be something in this lycanthropy bunk but, when it comes to fetching in strangers, you feel so damn stupid. I rather hoped," he ended, "that you'd tumble to it when I set you reading up the family dope."

"Well," said Meredith briskly, "we'll go to work on it, shall we?"

Yves smiled and impetuously thrust out his hand. "We certainly will," he nodded as Meredith took it.

CHAPTER XVI

PSYCHIATRIST'S OPINION

IT was a sign of Meredith's increasing strides towards normality that he did not flinch from the thought of the fatigues of another flying visit to London. He made his arrangements by telephone before leaving High Perwyl, but not from the house itself. He walked down to Stayley and telephoned from the post-office. He spoke first to General Sir Hector McAllister and from him obtained a second telephone number. When the exchange had eventually connected him with this Welbeck number he held a long, if somewhat guarded, conversation with the man at the other end and hung up with the knowledge that Mr. Hartley Frome would see him the following afternoon at three.

Meredith had no wish to commit himself in any way, yet the misery of Finella-Lou's little white face trapped him into speaking before he should have done, a fact which later he was bitterly to repent.

"My dear," he said, "don't think that we are out of the wood with regard to Martin, but I *can* tell you that I've got a glimmer of light."

The girl's reaction was instant and pathetic. It was as though the sun had suddenly burst through cloud on a rainy day. She was bathed in her own radiance.

"Oh, John!" she said breathlessly.

At three o'clock to the minute the following afternoon Meredith rang the bell of a discreet-looking house in Welbeck Street. He had noted before doing so that a brass plate upon the door proclaimed the consulting rooms of Mr. Hartley Frome and, as he waited for the door to be answered, his eye wandered to the other two brass plates with which Frome's shared the honours. The name on the centre plate meant nothing to him, but its fellow to the left bore the legend "Miles Langtry". Meredith frowned. The name was familiar and he knew that he had heard it recently. Then it burst upon him. He remembered that when Sir Hector had admitted bringing Hartley Frome down to see him he, Meredith, had made the disparaging query: "Nut-doctor?" He recalled, further, that McAllister, admitting this, had said that Hartley Frome and Miles Langtry were the king-pins of their profession in this country. And then he knew where he had heard the latter name before. It had been from Finella-

Lou, who had revealed that it had been Miles Langtry who had examined and treated Martin Lauder-Treaves on his discharge from hospital and the army.

The door opened and Meredith went into the house. He was shown promptly into an austere, colourless room furnished only with a thick beige carpet, a big arm-chair, and a most inviting-looking *lit-de-repos*. Hartley Frome stood near the fireplace, regarding him noncommittally as he entered. Meredith grinned and held out his hand.

"How's the Foreign Office?" he asked.

A twinkle appeared in the shrewd grey eyes in the strong face regarding him. "I wouldn't know," he replied, taking Meredith's hand. "Do you want me to ring up Ernie and find out?"

Meredith laughed and sat down uninvited on the big daybed.

"First of all," he said, the amusement dying out of his face, "I've not come to consult you about myself. I'm . . . I'm better."

"I can see that," the other man nodded.

"Yes," said Meredith simply. "I've come to talk to you, to ask your advice, about somebody else, but before going on with that may I ask you if Miles Langtry is a partner of yours?"

"You may and he isn't," replied Frome, "but we are colleagues and very often give each other a hand. You know, discuss cases and angles of approach."

"I see," said Meredith. "Then you would have no objection to having Langtry on the case as well—purely in a consultative capacity?"

"None whatsoever," replied Frome. "But why Miles?"

"Because Langtry saw this chap originally and . . ."

"My dear fellow," Hartley Frome broke in, "if he's Miles' case I couldn't possibly jump the claim. Besides it would be stupid, because Miles will have all the threads in his hands which I should have to begin from the beginning to unravel."

"Yes, but Langtry is the one man whom this fellow must *not* see."

Hartley Frome seated himself in the arm-chair and gave his visitor a cigarette. "Look," he said, when they had lit up, "supposing you outline the case for me and then, if I think Miles ought to come in on it rather than your going direct to him, I'll go and get him."

John outlined the case as he saw it and was vastly relieved by the other's prosaic approach to anything as esoterically silly as the subject of lycanthropy. When Meredith had finished speaking the other sat and regarded him in silence. "Fascinating," he said at length, "quite fascinating. We don't often get an obsession of this kind. I quite agree with you that Miles should come in on this."

A few moments later he was ushering into the room a long, gangling man of indeterminate age. Langtry had a face like a skull, but a skull with a most attractive humour and kindliness in its expression.

"Sir Martin Lauder-Treaves," he said after introductions had been affected. "Yes, I remember the case well, but there was no very considerable neurosis, just battle-shock in a fairly sensitive type."

"There was no suggestion whatsoever," asked Meredith, "*at that time* of any sort of suppressed fear, or whatever you chaps call it?"

Langtry shook his head. "Not a thing," he said. "Young Lauder-Treaves is an imaginative sort and what is usually called highly-strung. I would have said that he was an unusually brave man, using the term in its normally accepted sense, and I should think that he would, quite literally, have had to screw his courage to the sticking-point to go in and do the things he did as a Commando."

Meredith nodded. "If it isn't an impertinence for me to express an opinion in such expert company, I should entirely agree with you and, indeed, what you say is confirmed by his one-time Company Sergeant-Major. Briars, that's his C.S.M., told me that Lauder-Treaves exhibited, to those who knew him really well, symptoms of very genuine nerves before going in to the attack, but that once he got going nothing could stop him. What I want to establish is that when you, Mr.

Langtry, saw him he was not suffering under this particular delusion."

"I'd stake my professional reputation on it," said Langtry quietly.

"Then, in that case," Meredith pursued, "something must have happened between then and now to occasion his present mental condition?"

To his surprise and chagrin both psychiatrists shook their heads at this.

"I'm afraid it's not as simple as that, Sir John," said Hartley Frome.

"Hell," said Meredith, "why not?"

"Because," the other explained, "the root cause of his present condition may quite well have been there already, buried in his sub-conscious and quite without his knowledge."

Meredith leant forward and rested his forearms on his knees. "Right," he said, "I'll grant you that. Then let's get at it in this way. Given that the root cause might already have been stuffed away in his sub-conscious, something must have happened to shove it up to the surface?"

He looked expectantly at his companions, neither of whom spoke for a moment or two, and then the death-head smiled suddenly and nodded. "It's possible," he said.

"Damn it, it's probable," Meredith insisted.

"It's even probable," smiled Frome.

"Well, we're getting *somewhere*," Meredith grunted. "Look," he went on, "quite apart from the psychopathological aspect of the thing, do you fellows know anything about the beliefs in lycanthropy?"

"Yes," said Miles Langtry, "Hartley, there, does. Tell him the sad story, Hartley."

"As a matter of fact, Sir John," said Frome, taking a drag at his cigarette and sitting back on the day-bed at Meredith's side, "I started off by being an anthropologist, pure and simple. Among the kindred subjects which I found peculiarly fascinating was, not unnaturally, the whole field of folklore."

"Fraser's *Golden Bough* and that stuff," suggested Meredith frowning.

"Fraser and that stuff," agreed Frome. "The belief in lycanthropy is incredibly ancient. The word itself is generally presumed to come from the Greek *lukos*, a wolf, and *anthropos*, a man, though there is a school which claims that it originates from the name of Lycaon, an Arcadian, who, in the days when wolf-packs were making annihilating raids on the flocks, sacrificed a child to them by leaving it for them to devour. Lycanthropy is a generic term for the age-old belief of madness in which the individual imagines himself to be and acts like some animal. It is not necessarily a wolf. For instance, you have kuanthropy, which means a transition into a dog and boanthropy, which means transition into some bovine animal, usually a buffalo. As I say, the belief is very ancient, and you will find references to it in the Eighth Eclogue of Virgil. Similarly, there are passages in Herodotus which refer to it. I believe I could quote one of them now. It is when he is writing about a northern Balkan tribe called the Neuri." Hartley Frome leaned back and placed the tips of his thumb and forefinger into the corner of his eyes. "'It seems, that the Neuri are sorcerers, if one is to believe the Scythians and the Greeks established in Scythia; for each Neuri changes himself, once in the year, into the form of a wolf and he continues in that form for several days, after which he resumes his former human shape.'"

"Listen to the infant prodigy," scoffed Miles Langtry at the conclusion of this quotation.

"Not bad," agreed Frome smugly, "after all these years."

"Where does the word 'were' come from?" asked Meredith interested.

"Probably from the Latin *vir*, a man, or the similar Gothic word *vair*. The word for 'man' is much the same in a lot of languages. You have the Icelandic *verr*, the *vîra* in Zend; *wirs* which is old Prussian and its equivalent *wîrs* in Lettish and you even get similarities in Asia, for 'man' in Sanskrit is *vîra* and in Bengali the word is very like in *bîr*. But the word from which we, here in England, derive 'were' is probably the old Anglo-Saxon word w,e,r. Of course, in Great Britain, the belief in lycanthropy has seldom been associated with wolves, as such, since wolves were exterminated so early on in our history, but there are records of its association with the wolf in Wales. In Devonshire lycanthropy was associated with black dogs and at a place near Tavistock there are still people who believe that the Wild Huntsman rides at full moon with his wush-hounds. You must not, of course, confuse the werewolf with the 'church-dog' which was also known as a bar-ghest or pad-foit or, sometimes, as a wush-hound and was purely an evil embodied spirit which had no intimate association with man."

"This is all jolly interesting," said Meredith, "but, even supposing that Martin Lauder-Treaves believes he's suffering from this thing under an age-old curse, why should he have behaved as he has done with regard, for instance, to his toothbrush and the business of the glasses?"

"Oh, that's easily explained," replied Frome, smiling. "Given that the poor chap thinks he's got this thing, we may presume that he has some knowledge of the lore with which the whole subject is wrapped. One of the things which is probably worrying him beyond all others is the fact, or accepted fact, that the werewolf almost invariably satiates his horrible appetite on those nearest and dearest to him in his normal condition."

Meredith scratched his head. "I haven't the least idea what you're talking about," he said. "What the devil's that got to do with the toothbrush and cocktail glasses?"

Frome smiled. "I see that I've got to elaborate a bit more," he said. "You know, I suppose," he continued, "that the werewolf can be of two species. The first and the one more generally believed in is that in which the wizard or warlock or sufferer undergoes a metamorphosis from the human to the animal form while still alive. This involves the theory of bi-location to which I will return in a minute. The other type of werewolf is supposed at death to undergo a metempsychosis and for his spirit to enter into the wolf-shape. As I say, the former belief is the more common and there is a quantity of so-called evidence to support it and its kindred theory of bi-location or the ability to be in two places at once; that means that the warlock remains in his human shape in a state of stupor or coma while his astral body or other self, entering into the beast shape, is at liberty to move at will about the countryside and to satisfy his own peculiar and beastly appetites."

"Yes, I follow all that," said Meredith, "as far as it goes, but what about the toothbrush?"

Hartley Frome held up his hand. "Half a jiffy," he said, "I haven't quite finished with this business of bi-location. I'm sorry," he smiled apologetically, "but you asked me to tell you what I knew about lycanthropy and this *is* what I know and this is Hartley Frome telling you," he grinned.

Miles Langtry leant forward and whispered to Meredith: "You mustn't mind. He has a Narcissus-complex."

"To continue," said Frome, ignoring the insult, "as regards the theory of bi-location it is generally believed that the wizard or lycanthropist is himself vulnerable in his beast shape. By that I mean that it is generally supposed that if you wound the animal, a precisely similar wound may be found upon the body of the warlock. Numerous instances are quoted in support of this idea from half-a-dozen different countries, but chiefly from France where the whole business of the *loupgarou* was widely accepted for several centuries."

"You mean," said Meredith, "that if I run into a werewolf sniffing a tree in a suspicious manner and kick him up the rump, that his human or other self will at the same time receive a swift kick in the pants?"

"More or less," laughed Frome, "except that it wouldn't exactly be in the pants."

"Why not?" asked Meredith, "doesn't a warlock wear his backside in the same place as Old Faithful?"

Frome nodded. "Yes, he does," he replied. "There's no evidence of contortion, but the lycanthropist won't be wearing any pants."

"Nudist, too?"

"In a way. You see, in order to effect the metamorphosis

he has to be naked. The change can't take place if he is clothed. But to go on to your question about the toothbrush and so on. I can quite see why this poor devil was agitated at the idea that his wife might have used his toothbrush by accident. There are supposed to be various ways of contracting this magical disease and the spittle of a werewolf is more contagious than anything else."

"D'you mean," said John Meredith slowly, "that in this day and age a much-decorated Major of Commandos could seriously believe that, not only he was a werewolf, but that he might turn his wife into one too? It sounds absolute galls!"

"Of course it's galls," agreed Frome, "but we're dealing with the mind and the imagination, a realm where possibility is infinite. If Lauder-Treaves really believes this thing, then nothing could be more dangerous to his wife than his toothbrush. Similarly, the business of the cocktail glasses can, I have no doubt, be explained in the same way. Grant his obsession and he just couldn't take the risk. Another thing, I told you just now that a werewolf is supposed, when in his beast-shape, to single out those he loves best for attack. I have no doubt that that explains why young Lauder-Treaves has removed himself from his wife's bedroom."

"But surely," said Meredith, leaning forward and lighting a cigarette, "the chap just doesn't believe the thing for no reason. Surely there must be, at least to his mind, some evidence of his affliction."

"Not necessarily what you and I would regard as evidence. On the other hand, we can't, of course, be sure that subconsciously he has not been manufacturing that evidence, if it exists, himself."

Meredith stared at the two other men in bewilderment. "Do you mean to tell me that this poor devil might himself deliberately set about preparing the junk which is frightening him into fits?"

"It's entirely possible," Miles Langtry assured him, breaking in. "The human mind is tortuous in the extreme and there is a form of mental masochism well-known to psychiatry which takes a delight in fear. I had a case not so long ago of a boy of sixteen who, when he was much younger, had been terrified by reading Bram Stoker's *Dracula*. It had haunted him since first reading it, but at sixteen he was actually discovered to revel in his terror. He used to wait until the house was empty at night, and then turn all the lights out, put a chair in the open doorway of the drawing-room with his back to the dark hall and there read *Dracula* by the light of a single candle. He used to frighten himself literally into fits."

"*Chacun son goût!*" said Meredith dryly. "But getting back to Lauder-Treaves, what do we do?"

Hartley Frome hesitated and glanced at his colleague. "I rather think, Sir John, if you'll forgive me," he said, "that you'll do nothing. From what you tell me Lauder-Treaves will have to be handled very carefully indeed. In a case like this you can't just go up to him and say: 'Look here, old boy, what's this I hear about your being a werewolf?'"

Meredith did not laugh. He nodded slowly and said: "That's why I've come to you and, to be frank, I'm almost as much worried by Lady Lauder-Treaves' appearance. The girl's nearly out of her mind with worry."

"You say, Sir John, that Lauder-Treaves has refused to see a doctor?" queried Frome. "Well, I agree with you then that that rules Miles out of it altogether."

"Precisely," said Meredith. "I don't know if you will accept this idea, but I had thought that you, Frome, might repeat the histrionic display you gave when McAllister brought you down to put the rule over me."

"Go up and see him in some other capacity?"

"Yes," said John, "and I think the same one you adopted before. It's known at High Perwyl that I have connections with various Ministries and Government departments and it is also known that I have a very important report to write. I have no doubt I could arrange for you to come and stay there, at any rate for a few days, and thus give you an opportunity of having a look at the chap. I fully realise that for you to effect a cure you must have the willing assistance of the patient, but I feel that you would be more qualified to judge how the approach to him was to be made than anyone else."

"When would you want me to come?"

John Meredith smiled. "Isn't the answer always—as soon as possible?"

He left the house in Welbeck Street with the assurance that the eminent psychiatrist would be free in three or four days' time. It was arranged that Meredith should prepare the ground against his arrival at High Perwyl and that further details should be agreed by telephone.

CHAPTER XVII

VIRGINIA'S BIRTHDAY

MEREDITH caught an early train the following morning and arrived back at Stayley soon after three. He had made the additional effort since he remembered that he had promised to attend the small Virginia's birthday-party at Home Farm that afternoon. Before leaving town he had bought as many chocolates as he was permitted by the Minister of Food and these he had placed in an attractive box from the gift department downstairs at Fortnum and Masons.

On reaching the house in the station taxi he found the family already assembled to walk down and pay honour to the child on her sixth birthday. The presents, owing to their bulk, had been sent down to the farm by handcart.

Finella-Lou was dressed in a lovely printed chiffon and a huge picture hat, the whole ensemble more suitable for Ascot than a visit to Home Farm, but, as she explained, they always dressed up for Ginnie's birthday and that it was an occasion. Martin, remarkably spruce-looking in a lounge suit instead of his eternal polo-sweater and tweeds, seemed less drawn and hag-ridden than Meredith had ever seen him. Finella-Lou and her husband led the way, Yves and Meredith bringing up the rear.

"By the way," said the former as they started down the

hill towards the quarry. "You know that tyke we captured, or rather Brummy did? It's got a clean bill. Briars went over to Wrayne and there could be no doubt that the wretched dog was at home the night our sheep was killed."

"So the murderer is still at large?" commented Meredith.

"Seems so," replied Yves. "However, he hasn't added to his crimes so far."

The birthday party at Home Farm went with a swing. Ginnie, looking very appealing in her party frock, was completely ravished by the number and splendour of her presents.

"You really shouldn't have done, Sir John," said her mother, Susan Mills, when John produced his contribution. "You must have used up all your ration for the month."

"Never eat the things," said John with cheerful untruthfulness.

Finella-Lou, Martin and Magnolia had combined to produce a really magnificent present. It was a large dolls'-house made by Martin, who had also made the frames of all the furniture. Upholstering and decorating had been carried out by Mesdames Finella-Lou and Magnolia, the whole thing approaching something of a work of art.

"I'd no idea you were so skilled a carpenter," Meredith said to the young baronet.

Martin Lauder-Treaves gave one of his all too rare, attractive smiles and his eyes were very tender as he watched the small person standing in silent and overwhelming admiration before the toy.

"Oh, well," he said, almost apologetically, "it was for Ginnie, you see."

Meredith saw indeed. With the loss of his own boy he could understand very well what a tragedy it was that this young couple was still childless.

Finella-Lou sank down in a cloud of chiffon at the child's side and showed her how to open the house, where the electric-light switches were, how the curtains drew with little side-cords and all the joyous discoveries which still held Virginia in enthralled silence.

"O-o-oh!" breathed Virginia at last, her small hands clasped below her chin, the gentian eyes wide and awed.

"Say you like it, Ginnie," urged her mother. "Say thank you to Sir Martin and her ladyship."

The child turned her flaxen head and regarded her mother as though she couldn't credit the words she had heard.

"*Like* it?" she echoed, her underlip quivering dangerously. She turned and reached a small hand to Martin and another to his wife. "Oh, S'Martin! Oh, Lady Lou!" she quavered and burst into tears. The present was a success.

Martin Lauder-Treaves picked up the small Virginia and comforted her against her overwhelming pleasure and it wasn't long before she wriggled down to the floor now in a frame of mind where she could really go to work at appreciating the toy.

John's present was accepted gravely and shyly and her "brig-dear" was duly thanked. Yves' present proved to be almost as overwhelming as the dolls'-house, for he fetched in from one of the outhouses a part grown fox-terrier which immediately and amiably assumed that it was the centre of attraction. Ginnie was more than delighted with her new pet who behaved very nicely except for one momentary lapse on the valance of the sofa, but he was excused owing to the general excitement.

It was while they were all at tea at the big oak dining table over which old Mrs. Truelove presided that the adenoidal maid came in from the kitchen and said: "If you blease, mum, that there Brubby is at the back door and wats to cub in."

"Brown Brummy, what does he want?" exclaimed Mrs. Truelove.

"Says he's got a bresent for Biss Giddie."

"Oh, how lovely!" exclaimed Ginnie, "a present from Brummy! Oh, please Granny, may he come in?"

A moment later the little man entered the room, his bush of a face split in a dreadful grimace which revealed one tooth and which was undoubtedly supposed to be a pleasant smile. He dragged his indescribable hat from his head and leaped violently into the air to execute his double kick of greeting.

To everyone's astonishment, including his own, his present shot into the air from the folds of innumerable waistcoats and fell with a plop! on to the carpet. The present was received with very mixed feelings by the assembled company when they saw crouched on the floor a large white rat. What followed, followed very quickly. One moment the rat was looking round with an expression of surprise and the next it was quite dead. The young terrier had lost no time and had seized it expeditiously by the back of the neck, shaken it and laid it at Brown Brummy's feet with an expression of complete self-approval.

Chaos ensued. Ginnie emitted an ear-splitting squeal of distress. Brummy gave a roar of rage and aimed a savage kick at the terrier who danced away in evident delight at this new game. Briars tripped over the dog as he strove to restrain Brown Brummy from what was obviously murderous intent. It was the natural authority in Martin's barked command which restored order.

Brown Brummy stood by the door shaking with rage. "There be too many blarstid dawgs aroun' Perwyl these days, so there be an all," he snarled. "Blarstid dawg! Killed my liddle rat, so 'e did—the blarstid boogger."

"Shut up, Brummy," snapped Martin. "We're all sorry that the dog killed your rat, but it couldn't be helped."

The little old man regarded the baronet with evil eyes. "Shurrup, 'e says to Oi, and shurrup Oi will, Sur Mart'n, but facks is facks an' it don't alter it no 'ow. Too many dawgs, say Oi an' too many dawgs it is. Arh, Brown Brummy knows. Brown Brummy knows a mort of things wot some other folks don't know and mebbe 'tis as well they shouldn't know. Arh, Oi seen un, so Oi 'ave, runnin' loike the wind an' a gert big un, too. So big as a cart'orse. Oi seen un, Sur Mart'n, when other folks is close to bed." The bleary little eyes grew cunning. "Brown Brummy, 'e knows. 'E's seen un *an*' 'e don't go far from castle, neether."

There was a momentary silence when the little man ceased speaking, a silence in which three men in that room felt the same tension. The thing was absurd, of course, but Meredith knew a queer little cold feeling down his spine. He saw that Yves was looking at him, an anxious query in his glance. Martin Lauder-Treaves had paled slightly.

"You can go now, Brummy," he said quietly and the little man shuffled out of the room, muttering to himself as he went.

"What was Brummy talking about?" asked the small heroine of the occasion.

"Nothing, dear," said Meredith quickly—too quickly, he realised a moment later when he saw that Martin Lauder-Treaves was staring at him, lips slightly parted as though in horrified amazement.

Finella-Lou, always sensitive to atmosphere, realised without understanding that something serious was amiss. She plunged into a babble of talk with the child and her efforts were seconded by Yves. By common agreement, the party was not to be spoilt for Ginnie, but where before spontaneity was the prompter, it was now replaced by effort. In the parlour of the farm-house to which they retired after tea, Ginnie demanded that Lady Lou tell her a story.

"Not an ordinary fairy-story, please," she said, "tell me about when you were a little girl in . . . that place like your name."

"Louisiana," smiled Finella-Lou.

"That's right," said Ginnie, settling herself at the girl's side on the sofa and cuddling the terrier suffocatingly to her thin, little chest. "Tell me about that place. And tell me a birthday story. After all," she added, "it's your own birthday in a few days' time."

"Good gracious, child!" exclaimed Finella-Lou, "so it is." She had honestly forgotten the passage of time, being too preoccupied with other things.

"What sort of presents did you have?" demanded Virginia.

"Well, I had a dolls'-house," began Finella-Lou.

"Was it like my dolls'-house?" asked the child wistfully, "or was it much better?"

Finella-Lou smiled. "It was just like yours," she said, slipping an arm round the little shoulders.

"That's nice," said Ginnie, wrinkling up her nose, rabbit-fashion. "Go on."

"Well, then I had dolls, of course, and prams for the dolls and sweets."

"Like Brig-dear gave *me*?"

"Almost exactly the same," agreed Finella-Lou. "Oh, lots and lots of presents, but the one I liked best always was the 'morning-gift'."

"What was that?"

"Well, back home in Louisiana, we had fairies who used to bring a birthday present, to those they liked, first thing on the morning of their birthday."

"O-o-oh! I'd have liked *that*," said Ginnie, her eyes round with wonder. "What was it?"

"Flowers," said Finella-Lou. "A lovely basket of flowers, beautifully arranged and no matter how closely you watched you never saw it come. But there it was, when you woke, outside the door of the house. The little people were too shy to come into a human dwelling-place, but they would come as far as the door and there you would find it when you opened it first thing the next morning."

She didn't tell Ginnie that she had rumbled the Little People and had, on one ocasion observed Magnolia's vast bulk tip-toeing along the front of the house with that year's basket in her hand.

"And do they only do that at your own home, Lady Lou?"

"Yes," said Finella-Lou rather sadly. "Only way back home."

"Not never here at Perwyl?" the child insisted.

"No, darling, not here at Perwyl."

Ginnie laid a hand gently on Finella-Lou's cheek. "Poor Lady Lou," she said softly, "what a shame."

CHAPTER XVIII

THE MARK OF THE BEAST

THE following morning Mike appeared to be so much better that Meredith decided that the convalescent might be indulged to the extent of a real walk and the two of them set out amiably side by side soon after breakfast. Meredith didn't wish to take the dog too far and they strolled slowly down the long slope from the castle towards the old disused quarry. As they approached the gash in the hillside which was its entrance, Meredith decided to explore it, never having been inside. As he reached the old disused road, now grass-covered, which led to his objective, he noticed that a small landslide or fall of rock had almost blocked the entrance into the quarry, leaving only a gap of about two yards width by which to make one's way in. Meredith and the Sealyham walked through this narrowed entrance and found themselves in the ancient quarry. No workings had been undertaken, as Meredith understood, for more than two hundred years and the practically sheer sides, sliced and squared and boxed as they were, were now covered with sparse grass and a thin, rank vegetation. There was even a twisted, stunted tree growing out from what appeared to be a sheer wall of rock. What soil maintained it must have been thin indeed. It was early and the sun had not yet crept over the lip of this great stone cup. It was chill in this hollowed-out hillside and Meredith shivered as he looked around. Mike, too, appeared to find the prospect uninviting, for he made no offer to investigate its nooks and crannies, but stood eyeing it with disfavour at his master's side.

Meredith turned away from this bleak spectacle and walked back to the swelling comfort of Great Yield.

On a stile at the western end of the enormous field he rested awhile, Mike lying down at his feet. He frowned as he recalled that queer interlude which had shattered the happy atmosphere of Ginnie's birthday party. His reason, particularly after his visit to London and his talk with the two psychiatrists, rebelled at the thought in his mind. His reason rebelled but, deep down inside him, he knew a persistent qualm which was of the stuff of pure atavism. Angrily he dismissed his misgivings—and they promptly returned. Like a sensible individual, John Meredith realised that the thing would have to be faced and dealt with. First of all, what was it precisely that was worrying him? Well, it sprang from Brown Brummy's suggestion. It was the second time he had heard the little man claim to have seen something "so big as a cart'orse". He recalled that on the occasion when the little man had walked back with him from Home Farm towards the castle he had said the same thing. If Brummy was speaking the truth, and there was no evidence to the contrary, then there *was* some big dog or other running loose on the estate at night, probably the dog responsible for the death of the ewe over at Trennion Deep. Of course, Brown Brummy's claim as to its size was a half-wit's exaggeration, but the fact remained that, in all probability, there was a marauding dog loose at night. Meredith deliberately faced the uneasy implication in the fact. It was just one of those damned coincidences which sometimes happen. Just because he was thinking in terms of werewolves and kindred fantasies, it was foolish to permit himself to entertain such suggestive ideas. The obvious thing to do was to find and make capture of the four-footed trespasser and that would be that. Meredith nodded to himself. He had happily disposed of his problem and got down off the stile.

Then he stood suddenly very still. The impact of a further recollection fetched him up short. He realised with sudden discomfort that he had been concerned with *his own* reactions to the puzzle. He remembered, then, that Brummy's remark had affected others as well. The same contact had been occasioned in Yves Lauder-Treaves' mind. Meredith knew that. He had known immediately that the same thought had flashed through the young man's mind as had gone through his and he had seen the anxiety, unsuccessfully concealed, that the other was experiencing on his cousin's behalf. Damn and blast the thing! It was ridiculous, absurd. But there was nothing absurd in the recollections of Martin's sudden pallor. He, too, had immediately reacted and, to those who knew what was probably passing through his mind, it was pathetic.

Meredith, hands in pockets, moved slowly along the bank of the river with Mike walking sedately at his heels. Well, anyway, there was no occasion for him to worry himself about it. He had sought expert opinion and, presumably, the experts would cope. All the same, he wished to God Frome could get down a bit sooner. The thing was getting on his nerves.

Meredith lit a cigarette and walked on until he had turned the bend in the river, passed the sluices which fed the moat, and reached the small bluff above which the terraced gardens rose to the castle. This bluff was perhaps ten feet in height and extended for two or three hundred yards. It was overgrown with shrubs, bushes and brambles. From its foot the water-meadows, narrow at this point before swelling into the Duchies, extended flat as a billiard table to the river bank.

Here Meredith paused as the Sealyham seemed tired and reluctant to go further. He sought about him for something to sit on, for the grass was still damp from the night dews and, on the edge of the brambles, espied what appeared to be, at first sight, an ancient log. He tapped it with his stick and found to his surprise that it was a discoloured fragment of age-old stone masonry. What had brought it to this spot he could not conjecture, but he beat the brambles off one end of it and sat down.

"Here, old boy," he said to the Sealyham. "Come and lie down and have a breather."

Mike ignored the suggestion. His lethargic attitude of a moment back was gone. He was moving slowly over the grass, his nose to the ground. He was absorbed. Meredith watched the dog tolerantly and hoped he would not start a rabbit, for he was in no condition for a hunt.

"What is it, old boy?" asked Meredith quietly. "Bunnies?"

The dog acknowledged the remark with a faint wag of

his tail and then stood still and growled. Meredith remembered that it had not been far from this spot where Mike had had his fight with his unidentified enemy and he called the dog to his side and made him sit down. Mike still displayed every sympton of uneasiness and his hackles were by no mean smooth.

"It's all right, old boy," the man assured him, rubbing him behind the ears and the Sealyham settled down, maintaining an attitude of wariness and mumbling to himself under his breath.

Brown Brummy was frightened! The sudden thought came like a bolt from the blue and Meredith stared blankly across the river at the woods on the hill opposite. It was perfectly true. He had felt it more surely than anything else. Brummy was scared. Scared what of? He wouldn't be scared just of a dog. His behaviour in apprehending that savage-looking brute which he had brought in to Home Farm showed that. The little man wasn't frightened of animals—as such.

Meredith stirred restlessly. Here we go again. He'd have to have a talk to Brummy. It wouldn't be easy to get anything out of the little man unless he wanted to part. Still, he'd have to be made to talk. Brummy knew *something*. It was probably all poppycock. Still. . . .

Meredith rose and, walking round the end of the bluff, made his way into the lowest of the garden terraces and so up to the house.

．　　．　　．　　．　　．

As the day wore on it became increasingly evident that there was to be one of those sudden freak heat-waves at which the inhabitants of this country are invariably surprised and for which they are never prepared. The English climate is incalculable—damnably so—and by tea-time it was sweltering.

"It's hot enough to bathe," said Finella-Lou, as she poured out a third cup of tea for Yves.

"Where do you swim?" asked John Meredith. "In the moat?"

"Martin and I used to swim in it when we were youngsters," said Yves, "but it hasn't been drained and cleaned since the war and it's probably full of reeds now. No, our usual bathing place is that pool in the river straight opposite here. I think I'll join you, Finella-Lou," he ended, "if you're going in."

"What about you, John?" asked the girl. "I think it would do you good."

"I haven't got a bathing-dress," said Meredith.

"Oh, that's all right," replied Yves. "I think I've a spare pair of trunks and I know Martin has."

"Yes, I can lend you a pair," said Martin absently.

All four of them made their way down the hillside about half-past five, Meredith carrying Mike under his arm. The other three Sealyhams ran barking ahead.

"What about the invalid?" asked Finella-Lou solicitously. "I don't think he'd better come in."

"He won't," said Meredith, "if I tell him to stay put."

"He's a very good little dog," said the girl, gently stroking the dog's nose with one slim finger.

Meredith nodded. "Yes," he said, "and I've had him a long time."

The girl glanced anxiously at him, worried lest reminiscence prove too harrowing, but the man smiled down at her as they reached the river bank.

Finella-Lou piled her hair on top of her head and snapped on a snug, white bathing cap. She looked absurdly young in her two-piece nonsense of white and cherry and she was the first in, cutting the surface of the pool in a long, clean dive. Martin followed in a workmanlike manner, while Yves slipped in with all the ease and grace of an otter. Meredith came something of a belly-flopper, but made up for his exhibition by flashing across the pool with a perfect Australian crawl.

It was delicious in the water. The vast oppression of the atmosphere was lifted from them as they splashed and swam and floated and trod water. The headache which had troubled Meredith all afternoon was banished as he lay back in the water and stared up at the sky.

"Isn't it heaven?" said a voice in his ear and Finella-Lou popped up like a young seal.

For the first time since he had known her Meredith saw the natural fun and gaiety in this girl who had laboured beneath so great a load of anxiety. She looked years younger. She flashed away from his side and there came a sudden roar from her husband as she tickled his feet. "You little devil!" shouted Martin and, heaving himself out of the water, made after her with rapid strokes.

Meredith trod water and watched them. For a brief moment Martin was himself again as he chased his wife into the shallows, caught her, dragged her to deep water and expeditiously ducked her. They both bobbed up, shaking the water from their eyes and laughing like children. Yves looked on indulgently and smiled as he caught Meredith's eye.

Mike was obediently lying on Meredith's towel, but the other three dogs barked and slipped and slithered on the edge of the bank, excited by the antics of their demi-gods in the pool. Suddenly the bitch lost her footing, scrabbled wildly for a toe-hold and then fell with a startled grunt into the water. She was followed immediately by the two dogs and, what with one thing or another, the pool boiled.

It was in a happy frame of mind that the party made their way up to the house, their towels about their shoulders.

"Just dry yourselves off a bit," said Finella-Lou, "and we'll nip in and have one before dressing. We shan't catch cold. It's much too hot."

"Where shall I bring the ice?" asked Yves, as they entered the house and he turned towards the Inner Hall. "Lacquer Room?"

"Oh, no!" said Finella-Lou. "Let's have them in the drawing-room."

Meredith intercepted the glance which Martin shot at his wife and noted the tremulous little smile with which she met it. Blast it, he thought, here's the thing again. They hadn't used the Lacquer Room since the evening when Martin had smashed the cocktail glasses.

When they assembled for dinner, the heat seemed to be more oppressive than ever. The atmosphere pressed down ponderously on top of their heads. Everyone appeared to be slightly breathless and the magic of the pool had seeped out of them. Meredith glanced at his host as he came into the dining-room. Something about his eyes told him that Martin had been drinking a great deal more than he had imbibed when they were all together. The man was dull and lethargic and his conversation had once more returned to the monosyllabic. Watching her, John Meredith saw the bitter disappointment in the girl's expression. She looked tremulous, like a child about to cry. It was evident that the carefree romp during their bathe had been an oasis in the arid desert of loneliness and longing in which she had dwelt over many weary weeks.

After dinner Martin sat a little out of the circle in the drawing-room, drinking too many whiskies. He was morose, silent and abstracted.

When Meredith went up to his bedroom he flung aside all the curtains and opened the windows wide, seeking what little air there was. He noted, with thankfulness, that the servants had had the sense to dispense with the fire which ordinarily cheered him. He pulled off his clothes and walked naked into his bathroom. He ran a bath of cold water. He put one foot in and withdrew it again and ran some hot in. He got in and lay full-length and turned the cold tap on with his toe so that it ran very slowly. The water grew deliciously colder and colder. He lay there for about a quarter of an hour and then got out. The moment he had dried himself he was hotter than ever. There was a tiny hammer beating at the back of his skull, and his eyes felt as though their sockets were coated with sand.

Meredith swore. Surely to God, there must be a storm soon. The tension in the atmosphere was insufferable. The dog felt it, too, for he was restless, moving from his basket onto the carpet and from the carpet to the polished boards near the wainscoting. Once or twice he went over to his bowl of water and drank noisily.

"Me, too," agreed Meredith, helping himself to water from the jug on his bedside table.

He lay for some time with just a sheet over him. Then he threw that to one side and lay on his back with his hands behind his head. That wasn't much better and presently he rose and peeled his pyjamas and threw them across the foot of the bed and lay naked.

He must have dozed fitfully, for when he again glanced at his watch the hands stood at a quarter to one—and the heat and oppressive atmosphere were worse than ever. The hammer in the back of his skull had been replaced by a decidedly larger model. The whole back of his neck ached and he thought suddenly how nice it would be to sponge it down with cold water. The thought prompted a second. He wasn't going to sleep now, anyway. So, why not? No sooner thought than done. Meredith rose stiffly from the bed, thrust his feet into a pair of slippers and wrapped himself in his dressing-gown. He eyed his pair of bathing-trunks which he could see through the open door hanging over the basin in the bathroom. They would still be damp and he thought, what the hell, he'd be alone. He grabbed a towel and his ash walking-stick. Mike watched him with interest.

"I don't think you'd better come, old man," said Meredith, "I shan't be long. In any case, you can't bathe."

In the hall, Meredith helped himself to one of the electric torches from the big consol-table and opened the front door as silently as possible.

He went slowly down the hill, glad of the minute difference of the open air from the stuffiness of the house. He came eventually to that spot below the bluff where he had rested earlier in the day and, with the aid of his torch, found the heavy stone upon which he had sat. Here he dropped his dressing-gown and stick and went forward towards the river carrying his towel and torch. He did a preliminary reccy with the light to get his bearings before extinguishing it. He placed the torch on his towel and waited for a few moments for his eyes to accustom themselves to the darkness. There was a sudden flicker of summer lightning over to the south. The long-awaited storm showed signs of materialising. "Thank God for that," muttered Meredith, as he lowered himself gingerly into the pool.

If the water had been delicious and invigorating that afternoon, now it seemed, to Meredith, to be a panacea for all ills as he floated, supine, below the bank. He had been quite right. Cool water on the back of his head was what the doctor ordered. He ceased moving his hands and lay completely inert, allowing himself to sink down under the water, slowly, slowly, slowly. Then he dropped his feet suddenly and shot up to the surface. He swam lazily about the pool, listening to the night noises all about him. He felt young and invigorated. He recalled Finella-Lou's appearance that afternoon, her slight body still that of a girl. Perhaps the pool was fed from the Fountain of Eternal Youth. He lay again floating on his back and allowed his mind to speculate idiotically on the idea. Maybe if he brought Mike down to swim here, the Sealyham would emerge once more a puppy. He grinned to himself and then remembered that the other three dogs had undergone no metamorphosis on emerging. He frowned. Blast that word! Why the devil had it come into his mind? Meredith turned irritably over in the water and lashed the surface of the pool as he went round it at racing speed. He came up under the bank and put his hand out to hold on. The sudden physical effort had tired him. Still by no means fit, he thought ruefully. He brought his other hand up to hold onto the bank and, in so doing, inadvertently caught hold of one corner of his towel. The thing came away in his hand and he thrust his arm up to keep it from falling into the water. There was a sudden splash and he realised that his torch had slipped into the pool.

"Damn the bloody thing!" said Meredith, wholeheartedly, and clambered out.

It would be useless to attempt to find it in the dark. He would have to return tomorrow morning.

He dried himself on the towel and, as he did so, he became aware of the sound of a dog barking. He threw up his head and stood listening. It was Mike, barking in their bedroom.

The windows were wide open and the dog's voice was quite recognisable.

Meredith continued to towel himself vigorously. The little brute would wake the house if he didn't get back quickly and then something happened which took his mind off consideration of the household at High Perwyl. Something had moved about fifty yards away down the river bank.

Meredith stood and peered into the darkness. Once again that summer lightning in the south flickered momentarily and he could see that something, some dark thing which had not been there in daylight, was now only a little way from him along the water-meadows. His mind went to his stick and he walked the few yards to where he had left it with his dressing-gown. He picked it up by the ferrule and stood with it poised lightly in his hand. There was movement somewhere there out in the darkness, movement stealthy and purposed. Whatever the thing was, it had drawn nearer.

The quick glow of summer lightning at his back was almost constant now, as though some giant faulty electric bulb, concealed behind the hills, was flickering before expiry.

There came a sudden reflected gleam ahead of Meredith and the man knew that he had seen the flash of a pair of eyes. He knew what was coming and he braced his feet wide and raised the heavy ash stick to his shoulder.

From where Meredith stood he was gazing down the Perwyl Valley towards the Duchy Meadows where a dip in the slopes to either side provided him with a distinct skyline. This was an advantage of which he was to be glad, for suddenly the thing came.

More by instinct than anything else, Meredith realised that the thing was upon him and flung back the stout ash. Almost in the same movement he swung forward with all his strength and struck blindly. The skyline of his vision was, in a flash, blotted out and grown monstrous. Against that clear line Meredith saw the great pointed ears flattened back to the skull, the huge inverted triangle of the beast-head, the flash of vicious, cruel fangs—and then the full weight of his blow caught the brute in mid-spring down the shoulder. Came the sharp, decisive click of the big teeth which had missed their hold, a sudden half-grunt, half-yelp of pain and Meredith was sent sprawling by the sheer momentum of his adversary's body. Instinctively he flung one arm across his throat and landed a half-arm jolt into the side of the hairy thing. There was a sickening stench in his nostrils and then, as silently as it had come, it was gone.

Meredith, shaken and winded, scrambled to his feet, picked up his stick from where it had fallen and stared about him. As far as he could tell, he was alone.

· · · · ·

It was only afterwards, days afterwards, when he was reviewing the whole queer tangle of events at High Perwyl, that Meredith realised that it was at this moment that he made his fatal mistake. The course which he should have pursued stuck out a mile and yet, so shaken was he and soon, from that moment, was to be still more so, that he failed to see the obvious. It was an omission which was to have tragic results. I know how deeply he subsequently reproached himself, how bitterly he regretted his oversight, but in justice to Meredith I would remind you that he was, himself, far from fit and the events of that night were to prove sufficiently macabre to throw a completely normal man off his balance.

Satisfied at last that the brute, whatever it was, had gone, John Meredith became suddenly conscious that he was standing naked above a river bank in the dead hours of the new day. He shivered suddenly, but it was not with cold. He picked up his dressing-gown and slipped it on, collected his towel and, with his heavy stick still held weapon-fashion in his hand, started back up the hill. The ominous growl of distant thunder accompanied his going and, when it had died away, a deathly stillness blanketed the entire countryside. Meredith was conscious of something missing. It was the barking of his dog. The Sealyham was now mute.

In recording the many previous adventures of Sir John Meredith I have been apt, for the sake of the story, to draw him a shade bigger than life-size, in fact, the superman of detective story. I would protest that not all of it, by any manner of means, was exaggerated. Had he not been a very exceptional fellow his career would not have been worth chronicling at all, but, as regards the night which I am now describing, Meredith confessed to me later that there was little of the superman about him on that occasion. He admitted that on that lonely walk up to the house from the river bank he walked as softly as he could so that he might hear the better and that he kept an anxious eye peeled. The memory of what he had seen outlined against the night sky was still very fresh in his mind and no appeal to his common-sense would banish the fact that what he had seen was as much a wolf's head as ever was the engraving of the Lauder-Treaves' sometime crest on the frontispiece of Silas Whistle's history!

As Meredith crossed the causeway over the moat towards the front door, to his surprise, it opened. Yves Lauder-Treaves, wrapped in a silk dressing-gown, stood framed against the lighted hall.

"Good God, Meredith! What's happened?" he exclaimed.

"What are *you* doing up?" asked John.

He walked heavily past the other into the hall. Yves stood, his hand still on the latch, regarding him alarmedly. "Me?" he said stupidly. "I heard that dog of yours yelling his head off and, as you did not seem to be stopping him, I went along to see if anything were wrong, found you weren't in your room, came downstairs and found the front-door unbolted. I was just coming out when you arrived. I say," he ended, "you look a bit dickey. Are you all right?"

"Yes, yes," said Meredith impatiently, and then gave the lie to his words by sinking down weakly on an old leather watchman's-chair which stood near the door.

"You look as if you could do with a drink," said Yves, regarding him narrowly.

Meredith looked up. "I've just met that dog of yours," he said.

Yves looked startled. "Dog of mine?" he said. "What do you mean?"

"Not *yours*," said Meredith. "I mean the brute that's

been roaming round the estate at night. Presumably the beast that killed the sheep."

"Good Lord!" said Yves. "Where did you find it?"

"Down by the river bank," replied Meredith, leaning back as though slightly dizzy. "I couldn't sleep so I thought I'd go down and have a swim. As I came out the thing went for me. It's a bloody big brute, too. Thank heaven I had this heavy stick with me and I caught it a beauty, down the left shoulder, I should imagine. The sheer weight of the brute knocked me for six and I thought I was for it, but evidently I'd cooled it off with that one whack, because it bolted."

"Good grief!" exclaimed Yves. "One way or another you're having a hell of a convalescence here."

Meredith was silent for a moment or two and then he said: "I'm . . . I'm going up to have a look at your cousin."

Yves regarded him wide-eyed and then Meredith saw the swift sympathy and anxiety come into his eyes. He frowned. "You don't really think . . ."

John shook his head. "No, I don't," he said, "but . . . well, I thought I'd just have a look at Martin."

For a long minute Yves stared at him in silence. "Okay," he said. "I'll come with you. But first," he said solicitously, "I *still* think you could do with a drink."

"Maybe you're right," said John wearily, "I feel as if all the stuffing had been knocked out of me."

"One large brandy-and-soda," nodded Yves. "No, no," he added hastily as Meredith made to stand up. "I'll get it for you. I'd have to anyway as we only fetch out the brandy now on special occasions. I won't be long," he ended, moving away towards the door leading to Inner Hall.

Meredith sat still and closed his eyes. He felt horribly lethargic and reluctant to make the smallest movement. He was sweating again and wondered without interest whether he had a temperature. Quite likely brandy would be bad for him, but the prospect was very pleasant. He closed his eyes. He was very nearly asleep when the soft shuffle of Yves' slippers made him open his eyes. Yves looked flushed, as though he had been running.

"My dear fellow," said Meredith gratefully. "This is awfully good of you."

"Nonsense," said Yves, "I was as quick as I could be, but I had to open a new bottle and couldn't find the corkscrew." He held out a tall tumbler containing an attractive amber-coloured fluid. "There you are," he said, "one tumblerful of brandy-and-soda to be taken as the occasion arises."

Meredith finished his drink and felt better for it. "Now," he said, putting the glass down on an oak chest, "let's just take a look at your cousin."

They went, side by side, up Great Stairs, and, at the top, turned half right towards the door of the dressing-room which Martin now occupied since his self-banishment from his wife's bedroom. Meredith crossed the wide landing and knocked softly on the panels of the door. There was no answer. He knocked again. Still no answer.

"I say," whispered Yves nervously, "we don't want to wake Finella-Lou. What do you want to do?" he asked. "Just pop your head in and see that he's all right?" Meredith nodded. "Well, why don't you just go in? We can always trot out your sheep-killer as an excuse if the old boy wants to know what the hell."

Meredith nodded again and dropped his hand to the glass door-knob. He twisted it silently and pushed. Nothing happened.

"He's got the door locked," whispered Meredith.

"Oh blast," breathed Yves. "What's he want to do that for?"

He squatted down on his haunches suddenly and put his eye to the keyhole. Over his shoulder he turned a startled face to Meredith.

"I say," he exclaimed uneasily, "I don't much like this. The light's on in there and I don't think the key's in the lock. You have a look."

Meredith stooped and applied his eye to the keyhole. The room beyond was brilliantly lit and the keyhole was free of any obstruction. He could see a corner of the fire-place, a chair and that was all. He stood up, frowning, and knocked again on the door, this time a little louder.

"Take it easy," urged Yves at his elbow.

John Meredith stood irresolute. There was something wrong here, something very wrong. He could feel it in his bones. He made way for the other as Yves gently pushed him to one side and again squatted down at the keyhole. This time he applied his lips to the orifice and whispered, urgently: "Martin! Martin! Martin, are you awake? Martin! It's Yves."

He turned his head and pressed his ear to the keyhole. Meredith, standing over him, also had his ear pressed to the door. There was no reply. Yves stood up. He licked his lips nervously and said: "He's in there, Meredith. You can hear him breathing."

He stood aside for John to place his ear to the keyhole. Meredith could hear the occupant of the room now quite easily. The sound of laboured, stertorous breathing was distinct.

"That man's ill," said Meredith, straightening himself.

"He might be tight," suggested Yves miserably. "Old Martin's been whacking the bottle about a bit recently."

"Drunk or sick," said Meredith grimly, "I'm going in to that room if I have to kick the door in and wake every soul in the house."

"No need to do that," said Yves. "There'll be a duplicate key to the door in my office. Hang on half-a-jiffy and I'll nip along and get it."

There was a huge, round-topped Spanish sea-chest against the wall near the dressing-room door and Meredith sank down wearily onto this to wait for his companion's return. He noticed, to his surprise, that he was still clutching his damp towel and the ash stick which had been his saviour earlier on in the night. He dropped them onto the carpet at his feet and waited, his shoulders hunched up to his ears as though he were cold. A short while back he had been over-heated, now a chill, which had little to do with the atmosphere, was creeping through him. He knew a sudden premonitory shiver. He felt all at once weary to the very bones and wished to God he could just go quietly back to bed, but he felt a duty to the man beyond that locked door, that poor, deluded fellow who wandered miserably through the cold, lonely hell of his own obsession.

He turned as he heard Yves coming along the broad landing from Second Stairs. "Have you got it?"

"Here it is," replied Yves and placed a key in his hand.

John Meredith rose stiffly and went across to the door. He slipped the key noiselessly into the lock. He caught the door handle and pulled the door close against the jamb. Firmly and without noise he turned the key and gently thrust the door open.

For a long and very horrible moment Meredith stood and gazed. He was only barely conscious of Yves at his shoulder giving a kind of long, shuddering gasp which seemed to terminate in a whimper like that of a frightened child.

"Dear Christ!" breathed Meredith and put a hand out to steady himself against the frame of the door.

He stood, thereafter, in stricken silence for, for the first and indeed the last time in his life, he saw the mark of the beast!

CHAPTER XIX

"FROM THE POWER . . . O LORD DELIVER US"

STANDING on the threshold and staring into that brilliantly lighted room at High Perwyl, Meredith felt that, for a brief moment, he had looked into the Pit, itself. He knew, but was only dimly aware of, a discomfort in his scalp. His thumbs were pricking and, beneath the thin wrapping of his dressing-gown, his very flesh crawled. For the only time in his life Meredith felt that he was in the presence of the inexplicable and he was frightened, frightened to the core of him.

Gone were the matter-of-fact explanations of Welbeck Street and psychopathic study. These were banished in a moment to the limbo of forgotten things. Here, in this stifling room, this stifling room which reeked like a kennel, Meredith faced the old lore which was before science, that lore which ran when beast-men and half-men moved upon the earth and sought their kindred at many a black sabbath which shunned the clean light of day. Here, at High Perwyl, the whirligig of time was dancing widdershins and some dim corner of Meredith's mind and memory flashed momentarily brilliant with livid light and showed him that Perwyl had, in very truth, known much which is achieved in that grim border-land where nameless things are common-place. With a shrinking distaste, which sickened him to the point of nausea, Meredith went forward into the room.

Despite the overwhelming stuffiness of the night, a huge electric fire was burning with every bar alight, turning the room into an oven. In addition, the air in the room was foetid and stinking and the reek came from its occupant. To Meredith, the appalling thing was that he knew that stench, had encountered it earlier that night when he had lain momentarily beneath the body of his brute assailant below the bluff. It was something to shatter the imagination. White to the lips, he stared at the thing in the chair.

Stark naked and sprawled in the big winged-chair, as though in a coma, was Martin Lauder-Treaves, his mouth half-open, his bare chest labouring with the trouble of his breathing. But the sight which sent Meredith's mind tottering to the dreadful edge of insanity was the mark upon the man. *Down his shoulder, from the point of the shoulder almost to the centre of the left pectoral muscle, was a great livid weal, a long, narrow contusion which could only have come from a savage blow with some long, heavy, narrow object—such as a stick.*

Meredith extended a shrinking finger to that vast bruise as though he thought that his imagination was playing him tricks, as though he feared he were overwrought. He prayed silently that it might be so, that the thing would prove to be the horrid trick of a tired mind. But it wasn't. The thing was there. He could feel the discoloured flesh raised almost half-an-inch from its surrounding surface. To do this Meredith had been obliged to stoop above the man in the chair and the stinking emanation that came from him was not that of a man.

Meredith drew back and turned away from the lolling thing in the chair, feeling that he was going to vomit. He moved slowly to one of the windows and opened it. He put his head outside and closed his eyes while the sweat dripped from him. He stood like that for a moment or two and then turned back into the room, leaning his haunches against the window-sill. The high back of the chair was between him and the thing which it contained and he looked beyond it to where Yves Lauder-Treaves stood in the centre of the room. The man was standing with both clasped hands pressed to his stomach. He sagged inwards over them like a man who had just been shot in the guts and was about to topple forward onto the floor. His face, drained of all colour, was horribly witless as though he had actually taken leave of his senses. He was staring into vacancy.

"Turn that fire off," said Meredith hoarsely.

He, himself, went with dragging feet across the room and shut and locked the door on the inside. Whatever the outcome of this night's work, he was determined that Finella-Lou should not be a witness of a sight which might well blast her reason. As he took his hand from the key he saw that Yves had not stirred. Meredith went across to him and took him resolutely by the shoulders and shook him.

"For God's sake, snap out of it," he urged vehemently.

"Yes, of course," croaked Yves stupidly.

Meredith went past and switched off the electric fire and then flung wide the second window which had also been shut. Here he was obliged, for a few moments, again to rest against the window-sill while his mind boiled with the horrible implications held by that dreadful room. The warlock, or what-have-you, had to be naked. That's what Frome had said. Naked. Well, he *was* naked. So the metamorphosis could have taken place. Then there was that stuff about . . . what was it, bi-location? Well . . . there was no direct . . . circumstantial evidence, he supposed you'd call it. Of course the other thing had taken place in the dark. Hadn't it? Couldn't be certain, of course. But that was galls. Of course he was certain. He knew bloody well he'd scored on that brute's shoulder. His eyes wandered to the thing in the chair and he shivered suddenly, uncontrollably. He looked away. Then there was . . . that other thing, that Frome had made no mention of. The stink. There was no question about it. It was the same. Maybe Frome didn't know about that. He'd be able to give the expert points shortly. Practice, as opposed to theory. Bloody funny, that was! Meredith began to giggle and then suddenly got hold of himself as what was left of his sanity flashed him a warning of imminent hysteria.

"I say," he said huskily to Yves, "you haven't got such a thing as a cigarette on you, have you?"

Yves turned his head slowly and regarded him without expression. "Cigarette?" he said blankly.

"Yes," said Meredith.

Young Lauder-Treaves frowned, shook his head stupidly and then stirred himself from his lethargy and went across to the bedside table. He picked up a cigarette box and lurched back across the room with it.

"Here," he said, holding it out with a shaky hand.

"Thanks," said Meredith and fumbled with so much uncertainty that, between them, they spilt the few cigarettes to the floor.

Both men stood staring at the cigarettes, making no effort to retrieve them. Then, with a deep sigh as though the effort were too great, they both stooped at the same moment to pick them up. They banged their heads together.

"For God's sake," said Meredith wearily, while Yves looked as though he were about to cry.

They lit cigarettes and Meredith turned and again leaned his forearms on the sill of the open window and stood there smoking in silence. Yves went across to the bed and sat down upon it where he remained, huddled in upon himself, the cigarette drooping from one corner of his slack mouth. Neither of them made a move towards the man in the chair. It was as though they were resting between rounds, as though they must take time off before beginning to cope.

John Meredith flicked the remaining third of his cigarette out of the window in a wide arc. He watched the little trail of light and sparks and heard the faint hiss as the butt fell into the water of the moat. Then, since he was dropping with fatigue, he opened his eyes wide, took a deep breath and turned back into the room. It was less like an oven now with the windows open and the fire off and, with the air less vitiated, the smell which came from Martin Lauder-Treaves was less overpowering. The horrible paradox remained, however, and Meredith turned to his task with considerable distaste. "Come on," he said to Yves. "Get rid of that cigarette and give me a hand. We've got to get him onto the bed."

Dully, Yves rose to his feet and joined Meredith where he now stood, before that naked, lolling figure.

"I'll take his shoulders," said Meredith. "You take his feet."

As he stooped and slipped an arm beneath him, Martin stirred faintly and muttered something. Meredith did not catch exactly what he said, but the impression he gathered was of some reference to being caught by brambles and he knew a swift momentary return of his former panic as he recalled the bushes at the spot where he had had his encounter earlier that night.

"Are you ready?" he asked and glanced over his shoulder.

Yves Lauder-Treaves stood lumpishly in front of his cousin. He had made no move to take his feet. He just stood.

"Come on, man!" snarled Meredith. "Let's get this done. Catch hold of his feet, can't you? I don't want to stand here all night. He smells like a badger as it is."

"Yes," said Yves. "Yes."

But still he made no effort to do as he was bidden and Meredith straightened himself and said with an edge to his voice: "What the devil's the matter with you?"

The other shook his head slowly from side to side. His mouth was slightly open after the manner of a man with bad adenoids. "I don't . . . I can't . . . touch him," he said.

Meredith knew a sudden great anger. It swept through his brain like the swift jet from a flame-thrower—and it swept away all the cobwebs and horrors and hobgoblins. In that moment he wouldn't have cared a damn if a whole pack of werewolves had burst into the room, whipped on by the Wild Huntsman, himself.

He put out a hand and caught Yves by the front of his dressing-gown, gathering up the folds of silk and pyjama jacket beneath in iron fingers. He shook him until the man's head waggled.

"Get hold of his feet, you swob, or I'll pin your damned ears back."

Yves stared at him and the queer blank expression in the dulled eyes cleared.

"I'm sorry," he muttered, "I'll behave now."

"So I should hope," returned Meredith ungraciously.

They carried the unconscious man across the room and put him on the bed and pulled the eiderdown over him. The stertorous, laboured breathing had now ceased and his chest rose and fell in what appeared to be a perfectly normal manner.

"It must have been the suffocating heat in here that made him blow like a bellows," suggested Meredith and his companion nodded.

John Meredith seated himself on the edge of the bed and took one languid wrist in his hand. It was several moments before he found the pulse at all and he sat in silence, staring down at the floor with his fingers pressed lightly to Martin's wrist.

"As far as I can tell," he said, "it seems a bit slow, but nothing very much. All the same," he went on, "we'd better have a doctor look at him. What's the time?"

Yves turned and glanced at the clock on the mantelpiece. "Half-past two," he said. "Shall I go and 'phone Blackie?"

Meredith didn't answer at once. He sat and stared at Yves, his brows drawn down into a frown of concentration. And then he surprised the other by a question.

"Has Blackie always been your doctor here?"

Yves hesitated. "Well, he retired some years ago and the practice was taken over by his junior partner. Fellow called Harrington. Then, when Harrington joined the R.A.M.C., old Blackie came out of retirement to carry on in his absence."

"I see," said John Meredith. "What's your opinion of him as a doctor?"

"You think we ought to get someone else in?" asked Yves in surprise.

"I don't know," said Meredith impatiently. "You've not answered my question."

"Old Blackie? Well, I suppose he's really a bit timeworn and past it. He was quite sound in his day but, as I told you, he'd already retired from practice."

"Does he drink?" asked Meredith brutally.

The ghost of a smile appeared momentarily on the other man's lips. "Not exactly drink," he said.

John Meredith nodded. "Slightly fuddled the whole time?" he suggested.

"Well," agreed Yves grudgingly, "he likes his tipple. But you mustn't think from that that he doesn't know what hes' doing."

"H'm," commented Meredith noncommittally. "What's this medicine he's been giving your cousin?"

The other frowned. "Medicine?" he echoed. "Only bromide or something like that to keep his nerves quiet. Why do you ask? You don't think. . . ."

"I think," replied Meredith slowly, "and at a first guess, your cousin is drugged."

"Well, yes," agreed Yves, his voice puzzled. "I've just told you. He's been taking bromide."

"I don't mean bromide," said John and got up from the bed. He appeared to ponder for a moment and then said: "I don't think there's any harm in Blackie seeing him, but I think we could do with a second opinion. Don't you?"

Yves Lauder-Treaves hesitated. He shot a sudden swift glance at the other, ran his tongue over his lips and said quietly: "Look, Meredith, you're assuming that this is a case for a doctor."

John Meredith's eyes narrowed and he nodded. "That is precisely what I am assuming," he said.

Young Lauder-Treaves sighed, wrinkled his forehead and passed a hand wearily over his face. "I hope you're right," he said, his voice little above a whisper. "I hope to God you're right."

Meredith was saved an answer to this by the sudden muttering of the man on the bed. He turned in a flash and again caught that word which he had heard mumbled as he stooped above the baronet in the chair. He recalled that, at the time, he had had an impression that the man had been burbling something about being caught by brambles, but now he realised that the word had not been "brambles" at all but "briars".

"He's coming round," said Yves.

"Shut up," hissed Meredith from where he stooped above Martin's pillow, but the muttering died away again and Meredith was able to distinguish only the two words "caught" and "briars" before the unconscious man was again silent.

He remained bending over the other for a moment or so and then straightened himself.

"Briars," he repeated softly.

"What's he got to do with it?" asked Yves frowning.

"*He?*" queried Meredith.

"Sergeant-Major Briars," said Yves in surprise.

"Yes," said Meredith, "it's possible. My mind was confused by another association of ideas."

CHAPTER XX

LULL BEFORE THE STORM

WHEN Yves disappeared, bound for the telephone to call Dr. Blackie, Meredith dropped wearily into the big winged-chair near the fire-place. Despite his fatigue, however, he rose again from his seat almost at once for the upholstery of the chair still gave off that nauseating stench imparted to it by its late occupant. Meredith crossed the fire-place and seated himself in a high-backed Elizabethan oak chair.

In his mind he went once more over the startling events of the night. In spite of the clearance of his brain effected by that healthy gust of anger, there were still decidedly foggy patches in his thoughts, notably the horrid business of Martin's wound and the altogether inexplicable smell of him. For a few minutes Meredith played with the idea of that great welt down his shoulder and chest being self-inflicted. Though he had made no study of psychopathic-analysis he knew as much about it as the next man in the street. He knew, for instance, that in one of the psychoneuroses—he seemed to remember that it was hysteria—the sufferer, dominated by his own obsessionist preoccupation, produced certain physical manifestations which, to the uninstructed, appeared almost miraculous. There were authenticated cases of such instances with which the medical profession was familiar and which were recorded in the text-books. He recalled, as he sagged wearily in that uncomfortable oak chair, that it had been established that a marked religious mania, carried to the point of hysteria in a certain type of patient, had been sufficiently powerful to induce the sufferer to manifest the *stigmata* or Holy Wounds. If a psychoneurosis, a purely mental illness, could so affect the physical as to produce actual wounds and haemorrhage in the individual's hands, feet, side and forehead, would it not be possible, Meredith reasoned, for Martin, labouring under his morbid obsession, to produce on himself this particular wound? No, there was a snag there. The patient or sufferer had to have a desire for the condition which physically manifested itself and this was extremely unlikely in Lauder-Treaves' case. Besides, it presupposed that he was aware of what had taken place between Meredith and his assailant down by the river bank and Meredith refused to credit the possibility that Martin had been actually present. It was conceivable, he supposed, that by some incredible coincidence the man should, in some way, have injured himself without realising it and that the wound had happened to fit in with the thing which Meredith had momentarily feared. That didn't sound likely, either. It didn't . . . it seemed. . . .

John Meredith came to with a jerk. He had almost dropped off to sleep despite the discomfort of his chair. Feeling about a hundred he pulled himself up out of the chair and walked wearily over to the bed and looked down at the object of his speculations. The man appeared to be sleeping normally and the white face with its closed eyes looked very young and defenceless. John Meredith recalled the man's fighting record and knew a sudden tug of pity.

"You poor devil," he murmured and turned away.

He moved somewhat aimlessly about the room, largely to keep himself awake. He found himself standing in front of an Empire *escritoire*. Its centre drawer was slightly open and Meredith frowned down at what he saw lying half-concealed inside. He put in a finger and pulled the drawer open. He stood staring at a pair of handcuffs and a revolver. His frown deepened as he saw that the hammer of the revolver was back. The gun was cocked as though ready for immediate use. He picked it up, put his thumb firmly down on the hammer and gently squeezed the trigger. Very slowly he allowed the hammer to go back into the striking position. Then he broke the gun and saw that it was fully loaded. He emptied the six cartridges into his palm, snapped the gun to and slipped the whole lot into the pocket of his dressing-gown. The handcuffs he left where they lay and closed the drawer.

A few minutes after, Yves Lauder-Treaves returned saying that Blackie was on his way, but in no happy frame of mind at being fetched out at that hour. Meredith shivered suddenly. Though the promised storm had not materialised, the atmosphere was decidedly cooler and it was now the still dead hours before dawn when vitality is at its lowest ebb. He recalled suddenly that beneath his dressing-gown he was naked.

"Will you just stay with him," he asked Yves, "while I slip along and get some pyjamas on. I'm cold."

"Yes, of course."

Meredith did more than put on his pyjamas when he returned to his room. He ached to the very bones and he went into his bathroom and ran a steaming hot bath. He nearly went to sleep in it, but he was jerked suddenly back to the present by the thought that the arrival of Dr. Blackie's car would certainly wake Finella-Lou and she would want to know what was going on. He climbed out of the bath, dried himself rapidly and slipped into his pyjamas. He was about to put on his dressing-gown when he realised that it smelt from its contact with Martin and he took an overcoat from the cupboard and put it on instead.

He went along the wide corridor, past the closed door of Martin's room and paused outside a room further along. He knocked softly and then opened the door slightly. He heard the girl stir in her bed.

"Finella-Lou," he called quietly. "It's me, John. I've got to talk to you. May I come in?"

"John!" came the girl's voice in startled accents. "What time is it? Yes, of course, come in."

As Meredith went in and closed the door behind him Lady Lauder-Treaves switched on her bedside lamp and lay blinking up at him like a small, but attractive, owl.

"John, is it . . . is it Martin?"

The grey eyes, still slightly glazed with sleep, became increasingly troubled. Meredith sat down on the end of her bed.

"It's all right, my dear," he assured her. "Martin's in bed and sleeping, but I've sent for Dr. Blackie and I thought you'd better know as his arrival would have woken you."

"Dr. Blackie?" she echoed in stupefaction. "Then he *is* ill? I must . . ."

Without a thought to the proprieties Finella-Lou flung back the bed-clothes and made to get out of bed. Meredith put a hand to her bare shoulder and gently but firmly pushed her back against her pillows and then pulled the bed-clothes up around her.

"No, no, my dear," he said with quiet authority. "You be a

good girl and do as you're told. Martin's all right, I tell you. There *has* been some funny business, sleep-walking, but it's all over now although he's badly bruised his shoulder tumbling about and," he held her eyes with his own, "I know what's the matter with Martin and we're going to put it right."

"Oh, John," breathed the girl and burst into tears.

Meredith regarded her sympathetically and said: "Do you want my shoulder? You were good enough to lend me yours on one occasion."

Finella-Lou dabbed at her eyes with a handkerchief, whipped from under her pillow, blew her nose and smiled faintly. "Sorry for being a fool. But the thought of your being able to do something for Martin was . . . rather overwhelming. I don't know how I've borne it and I've felt simply wretched myself recently. But what did you mean about 'funny business'?"

Meredith hesitated. "Look," he said, "I don't know that I want to tell you just at the moment. Will you trust me?"

The girl leaned forward and put a hand over his. "You know I'd do that," she said impulsively.

Meredith nodded. "It's only for a little while now. I'm getting a really big man down from London to look at Martin. No, don't shake your head. He won't know he's a doctor. In fact, he's a cove who works with Miles Langtry and . . ."

"John," said the girl urgently, "you don't mean Martin's out of his mind?"

"I most emphatically do not," John assured her. "But he has been labouring under a perfectly frightful obsession. I'm convinced in my own mind that we can root the thing right out. After which Martin should be perfectly normal again."

"But what *is* this obsession?"

"How much of your husband's family history do you know?"

"Well, not an awful lot," she confessed. "Martin's always sort of soft-pedalled with regard to it. He's absurdly sensitive in some ways and I gather that the Lauder-Treaves have been a bit off-colour every so often. I believe some of them have been very definitely queer."

Again Meredith nodded. "Well, it's just that he's got some absurd bee in his bonnet about certain hereditary weaknesses."

The girl regarded him very solemnly. "John, if I ask you a straight question, will you give me a straight answer?"

The man gave her one of his crooked smiles. "You don't need to ask the question, Finella-Lou. I'll give you the answer without it. There is no foundation whatsoever in fact for this fear of Martin's. He has no hereditary taint whatsoever."

"Thank God," said Finella-Lou, leaning back against her pillows.

Meredith extracted a promise from her that she would not insist upon being present when Dr. Blackie came and shortly afterwards the doctor's old car was heard grinding up the hill and round to the front of the house.

Old Dr. Blackie puffed and wheezed and grunted as he came up Great Stairs and was exceedingly ungracious at being called out at that time of the day. He started bullying Yves at once, but Meredith chipped in and said: "Oh, just a minute, Doctor, I want you to listen to me."

"What is it, Sir John?" asked the other testily.

"Before you see Martin Lauder-Treaves," said Meredith, they were talking just at the top of Great Stairs, "I want to warn you that for many years I was a member of the Criminal Investigation Department. If it comes to the point I still cut a good deal of ice at Scotland Yard and, if I consider it necessary, I intend to have the medicine which you have prescribed for Sir Martin analysed."

"What the devil are you talking about?" blustered the old man.

"Exactly what I say," replied Meredith. "Are you convinced that the medicine contains nothing more than the bromide which you've prescribed?"

Dr. Blackie appeared to realise that the question was serious. "Perfectly certain," he replied emphatically. "But why all this thusness about young Martin's sedative?"

"Because," said Meredith, "I'm convinced that the man has been drugged."

"Let's have a look at him," said old Blackie quietly.

Meredith followed him into Martin's room and stood by his side while he made his examination. Finding that his patient did not wake upon being spoken to or shaken, the old man looked puzzled and proceeded to take his pulse.

"H'm, could be," he murmured. "Could be. The pulse is slightly depressed, between sixty and seventy. Let's see what his temperature is."

He had some difficulty in introducing the thermometer into Martin's mouth and placed it instead in the crease of his thigh.

"Slightly sub-normal," he said, peering at it short-sightedly, "but that's quite consistent with his general condition." He opened his bag and extracted a stethoscope. "Let's see what the heart is really doing."

He drew back the eiderdown and, for the first time, saw the huge bruise running down the chest of the unconscious man. "Jumping catfish!" he exclaimed. "What the devil's all this?"

"Don't know," said Meredith. "Suppose you tell us."

"But how did he get it?"

The old man seemed very startled and distressed, but eventually Meredith was able to elicit from him that Martin's condition was consistent with a drug-induced stupor and that in his opinion the wound could not have been self-inflicted.

"There's no question about it," the old man said firmly. "Somebody hit him, probably with a stick."

"In your opinion," asked Meredith, "is it safe to leave him alone now?"

"Oh, yes, but I'd like to have another look at him later when he's come round."

"We'd be glad if you would."

It was just on four when Meredith climbed wearily into bed and instantly sank into a deep sleep. It did not last very long, however, for, by eight o'clock, he was again awake. He felt like hell and shaving was an effort. Another boiling hot bath did much to restore him and about a gallon of tea set him ticking over again. He went to the telephone and called the Welbeck number. Despite the urgency of his request, however, Hartley Frome said it was impossible for him to get down that day, but would arrive on the morrow. He appeared to be more than interested in what Meredith could tell him over the telephone. Meredith hung up and made his way upstairs as Dr. Blackie's car once more appeared opposite the causeway over the moat.

"Hello, doctor," he said, as the old man appeared at the head of the stairs. "I wonder if you'd be good enough to come along to my room for a moment before seeing your patient?"

At the interview which followed the old man looked first indignant, then surprised, then astounded and finally frightened, but at length he agreed to do what Meredith suggested and they went together to Martin's room.

Yves, looking very white and tired, was sitting with his cousin who had not yet regained full consciousness.

"Well, my boy," said Blackie, going up to the bed, "you're a fine one. What have you been doing to yourself?"

The heavy eyelids flickered open and Martin frowned slightly as he attempted to focus.

"Hello," he said weakly. "I feel damn funny. Weak . . . kitten." The eyes closed again nor did they open when once more he spoke. "I've got it in the shoulder," he went on wearily, "thought at first . . . my leg. It must have been that bloody S.S. fellow. Didn't see him at first. Briars . . . in the way. He got him though. Saw him go over. Good old Briars! Let the bastards have it! Feel . . . tired."

It wasn't until more than an hour later that Martin really came out of his stupor. Blackie and Meredith were in the room at the time, talking over by the window, when a voice from the bed caused them to swing round.

"Hello, anything wrong? Christ, my shoulder! I say, what's happened?"

"This is your cue," muttered Meredith under his breath to his companion. The old doctor lumbered forward with an assumption of a hearty bedside-manner.

"Now you just relax and do as you're told," he boomed. "You've not been at all well. Had us dancing about half the night."

"What?" said Martin incredulously.

"Fact," nodded the doctor, "ask Sir John here. He heard you yelling your head off and came in to see what was the matter with you. Found you'd got out of bed and slipped or something and given yourself a great welt on the shoulder on the corner of the bedpost. And that's not all, Master Martin," went on the old man, nodding portentously. "I've had my eye on you for some time and you have now succeeded in achieving a nervous breakdown."

Martin dragged himself up against the pillows, winced as his shoulder hurt him and regarded the two men with deep suspicion. "What precisely do you mean by that?" he asked frowning.

"Good heavens, boy, what I say. For some reason or other you've had the willies for a long time. Probably never really got over being knocked about by the Hun, but you'll be all right now."

Meredith was watching closely and he saw the young baronet's face change. He saw the sudden, sickening fear leap to life at the back of his eyes. He turned his face slowly to Meredith.

"You found me?" he queried. John nodded. "What . . . what was I doing?"

Meredith regarded him quizzically and then smiled. "My dear chap," he said in a very matter-of-fact tone of voice. "You weren't doing anything. You'd knocked yourself out or something."

"Where was I and . . . had I got any clothes on?"

Meredith allowed himself to appear surprised. "Clothes on?" he echoed. "You'd got your pyjamas on, like any other civilised citizen."

The expression of undoubted relief which spread over the other's face amply repaid Meredith for his white lie.

"But why haven't I got anything on now?" asked the young man, pulling down the bed-clothes.

John Meredith laughed. "I'm afraid that's my doing," he said. "I found you'd fetched yourself a hell of a crack down the shoulder and wanted to be sure you hadn't got any other bumps and bruises. Then it was too much of a fag to dress you up again. What on earth were you up to? Must have been *some* dream. You looked as if you'd been engaged single-handed in wiping out the entire defences of the French coast."

Martin Lauder-Treaves looked up at the other incredulously. "Maybe," he said, "maybe that's what it was." He paused and plucked at the eiderdown and then said, as though it were an effort to put the question, "You didn't notice . . . anything else?"

Meredith knew very well to what he was referring, but he schooled his countenance into an expression of mild surprise.

"Anything else?" he queried.

"Yes. Anything queer . . . about the room, I mean?"

"About the room?" echoed Meredith in apparent puzzlement. "No," he said, "can't say there was. Should I have noticed anything?"

"No," said Martin quietly. "No," and he lay back on the bed and Meredith watched the eyes close and the small smile of extraordinary happiness which played about his lips.

Meredith and Blackie looked at one another and the former nodded. As though at a word of command the old man boomed: "Well, we can't take any risks with you, young man. You may not think now that there's been anything the matter with you at all, but you've been pretty ill. In a way it's quite a blessing you've had this . . . brainstorm, I suppose I'd better call it. It's like a boil, you see. Got to come to a head and bust and then you're all right," he ended weakly.

He forbade Martin to think of getting up and told him he'd have to take things very easy indeed for some days. He put a big arnica dressing on the enormous bruise and went away promising to return in the evening to give him something to make him sleep.

"What in fact are you going to give him?" asked Meredith as he accompanied the doctor down Great Stairs.

"Just a little luminol," said the old man and went his way.

The day was cloudy and overcast, but the excessive heat of the previous day was gone. John went and fetched Mike and took him at a slow walk down through the Duchy Meadows. Here, where thick woods came down on the eastern slope, they encountered Brown Brummy and Meredith hailed the little man, who came reluctantly at his summons.

"Do you smoke, Brummy?" he asked.

"Aye, so I du, an' all. Times when I can get owt to smoke," nodded the other, his bloodshot little eyes on the cigarette-case which Meredith produced. "Thank'ee kindly, sur. That's a mortal foine box you got to put 'em in, tu."

"It was given me by my wife," replied Meredith.

Brown Brummy shook his head. "Never 'ad none, meself. Wimmin is kittle-cattle. Oi got me beasts, so Oi 'ave an all." He fished an enormous ferret from inside his clothes and then stuffed it back again. "Oi don't need chick nor child nor kittle-cattlin' wimmin. If moi beasts don't do as Oi say, Oi bites 'em, so Oi du, and they bites Oi, but Oi bites a damn-sight 'arder. You can't du that, nor you can, with kittle-cattlin' wimmin."

Meredith nodded on solemn agreement. "No more you can," he said mildly. "They tell me," he went on, "you've a wonderful way with you with animals."

The disreputable little man nodded and smirked and gave a little sideways hop of satisfaction. "Aye, 'tis so."

"I'm told also," went on Meredith guilelessly, "that you know more about the estate here than anyone else."

"Du they say that, sur?" asked Brown Brummy in evident delight.

"That's what I'm told," John assured him.

Brown Brummy stepped up close to his companion and Meredith would have been glad to step away. It struck him that he was getting his fill of stinks what with one thing and another, but Brummy's smell was much more just unwashed humanity than had been the reek which had clung about the master of High Perwyl.

"They speak right, sur," nodded Brummy, wiping his nose on his fingers and then fetching the ferret, which had stuck its head out, a blow which Meredith thought might well kill the little brute. "Brown Brummy knows a mort of things as other folks don't know, no'ow."

"So I should imagine," Meredith encouraged.

"An 'ow true-right you'd be, sur. Oi'm a natcheral, an' natcher's things moi things, even when they seems onnatcheral."

"Unnatural?" repeated Meredith, allowing a trace of disbelief to appear in his voice.

"Aye, sur, onnatcheral. Oi been 'ere a long toime an' moi folks on moi mother's side 'ave been 'ere, ooh, a mort o' years. Longer, they du say, than Sur Mart'n an' his folks, up to Perwyl. Moi ol' mother tell me when Oi was a bye nor bigger nor that, about the weakness that was up to Perwyl."

"Weakness?"

"Aye, sur, weakness. There be them now that say it be nought but awld woives' tales, but Oi wouldn't stir o' nights without this," and from his pocket he pulled a withered little bunch of some herb.

"What's that?" asked Meredith curiously.

A look of intense cunning came into the little man's face as he returned his hand to his pocket. "Brummy knows what 'tis. Aye, sur, 'tis what some folks call the bane an' others dawg's bane."

"Dog's bane?" repeated Meredith. "I've never . . . Do you mean wolf's bane?"

"Oi never said it, sur! Stroike me black-bloind, Oi never said it! 'Twas you, you, yourself, said it."

Looking down into those bloodshot eyes, Meredith could distinguish the sudden fright which had overtaken the dirty little man and he recalled a not unsimilar expression which he had seen earlier that morning at High Perwyl. Instinct warned him that at any moment the little man would shy away and he again brought out his cigarette-case and held it out to the other.

"Help yourself," he urged. "Take as many as you want."

"'Tis kindly, sur, rare kindly," said the little man and took the lot.

Meredith turned to walk beside Brummy in the direction in which he had been going when they met. "Seen no more of your sheep-killer, I suppose," he asked casually.

"N-no," said the other warily, "but Oi seen his marks, the marks left by his gert big feet, so Oi 'ave."

"Really," said Meredith, without apparent interest.

"Aye, 'tis true, but tho' Oi carry the bane, jest in case, Oi'll tell 'ee somethin'. 'E don't go spare, 'e don't." Meredith looked puzzled and the little man went on. "'E don't go spare on no foot, 'e don't. Sound-footed, 'e be. 'E ain't got no limp."

Before Meredith could comment on this the little man was off like an arrow from the bow, sprinting, for all his age, across the Duchy Meadows on his short bow legs. He left Meredith staring after him, as once before, his mind fully provided with food for thought.

CHAPTER XXI

ROSE WITHOUT A THORN

When Meredith returned to the house he found Finella-Lou in better spirits than he had ever known her. They had not met since he had left her bedroom early that morning and there could be no doubt as to the reason for the sudden change in the girl. John Meredith knew a momentary qualm. He hoped to God he hadn't opened his mouth too soon with regard to her husband. She came to him impulsively and took both his hands in hers.

"John dear," she said, "you've given me new life."

He smiled down at her. "My dear, we haven't got Martin out of the wood yet. All we've done is to discover the way."

"You will," she said with happy confidence. "After you left me last night . . . this morning . . . whenever it was, I couldn't go to sleep again for a long time and when I finally woke up this morning I remembered at once what you'd said to me about my poor sweet and, d'you know, I felt actually sick with relief. It's been . . . quite dreadful."

"Finella-Lou," said Meredith quietly, "you mustn't go flying off to the other extreme. I beg of you not to rush your fences at this stage. Your husband's been through a bad phase, and if he still shows some signs of aloofness or withdrawal you must respect that privacy. He'll come round, you'll see, but he is, at the moment, teetering on a very fine balance. We want to keep that balance level. At all costs we must avoid anything which will send it dipping in either direction."

The girl's eyes grew solemn. "I understand," she said, "but, oh John, please, don't let it be too long."

That evening after dinner, Dr. Blackie returned to the castle, expressed himself satisfied with his patient's condition and left a small box of little white pills for him to take before settling down for the night.

"Can he be left alone tonight?" Meredith asked.

"Oh yes, he'll be all right. There's no need for anyone to be with him."

When the old man had left, Meredith made his way through the west gallery towards the drawing-room and it was here that he had a sudden dizzy spell accompanied by slight nausea. He slumped down onto a Chippendale chair and, bending, stuck his head between his knees. In a few moments he felt better and leaned back in his chair, his face clammy, his heart thumping uncomfortably. He recalled that he had had a pretty sticky night the night before with precious little sleep. He felt so rotten that his thoughts turned instinctively to a drop of brandy. He didn't want to call attention to his condition. There was enough agitation and turmoil in the house without his adding to it. He sat quietly for a few minutes and then pulled himself to his feet and went, rather groggily, towards the kitchen-quarters. In the butler's pantry he found the man for whom he was looking. Old Plum was seated before a baize-covered table, slowly and methodically polishing the table-silver.

"Why, Sir John, did you want something?" he exclaimed.

Meredith leaned in the doorway and smiled rather ruefully. "I do indeed. I'm feeling thoroughly rotten and wondered if I could have a spot of brandy."

"Why, of course, sir," said the old man. "Come and sit down here, Sir John. You do look a bit green about the gills."

Plum jumped up and insisted on Meredith seating himself. The latter accepted the chair gratefully. The butler opened a glass-fronted cupboard and took from it an oblong silver tray on which stood a bottle of brandy, a siphon and four glasses of a type which Meredith remembered he had drunk his brandy-and-soda from the previous night.

"I'll have it neat, Plum, if I may."

"Certainly, Sir John," said the old man and poured two fingers of brandy into the glass and held it out to him.

Meredith drank about a half of it and put the glass down on the table at his elbow. He closed his eyes and presently felt better. He opened his eyes to find the butler regarding him anxiously. He smiled. "Better now," he nodded.

"You're a better colour, too, sir," said Plum. "You gave me quite a turn when you came in. Really bad, you looked. No, don't move, sir. Just take it easy for a minute or two. Would you care for a drop more?"

"No, thank you, this will do me fine. A real life-saver."

"That's funny," said Plum suddenly, regarding the bottle which he still held in his hand. "I would have sworn there was more in the bottle than this."

"'Fraid I'm the culprit," said Meredith. "Mr. Yves brought me a whacking great brandy-and-soda last night."

"Ah, that accounts for the glass I found in Great Hall this morning," smiled Plum.

Meredith sat regarding the bottle which Plum had returned to its tray. He looked puzzled. The bottle was only about a quarter full.

"I say!" he exclaimed, his tone speculative, "I couldn't have drunk all that."

"All what, Sir John?"

"Well, all the rest of the bottle, apart from what you've just poured out for me."

The old man shook his head and smiled. "Oh, no, Sir John, I didn't mean there was all that missing."

"But Mr. Yves opened a new bottle," insisted Meredith. "He told me so."

Plum looked puzzled. "A new bottle, sir. He couldn't have done. This bottle was on the tray with the glasses, one of which he used. He must have used this bottle, sir."

"Perhaps he didn't see it," said Meredith, "and scouted round for another."

"No, sir," Plum assured him. "I've got the key of the cellar and there's no other brandy out except this. There isn't a duplicate of the cellar key. It was lost some time ago and there's a new one being cut at the moment."

"I must have been mistaken," said John Meredith. "That's what I *thought* he said, but I was pretty dicky at the time."

Meredith finished the remainder of his brandy and then went up to his bedroom by way of Second Stairs. As he was about to enter, he glanced down the corridor and saw Finella-Lou emerge from her room. She beckoned him.

"John," she said quietly, when they were together. "Would it do any harm if I slept on the sofa in Martin's room to-night? I mean to go in, of course, after he's fallen asleep with this stuff of Dr. Blackie's."

"I can't see that it would do any harm," agreed Meredith.

It may have been the effects of the brandy but, whatever it was, the moment Meredith had got into bed he fell instantly asleep. The hands of the clock crept on inexorably. The house grew quiet. In his room, Martin lay sunk in sleep while his wife, curled up on the sofa with her eiderdown over her, lay staring wide-eyed into the darkness and listening to the even tenor of his breathing. The hands of the clock crept on inexorably. The house was very still, In his basket in Meredith's room, Mike, the Sealyham, moved uneasily and raised his head. He, alone, of all the living things in High Perwyl that night, knew that an evil thing was stirring. The house slept on. Mike remained wakeful, his every instinct on the *qui vive*.

. . . . .

A mile away, in a little bedroom at Home Farm, a small person sat up in bed and yawned sleepily. It had been a huge effort to stay awake, but the thought of what lay ahead curled up the corners of the childish mouth. Carefully, her every movement instinct with stealth, her little pointed tongue caught between her teeth, Virginia climbed slowly out of bed. She kept her hand on the spring where she knew it made a noise on release and stood up. So far, so good. She tip-toed, barefooted, across the floor and pressed down the electric-light switch very carefully so that it would make as little noise as possible. Then, still moving with great caution, she pulled her nightie over her head and proceeded to dress. She did not put her shoes on.

Once dressed, she went back to the narrow, painted bed and, stooping, raised the counterpane which hung down on the outer side almost to the floor. She had so arranged it herself when she went to bed. From under the bed she took the most paradoxical object imaginable. It was a small white jerry, with jolly rabbits painted on its side, but what made it so unusual was that it was crammed with roses.

She placed the jerry-full of lovely blooms on a table and stood back and admired it. She stuck out her lower lip in sudden doubt as to what her grandmother might say when she discovered the rape of her small rose-garden. She dismissed the thought from her mind as it was succeeded by the pleasanter one of what *someone else* might say. From the floor she took a small punnet to the handle of which she tied an ordinary luggage label on which was scrawled in childish characters eleven words. She grinned impishly and wrinkled up her nose excitedly as she read them over again to be sure that nothing was left out. One by one, she took the roses from their humble receptacle, dried them on her small face-towel and arranged them with fond artistry in the punnet. It is to be remarked that all the thorns had been painstakingly (literally) removed in case their recipient should be pricked.

She slipped the wooden handle of the punnet over her right arm, picked up her shoes and tip-toed to the door. She extinguished the light and, taking great care, opened her bedroom door. Her course along the landing presented little difficulty. She had thought it out before-hand and, in any case, she knew exactly where the rugs were even in the dark. The stairs, however, presented a very different problem, for many of them creaked abominably. She solved the business in her own way and, cocking one leg over the banisters, she slid silently down in the dark to the bottom. The front door she had ruled out entirely, with its chain and bolts and lock, as being altogether too dangerous and she made her way silently through the sleeping house to the stone-flagged kitchens and went out through the scullery door.

She had never before been up as late as this and certainly not out of doors. She sat down on the step and slipped on her shoes, knowing that she could jump straight onto grass from where she stood.

Still on tip-toe, while so near the house, she went resolutely upon her way. Once at a safe distance from Home Farm, she went more carelessly, striding along in real excitement at being abroad alone in the middle of the night. She clung to the path, rather than striking across country, for there was only a fitful moon to show her her way.

Ginnie smiled to herself as she glanced down at what she carried and her blue eyes grew round with pleasure at the thought of what it would mean on the morrow. She was half-way between Home Farm and the old disused quarry and she skipped along happy in her unusual freedom, happy in the purpose of her mission and happier still because she was just a healthy little girl filled with well-being.

· · · · ·

In the room above the causeway at High Perwyl, Finella-Lou lay sleeping. Across the room in the big bed her husband moaned and stirred restlessly, his head turning from side to side on the pillow. The bed-clothes were thrust back. Somewhere among them and kicked down impatiently were his pyjama-trousers. The jacket lay flung onto the floor at his bedside. He moaned again and jerked sideways on the bed as though he were attempting to avoid something. Then he lay still and muttered.

In another room a dog suddenly jerked his head erect and looked towards the window. Slowly, Mike rose up in his basket until he was sitting. Then, very slowly, he stepped from his basket and stood still, his tail erect, his ears pricked. He whined suddenly and ran forward a few steps and stood again and listened. Then he growled. He went swiftly to the window and reared up on his hind-legs. His head was up, sniffing He whined again and ran across the room and reared up and pawed at Meredith's bed. The man stirred, turned over and was still once more. The dog's whine become more urgent and he pawed repeatedly at the bed-clothes.

"For God's sake, go back to your basket, Mike. Shut up and lie down."

The Sealyham dropped back onto all fours and went uncertainly back to his basket as he was bidden. He got into it with obvious reluctance, but he did not settle down. He sat, staring into the darkness, every fibre of his small body alert and he whined softly. He whined at intervals for a long time.

. . . . .

Small Virginia had reached the point near the quarry where the path turned right-handed up the hill to the castle. She stood suddenly still, her fair head on one side as she listened. There it was again. She hesitated and then, instead of turning right-handed, she turned to the left and walked slowly towards the old quarry. She went more hesitantly as she neared the narrow entry, half-blocked as it was with tumbled stone. In the very middle of the narrow way she stopped and at that moment the pale moon swept beyond a drift of clouds and she saw.

"Oh!" said Ginnie, in evident astonishment and pleasure and held out her arms.

 . . . . .

The great house within its moat was still, but in an upstairs room a small dog whined and whined again. . . .

CHAPTER XXII

UNHAPPY BIRTHDAY

THERE was an incessant buzzing that went on and on. No, it wasn't a buzzing, it was a small insistent bell, dulled by distance. She closed her mind against it, but it continued and forced her consciousness to take notice. With a sigh Finella-Lou opened her eyes and found, to her astonishment, that she was not in her own room. Somewhere a telephone was ringing. She listened more intently and recognized the sound as coming from her bedroom. Damn, she thought, I'll have to go. Plum must consider it urgent to switch it through to me. She flung back the eiderdown beneath which she had slept, swung her feet to the floor and felt sleepily for her slippers. The room was practically in darkness as the heavy brocade curtains were drawn across both windows. The outline of her husband's bed was only dimly visible across the room. She listened for a brief moment and was reassured by the evenness of his breathing. Hastily gathering up her dressing-gown, she went swiftly into the corridor and ran along to her own room.

"Hello," she said breathlessly, as she picked up the bedside telephone.

The butler's voice answered her. "Good morning, m'lady, I'm so sorry if I've woken you, but I've had an urgent message from Home Farm. Young Mrs. Mills was in a rare taking. She says Virginia is missing."

"Missing?" echoed Finella-Lou stupidly.

"That's what she said, m'lady. It seems the child got

up and went out sometime during the night and has not returned."

"Good heavens!" exclaimed the girl. "Is anything being done about it?"

"I gathered, eventually, that half the estate are already out looking for her. They rang here, m'lady, thinking that perhaps the child had come up to the castle. Mrs. Mills is almost distracted, I'm afraid."

"Would you have a tray prepared for me at once, please, Plum, and ask Magnolia to bring it up to me? I'll dress right away. I must go out and help."

"Very good, m'lady, and, despite its alarming beginning, may I take the liberty of wishing your ladyship a very happy birthday?"

"Good heavens, I'd completely forgotten. Thank you very much, Plum. And you *will* ask Magnolia to hurry with that tray? Just a pot of tea and some toast."

Finella-Lou hung up, a small frown of anxiety wrinkling her forehead. She hoped to goodness nothing had happened to Ginnie. Whatever was that baby doing, going out during the night? She turned to enter her bathroom, remembered Martin and went back along the landing to his room. She thought, a little sadly, that her normal way of entry to his room had, in the last few weeks, become abnormal. She went in and drew back the curtains and then turned to the bed.

"Good gracious!" she exclaimed. "What on earth have you been up to, my pet. Oh dear, oh dear, I suppose he was too hot or something and I slept right through it."

She decided that it would be impossible single-handed to get his pyjamas onto him again and had to content herself with drawing the bedclothes up and tucking them round him. She placed a cool hand on his forehead. He seemed quite warm despite his having been lying naked. He never stirred at her touch but remained sunk in deep sleep. She thought suddenly how very young he looked, young and unguarded and helpless. Her heart seemed to turn over inside her and she knew the sudden prick of quick, foolish tears. Very lightly she kissed his forehead and then allowed her cheek to rest a moment against his hair. A big tear rolled down her cheek and fell on the pillow beside him. It was the first kiss she had been able to give him for more than two months. With a deep sigh, she turned away and hurried back to her room to dress.

.   .   .   .   .

Across the dining-room at Home Farm Benjamin Truelove faced his prospective son-in-law. Both men were anxious and hollow-eyed and old Truelove showed the weight of his years.

"I can't understand it, Albert," said the bailiff of High Perwyl.

"No more can I," replied Briars. "What on earth would possess the kid to go out at night, anyway?"

Both men had been out since a quarter-past seven that morning. It was now after nine and they had come in for a moment to break their fast with a cup of tea.

"She can't have gone far," Briars pointed out. "Her bicycle's in the shed and her pony's still in his stall. She must-a gone out a-purpose."

"What have you covered so far?" asked Truelove.

"I've been all over the farm itself, then on to both Great and Little Yield, walked up the river to the back of Hollow Hill, back over it to the bridge, covered all five Duchies, round the back of the castle, and so home. The chaps from Trennion's Deep are covering their own ground and the Ga·vp and Hordle Hold and Stayley side."

"What about Hemsley at Nocking Thicket?"

"He and his lads are taking the Shrewsbury road and the Slopes. If we don't hear anything by half-past I'm going to ring the police."

"I've already got the Stayley bobby on the job," replied the other.

"Have you seen Susan since you come in?" asked Briars, his honest, battered face drawn with anxious enquiry.

"Aye," replied the old man. "She's taking it hard, lad."

He put down his big breakfast-cup with a shaking hand. The cup clattered noisily on its saucer, but not noisily enough to drown a dismal, muffled howl which came from across the courtyard of the farm buildings. Briars smiled faintly. "He's been at it all the morning," he commented. "I thought he'd better stay shut up, though. Only get in the way."

Benjamin Truelove jerked up his grizzled head and stared at the other. "I wonder," he said.

"Wonder what?"

"If he'd be in the way," replied Truelove. "He's taken to her something wonderful in the few days she's had him."

"You mean . . ."

"It's worth trying, anyway," said the old man, picking up his stick again and moving towards the door.

In the hall they encountered Susan Mills. Her blue eyes, so like the small Virginia's, asked an agonised question.

"Not yet, dear," said her father, laying a hand awkwardly on her shoulder. "But it's early yet. The little monkey'll probably walk in on us any moment of her own accord."

The young mother's eyes betrayed no consolation at the words. Her gaze went to the square man standing at her father's side. There had been few endearments between them in their oddly formal courtship, which came of an instinctive tenderness in the ex-Commando in his usage of a young widow. Now, in this moment of her travail, he moved forward and placed an arm about her. She dropped her head to his shoulder and, for a moment, he rested his face against hers. They did not kiss. No word was spoken between them but, as he turned to follow her father through the front door, she was oddly comforted.

Side by side the two men crossed the yard to a disused stable the other side. As their approaching feet rang on the cobble-stones, the howling which came from inside the half-door changed to excited yapping. Briars slid back the bolt and the occupant of the stable pushed open the door. It was the part-grown fox-terrier which had been Yves' birthday present to Virginia. He jumped up at them, barking and waltzing in circles with pleasure at being released.

"We'd better have something of the child's for him to smell," suggested Truelove and Briars ran back into the house and emerged a moment later with a small woolly cardigan. He held it out to the dog who, thinking it was a game, seized it in his teeth and pulled.

"No, boy!" admonished Sergeant-Major Briars. "Give over. Here, here, come 'ere. That's better." He picked the wriggling dog up and held him under his arm. Old Truelove helped to extract the woolly garment from the dog's mouth. Briars talked quietly and calmly to the terrier and presently he quietened down and appeared to listen. "This isn't a game, old boy. We want you to find Ginnie, eh? Ginnie, Ginnie, Ginnie! You know, boy, Ginnie. Find her. Where is she?" He held out his hand and Virginia's grandfather gave him the little cardigan. He held it close to the dog and repeated: "Ginnie! Where's Ginnie! Find her."

He put the terrier down on the ground who looked up at him and barked.

"That's right, boy. Find her! Go seek Ginnie!"

The fox-terrier cocked his intelligent little head on one side, wagged his tail and then ran across the courtyard on his swift, springy legs. Briars ran after him, exhorting him all the time to go seek Ginnie. "That's right, good boy."

The dog flashed round the corner of the house and out of sight, with Briars running lightly behind him. Benjamin Truelove stood where he was. He knew well that if the little dog were really running on a scent he would never make the pace and Albert, well Albert was the same as himself.

The terrier ran swiftly to the back-door. Here he cast about a bit, stood for a moment unmoving, head up, and then whined and ran back to the step before the scullery-door. He yelped suddenly and excitedly and then was off like a shot from a gun round to the front of the house and went bouncing along the footpath which headed almost due west and then turned off up the hill to High Perwyl. Briars sprinted after him. Once or twice he called out: "Good dog, that's it. Good boy!" but thereafter saved his breath against the speed of his going. Albert Briars felt his spirits rise.

Why the hell hadn't they thought of it before? Then a momentary doubt assailed him. Maybe the pup was only being a fool dog, after all. However, now, there was nothing for it but to follow. Sergeant-Major Briars ran on.

The dog rapidly outpaced him, but he had seemed to be following the path and Briars stuck to it. He came at last to where the path turned right and up the hill and glanced up the slope towards the castle. There was no sign of the terrier. And then the dog howled suddenly. The sound came from behind him and Briars turned slowly round, the blood in his body turning to water.

Briars was not a particularly imaginative man. That factor had served him in good stead as a Commando where, in that company of brave and courageous men, he had earned a reputation for utter fearlessness. Briars was a Cockney. He did not come of fey stock but, in that moment, he knew and the knowledge set him shaking suddenly and uncontrollably as though he had an ague. He heard queer, broken sounds and realised, with half his mind, that he was making them. His body, over-heated with the sweat of his rapid running, was now wrapped in ice-damp cloths. His heart was leaping like a maddened prisoner at the walls of his cell. He was strangling, suffocating. . . .

Again the dog howled, a long-drawn note of grief and dolour inconsolable, that long, sad note, instinct with melancholy, with which the canine breed recognises and signals death.

Briars went stiffly forward to the entry into the quarry.

He looked down. Almost at his feet sat the fox-terrier, his head thrown back, his muzzle pointing to the sky. The small, hairy mouth was opened in the pathetic O of a dog's desolation as he poured out his requiem for his little mistress. Within reach of his paws Ginnie lay upon her side. It must have rained since she fell there, for the child's clothing was sodden and she resembled more a tumbled bundle of old clothes than a little girl. She was dead. For the moment, the dreadful wound in her throat was mercifully hidden, for she lay with her face to the ground. But there was no need to see that wound to know that the small Virginia had run her brief course.

The man stood looking down, immovable. Still clutched in one small hand was the handle of a wooden punnet. It was filled with roses. It had a label, a luggage label, tied to it. As in a dream Briars knelt down and turned the label over. The ink had run a little, with the rain, but the childish handwriting was still easily decipherable. He read: "For darling Lady Loo on her burthday from the Litel Peepul."

CHAPTER XXIII

THE ACCUSATION OF THE DOGS

IN blissful ignorance of the appalling tragedy which had taken place in the quarry, Meredith rose from his solitary breakfast at High Perwyl and addressed the butler who had just come into the room.

"Is her ladyship up yet, d'you know, Plum?"

"Oh yes, sir, she's been up some time," replied Plum. "Up and abroad. She's gone down to Home Farm to see if she can help."

"Help?" repeated Meredith.

"Indeed, I was forgetting, Sir John. You are, perhaps, unaware that the little girl, Virginia Mills, is lost."

"I'm sorry to hear that," said Meredith, with very real anxiety. "What's happened, d'you know?"

Plum told him what little he knew and added: "Her ladyship is uncommon fond of the child. She was up and dressed and out in record time, as soon as she knew the facts. I saw her striking across the fields straight for Home Farm. She was evidently in too great a hurry to bother with the footpath."

"Is there anything, I wonder, that I could do?" Meredith volunteered.

"I doubt it, Sir John," Plum assured him. "I gather that the whole estate is already out and about and it can only be a short time before the child is found."

Meredith lit a cigarette and went thoughtfully through the house to the front door. As he was crossing the causeway, a car, which he recognised as the Stayley station taxi, swung round the corner of the moat and drew up opposite him. From it descended Mr. Hartley Frome.

"Good heavens!" exclaimed Meredith. "How on earth did you get here at this hour?"

The two men shook hands after Frome had paid his taxi-man and retrieved his suitcase.

"I got to thinking over what you told me on the telephone and thought I'd better get up here as soon as possible," replied Frome. "So I caught an early evening train yesterday, spent the night in Shrewsbury and came on first thing this morning."

"It's awfully good of you," said Meredith. "Here, let me take that. Come along in and we'll have a *bukh* before you see Lauder-Treaves."

"By the way," said the psychiatrist as he followed the other into the house, "am I doctor or one of the Foreign Office boys?"

"You're yourself," replied Meredith, "and incidentally, are you?"

"Am I what?"

"I suppose I ought to apologise for not knowing, but it never occurred to me to look you up or to check with McAllister. What I mean is—are you a qualified physician?"

Frome's grey eyes crinkled up at the corners and the strong mouth twitched as he replied: "As a matter of fact, I am. It helps, you know," he added smiling.

"With other sawbones, I take it?" suggested Meredith.

"With the body-hacking fraternity, precisely," agreed the eminent psychiatrist.

"That's a blessing," said John. "Then you'll be able to take full charge of Lauder-Treaves and . . ." He broke off and glanced down at the suitcase he was carrying. "Got any of your devil-brews in here?"

"The complete works," said Frome.

Meredith led the way into the library in the eastern wing

of the house. They seated themselves in two massive Jacobean chairs facing each other across the great fireplace.

"This is a very wonderful house," commented Hartley Frome.

"Yes," said Meredith. "It's also by way of being a haunted house. Haunted, that is, by an unhealthy history. Though, I must admit, the other night I really thought that there *was* a pretty solid ghost, if ghosts are ever solid."

Meredith broke off for a moment as though to collect his thoughts. His *vis-à-vis* sat quietly regarding him, his strong face impassive, the deep grey eyes half-closed.

"When I came to see you the other day," began Meredith frowning, "I described to you the case-history, as it were, of Martin Lauder-Treaves. That is, as far as I was in a position to know it. A good deal of it was, of course, largely deductive guessing, but you seemed to accept the general structure of the thing without any great surprise. When I had finished detailing the thing you described it as an obsession. Correct?"

"Correct," Frome confirmed.

Meredith nodded. "I want to ask you a question," he went on, "before telling you of the latest developments. Can someone with an obsession also be an hysteric?"

"Certainly," replied the psychiatrist. "Many sufferers from a psychoneurosis labour under an hysterical obsession."

"You must forgive me, Frome, if I appear awfully woolly about all this sort of thing, but you chaps use words in ways which are quite foreign to ordinary ways of speech. For instance, the word hysterics merely suggests to me a woman going off the deep end and enjoying a lovely go of the vapours. Of course, I know that the definition of hysteria is some sort of disturbance of the nervous system, but that is a very generic term. I believe that in medicine, and particularly in your line of country, an hysteric means something quite different, isn't that so?"

"Y-yes," agreed Hartley Frome cautiously. "Of course it means both the things you're saying. Look," he added as he leaned forward, "do you want me to give you a brief lecture on hysteria? Why are you harping on this?"

Meredith leaned back in his chair and regarded the other very directly. "Because," he said slowly and seriously, "it largely depends upon your answer to another question which I'm going to put to you whether Martin Lauder-Treaves' case could best be handled by you or by me."

The psychiatrist looked startled and then smiled uncertainly. "Setting up a rival shop?" he queried humorously.

John Meredith laughed and shook his head. "Not exactly," he said, "but just let me go on, will you? I believe I'm right in saying that in cases of acute or well-advanced hysteria the patient or sufferer has quite often been able to induce physical manifestations which are the product entirely of his own mind."

"Go on," said Hartley Frome softly. "I think I know what you're getting at."

"It's awfully difficult for me to explain," complained Meredith, "because I'm only a layman in these matters and I'm probably using all the wrong phraseology and terms."

"That's all right," said the other. "You're doing fine."

"Well," continued Meredith. "Let me put it this way. Medical science has knowledge of, indeed has, I believe, recorded actual cases of people, both men and women who have received the *stigmata*."

"Yes," agreed Frome. "That is so. It was, I believe, a more common phenomenon some centuries ago. Certain saints, notably Francis of Assisi, were known to have reproduced the wounds of the Crucifixion. There can be no doubt but what the individual himself induces these extraordinary manifestations urged by an amazing development of what you would call wishful-thinking."

Meredith nodded. "Yes," he said, "and I've met people in India, when I was a boy, who could, undoubtedly, do the most amazing things with their bodies by pure thought-control; Buddist lamas, for instance, and certain *fakirs* who were adepts in *yoga*."

"I don't wish in the least to hurry you," said Frome, "but what exactly has this got to do with my patient—if he is to be my patient."

"Just this," replied Meredith. "Do you know of any case in the whole of medical history where an hysteric has induced a smell?"

"What?"

"It's true," said Meredith. "That's exactly what I want to know."

"But I don't quite follow," said the psychiatrist, frowning. "I don't quite understand what you mean by inducing a smell. What kind of smell?"

"A smell," said Meredith, "a smell or rather a reek which is quite foreign to the human body and which I, myself, smelled on the body of an animal."

"D'you mean to tell me," said Hartley Frome, leaning forward, his face alight with interest, "that this chap stank like an animal?"

"Yes," said Meredith.

"And you want to know whether I can recall any recorded instance of such a phenomenon?"

"It sounds silly, I know," said Meredith, "but that *is* what I want to know."

"Well, I can't," said Frome quietly.

"Ah," said Meredith, "that's all I wanted to know."

. . . . .

It was shortly after Meredith and his companion had entered the library at High Perwyl that a small dejected figure could have been seen making its way slowly up the long slope from Home Farm to the castle on the hill. Finella-Lou went slowly and painfully, as though every step were an effort, though, in fact, she was quite unaware of the steady uphill trudge. From her almost nerveless fingers there hung a small wooden punnet filled with roses. Sergeant-Major Briars had said to her huskily as she left: "Please take it, ma'am. She'd have liked you to have it."

Finella-Lou felt empty with pain. It was as though some giant scoop had taken out the whole of her inside, leaving her completely void. She strove to shut her mind against what she had witnessed and undergone at Home Farm, but a devil's accompaniment followed ever after her. "Oh, my lady, oh my lady." Susan's distraught voice echoed and re-echoed through her brain. "Oh, if *only* you had never told her that story. Oh my lady, if only it hadn't been your birthday." Mental anguish can become a physical thing, a hurt scarcely to be borne. The wistful and agonised longing of a distraught young mother had been instinct with unspoken accusation. If only she hadn't told Ginnie that story of the fairy birthday-present. Oh God, if only she hadn't told her! The ache and anguish of that stricken household went with her like a fog from which there was no escaping. She wandered in a miasma of misery. Even now the thing was barely credible. The small Virginia had been a very real and lovable little personality, a familiar and happy and integral part of life at High Perwyl. She recalled the spontaneous gaiety of the little girl and the touching solemnity of her more sober moments. She remembered the unfailing welcome in the blue, blue eyes and the shy smile of the tender mouth whenever they had met. Childless herself, Finella-Lou had discovered a great tenderness for Ginnie.

Quite unconscious of the fact that slow, hopeless tears, welled from her eyes and rolled unheeded down her cheekse Finella-Lou walked blindly and unseeing across the causeway and entered the house. The appalling shock of the tragedy had dispelled the custom of past weeks and she went up Great Stairs, heading instinctively towards her husband's comfort. She went into his room. He was lying propped up against his piled pillows. He turned his face to her as she came in and then, startled, exclaimed: "Whatever's the matter, dear?"

"Oh, Martin! Oh, Martin, I can't bear it!"

She went towards his bed in a stumbling run. She flung herself down at his side and buried her face on his chest. He winced with pain as she blundered clumsily against the dressing over his wound. He put an arm about her heaving shoulders and gently stroked her hair.

"There, there," he murmured. "There, there, darling. What is it, my sweet?"

She raised her head and turned swimming eyes to his. "It's Ginnie," she sobbed. "Our darling little Ginnie."

"Ginnie?" he echoed in a whisper. "What's the matter with the child?"

"Oh, Martin, she's dead!"

His jaw dropped as he stared at her and he drew his breath sharply as though with sudden pain. "Dead?" he gasped.

"Yes, yes. Dead," sobbed his wife. "Killed, horribly."

Martin's face drained of colour. "Killed?" he repeated incredulously. "But I don't. . . ."

"Yes, killed," said Finella-Lou choking on the word. "Killed by that brute, that filthy sheep-killer that's been about. Oh, Martin, why didn't you have the beast traced and shot?"

For a long moment they stared at each other in common misery and then something quite terrible happened. The man's face cracked. It was just as though his face had previously been a wax mask which had suddenly been shivered by a blow, revealing the dreadful thing it had concealed. His whole face twisted. The eyes assumed an expression which she had never before seen in any human face. The lips rolled back, revealing the teeth in a beastly parody of a smile that wasn't sane and from those same lips there issued a dreadful bubbling chuckle.

"*Martin!*" she gasped.

"*Get out!*" he yelled and Finella-Lou, starting up from the bed, put both hands up to her face and screamed.

Half-way up Great Stairs, Meredith and Hartley Frome heard that scream. Neither man glanced at the other, but they leaped up the remaining stairs like sprinters at the starting-pistol. They burst into Sir Martin's room. The man had one foot out of bed and was crouched as though to spring. Not three feet distant, his wife backed slowly away from him. Meredith took one glance at the scene and barked: "Get the woman out of the room. I'll attend to the man."

What happened, happened very swiftly. Without so much as by-your-leave, Hartley Frome put his arms round Finella-Lou and carried her out into the corridor.

"For God's sake, what *is* this?" she cried. "Who *are* you? My husband. . . ."

Hartley Frome set her down on her feet and pulled the door to behind him. "Listen, Lady Lauder-Treaves," he said, his voice quietly controlled. The very measure of his tone carried with it the reassurance of sanity. "Listen," he said, "my name's Hartley Frome, I'm a doctor. I've come down to see your husband. What was it, can you tell me, that occasioned this outburst on his part?"

Finella-Lou put a hand miserably to her forehead. "I can't. . . ."

Hartley Frome took her firmly by the shoulders and gave her a gentle shake. "You've got to pull yourself together," he said, still in that eminently reasonable tone of voice. "Much may depend on what you are able to tell me. What has just taken place between you and your husband?"

The girl made an obvious effort and recovered some measure of composure. "I've just told him about Ginnie," she said hoarsely. "Oh, of course, you don't know who Ginnie is. She's the granddaughter of our bailiff. She's a little girl and she was killed last night by a beastly sheep-killer, a dog which has been around the estate for some time."

"I see," said Hartley Frome quietly and saw a lot. "And what happened after you told him?"

Finella-Lou raised a tear-stained face to his and looked as if she were about to cry again. "It was then," she said shakily, "that he seemed to go mad."

"I see," nodded the psychiatrist. "Yes, it all fits in," he went on, as though speaking to himself. "Try not to worry too much, I know you've had a frightful shock, but I know all about this condition of your husband's, thanks to Sir John Meredith, and I think we shall be able to get him well."

At that moment Magnolia appeared running up the stairs. "What ails you, honey-chile?" she cried. "I heard you holler."

THE ACCUSATION OF THE DOGS

The girl turned instinctively to her old Mammy and Hartley Frome, realising she would be looked after, went back into the bedroom.

Martin Lauder-Treaves was back in bed. He lay as though exhausted against his pillows. His face was quite colourless, even to the lips. He looked like something that had been dug up.

"Don't worry." Frome heard Meredith saying to him. "We won't allow her back."

Meredith turned as Frome entered the room and the latter caught his eye and jerked his head over to the further window. "Do you," he asked in a whisper when they stood as far as possible from the bed, "do you know a child called Ginnie on the estate?"

"Yes," replied Meredith in the same tone. "She lives with her people down at Home Farm. But she's lost."

"She's dead," said the other. "Killed by a dog."

For a moment Meredith said nothing. He regarded the other with incredulous horror. "God's curse on the thing!" he breathed. "And I suppose," he went on slowly after a pause, "she told *him*," and he jerked his head towards the bed.

"Yes," said Frome.

"Oh, my God, my God!" sighed Meredith wearily.

. . . . .

It was about half-an-hour later that John Meredith emerged from Martin's bedroom and went in search of Finella-Lou. He found her in the drawing-room, curled up on a big Knole sofa and cuddled to the vast, motherly bosom of Magnolia Lincoln. She had evidently been crying bitterly, for her face was red and puffy. She looked up at Meredith's entry, her eyes all anxious enquiry, and he walked across and stood looking down at the two women and then smiled.

"He's better now," he said.

"Oh John," said the girl tremulously. "It was horrible. Does what you said to me the other day still hold?" The man wrinkled his brow in enquiry. "I mean about Martin's getting well?"

"Yes," said Meredith.

"But I don't understand."

"Be patient a little longer, Finella-Lou," said Meredith. "I know it's awfully hard for you, but were I to tell you the thing so far it would, in itself, sound completely crazy. Be assured, my dear, that Martin *will* be all right. Why don't you go to your room and lie down? And I'd like you, Magnolia, if you would, to stay with her."

"I sho will do jest that," nodded the big woman firmly. "I don't know what's gwine on around this place, but it sho' is mighty onpleasant."

"You're quite right, Magnolia," agreed Meredith, "but it's not going on for very much longer."

"Well, I sho is glad to hear that. Come along, Miss Lou. You best rest awhile, like the man says."

It was as they were all leaving the drawing-room that Plum appeared in the gallery and spoke to Finella-Lou.

"Mr. Briars is here from Home Farm, m'lady, and is asking to see you."

Finella-Lou turned a face of entreaty to Meredith and said: "Oh John, I don't think I can cope with him, would you mind?"

"Of course not," he replied and followed the butler into the hall, where he found Albert Briars standing just inside the front door.

"Anything I can do, Briars?" he asked. "Lady Lauder-Treaves isn't feeling too good just at the moment."

"I didn't really want to come botherin'," said the ex-Commando, his square face grimmer and more craggy than usual. "I just came to report, so to speak."

Meredith nodded and said gently: "I'm very grieved indeed to hear the news, Briars, and you must be feeling it a great deal more deeply."

"Arh, that's true, sir," he said heavily. "It's cruel hard, too cruel. My pore Susan, it's knocked her for six, sir. It's too 'ard, sir, for a woman like my Susan to lose her man and her child, but to lose young Ginnie like this is. . . ." He choked and then a dreadful expression came over the battered face. The powerful jaw thrust forward into the ghastly parody of a grin. He looked completely ruthless. "If I could catch that black mugger or even the bloke what owns 'im, so 'elp me, I'd tear the bloody guts out of 'em."

There was a short silence between the two men, during which both stood in preoccupation with their own bitter thoughts. Briars' train of thought had nothing complex about it. He was shocked and grieved to the very soul of him, but he had a terrible anger to bear him through. The turmoil in John Meredith's mind was far more tangled and far more bitter. His mood was instinct with self-reproach. He blamed himself terribly for what had happened. He knew, in that moment, that he had had a hand, maybe very indirectly, but still a hand, in the death of this child. He knew, in that revealing moment of deep and gloomy introspection, that it had been, in part, his fault; that he could have averted the tragedy had he been quicker off the mark. The fact that he was still not quite himself he did not recognise as an excuse. On the night when he had been attacked by that brute down by the river bank, he should have kept his wits about him. He should, of course, have got dogs from somewhere, dogs that were not trained in the unnatural manner of the estate dogs, and he should have taken them down right away to the bluff below the terraced gardens and trailed his assailant without further delay. The fact that such a course of action should have been blasted from his mind by the frightful discovery of Martin's condition that same night was not allowed to weigh with him. He had failed to do the obvious and he cursed himself with an intensity which his failure in no way really merited.

He glanced up from his gloomy abstraction and said to Briars: "What was it you came to report?"

The other man straightened himself, sighed and said: "I just came up, sir, to warn the house that the police-sergeant from Dulbury is on his way over with his dogs. They been used before for this sort of job, so I'm told, and they're that artful they can follow anything. We're going after this bastard this time, sir, good and proper."

"Good," said Meredith, "I'm glad to hear it. Is there anything I can do, Sergeant-Major?"

"I don't think so, sir. Thank you very much."

"When are these dogs arriving?"

"They ought to reach Home Farm in about an hour."

Briars then took his leave, after sketching a brief salutation with the hat clutched in his hand to someone standing just behind Meredith. John swung round and found Yves Launder-Treaves at his elbow. The man looked white and ill. His eyes had sunk back into his head. He was drawn and hollowed like one in the last stages of consumption. Meredith noted that the pale lips looked wet.

"Pretty bloody, isn't it?" said Meredith.

"Ghastly," said the other huskily. "Terrible." He paused, regarding Meredith miserably. "Did I hear Briars say they were going to try and trail the . . . the thing?" John Meredith nodded. "It's about time," Yves went on, "I warned Martin he ought to track this brute down, but he seemed queerly reluctant to do anything about it."

"Did he?" asked Meredith softly and looked queerly at the other.

They held each other's eyes and in Yves Lauder-Treaves' expression Meredith saw a very real fear. His own eyes narrowed.

"What are you thinking?" he asked, still in that quiet tone of voice.

The other didn't reply immediately. He closed his eyes and shook his head as though refusing to acknowledge what was in his mind. "Nothing," said Yves. "Nothing," he repeated on a rising inflexion.

Meredith stepped forward and caught him savagely above the elbow. "Look at me, man," he urged. "Look at me!" With real reluctance the other opened his eyes and stared as though fascinated into Meredith's face. "You're afraid, aren't you?" went on Meredith brutally. "You're afraid because, like all your family, you're so steeped in the putrid superstitions of your own family story that you pay a grudging tribute to an impossibility. You're afraid, aren't you? You're afraid even to think what I'm going to say. You're afraid, just as Martin is afraid, that *he* has something to do with this, aren't you?"

Yves opened his mouth as though he couldn't draw enough air into his lungs, as though he were drowning. "No, no," he moaned. "I don't. . . ."

"Don't equivocate, man!" snarled Meredith. "You know bloody well what I say is what's going through your mind." He released the other man's arm and half turned away from him as though in disgust. He said over his shoulder: "There's no real blot on your family escutcheon, but it could do with a damn good wash."

With this Meredith brushed past the other and went with great strides towards the stairs. In Martin's room he found its owner lying quietly in bed, staring with wide eyes at the ceiling. Hartley Frome was sitting in a chair across the room smoking in silence. At Meredith's entry he got up, walked to the door and beckoned him out of the room.

"He seems quiet enough now," he commented as he closed the door behind him, "but there's no getting at him. He won't open his mouth. He did condescend to make one remark a little while ago when he acknowledged my presence with the words 'another blasted doctor'."

"I thought I'd better let you know," said Meredith, "that the police are arriving shortly with hounds to trail the brute that killed little Virginia Mills. They may run mute or they may not. If they speak, won't it upset that poor devil in there?"

"In the circumstances, most decidedly so," replied Frome quietly. "We must warn him of what's taking place. Are you ready to do your stuff yet?"

"No, I'm not," said Meredith uneasily, "I've got to think. I haven't had an opportunity really to think about the thing as a whole."

"Well, you'd better do your thinking pretty quickly," suggested Hartley Frome with painful directness.

Meredith nodded wearily. The psychiatrist turned and re-entered the bedroom while Meredith went slowly along the corridor to his own room. He went in and pushed the door to behind him, walked across to an arm-chair near the foot of his bed and sank into it. The chair was facing the door and he saw with annoyance that the door had not shut. It had swung open a good six inches again. Meredith regarded it with weary disfavour. He felt so filled with lassitude that he was reluctant to get up and close it. He stayed where he was. He felt extraordinarily averse to thinking at all. For a few moments he was afraid he was going to have another of those dreadful attacks of complete inertia and he clubbed his mind into obedience to his will. He began to think. He began to think back. He sat very still. He was barely conscious of Mike, climbing with great difficulty onto his knee. The dog dropped his head down the side of his master's thigh. Together they remained immovable for a long time.

It was the behaviour of the dog which jerked Meredith back to his immediate surroundings. The man's hand was lying idly across Mike's shoulders. He was still staring into vacancy when he felt the Sealyham's head jerk up into an alert position. Mike sniffed once or twice and then Meredith distinctly felt the hackles on the little dog's back stiffening under his touch. The dog was staring towards the partly open door. The small body was tense. Meredith felt, rather than heard, the beginnings of a deep growl. More by instinct than by reason he caught the dog's muzzle in his hand and, stooping, whispered urgently into the velvety ear, urging silence. Mike obeyed. The growl was still-born, but he remained staring eagerly towards the door. Something moved along the corridor, but Meredith was unable immediately to discern what it was. Once more he spoke softly and urgently into the Sealyham's ear and, with him tucked under his arm, rose to his feet. He went softly to the door and swung it noiselessly open. He glanced out into the corridor.

He saw Yves Lauder-Treaves. He had evidently come from Second Stairs, past Meredith's door, and was moving slowly, very slowly along the corridor. The man's whole attitude bespoke a deep despondency. His head was sunk upon his chest, his left hand hung limply at his side. One finger of his right hand was hooked through the collar-loop of a mackintosh which hung down, apparently unnoticed, and trailed negligently along the floor behind him. He moved slowly and heavily, like a somnambulist. He came to his cousin's bedroom door and there halted. He stood for a while very still and then, as though he had changed his mind, he turned wearily away and came back along the passage, retracing his own footsteps.

Meredith had no wish at this moment to talk to anyone and he stepped back softly and gently pushed the door to until he judged the man to have passed. Then he glanced out again and saw Yves, still absent-mindedly dragging his mackintosh after him, disappear down Second Stairs.

It was at this moment that a sound was heard which caused Mike to jerk his head up once more and which sent a quick anticipatory thrill through his master.

It was the voice of a hound, baying from afar off.

· · · ·

There must have been nearly three dozen men who had turned out for the hunt for Virginia's slayer, but the great bulk of them had wisely been kept at a distance so as not to confuse any possible scent. They were clustered in small groups halfway along the footpath between Home Farm and the quarry. One or two of them had shotguns, the others were armed with stout sticks or cudgels. Standing slightly apart from the foremost of these groups Brown Brummy stood lumpishly, a bunch of desiccated weed suspended round his neck by a piece of string.

At the quarry itself there were only the police-sergeant, Briars and the former's two great dogs which were half-lurcher, half-hound. Each man held one of the stout leashes. The dogs appeared eager enough and cast about, their sterns waving with anticipatory pleasure. The dogs were in striking contrast to one another, one being almost jet-black, the other a pale liver colour. It was the black dog which first gave tongue. He had dropped his heavy jowls to a corner of one of the great tumbled stones which half-blocked the entry into the disused quarry, had then stood erect, gazing excitedly towards the river and then had spoken in the deep bay which had been heard by all the household up at High Perwyl.

In Martin's room Hartley Frome lifted his head and then glanced at his patient. Martin Lauder-Treaves had raised himself on his elbow and remained thus, listening with a painful intentness.

"What was that, Magnolia?" asked Finella-Lou.

"Hush, now, Miss Finella-Lou," admonished the old negress. "It was only a dawg hollerin'."

Yves Lauder-Treaves, then crossing the library, stood suddenly still, his face ashen. He buried his face in his hands. "Oh, my God," he said. "Oh, my God."

In his room John Meredith put Mike into his basket and turned to go out of the room, but the dog refused to stay put and shot between his legs into the corridor.

"Damn you," said Meredith. "Come here, Mike!" But the dog ignored him.

The Sealyham stood squarely in the centre of the corridor, his lip curled, exposing his teeth, every line of his stocky little body bespeaking a dangerous temper. He dropped his nose to the carpet and began to run along the corridor when Meredith caught him by the scruff and hoicked him up into his arms. "For God's sake, Mike!" snapped his master and put him unceremoniously back into his basket and closed the door on him. As he made his way downstairs, Meredith heard the dog scratching at the door and barking in protest.

As the big black dog gave tongue his fellow flashed to his side and then, then were they off, baying excitedly, Briars and the police-sergeant hanging onto their leads as best they could.

Once it was seen that the dogs were running on a scent, the field closed in behind with Brown Brummy, for all his years, well in the lead. The hounds ran true and clean straight to the banks of the Perwyl and turned right-handed, following the river's course. They rounded the bend due south of the castle and made good time past the old stone sluices which fed the moat. By this time the hunt was in full view from the castle windows and Finella-Lou and Magnolia at their window and Hartley Frome at his could see the great dogs leaping down the water-meadows towards the bluff.

"Good dawg, that's it, boy, fetch the swine out," roared Albert Briars, running and leaping with an excitement no less than that of the dog he followed.

"Seem to be going right past the castle," gasped the police-sergeant at the end of the other lead.

Meredith was standing across the drive from the causeway, looking down over the garden terraces, as the hunt swung into view.

"Hey, boy, what's the matter?" cried Briars suddenly, for his dog had swung unexpectedly right-handed and headed straight for the bushes which covered the face of that ten-foot bluff which terminated the water-meadows at this point.

Meredith saw, with quickened interest, that the dogs had turned at the spot where he, himself, had encountered the thing which they were undoubtedly hunting.

"Good heavens, man!" said Hartley Frome. "What are you doing? Get back into bed."

Sir Martin Lauder-Treaves was standing at the other window of his room, staring out, his face grey, the knuckles of his hands white with the grip he was maintaining on the window-sill. "Did you see that?" he gasped. "Did you see that? They've turned . . . towards . . . the house." He turned a horrified face to the psychiatrist. He was breathing rapidly, as though he'd been running. Frome could see the sweat standing out on the pallid features turned to him. "I knew they would," gasped Martin. "I knew they would! I knew they would! I knew they would!"

He broke off his parrot-repetition suddenly and his look of horror was replaced by one of incredible cunning. He almost smiled. Before Frome knew what he was about, he had turned and run across to a piece of furniture against the further wall. He jerked open the drawer and then stood staring down as though he couldn't believe his eyes. He swung round on the psychiatrist, his face livid with fear and rage.

"You've taken it!" he accused. "Damn you, you've taken it! Even *that* is to be denied me."

"I've taken nothing, Sir Martin," said Frome, his voice quite even, his tone unhurried. "Now don't you think you're behaving unreasonably? Get back to bed, like a good chap."

"My revolver," hissed Martin. "It's gone."

The psychiatrist's expression did not alter. He nodded calmly. "Yes," he said, "it's gone. Sir John Meredith took it, if you want to know. He did quite right to take it, otherwise you might have shot yourself. You see, Sir Martin," Frome went on, talking ever in that casual voice which was almost impersonal, "you've been ill for a long time. You think you've got something wrong with you but, in point of fact, you have nothing of the kind."

The sudden rage which had followed his discovery of the theft of the revolver had died out of Martin's face, leaving it dull and hopelessly apathetic.

"You," pursued the psychiatrist, "think that you're suffering from something called lycanthropy."

Martin's jaw dropped at the other's use of that forbidding word.

"I am here," Frome continued, "to assure you that this is not so."

"Why, you poor fool," said Martin Lauder-Treaves, "what do doctors know about these things? I tell you I've had all the proof I need. I'm not a fool."

"It's because you are not a fool," Hartley Frome agreed, "that your condition was capable of induction."

"I don't know what you're talking about," said the other, a world of misery indescribable in his voice. "All I know is that something's happened now which I can't bear."

"You mean the death last night of the little girl, Virginia?" said Frome quietly.

The master of High Perwyl sank down into a chair and buried his face in his hands.

"Why, man alive," said Frome cheerfully, "you had no more to do with that than I had."

The baronet raised a dreadful face to his at the words.

"You think not?" he said in a strangled voice. "You think not? You'll see," he went on. "You'll see, Master Sawbones." His voice rose to the high pitch of hysteria. "You'll see," he insisted. "I don't know how but, God help me, those dogs will run the scent to me."

Thanks to the height of the bluff above the water-meadows, it had not been possible for the watchers up at the castle to see what exactly had been taking place after the dogs had made that sudden swing to the right. Moreover, the deep baying of the big dogs seemed to have ceased.

And then something happened which sent Hartley Frome's bland reassurances crashing about his ears and brought John Meredith at a rapid sprint across the causeway. The baying of the hounds was heard again and though still muffled, there was a new note in it which was unmistakable. *The hounds were in the house and still running upon the scent!*

"What did I tell you!" screamed Martin, starting up in a frenzy to his feet. "*Now* do you believe?"

A door must have opened somewhere, for the deep voices of the dogs were louder and coming ever nearer. Meredith, standing at fault in the hall, listened intently. There was no doubt about it. The hounds were in Inner Hall. He raced across and flung open the door to see the police-sergeant and Briars leaning back with all their strength on the leashes of the two ravening hounds. Both the men looked as if they had been rolling in a muck-heap. They were smothered in filth from top to toe and great sodden patches of wet darkened their clothes about their shoulders and knees. At that moment Plum opened the door to the kitchen quarters and the three Sealyhams shot past his legs and flew at the big intruders. The noise was deafening. Men shouting, hounds baying, the small dogs snapping and snarling.

"What the hell's happening?" yelled Meredith at the top of his voice.

"Don't ask me, sir!" roared the police-sergeant. "I'm muggered if I know."

"But where have you come from? How did you get in?" bellowed Meredith.

"We come up a sockin' great drain or somethin'," was Briars' shouted reply.

At that moment one of the Sealyhams shot between the police-sergeant's feet and he fell over on his side, releasing the black hound's lead. The great dog immediately went bounding up the staircase, his deep voice heralding his coming.

"For Christ's sake get a-hold of him, someone," yelled the recumbent man and Meredith went tearing up the stairs in the wake of the big dog, only to be flung to one side as its fellow shot past him with Briars still hanging onto his lead.

"I can't 'old 'im, sir," shouted the ex-Commando and they lurched on up the stairs together.

In Martin's room, Frome had his hands full. There could be no question as to the baronet's intention. If he could, he was going out of the window and the two men staggered backwards and forwards about the room, locked in a dreadful wrestling match. When the deafening accusation of the hound's bellowing reached the door and it jarred under the sudden impact of a heavy body hurled against it, Martin's strength seemed suddenly to be redoubled. He tore himself from the other's grip and swung round towards the window. He had taken but one step when Frome flung himself full-length and tackled him low. But he was fighting with a sometime Commando and when they again grappled he felt a sudden dreadful pain in the groin and knew that it would only be a few moments before he would have to give up. He called out as loudly as he could: "I can't hold this fellow! For Christ's sake! He'll kill himself!"

He felt his grip slackening. The maddened creature in his arms was frantic and he was getting away. His grip slipped down the man's thigh to his knee, from the knee to the ankle and at that moment the door leading into the bathroom flew open and Meredith caught Martin Lauder-Treaves by the shoulder and flung an arm about his neck from behind. He caught his wrist with his other hand and locked the man's body to his own.

"All right," he said between his teeth, "I've got him, but I can't hold him for long. Now then. *Open that door!*"

THE ACCUSATION OF THE DOGS

Frome rose dizzily from the floor and regarded him incredulously. From beyond the door the noise was deafening, men shouting, hounds baying, and then the sudden thin wail of a woman's unbearable distress.

"Open the door!" repeated Frome. "Don't be a fool! Do you want this poor devil to go right over the edge?"

Meredith didn't reply immediately. He moved slightly so that Martin's face was turned towards Frome. The man had ceased struggling and Meredith wanted to be certain of one thing.

"Is he conscious?" he asked the psychiatrist urgently.

"Yes," came the reply.

"Listen, Lauder-Treaves," said Meredith, his mouth close to the other's ear, but still holding him in that iron grip. "You've got to listen to me."

John Meredith was speaking in short, sharp sentences, but he spoke with an authority which was absolute. "No time to deal with your case-history now. The immediate thing is the dogs. You think they've trailed you. They *have* run the scent to your door. But they're not trailing *you*. I swear it. We're going to open that door. You'll see for yourself. I swear it."

With a sudden movement Meredith released the other from his hold and stepped back. Martin stood swaying as though he were about to topple over.

"Now then, Major Lauder-Treaves," said Meredith quietly, "you're going to do something tougher than anything you were ever decorated for. *You, yourself, are going to open that door!*"

Martin turned and stared dully at his adviser. He looked away towards the door. He closed his eyes, took a deep breath. He squared his shoulders and moved very slowly towards the door.

"One last thing, Major Lauder-Treaves," went on Meredith quietly, "as you open that door, step to one side, because the hounds will certainly come bounding into the room, but they won't touch you, *because you are not the thing they are hunting.*"

H

Frome appeared to have little faith in what Meredith was doing. He picked up a small standard-lamp in one hand and dragged the flex out of the wall. He stood with the weapon poised in his hand and followed the baronet to the door.

Major Sir Martin Lauder-Treaves, D.S.O., put out his hand, opened the door and stood quietly to one side. It was one of the bravest things Meredith had ever witnessed.

The hounds shot into the room and then, then they checked. They ignored its three occupants and ran eagerly about the room and then raised their muzzles, quite obviously at fault. One of them ran into the corridor again and then his fellow followed.

Martin Lauder-Treaves had not moved from where he stood after opening the door. He turned unbelieving eyes to where Meredith stood smiling at him.

"You see?" said the latter gently. "I told you so."

Hartley Frome replaced the standard-lamp on its table and mopped a sweaty face with his handkerchief.

CHAPTER XXIV

DARK EXIT

ANY question as to what was then to be done with Martin Lauder-Treaves was answered for them by his sudden collapse in a dead faint.

"I can deal with this," said Frome, "if you'll give me a hand with him onto the bed."

As the two men carried the baronet across the room, Finella-Lou ran in, her face the colour of paper, demanding to be told, for pity's sake, what was happening. Meredith turned a worn face to her and said gently: "Nothing more is going to happen to Martin, my dear. From this moment on I can promise you he's going to get well."

"But these dogs and the police and . . . ?"

Meredith took her gently by the shoulders and said: "Stay

here and help Frome. Martin's only fainted. I must go. I've got things to do."

He went out of the room and closed the door behind him. In the corridor he encountered Briars and the police-sergeant, who now had their dogs firmly by the collar. In the background, Magnolia and the old butler stood watching wide-eyed.

"It's quite evident," said Meredith firmly and addressing himself largely to the bewildered sergeant of police, "that somewhere or other these dogs have switched to another scent."

The sweating policeman nodded, while attempting ineffectually to brush off his filthy, sopping uniform.

"I can't understand it, sir, it's the rummiest go I ever see."

"Oh, the house part of it's quite easy to understand," said Meredith airly. "Once into the house they'd pick up any one of half-a-dozen trails. There are three Sealyhams belonging to the house and my own dog as well. No," he went on, in a more speculative tone of voice, "what I'm interested in is how you got into the house from the water-meadows."

"I'd like you to have a look, Sir John," said Briars quietly.

"Just what I was going to suggest," agreed Meredith. "Take me back over the trail exactly as you followed it."

The two half-bred hounds also showed that they thought retracing the trail was a good idea, their instinct, once at fault, being to cast back in search of a fresh scent.

Meredith followed the two men along the corridor and down Second Stairs. They crossed Inner Hall, passed the kitchen quarters, went through the library and into the north-east gallery. The two dogs lunged ahead at the end of their leashes, entered and crossed, without pause, Yves' big circular study to the door in the far wall. Here they swung down narrowing stone steps which were broken half-way down their flight by the enormous timbers of an ancient trap-door.

"This was shut when we came up, sir," Briars remarked.

"How did you get up, then?" asked Meredith.

"It was dropped down but unbolted," replied Sergeant-Major Briars, "and as them dogs seemed crazy to go up, we just give it a push."

"I see."

Below the trap-door the stairs continued, debouching finally from their flanking walls into a gloomy chamber of the same floor proportions as the room above, but not more than seven feet in height. This, presumably, was the lumber-room to which, Meredith recalled, Yves had once referred. It had, undoubtedly, at one time in the dim past, been a prison or dungeon.

It was filled with the accumulated rubbish of years. Broken pieces of furniture, old garden chairs and tables, discarded books piled carelessly against the walls from which, at intervals, depended great rusty chains, terminating in dull, iron collars. There was another reminder of the grim past as Meredith saw at once. Standing by itself was an enormous iron spit. Despite the urgency of the moment he was obliged to pause beside this and stare down at it. On this, he had no doubt, Rhodri Mawr had died so horribly all those long centuries ago and from these few pieces of corroded and time-worn iron had sprung the horror which had so recently driven a man almost to the point of madness and death. Meredith shuddered. He did not believe in bogies or family curses, but this queer freak of fate displayed a terrifying coincidence.

"This way, sir," said Briars' voice at his elbow, and wrenched him back to the immediate present.

Standing near the wall to their right was a huge piece of discarded furniture. It was a massive *armoire* of rotting and worm-eaten Spanish oak. It was of colossal proportions and stood nearly seven feet from the floor. It was black and rotten with age and looked vaguely sinister.

"We pops behind the wardrobe, sir," said Briars, speaking in the voice of sanity.

Meredith discovered then that this gargantuan piece of furniture was not flush with the wall, but that it stood away from it at one end about eighteen inches. The hounds took this strange exit in their stride, for an exit it proved to be. Behind the *armoire* was a small recessed doorway, the rough-hewn timbers which guarded it now flung back upon crazy hinges against the further wall.

"One of them secret passages or somethin', sir," said Briars, but the police-sergeant shook his head.

"May 'ave been used as one sometime," he said disdainfully, "but a lot of these old 'ouses, the ones as is really old, 'ave these things. Original-like they was drains."

"Quite right," nodded Meredith.

"Arh," nodded the country policeman. "I seen another like this in my time. Over at what's left of the Old Priory at Stayley."

Meredith hesitated, peering down the gloomy tunnel which stretched away under the moat from where they stood. "I don't think it's necessary to go back the same way," he said. "It comes out, I suppose, in the bluff down at the bottom by the river?"

"That's right, sir," said Briars. "This chap and me couldn't see what the dogs was getting at at all when they tried to get in. There must a-been ten yards thick of brambles as 'ad grown over the mouth of it. 'Owever, when we saw that the dogs really wanted to go through we call up the other chaps and they beat the 'ole bloody lot flat. And there it was, large as life."

"I see," said Meredith and in that moment saw the complete truth.

CHAPTER XXV

THE KILL

HALF-AN-HOUR had gone by. During those thirty minutes a bewildered and dishevelled representative of the County Police had departed with his dogs, Briars, at Meredith's request, returning to the castle. The ex-Commando had accompanied the police-sergeant back to the water-meadows and there, again at Meredith's suggestion, had dismissed the estate employees who had turned out for the abortive hunt. Meanwhile, Meredith himself had gone upstairs to Sir Martin's room, where he found the baronet round from his faint and sitting up in bed holding his wife's hand. With an occasional word interjected by Hartley Frome in support, John Meredith then had a straight talk with the master of High Perwyl, during which Finella-Lou's eyes grew round with horrified wonder while her husband's face gradually darkened with anger.

"Can you prove all this?" he asked in a quietly dangerous voice when Meredith had ceased speaking.

John shook his head. "No, not yet. *But*, leaving out the explanation which, for so long, you have been induced to believe, it *must* have happened as I deduce. I'm not suggesting that I have as yet got all the details filled in, but the broad outline of the thing is perfectly clear. I realise," he went on after a pause, "that this is a pretty frightful thing for you to swallow, but, if you'll look at it reasonably, you'll realise that it is far less unpleasant than what you have been imagining. Frome, I know, will confirm what I say and, furthermore, that you are completely sane and have been suffering from a delusion which you now see to have no foundation in fact."

Husband and wife regarded each other in silence and then Finella-Lou put up a hand and said unsteadily: "My poor sweet, you are a silly goop, aren't you?"

The very inadequacy of the homely words added enormous poignancy to the remark and Frome and Meredith instinctively turned away from the radiance that was between Martin and his wife.

It was a few minutes after this that Meredith collected Albert Briars from where he was waiting in Great Hall. He had made some effort to clean himself up a bit, but still betrayed much evidence of his crawl through the centuries-old drain.

"Hello, Briars," said Meredith quietly. "I want you to help me out with something, but I want to ask you something beforehand. I want you to behave yourself."

The other glanced at him enquiringly. "I don't understand, sir."

"I want you," Meredith explained, "just to listen *and do nothing else.*"

The ghost of his normally wide grin twitched the man's

firm mouth momentarily as he nodded and said: "Don't sound too difficult."

"You may find it so," Meredith warned.

They made their way side by side through the house until they arrived at Yves' big study in the old keep. It was empty and Meredith went across to the staircase beyond the further door and called up it.

"Hello! Are you there, Lauder-Treaves?"

The door above their heads was heard to open and Yves' voice queried: "Who's that?"

"Meredith. Could you come down a moment? I've got Briars here and I think between the two of you, I shall be able to work out something that will materially help your cousin."

"Yes, of course," replied Yves and descended the winding stone stairs from his bedroom.

He looked white and exhausted, like a man after a long illness. He followed Meredith slowly into his study and quietly closed the door behind him.

"I don't quite see," he said, "what I can do. You know as well as I do what's the matter with old Martin."

"Excuse me, sir, but what's this got to do with the Major?" put in Briars. "Is he took bad?"

"Sir Martin," said Meredith quietly, "has been a sick man for quite a while now."

"That's right," agreed Briars sombrely. "Not been himself at all."

"Well, we're going to put that right," Meredith assured him. He turned to Yves and added: "Shall we sit down?"

Yves Lauder-Treaves looked vaguely round him and motioned to two chairs at the corners of one of the big tables at which he was accustomed to write. The other two men moved to these and sat down. Briars' honest face was creased in worry and enquiry. Meredith was quite impassive. Yves sank down into a chair which faced them at the other side of the big table.

"Now then," said Meredith quietly and addressing himself

pointedly to the ex-Commando, "I want you fully to understand what exactly has been taking place."

"Very good, sir," replied Briars, much as he might have done in company-office.

"You won't find it easy to take in," Meredith went on, "because the whole thing involves the elements of a fairy-tale—a wicked fairy-tale."

"You mean, sir," said Briars scratching his head, "the sort of stuff I seen in pantomimes when I was a nipper?"

"I'm afraid not," said Meredith seriously, "but I expect you will have heard of family curses, you know, the sort of dreadful secret which is supposed to be passed down from father to son, usually in very old families with a long and bloody history?"

Sergeant-Major Briars looked steadily at Meredith. "Well, I have heard tell of 'em, sir, but I never thought there was much to it."

"There isn't," said Meredith and Yves stirred uneasily in his chair.

"Well, I don't see," Briars began, when he was cut short by Yves Lauder-Treaves leaning forward and saying: "Look, Meredith, I can't conceive of what your motive is but, damn it, do we have to air all this in front of"—he hesitated suddenly and Meredith knew instinctively that he was about to say "in front of a servant"—"in front of Briars?" Yves ended.

"I think it's very important that it should be given an airing and Sergeant-Major Briars is just the man to infuse into the whole unpleasant business the kindly wind of sanity."

Briars moved impatiently. "Look, gentlemen," he said, "so far I've not understood a blinkin' word."

"Right," said Meredith, "now listen. First of all I'll have to teach you a little of the Lauder-Treaves' history and then introduce you to the esoteric subject of lycanthropy."

Briars said nothing and Meredith went ahead and outlined for him the story of what had happened at High Perwyl centuries ago, the tale of the curse of Rhodri Mawr, the gist of Ranulf's chronicle and finally embarked on a matter-of-fact discursion on the whole subject and belief of werewolfery.

Meredith talked for the best part of half-an-hour, during which he carefully watched the incredulous but intelligent face of the man to whom he was only partly addressing himself. During Meredith's long recital, Yves leaned back in his chair, one elbow resting on its arm, his hand over his eyes.

Briars took a deep breath and leaned forward, his forearms on his knees, the fingers of both hands loosely interlaced. "I've listened as you tell me, Sir John," he said soberly, "and though it seems a bit of a do, I suppose as I've got to take your word for it. But what I *don't* understand," he went on vehemently, "is that a man like the Major, a man as I've served with and know . . . like me own brother, if I had one, could have believed in all this 'ere tommy-rot. It don't seem *natural* to him, somehow. I know the Major and he's not balmy. I've served with him and I *know*. He's sensitive, I know that, but I'd have sworn he hadn't got a screw loose. Why should a man like that believe all that bloody nonsense?"

Meredith smiled at the bewildered man and then asked: "What was that last thing you said?"

Briars looked at him in astonished enquiry. "The last thing I said, sir? I said I couldn't understand why a chap like the Major as is, to my personal knowledge, absolutely sound right through should believe all this stuff."

"Precisely," said Meredith quietly, "your common sense, Sergeant-Major, has put its finger on the crux of the whole beastly puzzle. Why did Sir Martin believe in this rotten business? What induced a comparatively normal man to admit even of the possibility of such a thing? Because," Meredith went on, his voice suddenly cold and judicial, "because he was encouraged to believe it, because it was deliberately inculcated in him."

Briars frowned. "You mean, sir," he asked, "that someone deliberately did something with the idea of making the Major think this?"

"Yes," said Meredith.

The word dropped into the ensuing silence like a pebble into a pond. That one word was both a statement and an accusation and the ripples of disbelief and fear spread through that vast circular room like something tangible.

"But . . . but who would have done such a thing?" asked Albert Briars, his big hands clenched into fists.

"He did," said Meredith quietly and nodded at the white-faced man across the table.

Briars stared for a long time at his informant's face. He searched Meredith's eyes with his own, as though he were incredulous of what had been suggested. Then, very slowly, he turned his head and looked at the other occupant of the room and finally his eyes narrowed, much as does a fighter's when the gong has gone and he steps out from his corner into the ring. He said nothing.

"I've watched this coming, Meredith " said Yves Lauder-Treaves, a small contemptuous smile lifting one corner of his expressive mouth, "during your learned discourse to our friend here." He allowed his glance to move to Briars' face, but what he saw there wiped the superior little smile from his own. "You know, Briars, why Sir John came down to High Perwyl, don't you?"

"He wasn't well," replied Briars, hardly moving his lips.

"Exactly," nodded Yves Lauder-Treaves with apparent ease, "he wasn't well. He came down here for rest and quiet, as he was a neurotic. It would appear that we have two pathological cases at High Perwyl now, my unfortunate cousin and our friend here."

Meredith laughed. "Quite neat," he said indulgently, "but not very effective."

"Perhaps you'd be good enough to tell me," Yves went on, "how exactly I induced this belief in Martin?"

Meredith hesitated. "I can *prove* very little," he admitted, "but I can deduce a great deal."

Yves gave a short hard laugh. "Really, this is too puerile," he scoffed. "I don't know why I have the patience to sit and listen to you. Deduction! Another word for guessing, the bad guessing of a man broken down mentally and in general health, fumbling around with the symptoms of yet another neurotic. Rather a case of the blind leading the blind?" he ended, his voice acid with sarcasm.

"Shut up, you!" barked Sergeant-Major Briars suddenly. "I still don't know what to believe and what not to believe, but you let the Brigadier have his say. All right, sir, you carry on."

"Thank you, Sergeant-Major," said Brigadier Sir John Meredith mildly. "Well, to continue with my guess-work, I would ask you what you, yourself, think induced in your cousin the kind of—er—coma in which we found him the other night?"

"My *dear* Meredith!" exclaimed the other in a tone of exasperation. "I think you, yourself, must be out of your mind. How should I know?"

"Well, let's put it this way," said Meredith patiently. "Leaving out all question of this lycanthropy nonsense, what cause would you think was consistent with the condition in which we found him?"

"Knowing Master Martin's habits recently," replied Yves brutally, "I should say he was tight."

"A drunken stupor?" echoed Meredith. "It could be, of course. But it could also be that his condition was drug-induced."

"It's quite possible," agreed Yves Lauder-Treaves disdainfully, "but it's not very likely, is it? I'm not a doctor, so I wouldn't know."

"It's extremely likely," nodded John Meredith quietly, "and I put it to you that the drug was administered to him by you."

"And where would I get such a drug?"

"I'm not sure," admitted Meredith, "but I could guess."

"Guess!" snarled Yves, suddenly appearing to lose his temper and bringing his hand down with a slam on the table in front of him. "God give me patience!" he went on, his face a blaze of anger. "God give me patience to suffer fools gladly!"

Hitherto Meredith had conducted the interview in an eminently reasonable, not to say amiable, manner but, at the other's outburst, a new quality was infused into the business. Meredith was tired, desperately tired, and at Yves' disdainful shout a spot of anger appeared in either cheek. He said nothing for a moment, but when he did his voice rasped.

"You insolent, wicked swine!"

Yves sank backwards in his chair as though the words and the glance which accompanied them had been a physical blow.

Albert Briars nodded shortly. "Now we're getting some place," he said with satisfaction.

"I don't know," said Meredith, a dangerous edge to his voice, "just how your cousin would like this handled, because I have not yet had time fully to consult him."

"Fully?" echoed Yves. "Then you've. . . ."

John Meredith nodded. "Yes, I've told him. I saw no reason why he should suffer any longer, once, that is, that I was certain in my own mind."

"Why you impertinent, interfering . . ." Lauder-Treaves began when Sergeant-Major Briars came suddenly to his feet and the other broke off. There could be no mistaking the menace in the ex-Commando's whole manner.

"Sit down, Sergeant-Major," snapped Meredith in a parade-ground voice. "I warned you you'd have to behave."

The square, stocky figure sank reluctantly back into its chair.

"Now then," said Meredith, addressing himself to Yves. "You're going to keep quiet and I'm going to tell you what you did. One or two of my guesses, as you call them, may be wrong, but the general structure of the thing is perfectly clear. The whole thing starts a good many years ago, when you and your cousin were boys living here at High Perwyl. Your parents were dead and you had been brought here to live on the charity of your uncle."

Watching him, Meredith saw the other wince at the use of the word charity and went on inexorably: "Martin was a sensitive little boy, whose mother had just died and whose father took little notice of him. You and your cousin were much together. He was fond of you and almost entirely dependent on you for companionship. That fondness for you has continued until about an hour ago, when I told him the truth."

Meredith paused to allow the words to sink in. "I can't give you the details because I don't know them, but here we have two lonely little boys thrown much together and sharing everything. As soon as you could read, you explored the vast possibilities of the library and you became acquainted with the legend with which your family was associated. It was a thrilling discovery and one which made a great impression on both your young minds. I expect there was a measure of fear, in fact I know there was a considerable measure of fear in both of you. It was just the kind of bogy-story to impress itself on imaginative children of your type. You grew up together and, as the years passed, the thing faded into the background, but it remained in the background as a looming thing in which you did not believe, but did not actively disbelieve. What you, yourself, said to me one day along those lines was the truth. You grew up together and you went to school together and you went to the University together and in every single thing, in your studies and at games, Martin excelled, and you tagged along behind as the younger and less brilliant cousin. You have never been able to take a rebuff or accept a correction. Your whole history shows that. You wrote a most promising novel and because its successor did not get the notices you considered it deserved, you threw away your talent in a pet. You went on the stage, where you had some measure of success. Again, at the first whiff of criticism, you chucked it, though, heaven knows, I could testify to the brilliance of your histrionic ability, for you have most successfully smiled and smiled and been a villain. You hated Martin because you were jealous of him. As I say, invariably he excelled and you couldn't bear it. But most of all, he was the man who owned High Perwyl, which is and has been the overruling passion of your life.

When the war came you were not called up into the services because of your weak heart and your cousin's going left you with an almost completely free hand here at Perwyl. His return necessarily curbed your activities, but you had had a taste of what mastery of High Perwyl would mean, the very real joy of caring for it which is probably the best thing in your entire make-up. You might even have been all right had your cousin agreed to employ you as his bailiff, for you would still have had the care of the estate which you genuinely love, but Martin wouldn't consider you and you know why. Your own record of inconsistency and change, of easy discouragement and petulance was not that of the man to whom Martin cared so largely to entrust the estate. Your cousin did more than show that reluctance, he underlined it by bringing back with him Sergeant-Major Briars, here, to train for the job. Having tasted the, to you, overwhelming pleasure of absolute authority, you could not resign yourself merely to living here on the charity which your cousin extended to you with the natural generosity which is his. What prompted you to the beastly thing you had recourse to I can't be sure but, I should imagine, that it was your cousin's jittery condition when he came out of hospital after being so badly knocked about. You realised, you must have realised, that he was slightly off his balance and that here was your opportunity. What an opportunity, what a dirty, filthy, rotten opportunity! But, by God, you took it!"

Yves Lauder-Treaves was leaning back in his chair, white-faced and sweating. His eyes were closed as he listened to the indictment, but he shook his head from side to side as though not only in negation but also in pain.

"It's not true," he said hoarsely. "It's not true. It started as a joke."

"A joke?" snarled Meredith.

"Yes, yes, a joke," replied the other. "I never meant . . ."

"Great God, what kind of a man are you?" wondered Meredith aloud.

"I only thought . . . I didn't at first. . . ."

"I see," said Meredith softly. "The thing grew on you, did it? You were surprised at your own success—was that it?" He paused, looking at the other in genuine disgust. "You make me sick to breathe the same air with you," he commented.

"How did this bastard do it?" asked Briars dangerously, his eyes never leaving Yves Lauder-Treaves' face.

"That's what I can't be sure of, Briars," replied Meredith, "but I can guess. You know that the Major's been taking medicine at night?"

"Yes, for his nerves, or something."

"Yes, bromide. Well, hydro-bromide has a pretty nasty taste and you usually swill it down at a gulp. I haven't the least doubt this man doped that bromide. I'd further hazard the guess as to where he got his dope from. Dr. Blackie here is a fuddled, tired, careless old man. I'll bet you, when we check up with him, he'll find that some of his dangerous drugs are missing. So I'm right?"

Meredith suddenly barked the question as he saw the fascinated expression in Yves' eyes.

"It had to be that," nodded Meredith, "but I'm glad I guessed right. Hartley Frome suggests that it was probably hyoscine. Was it?"

Yves made no reply and Meredith continued: "Well, we don't need to bother, we can check that later. You must remember that the curse was supposed not to take effect until after the heir's thirtieth birthday. Sir Martin's birthday was about ten weeks ago, but before that he had been reminded of that uncomfortable date by your re-writing of the family history. Maybe you embarked on that project solely with the object I have suggested? Anyway, it doesn't matter, you succeeded in preparing your cousin's mind for the reception of the poison which you intended to instil. Let's look at it from his point of view. On several occasions he woke feeling jaded and listless and remembering nothing of the night and woke to find himself naked. You will remember, Briars, that it is conditional on the man's being naked for the change to the beast-shape to take place."

Briars nodded shortly, impatiently. When he spoke, his voice was a growl. "I don't give a bloody hoot how this swine did it. I'm only interested in the fact that he done it." He turned his smouldering glance upon Yves. "I'm going to ask you a question now," he said. "Did you own the dog as has been runnin' loose of nights?"

Yves made no answer. He closed his eyes against that searing stare which the other directed at him.

"I can answer that one," said Meredith quietly. "Yes, he had a dog."

"Where is it now?" growled Briars.

"Almost certainly dead," replied Meredith, "and I'd bet a million to a china orange that its body's in the moat."

There was a long silence, during which Albert Briar's honest mind churned away at the staggering facts to which he had been made privy. At last he raised his head from his absorption and stood up. The threat and menace which had informed his whole attitude a short while ago was now gone. He stood lumpishly, regarding the white-faced man across the table with an expression faintly puzzled.

"I've sat here," he said quietly and calmly, "listenin' to what the brigadier has had to say. Though I've taken it all in, it still don't make sense to me. I'm just an ordinary sort of chap and all this monkey-shine with drugs and old supers . . . supersti . . . beliefs don't ring a bell. It seems nuts to me, but I gotter accept what the brigadier here has said and I'll tell you for why. Because he's a gentleman as makes sense, even out of nonsense. As I say," he went on, still in this reasonable tone of voice, "as I say, the why and wherefore and how is a fair puzzle. What sticks in me mind, Mr. Yves, is that you done it. The Major's as fine a bloke as I ever want to meet and it seems to me that you done worse than just take a stick and beat him over the head and kill him, as a decent man kills his enemy. You done somethin' much worse, somethin' horrible. You deliberately tried to murder his mind. I think it's the dirtiest thing I ever heard and fit only for a Jerry."

Meredith watched Yves Lauder-Treaves' face intently. Under the accusation of his own indictment the man had seemed to wilt, but the lash in the quietly accusing voice of the sometime Sergeant-Major seemed to make him disintegrate. The wet mouth in the pallid face hung slightly open. He seemed to be only semi-conscious. He appeared to have lost all shape and lolled in his chair like a sack of coals. It was not a pretty sight.

"But there's another thing," Briars' quiet voice went on. "Thanks to the brigadier, here, you didn't succeed with the Major, but you done fine with my Susan's Ginnie."

"No! No!" gasped Yves, his eyes starting from his head and then Albert Briars' slowly smouldering rage burst into flame.

"By Christ, you did! You wicked, murderin' swine!" he roared and flung himself forward to the table, reached across it and caught the other by the front of his jacket and yanked him up to his feet. "You bloody swine!" he shouted shaking the other as a terrier shakes a rat.

"Watch what you're doing, Briars!" snapped Meredith, coming to his feet. "The man can't stand that sort of thing."

"Can't 'e!" snarled the ex-Commando, dragging Yves towards him half across the table, "by Christ, he's goin' to stand a bit more before I'm through with him. You killed my Susan's Ginnie, you dirty bastard, just so sure as if you torn her throat out yourself!"

Briars slowly raised one leg-of-mutton fist and drew his arm back for the blow. Meredith saw it coming and flung himself forward and caught his arm and held it. For a long moment the group swung this way and that and then, strong as he was, Briars was no longer able to maintain the weight on his other arm. It was suddenly, unaccountably, increased. He released the front of Yves' jacket and the man slumped untidily across the big table. Then, very slowly, he began to slip down. He fell between the table and his overturned chair.

"That'll do, Sergeant-Major," said Meredith quietly and saw the red glare die out of the other man's eyes.

"So 'elp me," said Briars dazedly, "another moment and I'd 'ave done for the swine."

Meredith walked round the table and knelt by Yves Lauder-Treaves. He stared impassively for a moment at the clammy face and the figure which proclaimed complete collapse. He took the thin wrist in firm fingers and remained still, feeling with sensitive finger-tips for something he did not expect to find. Presently he raised his head and looked across the table at Briars.

"This man," he said quietly, "is dead."

CHAPTER XXVI

MEREDITH EXPLAINS

It was not until after dinner that night that Meredith and his host and hostess were able to have a quiet hour to themselves in which finally to thrash out the details of the thing which was now past. Meredith had done some quick thinking when he discovered that Yves was dead. The whole thing was nicely wrapped up in a neat parcel. Briars was not likely to talk and Dr. Blackie had swallowed Meredith's story, hook, line and sinker.

"He's been off-colour ever since I've been down here," Meredith had suggested. "And with all the excitement and the shock of young Virginia's death, I suppose he couldn't stand up to it. Though why the devil he went and swiped all that hyoscine from you to dose himself with, God alone knows."

"I'll never understand that," the old doctor had replied, shaking his head. "Why couldn't he have just come to me, instead of practising fool-medicine on himself?"

"Between you and me and the gatepost, doctor," Meredith had said quietly, "the less said about that the better. Don't you agree?"

"Indeed, yes."

"Sir Martin doesn't want any fluff about this or any

enquiry, and I'm sure you don't. You were his physician in attendance. You knew that he suffered from a weak heart. There's no question about the cause of death. So I suppose you'll be prepared to sign a death certificate?"

"Certainly," old Blackie had replied with evident relief, "there's no mystery to it. The boy *had* a heart and I shall say so. Don't want any fuss with young Martin in his present condition."

"I couldn't agree more."

And so the thing was accomplished.

It was with very mixed feelings that Meredith, Martin and Finella-Lou waited for Plum to leave the drawing-room after serving the coffee that night.

"Well," said Sir Martin, dropping the word suddenly into a pregnant silence.

John Meredith leaned back in his chair and regarded the two young people who sat, side by side, facing him on the Knole sofa. He noticed with pleasure that they were holding hands.

"Well," he said, "I had thought at first that it was a pity Hartley Frome couldn't stay to confirm anything I may say, but I don't think it would really have been necessary, because I don't propose dealing with the obsessionist side of this business. That's done with and dead with its originator. I feel first of all that I ought to apologise to you, Martin, for not cottoning on to this thing sooner. But the devilish beauty of it was that no one in his normal sane senses would have credited it for a moment. It was only when I had sure knowledge that certain phenomena could not be explained scientifically that I was in a position to know that there was a case to deal with at all."

"I can't see that you should blame yourself in the least," said Martin calmly. "After all, *I* was the bloody fool."

"That's as may be," replied Meredith heavily, "but I blame myself terribly for not getting after that brute of a dog sooner. Had I done so, young Ginnie would be alive today."

He paused momentarily and drew at his cigarette, frowning through the smoke which he exhaled. "I'd like you, if you would, Martin, to describe the symptoms which led you to suppose that you were suffering from lycanthropy."

"It all sounds so damn silly now," said Martin shyly and smiled at the pressure of his wife's fingers. "However, for what it's worth, here it is. I never had, that is until recently, any real belief in the possibility of the thing but, not very long ago, Yves started on the family history. I went into his office one day and found him engaged upon it. At his side he had open the Stayley document. I hadn't seen the thing since I was about ten and Yves gave it to me to read again."

"Preparing the ground," nodded Meredith.

"Yes," said Martin, "it . . . it sort of brought it all back again. I mean the sort of half-baked terror which we'd known as kids and I began to worry about the approach of my thirtieth birthday. Seems damn stupid, doesn't it?" he ended rather miserably.

"It doesn't sound stupid at all," John assured him, "it's most interesting. Do go on."

"Well, I'd been a bit under the weather about that time. My wound was hurting me again and making me nervy and irritable. That's why I got old Blackie to give me that bromide of his. And then, quite suddenly, the thing came upon me out of the blue."

"Yes, this is what interests me," said Meredith. "How on earth did he get at you when you were still sleeping in Finella-Lou's room?"

Martin shook his head. "He didn't. The cunning . . ." He broke off, his mouth twitching with reminiscent anger. "He must have planned the thing like a campaign," Martin went on. "Every so often he and I used to go over the estate accounts together and it was invariably after dinner. It was Yves' own suggestion and I saw no reason not to fall in with his wishes. It meant that we worked late and so as not to disturb Finella-Lou I used, on those nights, to sleep in my dressing-room."

"And I suppose that you woke up feeling pretty muzzy and without your pyjamas on?"

"Yes."

Young Lauder-Treaves stared blankly into the bleak and recent past.

"I didn't attach much importance to it the first time. We'd had a couple of whiskies while we'd been working and I thought maybe mine had been a bit stiff. As for the pyjamas, well, I supposed I'd got too hot and chucked them off. Then it happened again and this time I came-to lying on the floor."

"You recall nothing of how you got there?"

The other shook his head. "No," he said, "but then the hyoscine would explain that, wouldn't it. I mean, even if I had been semi-conscious of what was happening to me, I wouldn't remember it afterwards?"

"Yes, that's quite right," Meredith agreed. "It's the stuff they use for twilight-sleep."

"Anyway, after it had happened three times I began to get scared and then something else happened, something that damn nearly sent me off my rocker. I came to after one of these goes and found that I stank." He broke off and banged one fist into the palm of the other hand. "Again I suppose the thing sounds ridiculous but . . ."

"I smelt it too," said Meredith. "I know what it was like."

"But how the hell did he do it?" asked Martin.

"The time I found you, the night that dog of his went for me, the windows of your room were closed and the electric-fire was full on. I have no doubt whatsoever that you had been wrapped in the brute's blanket or rug or what, ever it had to sleep on and with the full blaze of the fire-you had been simply saturated in the stink."

"My poor darling," said Finella-Lou. "How utterly vile."

"You must remember," said Meredith, "that's Yves' mother was Spanish. The streak of cruelty which runs right through the whole of this beastly affair is quite un-English. It's far too refined and subtle for our direct characteristics. I suppose," he went on, "that by this time your fear had crystallised?"

"Yes," replied the master of High Perwyl, "I was really badly scared. Everything fitted in so perfectly, but the thing that seemed to confirm it in my own mind was Yves' own attitude."

"I don't understand, darling," Finella-Lou interjected.

"I hardly like to tell you," replied her husband unhappily, "it seems so . . . Anyway, what really clinched matters in my mind was the fact that Yves appeared also to be frightened."

"You mean," said Meredith, leaning forward and frowning, "that he allowed you to see that he was afraid for you, is that it?"

"Yes," said Martin and there was silence between them as they contemplated the devilish deceit which had characterised Yves' horrible campaign.

"You see, my sweet," Martin went on and turning to his wife, "when I . . . when I really thought I had this . . . this thing I went and mugged up all I could find about it and . . ."

"And you found that the sufferer was reputed to turn upon those nearest and dearest to him," ended Meredith for him. "I understood that fairly early on but, of course, I had no reason to suppose that the thing was not just a pure obsession in you."

"I got to the point where I was so afraid of . . . of doing anything to Finella-Lou that . . . that I tried handcuffing myself to a chair at night."

"Oh, Martin, dearest!" wailed the girl.

"Yes, it was bloody."

Meredith nodded. "There's not a great deal more to explain now," he said. "I don't suppose we shall ever know where your cousin got the dog from, but it must have been a very well-trained Alsatian. I saw it very briefly, you remember, one night."

"I don't understand why it should have gone for you, though," put in Finella-Lou.

"Simple, really," said Meredith. "Yves kept the brute in the old dungeon which you use as a lumber-room. That, from his point of view, had two advantages: it was in a part of the house where no one ever went and, indeed, could not go without his knowledge and it had an exit which enabled the brute to go in and out without being observed."

"But how did he control the damned thing?" asked Martin.

"Oh, it's fairly easy to imagine, if you think it out. He only let the dog out at night, long after everyone had gone to bed. I know that for a little while, when he first got it, he would take it out himself. Alsatians, as you know, are remarkably sagacious dogs and your cousin, in any case, had an extraordinary way with animals."

"But how," asked Finella-Lou, "when he let it out alone, could he ensure its returning when he wanted it to?"

"With this," said Meredith and took a small whistle from his pocket.

"But we'd have heard it when he blew it," the girl protested.

"Think so?" said Meredith. "Watch. Watch Mike."

The Sealyham was lying on the hearthrug, supine and with his eyes closed. Meredith put the whistle to his lips and blew. To all intents and purposes, as far as the three human beings were concerned, not a sound came out. The effect on the dog was electric. He jumped to his feet immediately, ears pricked, staring enquiringly at his master.

"Too easy, really," said Meredith, "it's one of those soundless dog-whistles. I found it in the drawer of his desk. I knew it had to exist. It produces a note too high in the scale for the human ear to detect, but is distinctly audible to all animals. You could get them at any dog shop before the war. The real detective in the whole of this business, if I'd had the sense to realise it, was that little chap there. Mike knew when Yves was calling his dog back and it worried him. Your own dogs heard it as well and raised Cain, if you remember, the night Mike had his fight down by the bluff. Incidentally, he gave us another pointer that night. When Yves attempted to doctor him, he growled at him. I have no doubt your cousin had just handled his dog on its return and Mike would smell it on his hands. Yves' big brute went for Mike for the same reason as he went for me, because we both stood near the entrance to the old disused drain which was his means of entry to the castle. In some ways it was for the same reason that he savaged and killed that child. I have no doubt that Yves schooled him pretty rigorously. Maybe if he didn't come as soon as he was whistled for he got a hiding and, in consequence, when he heard the whistle he came at once. Your cousin let the brute out at night quite deliberately that it might establish the fact that a wolf-like thing was loose on the estate by night. He reckoned that sooner or later you would get to hear of it and that it would be, quite literally, one more nail in your coffin. On the night that Virginia was killed, she was coming, as you know, to bring a birthday present up here."

The girl put her hands over her face, but Meredith pointedly ignored the gesture and went quietly on.

"When she reached the corner of the footpath near the quarry she must have heard the brute moving and gone to see what it was. The entry to the quarry is very narrow and it was that fact which occasioned her death. The dog must have been inside the quarry when he heard his master's whistle. Ginnie must have been standing between him and his means of exit. You both know what the child was like with animals. It didn't matter to her how big the dog was or how fierce it looked. She just walked up to it and put her arms round it. Probably that is what she did with this brute of your cousin's and the dog, frantic that it would not be able to get back when it was called, just snapped blindly. It was a big dog and Ginnie was a little girl. It killed her."

Again there was silence in the room. Meredith stubbed out his cigarette and lit a fresh one. Finella-Lou rose and mixed two whiskies-and-soda. She put a glass into Meredith's hand and handed the other to her husband.

"What about you, darling?" asked Martin, accepting it.

"I only want a sip," she replied, "I'll have some out of your glass."

"How in God's name," wondered Martin, "was the trail laid to my door when that police-chap and his dogs came barging into the house?"

MEREDITH EXPLAINS

"Again it was Mike who really rumbled it," said Meredith. "I actually saw Yves doing it. He came mouching along the corridor, dragging his mackintosh behind him. Folded inside that mackintosh *must* have been the dog's blanket, or a sack or whatever it was it slept on. Even after the death of little Virginia he couldn't resist going on. By that time, I should imagine, the thing itself fascinated him."

"My God!" said Martin breathlessly. "But how did you know it was Yves?"

"I saw him," said Meredith.

"No, I mean, how did you come to suspect Yves?"

"Well, once suspicion was aroused," John replied, "the field was a pretty narrow one, but I had caught him out in a deliberate lie."

He then told them of the episode of the brandy and how, the following day, Plum had given the show away.

"At the time I didn't attach all that importance to it," Meredith explained. "It didn't seem worth bothering about, but when I was satisfied that certain things could not have been achieved by you, wittingly or unwittingly, then it gave me furiously to think. While I was downstairs in the hall, waiting for that brandy-and-soda, your precious cousin slipped up to your room and beat hell out of you with a stick so as to reproduce the wound which I had just informed him I had inflicted on his blasted dog. At the same time, since he knew that I was coming up to have a look at you, he removed the dog-blanket in which you had undoubtedly been wrapped."

Finella-Lou shook her head and frowning closed her eyes momentarily. Then she looked across at Meredith and said, her voice very low: "You know, John, it's almost impossible to believe that . . . that someone who's been so close to one as Yves could have done this."

"He did it all right," said Meredith grimly. "I think," he went on, after a pause, "that there was one person on the estate who had some idea that something was up, but, of course, he hadn't the inside knowledge to add two and two together. That was that queer cuss of yours, Brown Brummy.

I went down and saw him this afternoon and got a bit more out of him. He knew that dog belonged to Yves. He'd seen them together, presumably when Yves was training the brute, and the little man was scared. He's quite conversant with your family legend. I suppose the thing has been handed down among the country-folk here for generations and he was worried. He did say one very significant thing to me, however, on a former occasion. He told me that the brute hadn't got a limp."

Martin looked up. "And I have?"

"Precisely," said John, "it was a sort of reassurance. Well that," he added slowly, "is about all I can tell you except . . ."

"Except?" echoed Martin.

"Except perhaps the one thing which might clinch matters in your own mind. I've wondered whether I'd tell you this, or not, but I think you ought to know. I'm afraid you'll receive this information with very mixed feelings."

"My dear John," said Martin, smiling rather ruefully. "I've got to the stage where any further shocks would just bounce off me."

"I hope so," said Meredith, looking at him rather whimsically, "as there never was any occasion for you to be worried by this family curse business, because it was the Lauder-Treaves' family which was reputed to be affected."

Martin frowned at him. "But that doesn't make sense," he said. "I know it was my family."

John shook his head. "The Lauder-Treaves' family, yes," he agreed, "but not yours."

The two young people looked at him as though he had taken leave of his senses, but they saw that he was regarding them with an expression which appeared to be quite sane, if somewhat apologetic.

"The people on whom Rhodri Mawr's curse was supposed to fall were the lineal descendants of the old Breton family who came from Tréves and who wrote themselves Loup de Tréves. The family later adapted its name to the present one. You, Martin," said Meredith, "have none of that blood in you at all. I got a half-glimmer of the truth one day when I was turning over some of the documents in your cousin's study. I remember, now, that he looked inexplicably apprehensive when he saw what I was looking at. I didn't, of course, realise at the time what dynamite I held in my hand. It was a letter from Lucinda Lauder-Treaves, who was the wife of 'mad, bad Treaves', Prinny's disreputable pal. This afternoon, going through the papers in your cousin's study, I found further letters which shed considerably more light on the thing which so vitally affects you. Lucinda, as you doubtless know, had three children. The two elder boys died and the name and title fell to Roderick, the youngest. I'm afraid there can be no doubt whatsoever that Roderick was his mother's son all right, but that his father was Peregrine Fallow who, you will recall, had been tutor for some years to the boy's elder brothers and who, after Buck Treaves' death in America, married your ancestress. So you see, Martin, you *had* a skeleton in the cupboard all right, but it's a very natural one in comparison with what you have been afraid of."

There was a short, pregnant silence. Then Martin drank his whisky-and-soda at a gulp. He lowered the glass and rubbed his forefinger across his jaw, looking rather helplessly at Meredith.

"Then we're . . . we're interlopers," he said quietly.

Meredith shook his head and smiled. "Not really," he said, "and certainly not according to the law, for Buck Treaves recognised the child as his. Indeed, it's practically certain he didn't know that Roderick was not his son. Buck Treaves was quite literally the last of his line, so you need not feel that you have done anyone out of their rightful inheritance. If I were you I'd simply forget this except to be thankful that you come of entirely healthy, sane and decent stock."

Martin sighed and looked at his wife. "What do *you* feel about the family you've married into, my sweet?"

Finella-Lou laid her hand on her husband's and said: "I married you, darling, not your family, but as regards the family, I really think I prefer it John's way round."

CHAPTER XXVII

COMING EVENTS

It was towards six o'clock on the following evening that Meredith emerged from among the trees which crowned the brow of Hollow Hill with Mike at his heels. Side by side they stood, looking over the quiet valley which lay between them and High Perwyl on its hill opposite. The man sighed suddenly, for it was time for him to be leaving this place. Though he had known much that was horrible and vile during his stay here, he had grown to know and appreciate the rare loveliness of High Perwyl and its beautiful surroundings. He had grown to know also its people and to like them well. One especially. There would always be a very warm corner in his heart for the young *châtelaine* of High Perwyl, not only because she was young and fair to look upon, but because she had proved so staunch and understanding a friend in his own black hour. Yes, it was time for him to be moving on. He had been able to achieve much during his stay and he, himself, was rid of the uncleanly thing which had burdened him so greatly as a result of his years in Germany. Physically, he felt a new man.

With the Sealyham walking sedately at his side he went on down the hill and, as he neared the stone bridge across the Perwyl, a sturdy figure appeared striding along Duchy Meadows the other side.

"Hello, Briars!" he said, "how're things?"

"Evening, sir. Might be worse."

"How's Mrs. Mills?" Meredith enquired.

"She'll be all right, sir," replied the ex-Commando. "There's good stuff in my Susan and," he hesitated a moment and then went on quietly, "we've had a talk, sir, and we've decided to get married quite soon. You see, I'll be able to take better care of her that way."

"Very sensible," nodded John. "I wish you both every happiness."

"Thank you very much."

"She's still very young, Briars, and most of her life's before her. You're to be envied, she's a very charming girl."

"She is that," agreed Briars warmly. "There isn't nothin' I wouldn't do for her." The ex-sergeant-major looked away up the river as though embarrassed by his own declaration. "Touching that other matter, Sir John," he went on.

"What other matter?" asked Meredith blankly.

The other glanced at him in surprise. "Why, what happened the other day." And as Meredith's expression still remained perfectly blank, he added: "Mr. Yves' death."

"What about it?" asked Meredith. "He had a heart-attack. Dr. Blackie signed the death-certificate."

"Yes," said Briars uneasily, "but you and me, sir, know different."

"My dear Briars," said Meredith quietly, "what occasioned that heart-attack is no concern of mine. Who am I to improve upon the findings of the medical profession?"

Briars looked momentarily shy and then he grinned broadly as he said: "I'd like, if you wouldn't mind, sir, to shake hands with you. You'd have made a good Commando."

Meredith grinned as widely and the two men solemnly shook hands.

. . . . .

Finella-Lou swung slowly round from her dressing-table and regarded the other woman as though she could not credit the evidence of her own ears.

"Sho, I'm sho, honey-chile," nodded Magnolia, her big black face beaming, the dark eyes dancing mischievously. "Why, Miss Finella-Lou, I'se been waitin' for this, I'se been waitin' for this ever sence you was a little gal. I'se said to myself, 'Magnolia Lincoln, one day you'se gwine to have to go to work all over again'."

Finella-Lou put a hand to her cheek and stared at her old Mammy, her lips parted in eager amazement. "With all that's been happening," she said in a voice of wonder, "I've sort of lost track of . . ."

She broke off, leaving the sentence unfinished and, with

a sudden flick of a brief skirt, had shot out of the room and headed for Great Stairs. Down these she went on flashing feet and her high heels echoed across the tessellated floor of the big hall. She flung open the door leading into the west gallery, leaving it to slam back against the wall, and ran frantically towards the drawing-room. She burst in upon her husband, who was sitting in a chair at the far end, making an undignified entry as she skidded on one of the rugs.

"Martin, darling!" she shouted at the top of her voice, her face flushed with her excitement. "I'm going to have a baby!"

. . . . .

Despite the tragic circumstances which still overhung the house to some degree, dinner that night was a really festive affair. Martin was in the highest spirits. It had been with the greatest difficulty that Finella-Lou and Meredith had restrained him from sitting down there and then and writing to his old housemaster at Eton to put the boy down—because, of course, it would be a boy. All the servants knew, for Magnolia had heralded the glad tidings in her deep, booming contralto, which was accompanied by constant outbursts of delighted laughter. Champagne was brought up from the cellars and Martin sent a bottle out to the servant's-hall. Towards the end of dinner, Meredith more than suspected that old Plum was a bit blurry and uncertain. The old man muttered continually to himself and, at one stage in the proceedings, was observed to be standing beside a serving table crying happily and quietly to himself. The affair was rounded off by Martin coming to his feet towards the end of the meal, his brimming glass in his hand.

"My sweet," he said, a shade unsteadily, "I give you your very good health, and, with the toast, I would like to couple a second. I give you your health and John, to whom we owe so much and who, I hope, will not disdain to be a godfather."

It was soon after dinner that night that Meredith left the young couple to themselves and went up to his room. The sight of their happiness together was a poignant reminder to him of his own lonely condition, but he was none the less glad, very glad, for their sakes. He sat for a long while at the open window of his bedroom with Mike on his knee. The little dog was almost recovered from his injuries and did not appear to wish to settle down. Meredith glanced down at the small bearded face which was turned to his.

"Walkie?" he asked suddenly and the brown eyes under their fringe of hair sparkled with gay anticipation. "All right, old boy," said Meredith, getting up and putting the delighted dog onto the floor, "but first of all I want to make a 'phone call. Can you wait that long?"

Mike signified his agreement provided the call was not of too long duration and the two of them went downstairs.

Meredith gave a London number and waited. Presently he heard the voice of the man to whom he wished to speak.

"Sir Hector McAllister? . . . John here. John Meredith . . . Look, Sir Hector, about that report. You can get hold of Gérard and tell him we're going to work."

THE END